ABOUT THE AUTHOR

When Chris Behrsin isn't out exploring the world, he's behind a keyboard writing tales of dragons and magical lands. Born into the genre through a steady diet of Terry Pratchett, his fiction fuses a love for fantasy and whimsical plots with philosophy and voyages into the worlds of dreams.

You can learn more about his fiction and download two free books at his website, chrisbehrsin.com.

facebook.com/chrisbehrsin

twitter.com/chrisbehrsin

goodreads.com/cbehrsin

bookbub.com/authors/chris-behrsin

BOOKS BY CHRIS BEHRSIN

DRAGONCAT SERIES

A Cat's Guide to Bonding with Dragons

A Cat's Guide to Meddling with Magic

A Cat's Guide to Saving the Kingdom

A Cat's Guide to Questing for Treasure

A Cat's Guide to Travelling through Portals

A Cat's Guide to Vanquishing Evil

A Cat's Guide to Serving a Warlock (Prequel Novella)

SECICAO BLIGHT SERIES

Sukina's Story (Prequel Novel)

Dragonseer

Dragonseers and Bloodlines

Dragonseers and Automatons

Dragonseers and Evolution

More works available at: https://chrisbehrsin.com

DRAGONSEER

SECICAO BLIGHT BOOK ONE

WORLDWALKERS
PUBLISHING

Copyediting by Wayne M. Scace
Cover Design Layout by Chris Behrsin

ISBN: 978-1-915866-29-3 (paperback)
ISBN: 978-1-915866-38-5 (hardcover)
ISBN: 978-1-915886-24-8 (e-book)

Published by Worldwalkers Publishing

To my wonderful mother.

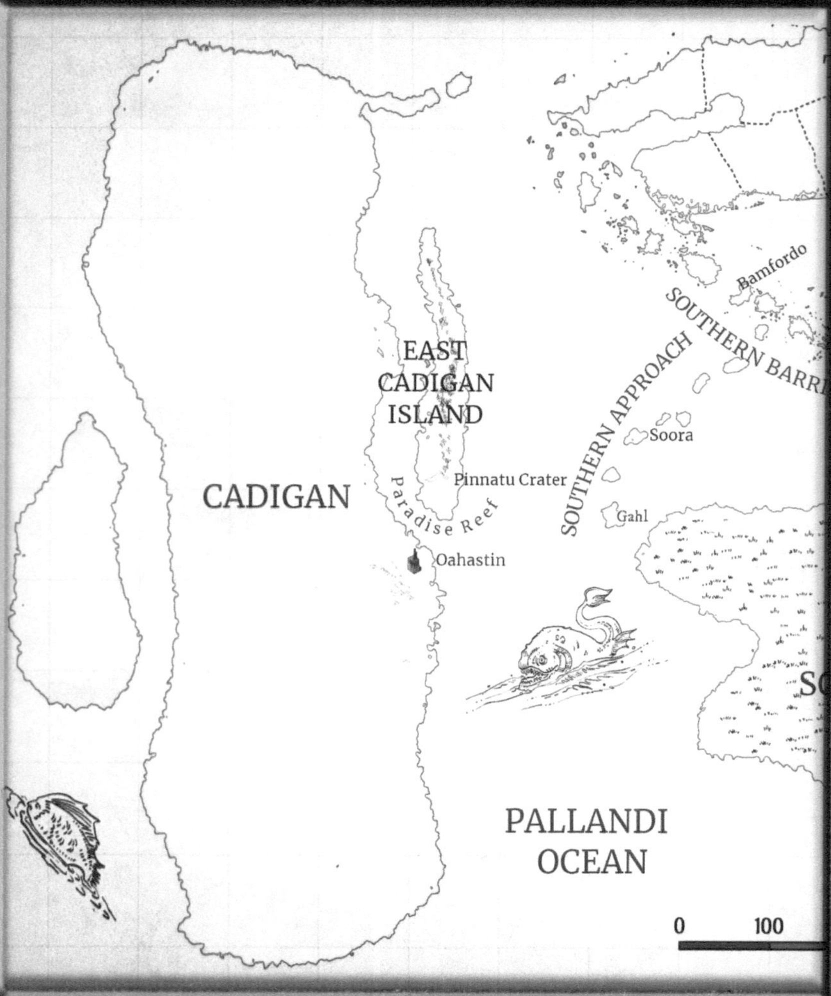

CADIGAN
EAST
CADIGAN
ISLAND
Paradise Reef
Pinnatu Crater
Oahastin
SOUTHERN APPROACH
SOUTHERN BARRI
Bamfordo
Soora
Gahl
S
PALLANDI
OCEAN
0   100

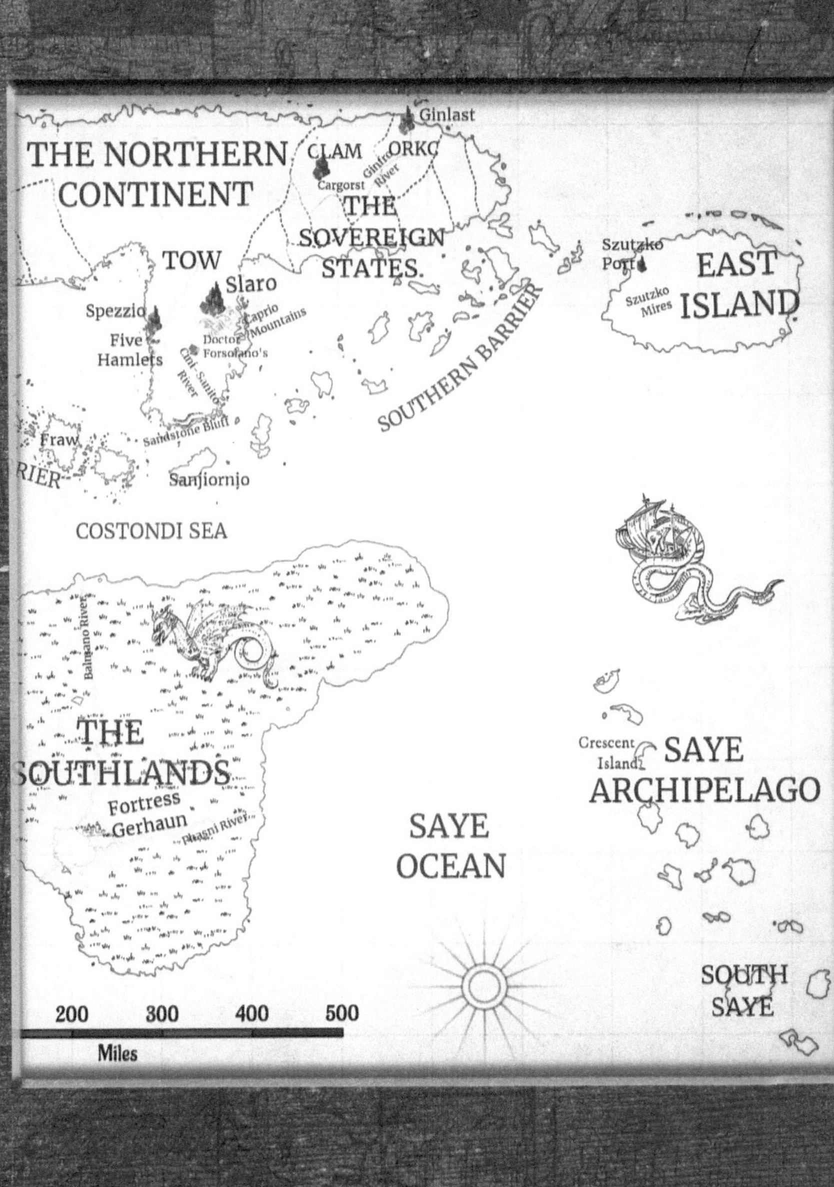
THE NORTHERN CONTINENT
Ginlast
CLAM
ORKO
Ginfro River
Cargorst
THE SOVEREIGN STATES.
TOW
Slaro
Spezzio
Caprio Mountains
Five Hamlets
Doctor Forsofano's
Cini-Sanito River
Szutzko Pott
EAST ISLAND
Szutzko Mires
SOUTHERN BARRIER
Fraw
Sandstone Bluff
RIER
Sanjiornjo
COSTONDI SEA
Balnaano River
THE SOUTHLANDS
Fortress Gerhaun
Phagni River
Crescent Island
SAYE ARCHIPELAGO
SAYE OCEAN
SOUTH SAYE
200
300
400
500
Miles

PART I

FASO

"Secicao-powered automatons are the future of mankind."

— FASO GORDONI

The wind from the airship's propellers came in chilly and strong. I bowed my knees and widened my legs to brace myself against the gale. Beside me, Faso got knocked back a little, almost sending that infernal six-legged automaton, Ratter, off his shoulders. Mr Sandorini, our mayor, was here too, wearing his monocle and tweed suit – much more traditional than Faso's pinstripes.

Soon, the propellers rotated on their gimbals to face upwards, causing the wind to ease off. This revealed the banner hanging down off the bowsprit, red with four white sabres radiating outwards from a circle, looking much like propeller blades.

"See that," Faso shouted in my ear, much louder than he needed to. "That's the king's insignia."

Faso stood there, high-and-mighty with his impossibly white skin, and his pin-stripe suit with the left sleeved flared out more than his right, to house his ferret automaton. Though Faso was in his early thirties, his skin was so unweathered by the sun that he looked like he was in his mid-twenties. The automaton in question, Ratter, sat upon his shoulder with those evil red eyes staring at me, cold and assessing.

"I know," I said. Being from a country town didn't make me ignorant.

"You don't sound particularly surprised," Faso said, with a smirk I wanted to knock off his face.

"Why should I be?"

"That's King Cini's airship, Miss Wells. I don't know about yours, but my letter said he was only sending an envoy."

"So what? Doesn't mean the king's come out to meet us."

"What century were you born in, lady? The king's airship always travels with the king on it."

The racket died down and the airship landed neatly within its allocated circle. Two guards dressed in scarlet, the king's elite redguards carrying Pattersoni rifles with fixed bayonets, came up on deck and kicked down the ramp. The king came up next, resplendent in white fur and a tall felt crown. Honestly, despite what Faso had said, I wasn't expecting to see him there. His clothes had some kind of sheen about them, and his face was powdered white with such perfection that he seemed to emit a radiant glow. Kind of handsome looking, in a way, although overdone.

"See what I mean?" Faso shouted with no respect for the delicacy of my eardrum. "That's King Cini."

The king didn't look at the world around him, but instead at the guards whom he motioned onwards with his hand. One guard proceeded down the ramp and King Cini followed him, with the other guard trailing rhythmically behind.

Mr Sandorini and Faso bowed and kneeled automatically when the king stepped off his ramp. In response, I dropped a deep curtsy, nearly knocking my knees hard against the ground. Ratter, as if he knew his place, ran along Faso's arm and concealed himself within Faso's widened left sleeve. The noise from the propellers began to die down and a slight balminess returned to the air.

King Cini III approached the mayor first and offered him his hand. Mr Sandorini stood up, then Faso and I followed. "Honoured you would come to such a humble town, my liege," Mr Sandorini said.

The king waved off his comment with a dismissive gesture. "It's these two citizens we rely on." He indicated Faso and me.

"Then I guess we better get started," Mr Sandorini said.

"Unfortunately, I can't be here long," Cini said. "I have other appointments. If you could just leave me alone with them..."

The mayor raised his hand and coughed against the back of it. "Very well. I'll be in the town hall if you need me." He walked back along the path towards town with a slight waddle in his gait.

King Cini III turned his attention to us. "So, Mr Gordoni and Miss Wells," he said. "I'll get straight to the point. We have a contract for you."

Faso stepped forward. "A contract? By all means, if you need more oil, I've been working on my automatons. Is it production speed you want? Because the more I create, the more I can supply. You'll get much more out of my technology than you can with a dragon."

Damn that man. I tried to step in, but Faso was blocking me off with his shoulder. So, I put my arm in front of him, feeling something cold and hard in Faso's sleeve – Ratter.

I took a step forward. "Surely it's quality you want," I said. "You can't get better than dragon roasted – a dragon who, I remind you, feeds on secicao."

Secicao was the lifeblood on which this country ran. A drink served out in cafetières that had significant augmentative properties. These properties were even stronger when the secicao was distilled into oil, allowed only in the military to create supermen of war.

Ratter now poked his head out of Faso's sleeve, ran up to his shoulder, and bared steel teeth at me with an ingratiating hiss. "Oh, secicao, secicao," Faso said. "If it's the power of secicao you want, you should see my latest technology. I've created—"

The king raised a white velvet gloved hand, cutting Faso off mid-speech. "What I want is for you two, both of you, to listen to your king." He walked up to the cliff edge that the airfield overhung and looked south. Two of his guards followed him, the sun's rays glinting off the bayonets of their rifles. "No doubt," King Cini said, "you're both aware that the skirmishes in the south have been on the rise lately. Not just that, but the dragons have been attacking the Southern Barrier forts that barricade in our beloved kingdom of Tow and keep it safe."

"I have heard that, my liege," Faso said.

The king gave Faso a scornful look. He hadn't given Faso permission to speak. I was beginning to learn how this game worked. "It seems," Cini continued, "that the Southlands dragon threat is becoming more severe. We have automaton weapons, but the dragons are learning to outdo them, always finding flaws in the machines before we know about them ourselves."

"With all respect, sir," Faso said. "If you need automatons, I can supply—"

"Obviously, Mr Gordoni, you don't like the sound of my voice." King Cini looked back to one of his guards who took his rifle off his shoulder and readied it with two loud clicks. A pocket of air travelled down Faso's throat.

Faso had now assumed a more startled posture, like a rabbit that's just seen a wolf. Ratter scurried up his sleeve and took refuge there. "I'm sorry, your highness," he said. "Speak away."

"Good," Cini said. "In short, we don't want more automatons. We want better augmented soldiers, and for that we need a better grade of secicao oil. Both of you produce some of the finest in all of Tow each, as you know, with its own characteristic effects. But we need more, and we need better to keep up with the war effort. I want you two to work together to combine your processes and surpass anything ever created before."

So, it appeared that Faso hadn't come to The Five Hamlets on his own entrepreneurial volition after all. I tried to hide my smirk. Faso's lips, on the other hand, were trembling as if trying to hide his scorn. "You want me to work with her?"

"Is there a problem with that, Mr Gordoni?" Cini glanced back over his shoulder at his guard.

Faso seemed to have been, figuratively, shot down enough times now to know not to really get shot. "No problem, your highness." Another lump travelled down his throat.

"With all respect, your liege," I said. "I'm not sure Velos will work so well with automatons. The advantage of my grade of secicao is it's produced the natural way. Bring automatons into the mix and there'll be less dragon spirit in your augmented troops and more of... Well, something else."

"Velos is your dragon, I presume?"

"He is."

"Then that is exactly why we want you to experiment. The Southlands have already shown us that dragons can't be trusted. There must be a better mix of ingredients. We've already been experimenting on how to combine your two oils for more positive effects. I'll send you the results, when we get them."

"As you wish, my liege," I said with a slight curtsy, while biting my tongue to stop me saying the wrong thing. I wasn't sure what was worse to be honest: the fact I would use Velos to support a war against dragons or the fact I'd be forced to pair him with automatons.

"Very good," Cini said. "Then we're in agreement." He turned back to the less threatening looking guard, who had a puppy like jowly face. "Contract please, Sergeant Orlo."

The guard nodded; he had two envelopes tucked under his arm. He stepped in front of the king and handed them out to us.

"Your mayor can distribute the signed copies of these with the next shipment," King Cini said. "Now, for all effective purposes, I shall consider this agreement complete."

I had in my hand a manila cardboard backed B4 envelope. Before I even had a chance to open it, the king bowed his head slightly and paused. As if by reflex, Faso forced himself down onto one knee and lowered his forehead. I followed suit, causing another jolt of pain against the tenderness there. The king turned on his heels and walked up the airship ramp.

I waited until King Cini had vanished into his cabin before I turned to Faso and let out my prepared speech. "Whatever it costs to work together, you will keep those automatons away from Velos or we'll both fly over and bake you within your metal abode. Do you understand?"

Ratter stared at me with its red evil eyes from a convenient perch on Faso's shoulder. Automatons like Ratter had been notorious for the extermination of dragons in the Northern Continent twenty years ago during the Dragonheat Wars. My dragon, Velos, had somehow survived all this and then he'd just turned up one day on our doorstep when I was seven years old.

We'd kept him secret for a few years, but it hadn't been long until the new king, Cini III, had discovered him. Fortunately for us, my parents had managed to convince him he'd be worth keeping as some kind of novelty, and the king had also come to understand Velos' value in enhancing the secicao refinement process.

But still, with Faso's automatons around, I couldn't help but feel Velos was under threat. I looked at Faso, waiting for a response. But he didn't say anything and had that arrogant smile on his face, as if whatever I threw at him couldn't affect him.

I huffed and stormed off.

"Love you too," Faso called back, but I didn't offer a parting glance.

I FOUND my parents waiting for me on the swing near the front door, wearing their parkas to shield off the bitter wind. Sunset was approaching, and Velos was asleep in his stables, exhausted after our recent run south, just a few days past. I decided it best to leave him be.

Instead, I invited my parents into my cottage, built only a stone-throw's away from their farmhouse. It was then that I told them the news.

"Dragonheats," Mamo said once we were seated. "Not only has Cini sent you out into the fire but he's done so as if you've a bottle of paraffin on your back."

She sat on the recliner next to my coffee table. It was a little late for secicao, so instead, three cups of chamomile tea were placed there. Papo was in the other recliner, his feet on the table and today's magazine in his hands.

On the front of the magazine was a picture of Alsie Fioreletta, the king's right-hand maiden, her expression characteristically straight and a soft lustre on her raven black hair. She had her hand on the head of the king's nephew, which was strange, as all news the last few days was about how he'd recently been abducted.

I sat on the loveseat that looked out over the stables although, admittedly, it was a little dark to see anything right now.

"Say, the king's even in here today," Papo said. "An interview with him. He says he wants to wipe out all the dragons with seci-cao-powered automatons."

Mamo jumped off her seat, almost knocking her teacup off its saucer. "Melting wellies, the man's a psychopath. There must be a way out of this, Pontopa."

"Versalina," Papo said. "You're talking about a king's edict here. It's not just a contract. She can't just tear it up and say no."

"But she can delegate," Mamo said. "Get Faso Gordoni's automatons to do the extraction, dear. They can harvest the secicao without anything getting you in danger. Velos can feed and roast at home." There we went again. Her logic – deprive Velos and me of everything we lived for.

"There's no way," I said, "that I'm letting those dragon-killers do anything in place of Velos."

"Not all automatons are dragon-killers now," Papo said. "Times have changed."

"Papo, Faso's contraptions are made out of old war-automaton parts. How can we possibly know there's not some killer instinct left in them?"

"I'm not sure that's how machines work," Papo said.

"Really? Have you ever created an automaton yourself?"

"Can't say I have."

"Pontopa, Cipao," Mamo said. "Please, can we please be peaceful here? Pontopa, don't raise your voice to your father like that." You would have thought I was still a child.

"All, I'm saying," Papo said, "is that you should put a little more trust in the man."

"And why, exactly?" I asked.

"Faso Gordoni's a genius. It says so in the magazines. You never know, if you two can learn to get along... You're twenty-one, Pontopa, and I'm dreading I'll never see a ring on your finger."

I laughed. "You really think he and I are compatible material? Hell, if you met him, you'd realise what a buffoon he is."

"I'm sure I will meet him one day, and I'm not sure I want to rely on your prejudiced impressions right now. Just because he works with automatons doesn't make him a bad man."

"I don't want to work with automatons! Why is that so hard to understand?"

"So, you'd rather fly into your death. Do you have any idea how much we worry about you?"

"How much you worry? How hard do you think this is for me? Someone has to feed this family. Where would we get money from otherwise?"

At that, Papo banged his fist down on the table, almost sending my teacup flying. He wasn't usually the aggressive type, I have to admit, but he did tend to keep everything bottled up inside. Push him far enough and he'd lose his temper.

"Dragonheats, Pontopa! Is this what this is about, money? How many times have I had to tell you that we can survive on less? We can move out from the farm. To the city, if we must, and get good paying jobs there. Or outside the border. Emigrate to Orkc or grab a steamer to Cadigan."

There it was again. Completely leaving Velos out of the equation. I stood up and pointed a finger at Papo. "I'm sick of having to explain this every time. Just... just, stop coming into my house and telling me what to do!"

"Your house?" Papo stood up, towering over me. "I remind you about the stones, the labour, the men to build the stables, all that imported food for Velos, even those stupid Sukina Sako books. Who provided that, exactly? Who tilled the soil and stayed out in the cold? Who waded through storms and lugged around heavy stones to build your cottage walls?"

"I'm repaying you by the work I do now!"

Mamo, who had been hovering nearby, came in to break us both up. "Stop it!" she said. "Dragonheats, Cipao, this isn't the way to handle this, and Pontopa, don't attack your father like that."

Papo took one hard look at her, and then sat down. I did the same.

"Pontopa," Mamo said. "Your father means well, but you're quite right to want your independence."

"Too right I am."

"But we worry about you," Mamo said. "You have a good life ahead of you and we're getting old. We don't want to see you throw your life away. Please, just think about this rationally."

"I'm not throwing my life away," I snapped back. "I've never been more alive."

"Oh, for wellies sake," Papo said. "When will you ever come to your senses, girl?" He turned to Mamo. "Versalina, you know what we talked about, right?"

Mamo shook her head. "Not now, Cipao."

"Yes, now!"

"Cipao, don't..."

But Papo had already stood up, holding his anger under his breath. He spoke through his teeth. "You don't need to do the runs anymore, Pontopa. I'll do it. I'll fly Velos, work with Faso Gordoni and his automatons."

"I—" Really, I didn't know what to say. I sputtered out some words, stopped myself, sputtered out a few more, took some deep breaths. My tea had cooled enough to drink and so I took it down in one gulp. I stood up and walked towards the door. I stopped there, tears in my eyes. "I've flown Velos all my life. What do you think I'd do without him?"

"You can still do the roasting and the processing," Papo said. "You'd have plenty more time for your books."

"Papo, you've never even dared to fly in the past, and you have the arrogance to think you can do so now."

"He was one of the best jockeys around," Mamo said.

Of course, they would have to pull the jockey ruse. I'd heard his story so many times. He'd won a lot of races until he fell off and broke his leg, trampled by his own horse. It had taken one of the best surgeons in Slaro, namely his old friend Doctor Forsolano, to install the titanium pins in his knee joint that allowed him to walk again. Now he couldn't ride without canting to the left a little, risking a fall.

"Pontopa," Papo said. "I'm old enough to have learnt from my mistakes. I won't be so carefree as I was then."

"Not so carefree? Riding a dragon isn't like learning to walk, you know?"

"I'll learn fast."

"No, you won't learn, because you'll fall off like you did the horse, and it will kill you. But you don't care, do you? As long as I stay 'safe'."

"Mind what you say, Pontopa," Mamo said.

But I was already outside and slamming the door shut.

I COULDN'T STAND BEING around the house any longer, so I went outside to get some fresh air. There, I saw Velos, sleeping soundly, despite the row that had just taken place in the cottage. The sun's waning red light glinted off the resin that plastered his skin. This resin really drained him. Eventually it would harden and flake off. This usually took a couple of weeks, but a bit of soap and water seemed to speed up the process. Although sometimes I felt guilty for not having the energy to do it as soon as I got back – I found the runs pretty draining too.

Velos lived in stables that Papo had converted to hold a dragon. Straw was littered across the ground for softness and the outer walls and inner rooms had been knocked out, leaving just the timber frame with a kiln placed at one opening for roasting the secicao beans. These were the fruits of my runs from the Southlands. I had arranged them in a pile, dropped in from Velos' own claws.

My cottage overlooked the stables, arched like a smile, or at least I hope that's how Cini's airships saw it when they passed overhead. On the ground it looked kind of glittery with its frosted windows and hewn stone corners, curving around Velos' abode. Behind the cottage was the farmhouse where Mamo and Papo lived, and beyond that vineyards spread into the distance, vines bare and barren through increasingly frosty winters. The farmstead stood between the Five Hamlets and a precipice, with sandstone cliffs that dropped down dramatically into a harsh, churning sea.

I took Velos' water bucket and emptied it. I scraped some more bark off the secicao tree we'd brought from down south and put it in his basket for food. The stench when I did so was always nauseating at first, but eventually had a slightly intoxicating effect on the senses, drug that secicao was.

I proceeded to gather up any beans that had fallen off the wiry branches and put them into a separate bowl for processing. Each had within it the power to augment the ability of a man for several hours. It was Velos' staple. When its power was roasted, ground, and served in a mug warm, it caused people to see more clearly, lift greater weights, jump higher, heal faster. The effect could be up to three times stronger if I processed it into oil, which was incredible in comparison to what you got in a cup.

As I perched myself next to the drowsy dragon, his breath balmy against my back, I ran my hand along his blue waxy skin. My hands nursed his countless scars and with each came a memory, deep grooves from automaton bullets, a pitchfork wound from the farmer who couldn't accept his 'monstrous roars'. After all, he did roar in his sleep sometimes, and if it weren't for the compensation levies I'd agreed to pay to the town hall, he wouldn't for much longer. Scales ran up his tail, up his back, up his neck towards the central steering fin that I liked to cling on to whenever I rode him south.

He lowered his neck, and I tousled his scaly head. Secicao was such a strange thing. I couldn't imagine life without it. Not just the effects of the drug, but the whole process to take it from plant to cup. The wind against my face as I flew south, the slight choking effect of the masks when the brown roiling secicao fumes of the continent of the Southlands hit us. It was always an adventure. For me and Velos, the world was our oyster.

I stroked Velos a little more until he started to let off a deep crooning sound from his massive snout, and then I went for a walk along the cliffs.

In the distance, gulls circled around fishing boats, waiting for some fish to flop back into the water. The sun now had fallen below the horizon. I hadn't even thought to bring a jacket and it was a little chilly. But I didn't care.

My parents were bad enough, always complaining about the apparent increasing dangers, saying I'd never be safe even though I had a fearsome dragon to protect me. Now Faso had entered the equation too and King Cini was forcing me to enter into a partnership with the man.

I had to do something about this, and I had to act fast.

So, I made a decision. Tomorrow, I would go to Faso Gordoni and set my own terms. I'd tell him that I would perform the runs south, drop off the secicao (leaving enough left over for Velos to feed on) and he could do the processing. We'd market it as secicao harvested from a dragon's claws and processed by automatons. That would keep us apart and the king happy.

Anything to get out of this farce.

2

Once the sun had set, I took the long road along the cliff edge towards Faso's at a casual pace. From below came the sounds of the sea swishing and the blurps of foghorns. It wasn't long until I saw the green lights peeking out from the horizon, like fireflies. They were all lined up in a row, just like the constellation of the sword. They didn't belong to Faso's workshop as such, but to the path leading there, as if they were rolling up to some kind of spectacle, whatever that might be.

After several more steps, the workshop came into view. The entire thing was aglow and not just in green. It seemed to shimmer like an oil pool, awash with all the colours of the rainbow, swishing over it in waves, the entire structure alive with luminescence. The structure rocked slowly from side to side on two spindly brass legs.

Miniature automated airships and other automatons zipped around it, carrying girders and obtuse bits of metal. Although the workshop had a roof, it still seemed unfinished, but building up rapidly, parts being fit into places with clanking and grinding sounds. There was a mouth at the base of the head, sealed shut.

Despite the dim light, I could see the guns, melted down at the ends and attached to cogs, which whirred around gear shafts, clearly powering this monstrous dwelling. I recognised the old cannons, now remanufactured into chimneys from where smoke and steam rose. Scattered around the workshop's facade were red glowing crystal eyes that had given the war automatons such accuracy. All embedded into the brass wall, with inanimate war-automaton heads, recognisable from the history books, now a part of the furniture.

In the house's centre, I could make out the tongue-like door, and I half expected to see Faso looking out from it. But instead a strange automaton, tall and on two wheels, with a camera on its domed head and a large green button on its face, wheeled up to me. Above the button was a sign saying, "Please press for attention."

I pressed for it. The camera clicked, and four blades popped out of the top. With a high-pitched whirr, the automaton floated up towards one of the workshop's slit eyes.

Eventually, the ramp came down, just in front of my feet this time, and Faso came sliding down on his haunches. I had to duck aside slightly so that he could land. He stood up, brushed himself off, and turned to me.

"Lady Wells. Why, pleased once again to make your acquaintance." He offered me his hand and I took it limply.

I'd already decided that the best strategy with this man was to get straight to business. "I've come to talk about how we're going to keep King Cini happy without losing our heads." I noticed something was missing. "Where's your ferret?"

"Why, upstairs, of course."

"I thought you took it with you everywhere?"

Faso raised an eyebrow. "Whatever gave you that impression? My creations are useful, but even a genius like myself needs to work on maintenance sometimes."

I smiled with desultory satisfaction. "You mean he's broken?"

"Broken is such a limited word. I'd rather say needing modifications. Say, I've been working on quite a lot of ideas for our little project lately. If you would allow me to escort you inside?"

He gestured up towards the top of the ramp and tried to take hold of my elbow, but I shook him aside. "I'd rather we talked out here," I said. "I think that we should – "

"Please, Pontopa," he interjected. "I have some things to show you. I've been hard at work and I'd at least appreciate it if you took a look."

He turned back towards the ramp and pressed a button. In an instant, the slats jumped up into a staircase, startling me.

"Come on," he said and beckoned me on. The first step bowed a little under his weight, but it seemed sturdy enough. He pressed a button on the panel on the side and the whole thing spun around in a spiral and carried him upwards without him having to walk a step. After about halfway, he turned and shouted down over his shoulder, "Don't be shy, lady. There's nothing in here that will kill you, I assure you."

I waited gingerly for a few moments, unsure whether I really should be following him up. But I shrugged off my doubts and decided that, annoying as he was, Faso didn't seem dangerous. I stepped on, letting the world revolve slowly around me. Soon, I was at the top, Faso standing next to me. His hand touched my shoulder and I shuddered. He noticed my reaction and retracted his arm.

"Remember we're on business only here," I said. "You've invited me into your workshop, not your bedroom."

"Of course, I would never dream of compromising. Please, allow me to welcome you into my abode."

I followed Faso inside. Surprisingly, despite its brass facade, the interior was covered in veneer, curved at the top and bottom like the insides of a barrel. But apart from the polished walls, the entire place was in disarray. Mechanical heads were strewn across the tables, cogs and gears were piled up on the shelves, brass clocks and robot parts hung askew on the walls with no semblance of order. Piles of junk were also heaped in random piles around the room, some of them coming up to my knee.

Faso seemed such a tidy man on the outside that I wondered how he could stay sane in such a place. But a little space did pool around some kind of bronze and steel rug laid out on the floor. I didn't even want to ask what this was.

"It's a pig-sty!" I said.

At that, Faso laughed. "Anything but," he said. "Everything here has its place."

"You mean there's some order to this?"

"An inventor always needs his systems. Of course, I wouldn't expect an average mind to understand how it works."

I decided to ignore the fact that he seemed utterly incapable of saying anything right. "So, where's Ratter?" I asked.

"He's over there." Faso pointed at a mahogany writing desk in the corner of the room. On it lay a corkboard with Ratter splayed out like it had been dissected.

I walked over, taking care not to knock over any stuff. I had to move like a ballerina, contorting myself into different positions, keeping my hands wide to keep balance, and then almost tripping over the metal rug.

Ratter looked a lot more complex than I'd imagined. Its spine had many more joints than a human's, and I couldn't even begin to comprehend how Faso had created the intricacies in its stubby little legs. It didn't have four legs, but six. Through its mouth ran some kind of spindle, connected to what looked like a revolver cylinder with twenty or so chambers.

Faso came over to join me. He stood awfully close, offputtingly so. He pointed to a sketch above the desk of the anatomy of a ferret. "Nature provides great examples," he said. "While many inventors rely on trial and error, evolution has been prototyping its designs for millions of years."

He turned and stared at me for a while, as if expecting me to be impressed. "A ferret doesn't have six legs," I pointed out.

"Why, of course. The two legs are a new addition. Ferrets are incredibly stealthy creatures, but the extra legs give extra gripping power for climbing those hard-to-reach places. The gun is also new. The ammunition can be changed by tickling him under the throat. He coughs it up, I put in the new ammo, and then get him to swallow it again. Really quite remarkable, don't you think?"

I snorted. "All I've seen it do so far is swat at mosquitoes. You're not truly trying to tell me this mechanical ferret is as good as the real thing?"

"Ratter's so much more than that. He's a damn useful machine who won't bite your fingers unless I ask him to. You want to know how he works?"

I sighed. Of course, I didn't. But then, in the interests of diplomacy, I thought I'd pander to his ego just this once. "How?"

Faso took a pencil from his desk and pointed at a green rubber pouch around Ratter's belly. "This bladder is one of my latest inventions. Ratter now runs on secicao oil, which powers a piston engine, here."

He pointed to a row of brass cylinders that ran along the torso. "The workings of which are incredibly intricate. In the absence of secicao oil, he can also be powered by an industrial spring."

He pointed to a second cylinder by the hip, which had a key sticking out of it. "By hand or a Gordoni steam-powered winder, a device which I patented myself. What do you think?"

"It's interesting," I said. What else could I say?

"Yes, quite..." He stared at Ratter for an awkward moment, until I thought I better break the silence.

"Look, as much as you may want to show off your work, we came to talk about the king's contract. I can see how, let's say, efficient your inventions are. So, I think it's best if your automatons work on the processing and I can run Velos down to the Southlands to harvest secicao every two weeks. That way we stay out of each other's way. How does that sound?"

Faso lifted his head. "I don't think that would work."

"Why not?"

"Cini said to combine our refinement processes. Not to work on separate processes, but to work together. Otherwise, he would have just shipped your harvested secicao over to me for processing and I wouldn't have had to come to this sleepy village."

I put my hands on my hips. "Okay, so what do you propose, mister know-it-all?"

"What I'm saying is that we need to find a way to meld our processes together. We can combine our strengths and I can help you eliminate your weaknesses. Which is what I've been working on." He gestured over to the metal rug on the floor. "Meet our new process."

I realised, for the first time, that the thing was shaped a little like a dragon. "Dragonheats! Please don't tell me you're building a dragon automaton."

"Heavens, no. It would cost a fortune to get together all the parts. Even I'm not that rich. This here, my darling, is dragon armour."

As I examined it more closely, I could still see some of the automaton eyes, those red laser crystals that used to belong to the dragon-killers. Otherwise, it was a convoluted mesh of pipes, screws, and pistons. A much larger pipe curled around what I assumed to be the back of it, connecting to two long stretchy rubber sacks that ran along each side.

"You've got to be kidding," I said. "If you think you're putting that on Velos, you've got another thing coming."

"I think it would quite suit him."

"Suit him? It's a monstrosity. Velos works quite well by himself, thank you very much. He doesn't need a coat of armour."

"It's much more than armour, darling. It's a machine designed to augment the dragon's abilities in the most astounding ways. Injecting secicao into him as he flies his runs. It will safeguard us from the dangers of the Greys and give him an edge if he ever needs to kill any of them. It will help protect us on our runs south."

"Us?"

"Of course. It's much safer than flying by airship with all those Greys down there. I still need to add harnesses, of course, to secure us in place."

I stopped for a moment to take a deep breath. I couldn't believe he actually thought I'd allow this. "Look, what did I tell you yesterday?"

He smirked, as if he'd bested me at something. "You told me you didn't want automatons near Velos. But this isn't an automaton. I've been careful not to include a central intelligence."

"It's still a machine."

"But not something which could take control of Velos' body."

"It doesn't matter. It's made out of dragon-killer parts. I'm not letting anything like that near Velos."

"Hah," Faso said. "So that's what this is about. You think that broken-down war-automatons could hurt your dragon? I've removed the cores, for wellies sake."

"I don't care. I know my dragon well enough to know he'll hate it."

"Why? Has he ever tried wearing anything like this?"

"Of course, he's never tried. Velos hates automatons."

"How do you know?"

"Because he's my dragon."

"Can you speak to him?"

"I just know. Not to mention the fact that you're implying we should install armour on Velos for the purpose of killing other dragons. Why in the dragonheats would Velos want to kill one of his own?" Greys may have been dangerous, but I'd never wanted to kill one, much like I'd never wanted to kill a lion.

Faso now had his hands out in front of him and had placed himself between me and the automaton armour, as if I could do damage to it. "Look, I know you're not so keen on the idea, but why not try it at least once? We can always remove it if Velos doesn't like it."

"We're not doing it," I said, "and that's the end of it. Now, if you'll excuse me, I want to get a breath of fresh air. All these oil fumes aren't good for my lungs."

I turned around but stopped when I got to the staircase. The stairs were still raised, but I worried they'd automatically collapse if I stepped onto them. If Faso was expecting me to slide down that thing, he had another thing coming.

"It will take you down automatically," Faso said, and I threw him a dubious look then stepped on the top stair. Faso pressed a button and the steps lowered me down gently to ground level.

Once I was at the bottom, Faso called out, "Goodbye, lady. Please think about what I said."

"No is no!" I shouted back and I walked as calmly as I could into the night.

3

Despite my best intentions, I didn't get to lie in much the next morning. Velos' roar woke me up just before dawn. Although he did it less frequently now, his roaring had never been popular with the villagers. It had attracted a lot of aggression at first – the cause of Velos' pitchfork wound on his right flank. But once we started bringing good money in, we agreed to pay levies to the town hall every time a roar occurred, which were consequently distributed amongst the villagers. They'd shut up about it then, happy to have extra cash in their pockets every time Velos had one of his nightmares.

I assumed nightmares to be the cause of the roars, anyway. It must have been tormenting for him to be separated from his mother at such a young age. I could always feel his grief within my chest. It made me laugh how people called him an animal. In many ways, Velos was more human than anyone I knew.

Papo was already waiting at the stables when I stepped outside. Velos' trough had been emptied of the brown mulched secicao bark, transferred to the kiln ready for roasting. Papo was flicking off more bark from the wiry branches with a knife.

"I've been to the village hall and paid the levy already," he said. "The mayor, as always, was very grateful."

"Thank you," I waited with my arms crossed to see if he had anything more to say.

"Look," Papo said. "I'm sorry about yesterday."

"Are you?"

"Your Mamo and I – we just don't want to lose you."

"Well, separating me from Velos is one sure way to do that."

"I know…" Papo looked out towards the sea. "I know."

I couldn't do anything but sigh. Papo meant well. I guess I was a little harsh the previous day too. "Just remember, flying Velos is my job. I do my best to stay safe, and I wouldn't unwittingly put myself in any danger. It's hard for me sometimes too, you know."

"I just wish there was something more I could do," Papo said.

"I'd appreciate any help you can give me in the stables," I said. "Really, if I have to work with this moron Faso, I'm going to need it."

Papo smiled. "Is he really that bad? Most people I've met who are that successful are quite nice."

"Oh, he's domineering and arrogant, Papo, like you wouldn't believe."

"I think I'd still like to meet him. I trust your impressions, Pontopa, it's just the magazine articles give him so much praise."

I snorted, then I picked up a pitchfork and started to help Papo shovelling secicao into the kiln. "He's probably paid the press to sing praises about him."

"You could be right. Say, my prayers have been answered. That looks like him now." Papo pointed down the path towards an approaching figure in a long coat and top hat, coattails trailing behind.

"That's him all right."

Papo clapped his hands together and stood up straight. "Be on your best behaviour, will you? I know you two don't get along, but you never know where he might be able to bring in a little extra cash."

Again, typical Papo. I could read him like a book. "I hope you're not suggesting that he'll pay us a dowry."

"Oh, please don't put the words into my mouth. But now you mention it…"

"I'd rather run away to a nunnery."

He raised one eyebrow. "And leave Velos behind? Say this young man's got quite a swagger on him."

"What did I tell you?" I said and I tucked into the work again, hoping that if I appeared busy enough, he'd go away. I watched Papo step up to him and offer his hand from the corner of my eye.

"Say, you must be Faso Gordoni, the entrepreneur," he said. "I've read all about you in the Tow Observer."

Faso stood tall as if basking in the admiration and let off a contrived smile. "Pleased to make your acquaintance. I came to talk to your daughter."

"Oh, Pontopa's told me so much about you." He draped an arm over Faso's shoulder. "Say, it's not often we have visitors here. Why don't you come in for a cup of secicao? My wife has baked a cake. She'll be so proud to meet you, I'm sure."

"I, er..." Faso looked at me and I lowered my eyes, tossed some secicao, trying to look busy.

"Please, Mr Gordoni. You couldn't possibly refuse such hospitality. Pontopa will be here later and there's so much we wish to learn about you."

"I guess I'll have to say yes, then," Faso said with evident undertones of chagrin in his voice.

"Pontopa," Papo said. "Would you like some cake too?"

"I need to finish up here," I said, "and I, er... Have an appointment with the mayor soon. But I'll be back later on this evening."

"Very well," Papo said. "Come on, Mr. Gordoni, I'll show you around."

I watched Faso flitter away in his swallow-tail coat, guided by Papo's arm, into the farmhouse. Now, it was time to enjoy my afternoon off.

I WENT into my own cottage to grab a book and yesterday's copy of The Tow Observer – today's was no doubt in the farmhouse, and I didn't plan on going anywhere near there. I gathered my knapsack and put the magazine and book inside, alongside my felt overcoat and scarf.

Outside, it was colder than it had been yesterday, and a fresh salty wind came off the coast. The sun was hiding behind a large grey cloud, and it would be chilly on the moors. But I knew of a sheltered spot behind a copse of beech trees, around half an hour south of my cottage on foot.

Every so often, as I walked, I would glance around at the faint outline of Spezzio in the distance – the port city where most of the secicao came in off the steamers. A little closer than that, I could see the glint of light off the boats, great armoured ironclads with large Gatling guns to shoot down any attacking grey dragons, or Greys. Here, the boats were under no threat. But once they crossed the Southern Barrier archipelago, they'd have to keep up their guard.

I found the shaded copse and sat down by a tree there, its bole sheltering me from the wind. I opened the magazine first, ignored the article about Faso, and instead focused on the double page feature on Prince Artua, the king's nephew who had been kidnapped. They claimed to have arrested two perpetrators, both of whom had been executed by rifle squad, but there was still no sign of the boy. There was mention of these men being linked to a terrorist organisation down in the Southlands. But no one knew much more. I had to admit, it all seemed pretty ridiculous. The clouds that the secicao plant produced made the Southlands uninhabitable, so how an organisation could exist down there, I had no idea.

I stuffed the magazine back into my knapsack. Instead, I opened up Sukina Sako's, my favourite author, novel "*The Dragon Boy*" and prepared myself for a riveting read.

Varion, the protagonist, had been taken hostage by a tribe in the Southlands and was now tied to a tree. The tribe had the abnormal power to breathe secicao – while I personally had to wear some kind of breathing device. These men had profited from the king's harvesting operations and they didn't like Varion's sabotage attempts. But Varion had something in his arsenal that the cannibalistic leader didn't know about. He could sing songs that called the Greys to his aid. He held off doing so, though, since he had a feeling that war-automatons were nearby that could shoot the dragons down. He wouldn't call them in unless he was at death's door.

I couldn't help but wonder how Miss Sako had written a book with so much empathy for dragons. One day, I would love to meet her. I had so many questions to ask her. Just the way she spoke about dragons reminded me of my own connection to Velos.

But how you came to meet an author like Sukina Sako, I didn't know.

Eventually, after what must have been three or four hours, it became a little bit too cold for sitting around and I started to get peckish. So, I lifted myself off my catkin carpet, brushed myself down, and headed back to the vineyard, hoping that by the time I arrived Faso would have gone.

What I didn't expect to hear was another of Velos' roars, booming along the coastline. It sent me from a casual walk into a jog, then a run – as fast as my legs and heart would carry me. Velos would only roar during the day if he was in danger or intense pain. Three times I had to stop, to catch my breath – I was never really a runner. But each time, I swallowed, clutched at my stomach to alleviate the stitch in my side, and soldiered on. The roar didn't come again which made me worry even more. What had Faso done?

I saw the converted stables, then something glistening underneath the tarpaulin covered roof. Something bronze, the same colour as Faso's workshop and the old war-automatons which it was made of. Even closer, I could see Faso's coattails blowing in the wind and Papo's bulky form. Both men had their backs to me, standing back from Velos a little with their arms crossed and heads high. A fleet of miniature airships floated away from the scene, the same machines that I'd seen piecing Faso's workshop together the other day. Even closer still and I could see Velos' head flat against the ground, dead to the world. Closer again, I saw Mamo emerging from my cottage with a tea-tray in her hand.

I sprinted, screaming expletives. Papo and Faso turned to me. Mamo almost dropped the tray. Closer still, I saw something sticking out of Velos' flank, and that horrible armour I'd seen on Faso's floor, on his body. Then, I was near enough to see Ratter clinging onto Velos, the automaton's lips clamped around a glass beaker of some kind that looked through my blurry vision like some kind of a syringe.

I used whatever energy I had left when I got there to take a huge swing and I punched Faso in the face. He wasn't fast enough to dodge out of the way. My knuckles cracked when they made contact right on the bridge of his nose. It probably hurt me more than it did him, but I was past caring.

"Pontopa!" I think the call came from Papo.

"Shut up!" I shouted, shaking my fist. "Faso, you filthy, swine-eating piece of swill. I told you not to put the armour on Velos... So, what do you do? You're a swine, Faso... A swine in a suit!"

Faso raised his hand to his face and wiped away some blood that had begun to trickle out of his nose. Papo loitered a little further back, probably trying to work out how best to break this up. Mamo quickly placed the tray down and stepped in between me and Faso and held out her arms. "Pontopa, we—"

"Don't talk! Just..." I was already sprinting towards Ratter, new energy coming from somewhere. I took hold of the automaton, pulled it out of Velos and threw it onto the ground. The syringe shattered out across the gravel, a piece brushing against my leg but not scratching. I stamped on him a few times hoping to break it into pieces. But somehow that damn machine rolled away and scurried back towards Faso. I ran to Velos, placed a hand on the bridge of his nose, then I put my head down against him to listen for breath. Fortunately, he was still breathing. I turned to Faso.

"You could have killed him, you arrogant bastard!"

"Oh, for wellies sake! He's just sleeping off the effects of the sedative."

I took hold of a heavy piece of firewood lying around near Velos and threw it at Faso's head. This time he dodged out of the way. "Why, you bastard? Why?"

"Pontopa, get a hold of yourself," Mamo said. "Faso, I think it's best if you left."

"Pontopa, I..." Faso said.

"Get out of here!" I looked up at him, my vision kind of hazy with tears. Faso stood there staring, clearly unsure what to do.

"Go!" I screamed and he turned on his heels and walked away, Ratter peeking up over his collarbone.

"I better be able to get this thing off him," I shouted after Faso. He glanced back over his shoulder, clearly had nothing better to say and then carried on his way. I returned my head to Velos, listening to his breathing, almost like a snore.

Papo stepped forwards. "Pontopa, Faso said—"

"I don't care what he said," I snapped. "I told you he wasn't to be trusted and you let him do it. You're no better than him."

"But—"

"Just go, Papo!" I screamed and I looked around for something to throw at him but found nothing.

"Come on dear," Mamo said. "Best leave her be for now." She took hold of his hand and led him past the cottage to the farmhouse. I stayed put for a while, trying to piece together what had just happened.

I had left them alone with Faso and he'd talked to them and convinced them to betray me. In a way, I wanted to know why they did it, but then I didn't want to hear their excuses. I didn't want to hear their patronising tones and the fact that they thought they knew better and they didn't trust me to make decisions on my own.

I'd have to talk to them eventually. With Velos sleeping like this, there was no way I could just take him and run away. But the thought of talking to anyone sent me into a fit of rage. So, I examined the armour, tried to find a way of taking it off. I thought of lifting it, but the thing was covered with screws that had somehow pierced Velos' scales where they folded down above his skin. Did it hurt? I wondered. Did he need the sedative because he was in so much pain?

Eventually I spotted Mamo loitering nearby. When I looked up, she approached gingerly, and I watched her through blurry eyes. She placed herself on a trestle stool a few yards away from me and looked out towards the waning sun.

"I'm sorry, dear," she said. "I didn't know Faso and your father – I mean, I would have stopped them if I knew, or at least asked them to wait until you got back."

"Just leave me alone," I snapped.

Mamo dipped her head. "I'm sorry," she said, and then she turned to leave.

THERE WAS a bottle of brandy in the cupboard in my cottage, twenty years matured. I didn't really drink much – didn't have the head for it really. So, the bottle remained largely unused, reserved for sombre occasions like tonight. I took the bottle, a sherry glass, and a spiral citronella candle and sat outside under the moonlight on the trestle stool. There I waited, watching Velos for any signs of life.

There's something about strong emotions that allows alcohol to travel fast down the gullet and the stomach to open up and accept it with ease. As I drank, I sat listening to the occasional hoots of owls, and a bat sometimes fluttered over the moon, cutting out its glow for a fraction of a moment. In a way, I wanted to read some more Sukina Sako to at least try to cut off the thoughts. But even my favourite author had no chance of cheering me up.

So instead, I decided to play a little game. Every time I thought of a man, I would flick him out of my mind with a swig from the glass and refill. If I thought of Faso and what a swine he was, the subsequent burn in my chest would erase him from my train of thoughts. If I thought of Papo, always trying to control things, down another swig would go. If I thought of men in general and their thirst for prestige or power, then the golden liquor would be travelling down before I could even think of who those men were. I drank to forget my ego. I drank to forget about those men who wanted to have reign over my life. I drank, in short, to be free.

After a while, I decided to move closer to Velos. The dragon was really my best friend in the world, and it pained me to know that Faso could even think of sedating him. But he'd wake up, surely, he would. I stroked his rough scales. "It will be okay," I said. "We'll get through this, Velos. We'll get that ugly suit off you then show Faso who is really boss around here."

Usually, even in his sleep, he'd raise his head when I stroked him, and start to croon from the bottom of his neck. But there was no response from him. I felt empty – as if part of me had left this world.

Soon, I found myself imagining myself as Varion the Dragon Boy and his songs. As I watched Velos, listened to his soft snores, I wondered if I could indeed sing to talk to him. Enough out of my senses not to feel foolish, I decided to try my hand at it. Varion's songs were meant to be without melody, so I hummed as if singing chants from an ancient temple. My voice didn't really have much tune, nothing intrinsically memorable, yet there still seemed an innate beauty to the song. Maybe I saw Velos stir and tilt his head, maybe I imagined it, but I certainly felt a strange sense of connection, almost as if I was in his body with my eyes closed, dreaming dragon dreams.

I awoke, shivering and cold. I went inside and crawled into bed.

THE NEXT DAY, I was woken up at daybreak by a heavy rap at the door. I put on my dressing gown and opened the door, half expecting to see my parents or Faso there. But instead, there was the mayor's son, Domio, a gangly boy of about fourteen with long ash-blond hair. I squinted at him.

"Miss Wells," he said. "If you'd please excuse me, I didn't mean to wake you."

"What is it?" I asked. "Why so early?"

"I'm sorry, Miss Wells, but my father didn't think you'd want to miss this. It's just, you see, the author Sukina Sako is in town and she's requesting an audience with you. Would you please accompany me to the town hall?"

I blinked off the surprise. That certainly was an exciting turn of events, my favourite author actually requesting to meet me when I was expecting another row with my parents. "Of course she can," I said. "I'll get showered and be there in half an hour."

PART II

SUKINA

"Varion was a boy who could talk to dragons, and he did so not through words, gestures, or expressions, but through a harmonic and beautiful song."

— FROM 'THE DRAGON BOY' BY SUKINA SAKO

4

Before I was born, the Five Hamlets – Drani, Forst, Pagla, Boroti, and Girn – were independent in their own rights. Not only that, but they competed for the position of the best wine exporter in all of Tow. Each hamlet supplied the surrounding vineyards. Initially, they'd just consisted of cottages and farmhouses, but the vineyards became lucrative enough, and the scenery was so beautiful that retirees emigrated here from Spezzio, causing the hamlets to expand into villages.

They didn't start to merge, until I began importing secicao at fourteen years of age. This had created such a boom to the Five Hamlet's that the villages spread outwards to combine into one large town.

The town hall was no longer the unadorned assembly hall built of local timber I remembered from my youth, but a gothic wonder with gargoyle-topped towers. Flags hung from the eaves of the roof with the insignias of each of the original Five Hamlets. Another flag rose up even higher from the central tower, displaying the town's emblem – two curling vines wrapped around a dragon.

Inside, Sukina Sako was in conversation with Mr Sandorini, the mayor, both seated on upholstered velvet chairs in the waiting room. The author wore a green floral dress and had a strap over her shoulder leading to a canvas haversack on her back. She was petite – much smaller than I'd expected her to be.

Amusingly, the fading paintings of the patrons of the original hamlets had been removed from beneath the high arched windows and replaced with illustrations of scenes from Sukina Sako's novels. In each of them, I recognised Varion staring down at me with playful eyes. I couldn't help but smile. Until, that was, my hangover kicked in and part of me wanted to throw up instead.

Mr Sandorini stood up, his cheeks ruddy underneath his fuzzy moustache and his smile full of mirth. His eyes seemed pleading as if telling me to be on my best behaviour and represent the town well. Sukina rose too. She stood back with her hands folded towards her knees while the mayor spoke. "Ah, Miss Wells, I wasn't sure you'd be able to make it. Our wonderful writer, Sukina Sako has honoured us with our visit, and she has requested you."

"It's an honour," I said, and I nodded to Sukina.

"You know, she has over a million books in print." He gestured towards the paintings. "I had these commissioned especially for the occasion. I'm sure, she'll... you know... portray us well." That last part he gave in a mock whisper, loud enough for Sukina to hear.

"I know," I said, and I waited patiently, as I started to wonder why there weren't any paintings here of Sukina herself.

"Right then," the mayor said. "I'll leave you two ladies alone." He exited via the left wing.

Sukina offered me her hand. "Well, you already know I'm Sukina Sako from Orkc. You must be the famous dragon girl."

"Pontopa Wells, at your service." I took her hand. She had this wonderful marble-like face, so polished above her high cheekbones that she looked almost like a statue. Although her author bio said she was fifteen years my senior, she looked the same age. She'd painted her lips with a little pink lipstick which complemented her long eyelashes and almond, slightly slanted eyes well. Her hair was jet black and incredibly straight. Indeed, she looked very different from anyone I'd seen in Tow.

"Say, I've read virtually all your books," I said. Although, this was the first time I'd seen what she looked like, as she never displayed her picture in her books.

"That's good to hear." While I expected her to have a bouncy alacrity, she didn't seem to be the smiley type. Even when she looked at me, her eyes seemed kind of dreamy as if thinking of a far-off fictional world. "I guess you have some notion of why I'd visit you here."

"I don't. I mean, I kind of regret that I didn't write you a letter. That's what fans do, right?"

"Oh, it's of no consequence," she said with a dismissive wave. "I actually came to learn more about your work and hopefully to visit your dragon, for research purposes. It's the last remaining coloured dragon on the North Continent, you know?"

"I do. Although I've never quite believed it."

"Please don't misunderstand me. There are other dragons of colour – in Cadigan and the Saye Archipelago. But not here and all thanks to Cini II's war effort. There are none either in the Southlands, but that's for different reasons."

"Why exactly is that?"

"Well, for a dragon to gain colour, it has to live away from the secicao clouds for quite a while. No one really knows why. But, while Greys aren't fertile, coloured dragons are and – since there's less and less of them – they've become immensely important to the dragon queens."

My eyes widened in surprise. "Dragon queens?"

"Why, of course. All dragons need a queen. This world has eight. Haven't you read about them in my books?"

"Never... There's boy dragons and there's girl dragons, but none of them are queens."

"Yes, I remember," Sukina's eyebrows turned downwards. She turned to one of the paintings on the wall, just above the right-wing staircase. "Cini censored them all out. Didn't want you Towese knowing that there's actually a civilisation in the Southlands."

"What? Why would he do that?"

Sukina shook her head. "I guess it's easier if it's just the king against the dragons..."

I was lost for words. Eventually, I found the silence so awkward that I thought I'd better cut through it.

"Say, you came to see Velos, right? How about we go over to my place now? My parents are always honoured when a celebrity comes to visit." Although I wasn't sure I wanted to see them right at that moment, particularly Papo.

Sukina smiled and half bowed. "It would be an honour."

"Then let's go. If you want, I have some of those censored books at home."

We left the town hall and followed the path through the Five Hamlet's narrow alleyways towards the vineyard. En route, the smell of freshly baked bread and melons lying out in the sun made me slightly peckish.

Sukina and I talked a bit about our childhoods: how I'd been brought up by two parents and a dragon and about her nomadic ways travelling through the icy north when she was a child. Her mother died young and so, eventually, she and her father had decided to settle in Slaro. But they packed up their bags and left in a hurry several years later. Sukina didn't say why.

Once we hit the cliff-edge, I looked north towards the workshop. There must have been an expression of scorn on my face.

"There's something over there which troubles you," Sukina said.

"Oh, it's nothing. I mean, there's this inventor that's just set up there. I've been ordered to work for him, and you'll never believe what a swine he is. You'll soon see what he did to Velos."

"Ah, that must be Faso. I've heard he's moved here."

"You know him?" I felt a sudden fear that Sukina might somehow be chummy with that buffoon.

"I was in a relationship with him for five years. Fortunately, it didn't last. Faso is..." She stared up at the circling seagulls. "It doesn't matter."

I made a mental note to question her about it later. I didn't know how anyone could fall for such a swine for even a day, let alone five years. But for now, I thought it best to leave that stone unturned.

I wasn't quite ready to see my parents again yet. Fortunately, they were in the farmhouse when I arrived, oblivious to their celebrity guest. Sukina didn't seem too bothered about their absence. Instead, she was eyeing Velos up and down as we approached. Velos' armour glinted in the sunlight.

Sukina's lips tightened. "What is that thing on him?"

I shuddered, remembering Faso's atrocities the previous day. "That is what my father calls Faso's genius."

"Faso invented this... suit?"

"He did..." I said through clenched teeth. Much as I was angry with Papo, I didn't name him as an accomplice to this act. Deep inside, I guess, I didn't want Sukina to see him as an antagonist as well. "Faso installed it on Velos after I had vehemently told him not to."

Sukina furrowed her eyebrows and her lips curled downwards. "I might have known he'd still be up to his antics." She walked up to Velos and began to run her hands along the armour.

"I know... I'm honestly not sure I could have put up with him for so long."

I wanted to take that back as soon as the words tumbled out of my mouth. I'd had enough of a fall out with my parents that I didn't want to also offend my favourite author. But she just looked at me, blinked and then answered as if I had a perfect right to ask about her relationship, even if we'd just met. "People are evidently misguided when they're young. But how did you two get acquainted? You said that you have to work with him?"

"A contract from Cini. The king says he wants to improve the output of secicao from this town to aid his war effort. So, he has this idiotic idea that if Faso and I combine our processes, we'll be able to create the finest secicao oil in the world."

Sukina raised a hand to her chin. "I see. Actually, I did want to talk to you about that."

But before she could say anything else, she looked up towards Mamo turning the corner of the cottage and skipping towards us.

"Why, Pontopa, I thought I saw a guest," she said and offered Sukina her hand.

"Sukina Sako." She accepted the handshake.

"The author? Wow, I'd never have thought..."

"It's good to know that you are acquainted with my work," Sukina said. "Many don't find time to read nowadays."

"It's always such a pleasure. I'm Versalina, by the way. Say, Pontopa, why don't you put some secicao on for our guest. I'll tell my husband you're here. He'll be so eager to meet you, I'm sure."

"I'd be honoured," Sukina said. "But just tea would do fine."

"Whatever you need," Mamo said. "I'll be right back." She walked with a skip in her step towards the door.

"Come on," I said to Sukina. "I'll show you the cottage." I led her inside.

I'd been in such a rush to meet Sukina that I'd not had time to tidy up that morning. I'd left my nightie strewn across the sofa and there was a mess in the sink. So, I apologised to her, threw my nightie into the bedroom and put the kettle on the stove.

"You needn't worry," she said. "I don't mind a place looking lived in. It's hardly as if I have the personal luxury of a maid myself."

Now that surprised me. I'd always thought that a maid would be a given for a successful author like Sukina, probably living in a mansion and whatnot. It seemed rude to ask questions about it though. "You know," I said instead, "quite often my parents look after things here, while I tend to Velos. But we had a bit of a row..."

"It must be hard having parents so close all the time."

"Tell me about it."

Papo's voice came from outside and Sukina turned to the door. Papo entered the room. He flashed a toothy smile and held out his hand to Sukina. "Two celebrities in two days. It's my lucky week." This was the man who'd just called my Sukina Sako novels stupid the previous day.

Sukina greeted him and I ushered everyone into the living room while Mamo took over making the tea. Sukina sat down on the seat nearest the window and placed her haversack down on the side table.

In all honesty, most of the conversation that followed involved Papo asking questions as if interviewing for a magazine. I could imagine him mentally taking notes, planning what he'd put in his letter to the editor of the Tow Observer. Maybe he'd even try to write a short article for them.

Still, Sukina didn't seem annoyed. She answered the questions politely, her hands folded neatly across her lap. Soon Mamo came over with the cups of tea and she asked more personal stuff, in other words the kind of diplomatic small talk that mothers often give to their child's friends. Eventually, it all came to a standstill. Mamo excused both of them and dragged Papo through the door. Sukina and I watched them go.

"I can see there's tension there," Sukina said once they were well out of sight.

"How do you mean?"

"Between you and your parents, and particularly your father. He wasn't involved in Faso's install-the-armour escapade, by any chance?"

Never before had I met someone who could be so perceptive – even more so than my mother. "How can you tell?"

"Piecing things together. I figured that Faso wouldn't have been able to get that thing on Velos alone."

She finished her tea and placed her cup down on the table. I quaffed mine, put both cups on the tray and refilled them from the teapot. Sukina thanked me, picked up her cup and took another sip.

"Look, about that contract," she said. "I didn't just come to see Velos. I came to warn you about the dangers. Now I see I'll have to remind Faso about them, once again. Let me tell you now that secicao is endangering the world."

I looked at her, astonished. "You knew about our edict from the king before you came here?"

"I knew that the king wanted to improve his refinement process. I didn't know Faso was involved."

"So why would we need to stop it? I mean, I don't want to work with Faso, but this is an order..."

"I know it won't be easy. But allow me to spend some time to show you a few things." She walked up to my bookshelf and began to thumb through my books. "Do you have anything here by Gerhaun Forsi?"

"Say who?"

"Gerhaun Forsi. She's an anthropologist who lives out in the Southlands and studies the relationship between dragons and seci-cao. There's a book by her called *Dragons and Ecology*." She walked back to her seat and started to ruffle through her haversack on the side table. "Here, I have a copy of it. Gerhaun explains why secicao is a blight upon this world and cannot be trusted. The more we refine secicao, the more we endanger the planet. The only thing that

Cini's plans to automate your refinement process will serve is the entire annihilation of this continent. Oh, and the Greys are actually on our side."

"But then why would the king declare all-out war on them?"

Sukina looked at me knowingly. "Let me just say that the dragons are attacking the harvesters because they don't want to allow the secicao to spread north. When that stuff is flushed down toilets in human excrement, it's released into the soil which, in turn, becomes more acidic. This makes the soil so toxic to other plants, that only secicao can grow in it. Then one secicao seed carried on the wind over the sea is all it takes, and the stuff spreads like a blight."

"You mean to say it will kill us?"

"It could be in as soon as thirty years."

Outside, a sparrow landed on the window and began to tap on the ledge to pick at some ants. In the sky, an osprey wheeled overhead. The sun had begun to paint a red line just underneath the clouds. "All this life destroyed..." I said. "The fruits of mine and Velos' labour amounting to such destruction. Surely, it can't be true..."

Sukina looked at her watch. "I'm sorry to deliver it to you like this. But everyone who supports Cini's war effort needs to know the stakes. Ultimately, I'm sure the king has been told, and this is why he censors books. I guess it's no surprise you've never heard of Gerhaun Forsi."

"I guess," I said.

"Anyway, I have to also meet with Faso, and it sounds like, the way he's treated you, I have a bone to pick with him too." She deposited the book on the coffee table. "You'll read this won't you? Just don't let on that you've got it here." She turned towards the door.

"Wait!" I said. "I'm coming with you. I want to see Faso squirm and two of us are better than one."

"I guess you're right," Sukina said, and for the first time, I saw a slight grin. Despite the bomb she'd just dropped on me, it seemed I was beginning to make a new friend.

Sukina glanced once more at the bookshelf then she grabbed her haversack and we both headed outside.

5

Sukina didn't seem as moved by the sight of Faso's workshop as I'd been. In fact, I swear that she scowled when the doorbell automaton floated over to her. This time, it had been modified to include a lens that jutted out from its face. Sukina looked at the device, thrust her face right up to the lens and whacked the red button just beneath that with the side of her fist. "Faso, it's me, you buffoon," she said to the machine. "Come right down here this instant. I have a bone to pick with you."

The machine clicked, whirred a little, then flew back towards one of the high slit windows of Faso's workshop, where it disappeared from view. Sukina turned to me. "You've got to be direct with Faso. He doesn't notice when you're angry unless you show it explicitly."

I nodded, smiled. I'd hardly been skirting around corners with Faso. But then, I had a feeling he would respect Sukina as more of a woman not to be messed with than he did me, simply on the account that he'd known her longer.

"How long has it been since you last saw him?" I asked.

"Oh, I don't think since I left Tow all that time ago. Must have been around nine years."

We waited a moment for a response, but it didn't come immediately. The workshop simply swayed in the wind. The sky around it was hauntingly still, no sign of any airships doing construction work.

"Maybe he's out," I suggested.

"Not the Faso I know. He's probably watching from a window up there seeing if we'll go away."

Which was unsurprising really, given how I'd punched him in the face yesterday. "We should probably go," I said.

"No, no, let's see this one out. We can have some fun with this." Sukina cupped her small hands to her mouth and projected her voice with a power that belied her tiny frame. "Faso, we know you're in there. If you don't come out, we have a dragon that can roast you in there alive. I'm sure he'd find it a pleasure after what you did to him."

I smirked. "Will he really take you seriously?"

"If anything, I think he'll be surprised to see me. The last time was meant to be the final goodbye."

We waited for a while with our legs wide and hands on our hips. It seemed so long that I just wanted to turn around and give up. But Sukina didn't seem ready to move and, every now and again, hollered out assertions that we weren't going to go away so easily.

Soon enough, the ramp spiralled down from the workshop and Faso emerged at the door wearing a sharp black suit. Even from this distance, I could see the purple welt I'd caused beneath his right eye. "Ladies, ladies!" he called down. "Do you have to make such a racket? I'm trying to get some hard-earned rest." He was squinting. "Sukina, is that you?"

"Didn't your device record my message?" Sukina shouted back. "Or didn't you recognise my voice?"

"Why didn't you just press the button?"

"I did!"

Faso shrugged. "Oh, well, I guess I need to make some modifications. What do you want?"

"To talk," Sukina said, "and hopefully for you to apologise to Pontopa here."

"And tell me how to get that damn armour off him," I added.

"Hang on, hang on," Faso said. "I'll be right down." He went back into his workshop and then re-emerged a moment later with Ratter on his shoulder. He lowered himself onto his haunches onto the slide. As he slid down, Ratter watched me with those red menacing, crystalline eyes.

"Don't make any sudden movements," Sukina whispered in my ear.

"What, why?"

She remained silent until Faso approached. "First things first, Faso," Sukina said, "get that thing to take its sights off Pontopa. I know your tricks. Pontopa, right now, won't harm you."

"Dragonheats, did you see what she did to me?" Faso pointed to the welt on his right eye. I was impressed I'd managed to cause such a bruise. I hadn't, in all honesty, been in many brawls.

"Yes, and you bloody well deserved it," Sukina said. "But we're not here for fisticuffs. We need to talk about your contract."

Faso studied Sukina for a moment. "Oh, if you insist..." He tapped Ratter on its back three times and, thankfully, the automaton scurried down his arm and hid itself in Faso's widened sleeve. "So, let's talk. And don't be long, I've a busy schedule."

Sukina swallowed. Deep inside, I thought I could feel her seething.

"Very well," she said. "I came to convince you to quit the contract and come south with us. Fortress Gerhaun would welcome your skills, and we could give you a better life than you have here, living out of Cini's pocket. Gerhaun Forsi, in short, wishes to employ your services."

"For what, exactly?" Faso said.

"Because you're one of the best inventors in this land, and Gerhaun would rather you helped advance science for her cause rather than Cini's."

Faso cocked his head and scratched at the stubble on the side of his face. I'm sure that would have ballooned his ego. "I see," he said. "So, you did go south in the end? Here I was thinking that strange man – was his name Colas – had *really* sold you to a dragon queen."

"Gerhaun Forsi is real," Sukina snapped back. "If you saw her, you'd believe. For your information, she's much better to work for than a monarch who will backstab you at any opportunity."

Faso let out a desultory laugh. "Really? I guess you flew all the way from the Southlands on dragonback, without any of Cini's forces shooting you out of the sky."

"I have my ways," Sukina said.

"And wellies knows how many merchants you stowed away with to get through the barrier."

Sukina's lips tightened. "I can travel quite freely, thank you very much. It's a personal choice to travel via boat rather than air."

"Oh really? Didn't you see that article today in the Tow Observer mentioning the terrorist organization down south? It's only a matter of time before King Cini comes looking for you."

"Fortress Gerhaun had nothing to do with Prince Artua's kidnapping, and the king has no idea who I work for."

"Because you haven't published your photograph anywhere and you shy away from cameras? I would have thought you'd at least have considered a false alias by now, Sukina. I guess you're here to convince us of the dangers of the secicao blight. Gerhaun Forsi and her unscientific nonsense. I've read her baloney."

Sukina had her fists clenched by her side. "Gerhaun has conclusive, empirical evidence."

"Because she lives in the Southlands and calls herself a dragon queen? She's published no statistics; I've seen nothing in the scientific journals."

"You're a buffoon, Faso. You've not seen any statistics because Cini won't publish them. But of course there's evidence. You've been to the Southlands, haven't you?"

"Which is one piece of land with its very own characteristic ecosystem. What proof is there that what's going on down there will happen up here?"

At this point, part of me wanted to run away and leave these two to their bickering. But I felt this strange sense of feeling what Sukina was feeling. A kind of rage mixed with yearning, as if a thief had just stolen my necklace and then positioned me by a shop window where that very same necklace was for sale. In the same manner, part of me wanted to reach out with my mind and soothe Sukina. But that would be impossible, right? How could what's in my mind possibly influence what's in hers?

But Sukina seemed to sense something too. She stopped in her tracks, completely blanking Faso, and turned slowly to me. Meanwhile, Faso held his arms outwards and shrugged, clearly not liking to be ignored. Sukina raised one eyebrow at me. "So, it's true... I suspected as much."

"What?" I asked.

"I suspected it when I saw how you behaved around Velos. You can connect to the collective unconscious. There's more to you than meets the eye, Pontopa Wells."

Really, I was glad Sukina had decided to talk to me directly because I'd had enough of turning my head between these two in an attempt to make sense of it all. "Okay," I said. "Could you please fill me in here? Give me a little context, at least. You're talking about dragon queens, Fortress Gerhaun, Faso says you're a terrorist, and now this mystical thing called the collective unconscious. For wellies' sake, what is going on?"

Sukina turned to me and smiled. Her face had a kind of ethereal glow that seemed to tone down my emotions somewhat. "I think you might want to come south with me and see for yourself," she said.

"What? Why?"

"Because. It looks like you're a dragonseer."

Which left me absolutely dumbstruck. Understandable, given my favourite author had turned loopy all of a sudden. "What in the dragonheats are you talking about, Sukina?"

"Okay, this is going to be hard to believe, but there's a reason your connection with Velos is so strong. I came from Fortress Gerhaun, which is one of the eight fortresses in the Southlands run by dragon queens. Gerhaun Forsi is not only an anthropologist but a dragon queen and mother of two thousand Greys. I am a dragonseer, which means I work with her."

"You're a..." I was lost for words. Varion in Sukina's books was a dragonseer. Could my favourite author's fictional worlds in fact be constructed from her own delusions?

"Oh, this is just bloody marvellous," Faso said. He shook his sleeve and Ratter came back up to his shoulder. It swiped at a mosquito and knocked it right out of the air. "You decide there's no chance of getting me to come south, so you decide to work on my business partner instead. Hence, leaving me to explain her desertion and to pick up the consequences while hanging from the gallows."

Sukina's eyes narrowed. "Dragonheats, you can be impossible, Faso."

"And you can be so... treacherous."

It was kind of hard to concentrate with these two bickering away, but still I was trying to organise my thoughts. What Sukina had told me made sense when I thought about it – I'd always felt something with Velos. Plus, what Faso said didn't make sense – Sukina just didn't seem to be the terrorist type. Despite all this, and this really wasn't rational, but I somehow knew that Sukina was telling the truth.

Perhaps part of it was me not wanting to believe bad things about my favourite author. But also, something had started to grow in me, this strange sense of knowing a lot more about Sukina than I'd ever had a chance to learn.

The two had just reached that lull in their argument where they had run out of things to say. Faso had just about turned on his heels ready to go back inside. Sukina was furious: I could feel it, the rage also fuming inside me. At the same time, I felt kind of detached from the emotion. I had enough rationality at that point to take a few breaths and let it cool. Now seemed a good time to deliver my coup de grâce.

"I think I want to go south, Sukina," I said.

Sukina turned to me. She blinked a few times. "That's good to hear," she said after a short pause.

"Yes, it sounds like an adventure, and you... Your world fascinates me." Crazy as this might seem, I believed her. I couldn't really explain why. Partly, it just felt right.

Faso had taken a few steps and stopped, turned around. "Well, I didn't think you'd manage to convince her with such a phoney sales pitch. Pontopa, this is stupid."

"No," I said. "Stupid is getting me in such a rage that I make irrational decisions like punching you in the face. If you'd just asked nicely." Well, I still wouldn't have let him install the armour, but a man needs to learn how to behave.

Sukina was beaming. "So, that's settled then."

"Where are you staying by the way?" I asked.

"Well, I have a room booked in The Vineyardier."

"Oh, stay with me," I said. "The sofa's comfortable and I've so many questions."

"Fantastic idea."

Faso huffed and turned around. He punched the button that flipped up the slats of the staircase and then stepped on and let the device carry him up. Sukina watched him go, scorn tracing the line of her lips.

"Come on," I said. "Let's leave this moron to sulk."

WE TOOK a detour on the way back to cool off a little via the cliff-edge. It was drizzling and it felt a little chilly – we should have brought our coats, really. But still, we walked fast enough that we didn't get too cold.

Back at the cottage, the sink had been cleaned and a plate of chocolate biscuits was on the table – a peace offering, I was sure. My parents had left a note saying that they were going hiking then shopping and that they wouldn't be back until late evening. I made Sukina tea again – I realised now why she wouldn't want to drink secicao – and we talked a little until she was yawning out her words. I let her nap on the sofa, while I sat under the steady light from the reading lamp.

The latest Tow Observer had been placed in the magazine rack by my armchair – Papo must have been reading it while Mamo washed the dishes. I picked it up to try and get the latest on Prince Artua, but there was nothing new, only journalists who wanted to revive old news. So, they interviewed a farmer who thought he'd seen the boy who had turned out to be a scarecrow. At least in fiction stories got completed, rather than being revived and revived aimlessly.

Yawning, I picked up *Dragons and Ecology* and began to leaf through the book. It amazed me to think how a dragon queen could write such a thing and I tried to imagine her gripping the pen with her front claws.

While Sukina's explanation had felt like part of a dream, the information had flown by so fast, Gerhaun Forsi explained it in clear, succinct language. I felt entirely convinced, as well as mesmerised. It felt as if I was reading words written by my own kin.

Eventually, I drifted off to sleep. I later woke up to Sukina reading a censored version of one of her books, a scowl on her face. She lifted her head and we began to talk about the practicalities of going south.

We decided that when Velos awoke, we'd take him with us. Sukina said she could wait until then. But I felt anxious, really. Velos could take up to a week to wake up after a heavy run south and, for all I knew, he might never wake up again. Fortunately, Sukina kept me distracted from these horrible thoughts, and we continued to talk about life, dragons, and the Southlands until sunset when we were ready for sleep.

I looked outside to see if the lights were on in my parent's farm-house, but they didn't seem to be back yet. After I had checked on Velos, who was still dead to the world, I turned off the lights. Sukina and I slept until the late hours of morning.

I woke up with a groggy head but a decisive mind. Something was different – I knew it before I could put words to thought. I'd left the bedroom door open and the sun streamed through the front windows. Without bothering to get dressed or say good morning to Sukina, I put my slippers on and ran out into the yard.

Velos now had his head raised to the sky, but his eyelids were still droopy. The sun was out and already gave the air a latent heat, even though it was still early. The light gleamed off Velos' majestic blue scales and that ugly armour. Meanwhile, Velos lowered his head towards me and I rubbed the bridge of his nose. Sukina was soon out and standing next to me, fully dressed.

"He's amazing," she said. "He stands so much taller than the Greys."

I wouldn't know – I'd only seen Greys in flight. "Velos is certainly something," I said. "I can't tell you how happy I am to see him awake."

"You know, the armour..." Sukina cocked her head. "Come to think of it, it doesn't look so bad."

Velos raised his head and stood up proud, as if posing for a photograph.

"What are you looking so smug about?" I said and I glanced out towards Faso's workshop. I imagined the whole thing walking on its chicken feet towards us, chasing Velos through the woods and trying to shoot him down with its decommissioned war-automaton parts. I turned to Sukina. "This armour needs to be taken off him. A man might look good in an itchy suit until he takes it off and shows how red his skin is underneath."

"But Velos doesn't seem affected by it."

"Still, Faso was wrong putting it there and I'm sure it will do Velos no good wearing it."

Sukina smiled. "You are headstrong, I give you that. I think Gerhaun will like you."

"I hope so," I said, and I walked around Velos. His muscles were taut, and they felt strong again. He started to croon from the base of his throat. "He looks ready for flying," I said after my brief inspection.

"That may be. But take as long as you need."

Really, I had no reason to be sticking around. "I'll just go and deliver the news to my parents. I'll be back soon."

I literally danced around the side of the cottage towards my parent's farmhouse. The door was open, and the smoky smell of bacon and eggs wafted out. Mamo was in the kitchen holding a frying pan over the stove, light smoke rising from it. Next to her, on the counter, was a full jug of tomato juice.

"Ah, Pontopa, you're awake," she said. "I was just going to bring you breakfast. How did you sleep, dear? I've only just got up myself."

"A late one?" I asked.

"We ended up in the bar last night. Your father's still in bed." The frying pan began to spit, and so Mamo turned the heat down on the stove.

"Look, Mamo," I said. "Maybe we should have breakfast outside? Sukina stayed the night and we've both got some news."

"Sukina? Gosh! Okay, I'll just wake him. Look after the pan will you, darling?" While Mamo went towards the stairs, I moved towards the pan and turned the heat down a little more, so I wouldn't have to pay it much heed.

Creaks came from the staircase and then Mamo's footsteps passed by overhead. I hummed to myself, some kind of strange tune which you wouldn't even have recognised as having a melody.

After a while, I noticed the tune to be the same as that

harmonic progression I'd produced by the tree trunk the other day when I was reading *The Dragon Boy*. My voice seemed to reach out into the air around me like gentle shimmering tendrils, but I dismissed the effect as an illusion caused by the heat from the pan.

It must have been a good ten minutes or so before I heard Papo's heavy feet staggering across the landing and down the stairs. He walked in, bleary-eyed, his hair dishevelled, wearing a t-shirt and jeans. Mamo followed him into the room.

"We'll meet you at your place, darling," Mamo said. "Your father just needs a brief hair of the dog to whip him on his way."

I went back towards the front of my cottage. Sukina was just outside, crouched next to Velos' head, crooning a soft song to him. She looked up as I approached, and I told her breakfast would be ready soon. We went inside. Sukina helped me set up the coffee table with cutlery, crockery and placemats.

Papo soon came in with a sizzling frying pan, looking much better for wear. He looked at me and smiled, but I returned a sneer. If he thought I'd forgive him that easily, he had another thing coming.

Mamo followed with the tomato juice. We sat down and served out our food. Sukina said how fantastic it tasted. Mamo mentioned how we only used local eggs and bacon from the farms, which was much better than anything you'd find in the city. Papo asked whether Sukina had heard anything of Artua, seeming to think her celebrity status would give her inside knowledge. Of course, Sukina knew nothing. It was eventually Mamo who decided to get to the point.

"So, dear, what's this news you mentioned?" she asked.

I felt bad breaking it to Mamo. But really, I had no other choice. "Sukina and I have decided to visit her home in the Southlands," I said.

Papo almost spat out his food. "You're going where? But King Cini... What about your contract, Pontopa?"

"I'll only be gone a week or so, Papo. Sukina knows people that I want to meet, and I think this could be good for the business." Of course, I mentioned nothing about Faso's allegations that Sukina might be working for terrorists. But then, in all honesty, I found this hard to believe.

Mamo reached out and I saw her squeeze Papo's hand. "Where exactly are you going, dear?" she asked.

"The place is called Fortress Gerhaun," Sukina said. "I want to introduce Pontopa to my mentor, Gerhaun Forsi." She glanced my way. I gave her an approving nod. Wisely, she hadn't mentioned anything about Gerhaun being a dragon queen.

"But, Miss Sako," Mamo said. "I thought you lived in Orkc." Orkc was a country far to the northeast of Tow, part of the Sovereign States – independently ruled, even though King Cini claimed jurisdiction over them.

"She did," I said. "But now she lives in the Southlands. They have a whole colony of anthropologists down there, and they know things about dragons. Maybe I'll be able to learn more about Velos." I avoided mentioning anything about the Greys and dragon queens – that would have just tipped them over the edge.

"But how on earth can anyone live down there?" Papo asked. "Those clouds make the place virtually inhabitable. I've read it in the magazines."

"Trust me," Sukina said with a sly smile. "There are ways."

Mamo had been silent so far, but she was communicating with Papo with her eyes, the way that couples often do. She had her fork poised in the air with a bit of egg attached to it. Papo looked at me again, this time as if he wanted to tell me that he didn't approve of this decision. But I just huffed and turned away.

"Gerhaun Forsi," Mamo said after a moment's respite. "I think I've heard of her. She wrote that book, didn't she? Was it *Dragons and Ecology*?"

"Have you read it?" I asked.

"No. But I know a lot of people who have. It had a kind of cult following at the time."

"I thought it was banned?"

"That's never stopped university students passing it around the dormitory."

"Say," Papo said. "Is that Mr Gordoni coming down the path?" He pointed his knife at a familiar figure approaching in a suit, wheeling some kind of tank on a trolley.

"Wellies, what's he doing here?" I left my breakfast alone to apprehend Faso outside.

Faso waved once he saw me at the door, but I didn't return the gesture. Sukina came out to join me, then Mamo and Papo. Mamo glared at Faso with an expression of disgust.

"He better have answers for why he lied to you, Cipao."

"I'm sure it was all in good intentions, dear." That caused me to give Papo another hard stare.

"We'll see about that," Mamo said.

As Faso came closer, sunlight glimmered off the top of a brass tank that he was wheeling behind him. Closer still, and I recognised Ratter sitting there, guarding whatever Faso had decided to bring.

"What the hell are you up to, Faso?" I shouted.

"Well good morning to you as well, Miss Wells. How are you today?" He smiled toothily at Papo who smiled back. But Papo's expression fell as he turned to Mamo, who was shaking her head.

"You caused quite a stir here the other day, young man," Mamo said. "Now if you don't mind, please answer my daughter's question. She has every reason not to trust you."

Faso squirmed. "I just... Listen, Velos has awoken, and it's time to fuel his armour."

"How did you find that out so quickly?" I asked.

Faso pointed at the armour. "See that nook, just where Velos' heart is? There's a sensor under there that measures his vital signs. It told me that your dragon's heartbeat had quickened. I knew that either he'd awoken, or he was having nightmares, so I sent an automaton scout earlier this morning to check on him."

"I thought I bloody told you to keep automatons well away from Velos," I said. "You never told me that the armour had sensors on it. You said it didn't use automatons."

"I told you it didn't have a central intelligence. But a sensor can't make decisions. It can only send me information and hence, like the armour, it's not an automaton."

"Well, I'm glad you're here because it's high time you remove the whole thing."

"I can't." Faso scratched the side of his neck. "Once it's on there's a certain adjustment period while the scales heal around the boreholes. If we remove it, your dragon will feel weak for days. But, trust me, things are going to be better this way."

"I've trusted you far enough." I started to lurch towards him. I didn't want to hit him this time, only push a finger to his chest to assert authority. But Ratter turned its red crystalline eyes upon me, and I backed off. "You've done it again, you swine..."

Faso looked where I was glaring. "Ah, sorry," he said. "I have to get that glitch sorted out." He tapped Ratter three times on the back, sending him scurrying back up Faso's sleeve.

"Faso," Sukina said. "You can't force your will upon everyone like this. You were wrong to install the armour without permission and Pontopa has every right to be angry."

Faso put his hands on his hips. "Well, well, I'm genuinely offended," he said. "I came to talk this through with you before we make any more rash moves. You know, like rational people do."

I frowned. "So, have your say."

Faso turned to Sukina. "I've been considering your offer to go south, Sukina, and I think I'll accept it. I've put a lot of money into this dragon armour. Now, I want to see it in action."

I raised an eyebrow. I had a feeling that there was a lot more in this than Faso just wanting to see how the armour works. Granted, as a scientist, he probably wouldn't want to miss the opportunity to see something new as a scientist. But then, perhaps he still had feelings for Sukina that he wasn't letting on about. I glanced over at Papo who had a wide grin on his face. Mamo nudged him in the ribs and whispered something in his ear. Then she walked up to Faso.

"Mr Gordoni," she said. "You lied to my husband here and caused problems in the family. Why should we trust you with anything right now?"

"Why, what lie did I tell exactly, Mrs Wells?"

"You told my father that I'd given you permission to install the armour," I said.

"I didn't. I told him that we'd discussed the prospect and that you hadn't been opposed to the idea of installing a non-automaton entity on Velos."

"That's twisting my words!"

"Please, Pontopa, let's just think about this rationally."

Sukina was tapping her foot. "We're waiting."

"Mr and Mrs Wells, I've spoken to a few people in town and they've told me you're not too happy about your daughter's runs south with the dragon. Honestly, from what I've learnt about Pontopa, I'd say that you're not going to be able to stop her. But you can make sure she has the best protection money can buy. That's what I've created with this armour."

"Oh, please!" I said.

Mamo placed her hand on my shoulder. "Let's hear him out, dear." She had her hand on her chin and she looked as if she'd just seen a new carpet cleaning machine at the market. She'd gone from hating the salesman to thinking what a good buy his product could be.

"Thank you, Mrs Wells," Faso said. "The armour is powered by secicao via these soft pouches on both flanks. We can use any blend of secicao oil in it to augment Velos in any way we like, making him faster to escape automatons, for example. He'll never go hungry mid-flight.

"The armour has two sensors on each side that can warn via an audible alarm of nearby danger. Each of these sensors can be attached to one Gatling cannon, allowing protection from any threat. Harnesses can also be attached on the back to ensure extra safety in flight. In short, I can assure the armour and any automatons I bring south with me will protect your daughter and Velos from the Southlands. We'll be clear of any danger before it even has time to notice us."

He finished his pitch and embraced the silence that ensued. Eventually, Papo stepped forwards and started to examine the armour that he'd helped install. "I wish you'd told me all this before Mr Gordoni because I must say, I'm quite impressed."

"Of course, you are," I said sarcastically.

"Don't talk to me like that in public," Papo snapped back. "You know full well that your safety is my paramount concern."

"Exactly," Faso said. "Thank you, Mr Wells. But remember, this was a team effort."

He looked at Papo who tugged on his collar. "Yes, well..."

Mamo watched Papo with a resigned look on her face. She turned to me and spoke more softly in my ear.

"Look, Pontopa. You have to understand that this is incredibly hard for both me and your father. But sometimes we have to let go. Still, I've got to ask one more time, do you really have to do this?"

"I do," I said. "It's important." As much for me to have a holiday from my father as anything else.

The two men finished their inspection and came back to join us. "It's sold," Papo said. "Faso, we'll take the armour and your protection." There he was, playing matchmaker again with the man I wouldn't marry for the end of the world.

"Papo, the decision isn't up to you," I said.

"While you live under my roof, it is!"

I sighed. I'd just about had enough of Papo's bullish ways. But I decided not to chastise him for it this time. Better they were happy with my decision than we had another row. "Fine, but don't think for a moment I forgive you for what you did, Papo."

"Great," Faso said. "Then let's get on with the fuelling." He walked up to the tank and looked up to Velos. "I assure you, Mr Dragon, this won't hurt a bit."

It had better not, I thought. Because if Faso caused any noticeable pain to Velos then as soon as we were high enough, I'd throw him out of the sky.

SUKINA and I decided to stay one more day. I wanted to spend a little time with Mamo, but I avoided talking to Papo like the plague. This also gave Sukina plenty of time to explore The Five Hamlets, which she told me was one of the most beautiful places she'd seen.

For the first half of the day Sukina, my parents, and I sat and finished our breakfast outside, while Faso installed the tank. Mamo offered Faso a plate. He refused at first, but I guess he couldn't resist the smell, and he was soon tucking in and munching away. After that, Faso took some time to make what he called the finishing touches. I watched while he inserted a pipe into a spigot on Velos' underside and pumped into the armour what Faso described as his finest secicao yet. Papo helped the young inventor, seemingly interested in what he was doing. They were getting on ingratiatingly well.

Meanwhile, Mamo, Sukina, and I sat drinking tea around the outside trestle table. When Mamo asked how long I'd be away for, Sukina told her that it shouldn't be longer than a week. I decided to reveal nothing to Mamo of Faso's assertions that Sukina was a terrorist, or of her association with the Greys, for that matter.

After Faso had finished fuelling Velos' armour, he produced some harnesses from a hatch at the back of the tank and hooked them onto the brass seats that flipped up out of the top of the armour. A ladder led up to the central one of these.

Eventually, Faso and Papo stood back to examine their handiwork, adulation plastered across both their faces. Velos had his head lifted high, peering into the distance as if posing for a photograph. "You're meant to be on my side," I wanted to tell him. But I didn't say anything out loud. Even Sukina had started to support the idea of Velos wearing the armour.

"If it protects Velos, it can't be a bad thing, right?" she said. But it was a matter of principle really – maybe I wouldn't have minded so much if Papo and Faso had talked this over with me first.

Faso eventually left, saying he wanted to finish some things off at his workshop before he travelled. Sukina also asked for some time alone so she could do some research for her novels. Honestly, although I wanted to spend more time with Sukina, it felt good to have a day of peace before we'd have to carry that bumbling fool Faso south. I just hoped I wouldn't have to put up with him long after that.

7

It took a good couple of hours for the fog to clear the next day before it seemed safe to leave. After another breakfast of bacon and eggs – Mamo had decided to spoil me with my favourite meal before I left – I spent some time packing my clothes into a small bag. Faso had created some storage space underneath each seat on Velos' armour. Although I still wasn't happy about the armour, part of me appreciated the extra room for more changes of clothes.

Sukina had changed out of her green floral dress into black denim trousers and a white blouse. With her being so small, her clothes took up very little space, but even then, she seemed to be travelling with so little.

Airships patrolled the entire Southern Barrier, an archipelago arranged in a horseshoe that separated the Northern Continent from the Southlands. Every island had a guarded station, making it virtually impossible to slip by unnoticed. But Velos and I had passed through many times there before and after a while, both I and the customs guards agreed that there was no need to land every time and show my papers.

"We're best to take the Fraw route," I said. "They know me there." Fraw was the largest of The Barrier Islands, the most forti-fied since most ships and airships passed by it. That meant there was less bureaucracy. Everyone took it for granted that a criminal would try to take a less guarded route.

Usually, I'd speed through fast, giving that usual flirty smile to that good-looking guard stationed there. Admittedly, I'd never carried a passenger on the back of Velos, before, or had him pass through wearing armour for that matter. But this flying-by ritual had become so common that I'm sure the guard wouldn't bat an eyelid. Then, perhaps on my return journey, I could stop off there finally for a cup of secicao and get to know this man a little better.

Faso soon came down the path, wheeling another tank on a trolley, and with Ratter perched on his shoulder. "All ready?"

Sukina looked at the tank. "More secicao?"

"This is another blend, my dear. I won't put in much, but it should give Velos a little extra strength if he ever needs to defend himself."

I don't know why I trusted him, really, but I let him open the valve on one of the side balloons and pumped the contents of the tank into it. Mamo and Papo came outside, Mamo carrying a plate of blueberries and Papo with my hip flask. They'd bought this for me on my eighteenth birthday: gold plated, rust free, embossed like a tortoise shell, and perfect for tipping secicao oil down my throat on those rare times that I needed it.

"Don't forget this," Papo said.

I snatched it off Papo. "That's the last thing I'll forget," I said. I sloshed it up and down a few times to check it was full and then slung it over my shoulder without giving my father another glance.

The flask contained the very own secicao oil that Velos and I supplied to the king's military. A sip of that would give me the acuity to slow time around me and make me much quicker on my feet, plus allow me to heat my body up or cool it down to withstand extreme temperatures. Not enough to stop my skin from burning, however, just to alleviate discomfort. Sukina and Faso had their hip flasks too, but what blends they'd used and what kind of properties they had was anyone's guess.

"Look," Papo said and rubbed the back of his neck. "Your mother and I have been talking, and I wanted to say... well... I'm sorry about the other day. We only want what's best for you, and I wanted the armour to protect you. But it turned out for the best, right?"

This was a typical Papo apology, saying that he shouldn't have done something and then saying that he did the right thing anyway. I'd still rather be flying Velos without the armour; I would surely miss the feeling of his scales under my bare legs as the wind whipped against them. But if it got my parents off my back, it was best to stick with the armour for now.

"Just let me do my thing," I said. "I need some time away, Papo."

Papo shifted awkwardly on his feet. "Fine," he said, then turned to Faso. "You look after my daughter for me, will you? Bring her back alive..."

Faso smiled. "I have no intention of doing anything else."

Mamo then took her turn to step forwards. "Pontopa," she said. "Good luck out there and I hope you have an adventure. I was your age once and I know what it's like to be young and carefree."

"I know, Mamo," I said, and we hugged for a while.

"Okay," Faso said. "Bottoms up and time to climb aboard." He patted Velos' rump, and the dragon stood up on his haunches and craned his neck to the sky. Faso had spent the last moments installing two Gatling turrets on the armour. They made Velos look rather mean, like a weapon of war...

I climbed on first and took my place at Velos' steering fin. Sukina came next and seated herself behind me, followed by Faso who took the rear. I didn't think I'd need to use the harness, but then the seat seemed a bit slippery and I knew that, by the way Velos rolled about, it would be easy to slide off.

I ran the two harness straps over my shoulders and buckled them at my waist. I pulled the waistband tight. Then, I pulled back on Velos' steering fin. The dragon kicked back on his hind legs, took a huge run, spread his wings and launched us into the sky, Faso screaming, "Bombs away!"

The wind picked up and tossed back my hair, my favourite part of flying.

AFTER WHAT MUST HAVE BEEN an hour or so, I began to realise why travelling strapped to a harness wasn't ideal. My shoulders and thighs began to feel a little constrained and I was sweating underneath the straps. I wanted to loosen them somewhat, but I thought sliding around in the seat would only make things worse.

The fog had now lifted. The sun was even more searing, not just from above but also from its reflection in the water. Admittedly, the wind provided a little alleviation from the heat. But the harness strap and the back of the seat blocked off a lot of the airflow, causing me to sweat even more. I had to put up with this for the sixteen hours it took to reach Fraw, through sunset and sunrise. I just couldn't wait for the coolness of night.

The armour made me feel that I was a little more distant from Velos as well, as I could no longer feel his scales against my skin. Every so often. I found myself muttering under my breath, "is everything okay, Velos?" and I'd stroke the leathery skin underneath his steering fin. Even though I couldn't feel the croon rumble through his body anymore, I just felt deep inside that he didn't mind his situation one bit.

Every so often, I also remembered the song that I'd sung to Velos the other day, when I was drinking the brandy. Then, I would sing what I remembered, and for a moment, Velos' wings would relax, and then he'd soar in the sky a little before resuming the slow, steady beat of his wings.

Eventually, the outline of the Southern Barrier came into view. First came the glint off the ironclad flotillas and the tiny armed Hummingbird automatons that darted around the boats like wasps. All who travelled this way knew the rules. Anyone flying over or sailing through had to do so via one of the designated checkpoints on the islands. The spaces in between were guarded by boats with automaton technology, connected to air-torpedo launchers that could shoot anything larger than a seagull out of the sky.

Soon, I could see the coast of Fraw, the white foam lapping against the golden shores. There was no vegetation on this island; there was not much vegetation on any of the Southern Barrier islands, really. Here, the land segued from golden sandy beaches into a mosaic of red mudflats and then rocky grey hills.

The checkpoint stood between two brass watchtowers, with automaton technology built into them, so they could scan anything that passed nearby. To the outside of these, a line of ground-based shrapnel-flak automatons could shoot down anything that tried to veer from the checkpoint. A military airship was moored to the base of each tower, both of them bobbing up and down in the air as we approached.

I pulled back on Velos' central steering fin to brace him for passing through the checkpoint, and he slowed down a little.

"So, this is it," Sukina said once the wind had eased off. "I have to admit, I've never flown through one of these checkpoints."

"No?" I asked.

"I've never been a big fan of airships. You can probably imagine why I wouldn't pass a dragon through here."

Faso said something from the back, but he was too far away for me to hear.

The men at the top of both towers waved two green flags to signal us through. I pulled down on Velos' steering fin to speed him onwards. This was part of the ritual – pretending to this man I had no respect for authority, in the hope that one day he'd call me in. The wind picked up around us as Velos gained speed and was soon whipping my hair back again. Behind me, Sukina was grinning and Faso was looking a little green.

We approached the tower faster than most would, but these men knew who I was and so I could do this out of habit now. I turned my head to my left and got my smile ready for the man who I expected to see in the window, a handsome dark-curly-haired thing. Often, I'd wondered if I should just stop by and visit him at his post. But then that would ruin the mystery of not knowing who the hell he was.

Unfortunately, it wasn't him that I glimpsed behind the glass, but a middle-aged plump and toothy faced man, not looking happy to see us. Just as we passed, he was turning towards the big red button on the wall.

Soon enough, the alarm was sounding and Hummingbirds, two or three dozen of them, swarmed out of the airships and formed a wall in front of us. Part of me wanted to barrel right through them, testing the armour Faso had installed. But I did want to return home eventually and I certainly didn't want to impede my chances. Besides, I reminded myself, Sukina's harmless. She couldn't be a terrorist, surely.

"To your left, Pontopa," Sukina said, and I swung round to see the mooring rope swinging in the air no longer connected to the ground. The airship's propeller fans were making a racket and the balloon was careening fast towards us.

I turned Velos away from the Hummingbirds, towards the airship's flight path, ready to level out against it. Soon enough, a voice bawled out from the airship's loudspeaker. "You are harbouring a terrorist. On King Cini III's command, we order you to land."

I looked back into Sukina's wide eyes, her knuckles white against the handlebar in front of her.

"Land, damn you!" Faso shouted from the back. "Whatever the consequences of this, it's better than being shot out of the sky."

I don't know what possessed me to even hesitate, to be honest. Maybe, instinctively, I felt that Sukina really was in trouble and I didn't want her to get caught. "Sukina, what should I do?" I asked.

She didn't seem as anxious as Faso and me, looking at the airship with narrowed eyes, her hand on her chin.

"Land," she said firmly. "We'll deal with things on the ground." I nodded and pushed down on Velos' steering fin.

As we came in to land, I looked down at the sky-torpedo launchers and shrapnel-flak automatons. There must have been one every hundred or so yards. The Hummingbirds had come closer now, and they had their spark-guns pointed at each of us. If we even raised our flasks to augment, they'd shoot. The automatons guided us down to a landing platform just south of the fortress housing Fraw's marines. There, accompanied by two soldiers, a tall and lithe blue-suited officer stood waiting for us, tendrils of smoke rising from the cigarette he held towards the floor.

8

As soon as Velos touched down on the ground, the officer motioned his two guards forward while he kept his rifle trained on Sukina. Really, Velos could have roasted them alive if I'd only shouted the command. But we were still surrounded by those armed Hummingbird automatons, darting around us in every direction. Even if Velos had his armour, we had nothing to stop ourselves being shot out of our saddles. Plus, I wasn't a murderer.

Sukina climbed off the ladder first and I followed her down to the ground, Faso going last. The guards forced us to hand over our hip flasks, then frisked us. They didn't want us augmenting when they weren't looking – all it would have taken is one sip of the secicao oil and we might get enough superhuman speed to disarm them in an instant.

As the guard frisked Faso, Ratter started doing a little dance around his suit. It used its extra feet to cling on to the fabric and scurried away from the guard's hands whenever they came close, always staying out of their sight.

After the frisking, we handed everything over, including our passports, and the Hummingbirds then left us and buzzed back towards the hatches on the gondolas of the two airships.

A hut stood in front of us, with a corrugated blue-painted tin roof. Just beyond that were the two customs towers, with a guard seated at each lookout point. Behind us loomed Fraw fortress with artificial escarpments rising in front of its four stone towers. The building housed over two hundred marines and thousands upon thousands of Hummingbirds, on-call in case any dragons decided to attack the island from the south.

"I demand an explanation," Sukina said. "You accuse me of being a terrorist, but we're just three innocent travellers heading south for research purposes."

The guards moved back towards the officer, keeping their rifles trained in our direction. They dropped the hip flasks into a box by his feet and then gave the officer our passports. The officer ignored our forest green ones, and instead opened up Sukina's red passport to the first page and examined it with an eyeglass.

"Seliano Artino, I see..." he said. "Our orders have been to look out for a woman of your physical description by the name of Sukina Sako. You must wait there until my superior arrives." He looked at his pocket-watch. You would have thought that if Sukina was so important, the guard would have recognised her immediately. But the guy just didn't seem to know what was going on.

"What's taking him so long?" Sukina asked.

The officer shrugged. "Biscuit break, I guess. What kind of device is that?" He pointed at Ratter who had just perched itself on Faso's shoulder, its red crystal eyes focused on the officer. Faso looked down at it disdainfully. Clearly, he hadn't wanted Ratter to do that.

"It's my very own invention," Faso said. "Programmed to protect me when I'm under threat."

"Disable it immediately!"

"What? Why would I disable my only protection when I have guns pointed right at me?"

"I said disable it! Unless you want a bullet in your head."

Faso moved his hand towards his pocket.

"Slowly! Keep your hands where I can see them."

Faso carefully lifted his hand the rest of the way towards his shoulder. He tapped Ratter four times, pausing slightly before the last tap. Ratter buried himself inside Faso's left sleeve.

"Hand the automaton over," the officer said. He signalled one of his guards to move forwards.

"I'll do no such thing," Faso said. "That's my life's work. You've insulted me enough by ordering us to land when we're on a mission under edict of the king. Here, I have the papers." He reached into his pocket.

"I said, put your hands where I can see them!"

Faso put his hands to his sides and scowled. "Cini will have your head for this, you know?"

"I don't think he will… I remind you who's in charge here."

Reluctantly, Faso shook out his arm until Ratter tumbled into the guard's hands. "Look, just let me get my papers. You should see them too."

The officer gave Faso a nod. "Slowly," he said.

Faso reached carefully towards his pocket. From there, he produced a manila envelope. The guard took this, strode back to the officer, gave him the documents, and dropped Ratter on the floor. The officer opened the envelope, took the contract, scanned it and then turned to the page that contained the king's seal.

"Which one of you is Pontopa Wells?" he asked.

Before I could utter a word, Faso butted in. "That's her." He pointed at me. "I'm Faso Gordoni. No doubt, you've heard of my genius. I'm famous and still you treat me like dirt."

The officer didn't seem particularly interested. "Miss Wells," he said, clearly sick of Faso's whining. "Your dragon is registered at our station but who is your third passenger?"

I looked at Sukina who looked surprisingly calm given the situation. She nodded a confirmation and, instinctively, I knew exactly what to say. "This is Seliano Artino, a biologist. She's coming south to help with some research we need to improve our secicao refinement process."

The officer turned to Sukina and studied her. "So why do you travel, Miss Artino? I want to hear the words from your own mouth."

"I write about dragons and wish to research their relationship with the secicao down there. In return, I'm also going to help these two in their harvesting operations for the king. That's understandable, isn't it, officer?"

The officer squirmed. "Hang on a moment." He took hold of his talkie on his belt and spoke into it. "Captain Orson, I've performed the initial inspection and we're awaiting your arrival. What's your ETA?"

I couldn't quite hear the words over the talkie, partly due to the fact that Sukina started singing as soon as the officer was distracted. But I did recognise Sukina's song. It didn't have a tune, as such, but the way the music segued from one harmony to the next sounded just like what I'd sung by the tree that day.

It was simply a pastiche of notes, in which Sukina's lilting voice blended into a natural meditative harmony. This lifted me into a trance, and I imagined Varion with his silver staff and apple calling down his Grey from the sky. I felt as if I could drift away from my mind and travel into Velos' mind, calming the dragonfire that had built inside his stomach, his emotions raging due to our captivity. Or perhaps my mind could find its way towards the three score Greys that I somehow knew to be circling over the ocean somewhere nearby.

The officer lifted his head from and pointed his rifle at Sukina. "You, what did you do?"

"I just felt like singing," Sukina said. "That's how they chant in the North Eastern Ranese temples, you know."

"And why sing at a time like this?"

"To keep me calm in a moment of crisis, of course. Why do you hold guns against people who intend you no harm?"

The officer tugged at his collar. "Just don't try any funny business."

A voice came back over the talkie, but it was again too faint to hear clearly. A door opened at the top of the right-hand customs tower and a portly man emerged. He scurried down from the tower at an unbecoming speed, considering his size.

"Don't move a muscle," the officer said. "Captain Orson will be here soon."

"You know," Faso said. "There was once a time that prisoners of status were treated with a little civility. You could at least make us a cup of tea."

The officer didn't reply but stared Faso down with a hard look. Faso fell into a slouch and looked away. My gaze drifted to the captain, now sprinting towards us at a much slower speed than he had come down the ladder.

The officer's talkie crackled, and an urgent voice came much louder this time. "Dragons," it said, "coming from the south. Requesting red-alert. Requesting red-alert."

The officer screwed up his eyes and glared at Sukina. I hazarded a look over my shoulder to see a V-shaped line in the sky, like a flock of geese but longer. The portly captain stopped in his tracks and, since Sukina had stopped her singing, I could make out his words over the talkie.

"Granted," the captain said. "Soldiers, take your stations. Hopkinli, stay put with the prisoners."

The officer nodded and put down his talkie. He turned back to us. "You heard what Captain Orson said."

The captain was now running back to his station, much fleeter of foot now in his panicked state. He climbed the ladder even faster than he had climbed down. From the fort, klaxons sounded. I suppressed the instinct to raise my hands to my ears since we'd been warned about any rapid movements. The officer took a step towards Sukina.

"If I find that you'd had a part to play in this then I won't hesitate to hang you from the custom towers. The three of you!"

"How exactly can we be involved in this, officer?" Sukina asked.

The officer opened his mouth to speak but was interrupted by a roar from behind. A grey dragon rose up from behind the fortress, whose parapets were now limbed in fresh flame. Mortars boomed around us and steam-powered surface-to-air missiles screamed into the sky. One seemed to pass awfully close to the Grey, which managed to evade just in the nick of time to return to its flock circling over the fort. Then, the shrapnel-flak cannons started to create their own roar, and black clouds enveloped the sky, full of floating shards of metal that would tear through anything that tried to pass through – airship or dragon alike.

The officer again lifted his talkie, which gave Ratter from its position at the officer's feet an opportunity to take advantage of the situation. The automaton moved faster than a squirrel. It scurried over to the box on the ground. Then, in a motion that seemed to defy gravity, it sprang up onto its tail, took Sukina's hip flask in its jaws, and launched it towards her.

"Halt!" one of the guards shouted.

But Sukina already had the flask in hand. She flipped up the top and took a swig of her secicao oil blend. A guard fired at her, but Sukina spun out of the way almost faster than the eye could see, her blend clearly augmenting her reflexes. Then she was running towards the guard that had fired, her speed three times that of a normal human, and a faint green glow now visible beneath her skin.

Before the guard could lower his rifle, Sukina took hold of it and backflipped, kicking the guard in the chest and knocking him back against the wall. The other guard was turning towards her, just as she used the momentum from the flip to launch her procured rifle at his knees. It hit him there with a crunch. The soldier groaned and tumbled forwards onto the floor.

Sukina drew two curved daggers from her garters and stood in a half-crouch, breathing heavily, as if waiting for the officer's reaction.

He didn't hesitate. He popped the top off his hip flask and raised it to his lips. But Sukina was already upon him. She knocked him unconscious with two blows to the side of the head from the handles of the daggers.

By this point, the second guard had managed to lift himself onto all fours and reached out for his rifle. But he wasn't fast enough. Sukina had already drawn a concealed dart from her hip, which she threw at him. It burrowed into his shoulder and, after a couple of seconds, the guard collapsed under his own weight.

My jaw dropped, astounded. I mean, I'd seen soldiers augment before, but I'd never seen anyone use their augmented abilities to their advantage in such a graceful way. Sukina had moved with all the ferocity of a wild animal. Many would become incredibly clumsy once they augmented using oil, not being able to handle the sudden abilities they gained. It could make them pretty dangerous. Which is why King Cini III tended to keep military-grade secicao oil out of the hands of normal men. Which is also why it was incredibly important to get the blend right.

My heart was thumping in my chest. Sukina had performed an act of terrorism I would be named as an accomplice too. We'd given them our names and, once they woke up, King Cini III would hear exactly what we'd done.

Sukina took hold of the two remaining hip flasks and tossed one to Faso, then one to me. She took the dart and gave it to me to examine. "Sedative. Works in two seconds."

Ratter scurried back into its place on Faso's sleeve, with Faso's documents and our passports in its jaw. Faso glared at Sukina. "Sukina, you—"

"Look, Faso," Sukina interrupted. "It was Ratter who made the first move. You can't put the blame on anyone but yourself."

"I didn't set him to do anything," Faso said. "He acted of his own will. His central intelligence is the best I've ever designed, you know. In fact, I'm sure, the best you've ever encountered."

"But you could have kept him disabled," Sukina said.

"I merely put him on suspend to wake up if there was any true threat, like dragons attacking. It was you who decided to call those beasts in."

Sukina ignored his rambling. "I guess you'd both better augment." Augmenting was the term we used for drinking secicao oil. Sukina had already done so, of course, and the effects would last for quite some time.

I nodded and took a swig of the oil. A cooling effect washed over my body, and I was no longer affected by the heat of the island. Any mugginess in my head also cleared, and instead, a warmth pulsed through me, as lines of faint green began to seep along my veins. Together, the three of us rushed towards Velos, Faso slower than us due to the differences in our secicao blends.

Once I'd climbed the ladder and was seated below Velos' steering fin, I looked down to see Faso still running towards us. Part of me wanted to take off then and leave him behind. But Ratter, after all, had saved the day, and so Faso had proven useful. Plus, I had no idea what to do with Velos' armour – in fact, Faso was the only person who knew how to take it off.

Faso soon got there and jumped halfway up the ladder, revealing one of the powers he had developed into his secicao. He landed right at the back of Velos and strapped himself into his seat.

Velos knew what to do next. Without me even giving the cue, he launched himself into the air. Around us, war was waging. Torpedoes screamed. Artillery boomed. Gatling guns sputtered from the ground. I looked over my shoulder to see Faso turning some kind of spigot beneath his foot.

"What the hell are you doing?" I shouted back to him.

"Helping Velos augment," he shouted back. Ahead of me, faint green lines began to pulse along the skin on Velos' neck, just underneath the armour.

At the same time, Sukina was singing some kind of tune.

"On the right!" Faso shouted and I looked over to see a military airship coming from the fortress, much larger than the types that had been moored to the customs towers.

Just as quickly as we had spotted the airship, it shot out a fleet of what must have been three-hundred Hummingbird automatons, their round bodies wavering from side to side underneath their whirring propeller blades. Velos had never had to face-off with them before, but I'd read Sukina's stories of how they could easily swarm Greys. They would take the rider out first with a spark to the head before sending out a barrage of fire into the dragon's flank, eventually bringing the giant down to earth.

But Velos was now augmented with the concoction Faso had put into the armour. Just as soon as the Hummingbirds came into range, I felt a shudder through the armour and its Gatling turrets started firing, causing smoke to rise around us. Velos swerved away from the smoke faster than I'd ever felt him turn – and, at that point, I was grateful for the harness. He charged towards the automatons and, with a roar, beat his wings as fast as a sparrow, knocking a huge number of them away from their cluster. Velos broke through the swarm, circled around and let out a torrent of green flame, much stronger than his usual orange fire: the work of the secicao blend.

The flame washed over the Hummingbirds. All around us, automatons erupted into sparks as the Gatling turrets swivelled, rattled, and kicked, knocking even more automatons out of the sky.

Of course, the automatons were firing too. A couple of times, my enhanced eyes saw a bullet rapidly approaching and I quickly ducked out of the way. With Faso's lack of augmented speed, I wondered how he would survive back there. But I didn't dare turn around to look. Sparks flashed off Velos' armour around our feet but he seemed unscathed, merely letting his green fire rage into the swarm of Hummingbirds that had now started to retreat.

The remaining automatons regrouped and joined an even greater swarm that had emerged from hatches on the dirigible's hull. I looked at them in dismay – there were just too many of them.

"Get high," Faso shouted. "They can't reach you above four-thousand feet."

I didn't hesitate to react. I pulled back on Velos' steering fin and sent him upwards before the automatons could swarm us like locusts. We broke through a low-lying cloud layer and a sudden chill hit me, which went quickly away once my augmented body adjusted to the temperature change. I looked down to see the Hummingbirds wavering beneath us, unable to push up any higher. We passed over an encroaching black shrapnel-flak cloud. Velos wouldn't have been able to get high enough to do this if he didn't also have secicao running through his veins.

An aura of peace washed over the battlefield, or at least it seemed to from our vantage point. Somehow, I could feel how Sukina's tension had lifted and how the dragonfire had settled down in Velos' stomach, that horrible burning sensation now dissipating.

Sukina began to sing as we rose higher, but otherwise it was awfully silent here, except for the roar of the wind. Velos continued to sail upwards, so high we had to keep our breathing deep and steady. Up here, not even the airships would be able to reach.

"Under your seat," Faso shouted. "Mask!"

Between my legs was a compartment with a face mask inside. This had a long muzzle that went over the nose and was attached to an oxygen canister that extended out from the muzzle. It was one of those kinds of masks that made you look ridiculous, and they got incredibly sticky and stuffy beneath the rubber.

I preferred my much more compact bit-and-clip design, similar to what divers used, but without the mask. You clasped your mouth around the horizontal bit and used a clip to block off the nose, drawing oxygen from a small tank on the back while blocking out the secicao fumes. But I'd left this in the luggage behind my seat since I didn't think I'd need it before the stopover. I sighed and strapped the mask over my face.

Under Sukina's command, the Greys followed us. Beneath us now, I could see a few fallen dragons, spread out, with guards that looked like toy-soldiers stationed at their heads.

The wind whipped against us and made it hard to speak, let alone breathe, even with the mask on. Soon, the Greys regained formation and formed a protective V-shape in front of us. We followed in their wake.

PART III

GENERAL SAKO

"Blunders and dragonheats!"

— GENERAL SAKO

9

The dragon led us to a flotilla of ironclads that had been waiting for us to arrive. The sky had begun to cloud over now. We approached a large frigate with two dirty funnels puffing out brown smoke. We landed on the quarterdeck, so spotless and shiny, it looked like it had been swept and polished clean. I brought Velos down and a man in a navy-blue uniform came out onto the quarterdeck and waited for us to dismount.

I was the first down the ladder and the man extended his hand to help me off the final step. Not that I needed it, of course, but small, gentlemanly gestures are always nice. The man took my hand again, albeit limply, and shook it.

"The name's Sandao," he said. "Captain of the Saye Explorer," he swept out with his arm to indicate the vessel, "and admiral of Gerhaun's fleet. Pleased to make your acquaintance." He had a little charm to him, but a weak demeanour.

"Captain," Sukina said. "This is Pontopa Wells, who I'm taking to see Gerhaun, and this" – she gestured towards Faso – "is Mr Gordoni, who I was telling you about the other day."

The captain approached Faso, eyed Ratter upon his shoulder, and then he took some more cautious steps forward and offered Faso his hand. "Mr Gordoni, I'm glad to see you've chosen to come south to join us."

"Is that so?" Faso said and looked at Sukina. "Well, I wouldn't quite say I've chosen yet. Miss Sako's actions have, in fact, guaranteed that Miss Wells and I have no other choice."

"I beg your pardon," Sandao said.

But Sukina was already upon him. "A moment please, Captain," she said.

Sandao gave a meek smile and rubbed his Adam's apple. He then stepped aside and folded his hands behind his back.

"Faso Gordoni," Sukina said. "You knew perfectly well the risks before you chose to come here. I didn't know that King Cini would suddenly want me arrested. So, I will not bear any responsibility for bringing you here. By all means, you're welcome to take the next passenger ship home."

"What? I'm a wanted fugitive now. I'd have to be a stowaway and then where would I go?"

"I don't know. Tell the king I took you captive under duress. Go and work in his comfortable palaces again, putting cogs together on his royal divans and sipping his wine."

Faso held his hands out in front of him. "It was you who knocked the lights out of the officer. That's a crime punishable by death in itself."

"Whose fault is it, Faso Gordoni, that you can't look after your own automaton?"

"My automaton malfunctioned and aided you. You chose what to do with that hip flask, not Ratter."

Sukina put her hands on her hips. "What should I have done? Waited for the king's executioner to arrive so I would get hanged? You'd like that, wouldn't you, Faso? To see me hang..."

Faso scratched the back of his neck. "I never wanted to be associated with you in the first place. Why did you have to come back?"

"I came to you with an offer from Gerhaun, and you decided to accept it knowing what the consequences might be. You can't hold me culpable for that."

"Damn it, Sukina. Just damn it!" Faso stormed off to the other corner of the deck.

Now, I wanted to side with Sukina on this, but her logic was starting to distress me a little. I hadn't been aware of the risks either. Given Sukina and Faso had reached an impasse in their argument, I saw it a good time to express my doubts.

"I'm worried too, Sukina. I mean, I can't believe you're a terrorist. Or is there something you're hiding from me?"

"The king calling us terrorists is just propaganda, Pontopa. Terrorists spread terror and that's certainly not what we aim to do at Fortress Gerhaun. I've always been allowed to travel freely through Tow before. King Cini has always claimed that I have diplomatic immunity. Despite knowing who I work for, if anything happened to one of his kingdom's favourite authors then there could be quite a lot of public discontent. But today, it seemed, for some reason, he's changed his mind."

"Why would he do that?"

Sukina shook her head. "I don't know. But I have a feeling that it has something to do with whoever it was that kidnapped the king's nephew."

"But what about me?" I asked. "Am I really a fugitive now?"

"I'll find a way to clear your names, both of you. But Pontopa, I saw how you interacted with the collective unconscious up there. I could feel you reaching out to me and the dragons. There's so much more, I'm sure, that you'll want to learn."

"But what about my parents? I mean, what will happen to them?"

Sukina gave a curious frown. "You know," she said. "I know this might be a little tough to fathom at first, but you may want to consider if they truly are your parents. Your mother, she's a sweet lady, but I couldn't feel any sign of her reaching out to the collective unconscious. Nothing from her that might suggest she's a dragonseer."

I looked at her incredulously. "Sukina, that's ridiculous. I mean, I have my mother's eyes, don't I?"

"I guess, I guess. Maybe your mother lost her abilities with time. Although, I don't know if that's possible. The only dragonseer I knew was my own mother and she passed away when I was a teenager. During the dragonheats..." She looked out over the horizon, towards where the battle had been an hour or so ago. "Your parents will be fine, Pontopa. Cini III is not as bad as his father. He doesn't arrest people for being accomplices. They'll be much safer without you than if you're there."

"I'm sorry, Sukina," I said. "About your mother, I mean."

I glanced over at Faso, glaring out at the water, his shoulders hunched, his posture like a sloth. Much as I disliked the guy, I felt a little sorry for him. I mean, did he have family in Slaro too? He could be in the same situation as me. Would either of us be able to return to our parents now, after what we'd done?

I began to cry. Sukina noticed immediately and took me into her arms. "Hey," she said. "It will be okay." I don't recall how long she held me there.

ONCE EMOTIONS HAD STOPPED FLYING AROUND, Sandao invited us into his steel-panelled drawing room. We sat around a circular oak table, cups in front of us. We were already a little jittery after augmenting with secicao, and so Sandao offered some South Saye tea instead.

It had a smoky taste and calmed the nerves well. On the table, a map had been pinned out, on which Sandao had stretched out a piece of string to plot the boat's course. Fortress Gerhaun was in the southwest, so I would have expected our route to head west through the Southern approach and then inland via the river. But instead it headed east, right around the Southern Horn and then into a river leading inland. Sandao explained it for my benefit.

"Fortress Gerhaun lies between two rivers," he said. "The Balmano runs from north to south-west, the largest in the continent, and the Phasni west to east. Such an astounding piece of geography means that the rivers almost divide the entire Southlands, which allowed us to build a canal between them. Unfortunately, a reef connects the islands of the Southern Approach, making it too shallow for us to get through."

I looked at Sukina. "You must have planned this months ahead," I said. "If it took them so long to get here, I mean."

She smiled. "They'd been instructed to wait here for a week. My father always plans it this way whenever I need to travel."

"Your father?"

"He's Gerhaun's general. You'll meet him soon. But whether or not you'll like him is another matter." I didn't know what she meant by that and I'd taken in so much that day already that I didn't want to ask more questions – my brain was fried.

"Do you want to be escorted?" Sandao asked.

Sukina looked at me, then Faso. "Faso might. But I think it's better if Pontopa and I take the Southern Approach. Gerhaun will be eager to see us as soon as possible."

"Then I will join you," Faso said. "I came all this way to test the armour once it hits the Southlands. There's no way I'm letting you see what happens without me. That's going to be the best part."

Typical Faso, always putting science first. I guess we were stuck with the guy.

The Southern Barrier traced the bottom of Tow like a smile, and had been fortified by Cini's forces right, left and centre. These fortifications ran from west to east, but the archipelago also forked off at the central western island of Bamfordo. This fork ran southwest through another archipelago called the Southern Approach. The reef underneath the water here gave it a turquoise hue so beautiful it was a delight to fly over it.

The Southern Approach wasn't as well fortified as the Southern Barrier, but it did have various outposts that, although officially owned by Cini, were run by merchant traders. All of these tended to be stationed on the western side of the islands. During the week it took for an airship or steamship to travel south, the crew could stop off at these and drink beer or stay the night in a ramshackle inn.

Given our recent actions, it was best to stay away from these, so we kept on the eastern side of the Southern Approach, characterised by rugged shores and rocky basalt terrain. We'd packed some firewood, as the islands tended to get quite cold at night.

With Velos moving so fast, due to the armour, the journey along the Southern Approach was reduced from six (Velos could move slightly faster than airships) to three and a half days, with three stop-offs. For the first two nights of these, we slept most of the night, virtually as soon as we landed. It was only on the last that we really had a chance to talk.

"Do you still like him?" I asked Sukina. We sat at a campfire roasting some bread twists Mamo had packed in my food-pouch.

"Who?" Sukina said.

I tilted my head towards Faso, who was sleeping on a roll mat on the ground, snoring softly. It was Sukina's turn to stand guard and look out for any signs of Cini's airships, but I'd decided to stay up and keep her company. "Who do you think?"

"Faso, I – He's... Flaming wellies, have you seen how argumentative he can be? He's stubborn too." She looked over at him for a moment, probably to check he wasn't awake.

I smiled. "You know, I've never really been in love."

"No?"

"Don't get me wrong; I've had boyfriends. It's just I've never really found one that lasted."

"I guess it's because of Velos," Sukina said.

I laughed. "Velos takes a lot of my time, yeah." But something told me that wasn't quite what Sukina meant.

Like Faso, Velos was snoring softly, his hot breath occasionally buffeting the fire but never quite blowing it out. I turned back to him and smiled, and Sukina smiled too.

"It's wonderful this connection you have to him," she said.

"How do you mean?"

"It's just a long time since I've been connected to a dragon like that..."

"You don't have a dragon?"

"Not that I'm truly bonded to," Sukina said. "I mean, there's Gerhaun, of course, and I have a kind of connection with her. But she's a leader and not a partner. It's kind of hard to explain." The flames of the fire seemed to dance in synchrony with her words, almost as if she commanded them.

"Surely you could just bond with any Grey," I said.

"It's not like that. Dragons tend to choose you, and I'm guessing that sometime in your early childhood, Velos came looking for you." She was absolutely right, of course. Velos had turned up on our doorstep when I was seven, and I'd never actually realised, until that moment, exactly why he was there.

"Coloured dragons are more intelligent than Greys," Sukina continued. "They're special... Through ages past, every dragonseer used to be bonded with one. I remember mine, Charlick, a brilliant emerald green with waxy wings wider than any male dragon I've known. But King Cini's father took Charlick away when I was just a teenager, and now I live this life alone."

Her eyes were so expressive that the reflection from the flames seemed to dance in them, as if agreeing with her every word. Sukina looked away, took the bread twist that she'd been holding over the fire, blew on it and then took a bite. "Pretty good."

"I know, right? We used to sit outside and toast these when I was a child. I don't know why we still don't."

She shrugged. "People move on, I guess."

"I guess." Before my bread twist could burn to a crisp, I took a bite, forgetting to blow and almost burning my tongue. Really, Faso didn't know what he was missing.

"Say," I said. "Those dragonsongs are amazing. I loved them in the books, but I had no idea they were actually real. Are you as powerful as Varion?"

Sukina laughed. "Varion, no, he's fiction. In the real world, they say, males can't converse with dragons unless they're a dragon themselves. They just can't get the songs."

I gazed at Sukina in awe. "It's all so fantastic," I said. "So, you can hear their voices in your head and stuff?"

"Oh, no. Humans and dragons speak completely different languages even if we can both connect to the collective unconscious. It's only the dragon queens who know how to bridge the gap between us, through dragonseers. The original Ambassadors developed the songs as something dragons would recognise. Given time, we gained the ability to identify their own songs through the collective unconscious. They've become our way of communicating now."

Now she'd started entering that place where she assumed that I knew more than I actually did. "Ambassadors?"

"I'll leave that one up to Gerhaun to explain." Sukina looked up at the moon. From beside us came a groan from Faso, who was tossing and turning in his sleep.

"Ah, nightmares," Sukina said. "I guess he's not going to sleep well here."

"Come to think of it, I tend to get a lot of nightmares on these islands."

"It's the fumes. Having dragons around helps us to connect to the collective unconscious. But secicao blocks this connection and puts its own constructions in our heads instead. The blight is much more powerful than people realise."

"What is this collective unconscious, anyway? There's just so much to understand here."

Sukina smiled. "Why, it's simply the essence of our collective minds. Humanity and dragonkind interlinked through each and everyone's conscious and subconscious thoughts. It pulses through the world, particularly when great beings are nearby. Gerhaun has written some books on it, which I'm sure she'll lend to you if you like."

"Thank you," I said. "I'm certainly eager to know more. I still have so many questions. Like what exactly is a dragonseer, Sukina, and what does it mean to be one? I mean, I've read about them in your books... But I have a feeling that there's so much more to it than that."

"That's true," Sukina said. "Let's just say for now that we dragonseers are there to protect the fate of both dragonkind and mankind. As dragonseers, there are certain things that affect us much, much more than normal men. One of them is secicao. Did you notice how much faster you were than Faso at Fraw?"

"I thought that was just my blend."

"Partly," Sukina said. "Having the secicao roasted by dragon's flame certainly helps."

"But there's more to it than that?"

"The only time I drink secicao is when I need to take the oil. It's partly to set an example and protect the environment, but I've found myself much more powerful through training my body to be the best it can be in the absence of secicao. Once you do so, you'll find that you're capable of much, much more than you've ever imagined, especially when you augment. Although such discussion is a little hefty for late nights and you look exhausted."

I looked again at Faso, and despite the way he tossed and

turned, I envied the sand he lay upon – even if it wasn't as soft as my own bed. "What about you?" I asked. "Maybe we should at least wake Faso. It's about time he did a shift."

Sukina had an expression of calm on her face as the light from the fire sent shadows dancing across her skin. "Don't worry," she said. "I'd like to have some time to think, and I need less sleep than I used to. I'll be fine."

I didn't want to leave her there, but my eyelids were getting heavy. I took a position by a rock on the other side of the fireplace, put on my jacket and then I quickly fell fast asleep.

I didn't see the sun until late, as usual. It wasn't that I'd slept in late. But once you got far enough south down in The Southern Approach, you wouldn't see the sun until about eleven o'clock in the morning. It took some time, you see, for it to rise above the low lying brown secicao clouds to the east – the first sign of the blight that plagued the Southlands.

I opened my eyes to see Faso standing next to me, his delicate inventor's hands clasped around three steel cups of water. Behind me, Sukina had lain herself down on a patch of earth just by the campfire and was fast asleep. Faso offered me a cup. I took it and eyed it suspiciously.

"It's water," Faso said. "Ratter got it from the sea."

"Why in all the dragonheats would I want to drink salt water?"

Faso laughed. "I'd give you nothing of the sort. This, my dear, has been processed in Ratter's distillation chamber. One of the many modifications you saw me working on the other day."

I didn't like the idea of drinking anything that had been processed by a ferret automaton, although, to be honest, I was pretty thirsty. I'd stocked up on a few bottles of water on the Saye Explorer but, exhausted after the commotion at Fraw, I'd gulped them down pretty quickly.

"Drink," Faso said. "I wasn't going to offer – Ratter's resources are precious – but I saw you needed it, and it pays to be a gentleman, right?"

"Right," I said, thinking this rather uncharacteristic of Faso. Perhaps he had a soft side after all. I raised the cup to my lips. A metallic tang settled on my tongue. There was a slight rustle behind me. Sukina had just started to stir.

"She didn't hit the sack until I was awake," Faso said. "She looked absolutely exhausted. You could have woken me, you know. Ratter would have kept guard."

I frowned. "Kept guard while you slept through everything, more like. What would have happened if Ratter malfunctioned again?"

Maybe it would have been better to have woken Faso up, or at least insisted that I cover the shift. Sukina had hardly slept at all for the last three days. She hadn't seemed tired, but looking at her now, I could see how exhausted she actually was.

Sukina stirred again, opened one eye, and then pushed down on her elbow to prop herself up. Faso smiled at her and walked over to give her a cup of automaton processed water. She took the cup, sniffed it, tasted it with her little finger, and then gulped it down in one.

"Thank you," she said.

"You're welcome." Faso turned to look at Ratter. "Right, now we're all awake, I guess we should make some breakfast. That nice fellow, Hars, you know the chef on Sandao's ship, gave me some eggs and bacon. I thought I'd save it until our last day. Lucky you ladies have me around to take care of you, right?"

I sneered at Faso. "Lucky you have two ladies around to put you in your place." Although, to be honest, I did appreciate the eggs and bacon. Maybe, again, the softer side of Faso had latched on to the fact that this was my favourite meal. It smelled great. For the last few days, we'd been surviving on a steady diet of Mamo's breadsticks and the occasional apple.

Faso smiled and walked back over to Ratter. He opened a hatch on the automaton's back, pulled out a small brass box from beneath its vertebrae and then he hooked this up to some wires. The device had a complex array of tiny pins on each of its six faces, connected by a complex spider web arrangement of miniscule grooves. Faso took an eyepiece out of his breast pocket and started to shift the pins around with a needle. After a minute or so of concentration, he put the device back in Ratter's hatch, closed it, stood up and brushed the dirt off his suit.

"Ah," he said. "That's about right." He gave Ratter a light toe-kick in the flank.

The automaton scurried over to the supply chest on the back of Velos' armour. Before I could even blink, it dived in and emerged with several pieces of firewood, bound together with twine. Ratter carried the wood over to the firepit and threw it on. The automaton then opened its mouth and out hissed a green flame, much the same colour as the one Velos had breathed at Fraw. The fire jumped to life.

Of course, there was a tinderbox right by the firepit, meaning there was no need for such an ostentatious display from Faso. I'm sure he just wanted to show off.

Faso took a pan, placed the eggs and bacon in it, mixed them together, and held the pan over the fire. It was soon ready and, short of plates, we passed the food around by hand and munched away.

After we had finished eating, we let the fire die down and then Sukina beat it out with her foot.

"I guess we should get ready to leave," Faso said.

Sukina lowered her cup from her lips. "Just a minute, I'll call in some escorts."

"Escorts?" I asked.

"Greys, just in case we have any company from automatons in the Southlands. You never know how far Cini's forces might be ahead of us."

Faso put his hands on his hips. "You've got to be kidding. You think I'm going to let any of those dragons within a yard of me, you've got another thing coming."

"But you're okay getting close to Velos," Sukina pointed out.

"Velos doesn't bloody-well shoot down the king's airships and rip his harvesting automatons to shreds. We've gone far enough with the whole terrorism thing. I'm not going to let you drag me further into this."

Sukina turned to me. "He really can be tiring, can't he?"

I nodded, biting my lip.

Sukina turned back to Faso. "Look," she said. "I appreciate your concern here, Faso, but it's protocol for Greys to escort all visitors into Fortress Gerhaun. It helps us keep the location a secret."

"Secret? It's between two massive rivers, on one of the most obvious tactical locations you can think of. How can King Cini not know about that?"

"You think Cini's men want to go exploring through secicao and the gas? They keep to the fringes, Faso. They don't go anywhere near the rivers."

"It doesn't matter," Faso said. "I augmented Velos to be safe and I don't want to go anywhere near those disgraceful beasts. Pontopa, you tell her."

Once again, Faso was starting to get on my nerves. "Look, Faso," I said, "I see two options. Either you do as Sukina says, or we leave you on the island and your only way home will be to swim."

He glared at me a moment then looked out to sea and puffed out his cheeks like a blowfish. "Girls will always stick together, won't they? Never listening to reason. Always doing what they think is best. You're really making me not want this job, Sukina."

"Then I'll gladly send you on the next transport home. I'm sure King Cini would gladly accept you as his royal scientist again."

A look of disdain came upon Faso's face, and he walked over to the beach to sulk. Sukina watched him go for a moment then raised her head to the wind and began to chant that familiar, unmelodic song. I had a chance to observe her this time, and I could swear that the air shimmered around the notes that emerged from her mouth.

After around a minute she stopped singing and turned away. "They'll be here soon," she said. "Maybe fifteen minutes. Did you hear them?"

I shook my head. I'd only heard Sukina's voice and the susurrations of the wind.

"Dragons have very acute hearing," Sukina said. "You'll be able to read the signals eventually, if you want to learn, of course. I don't want to force you into anything."

"I know," I said.

In the distance, I thought I could hear a faint tune. A call from hundreds of miles away from another kind of creature. I heard Velos shift behind me and then I turned to see him cock his head to the wind and listen to the voices from afar.

I felt the urge to reach out to Velos then. So, I decided to sing him a song. Part of me wanted to communicate with him, excited to know that I had a means to do so as a dragonseer. At the time, I didn't know what I sang the song for. I just really wanted to tell

Velos how much I appreciated him being there, coming with us on the journey.

But then I learned something about him too, because I could feel what he felt, just as I was sure he knew what I was feeling too. He was about to meet others of his kind, and he was apprehensive to say the least. The only interactions he'd had with dragons since I'd known him had been with the Greys we occasionally saw in flight in the Southlands. Admittedly, he hadn't had a chance to interact much with them. I tousled Velos' head when he lowered it towards me, and he let out an appreciative croon.

11

After about fifteen minutes, the Greys arrived. They came in from the east, breaking through the brown clouds. Their formation was looser than it had been at Fraw. But there were less of them, so they had more freedom to flitter about, darting and diving over and under each other like swallows. I was glad of their arrival, for the sun was high in the sky and it was starting to get searing hot. It would be cooler under the secicao clouds and I now had my bit-and-clip breathing device ready to enter the thick polluted air.

Seven Greys arrived in total, but only one of them came in to land while the rest circled above. "It's a precautionary measure," Sukina explained. "They're keeping watch for approaching airships and automatons. If anything happens, they'll defend the Grey on the ground, giving him space to get us out quickly and lead the retreat."

As the Grey closed in, the wind from his wings whipped against us. Behind us, Velos stood up on his haunches and bared his teeth at the Grey. Then, he let out one of his ear-piercing roars and I raised my hands to cover my ears. Sukina immediately spun around to face Velos and let out a sharp song. Her tune was much more grating than the delicate harmonies from before. Velos yelped like a scolded dog and then turned away from Sukina.

"They're his brothers," Sukina said to me. "He'll have to learn."

I nodded. "I'll try and teach him…"

Faso had retreated to the beach. He was now squatting down beside the sea, staring out at the horizon. He seemed to be keeping as far away as possible from the Grey until it had landed. Then, he walked over a little but still kept out of neck's reach. He looked at the dragon with contempt.

"I guess you'll want to ride on one of those things," he said to Sukina.

"I understand that it will be safer on Velos," Sukina said. "Isn't that how the armour was designed?"

"It is. I just thought—"

"And I just thought that we should do what's safest for everybody. Isn't that right, Pontopa?" It seemed that Sukina was still in a bad mood with Faso, from their argument earlier.

I shrugged. Really, I thought I'd rather make this journey without automatons, which included Velos' armour. Of course, I'd rather ride Velos than an unfamiliar Grey. But still, I missed the feeling of Velos' scales underneath my legs. The armour just didn't feel quite the same.

"Very well," Faso said. "Then I guess before we reach another impasse, we should get on." He walked over to Velos and climbed up the ladder on the armour's flank. Faso took position at the back.

Sukina, on the other hand, launched herself off from a crouch then sprinted towards Velos' tail. Velos, as if reading her intentions, straightened his back and then let out a soft, affirmative roar. With an agility that I'd never seen from anyone before, Sukina scrambled up, using each of the fins as a makeshift ladder. I smiled, and considered trying the same (although I doubt I would have done it with so much agility), but Sukina already had to climb over Faso to get to her seat. I didn't really want to have to climb over both of them.

I took hold of my bit-and-clip device and secured my oxygen tank on my back. I hung the rest of the apparatus over my shoulder at the front. Then, I took the safe route up and took my place at Velos' steering fin. A quick pull on this launched us into the air.

IT WAS another good half an hour before my breathing started to become heavy, from the thickening secicao fumes. Soon enough, Sukina and Faso put on their gas masks, and I secured my clip onto my nose and clenched down with my teeth on the bit. Then, I put on my goggles and pressed them against my skin to secure them in place.

The temperature suddenly dropped when we entered the clouds of Secicao fumes, and the air became scathingly dry. As always, I kept my breathing shallow, sucking in only small bursts of oxygen from the tank. The clouds rubbed against my skin, causing a kind of itching sensation. It always made my skin feel like dried wood as if it was going to crack. These effects weren't permanent, and I was kind of used to the sensation now. But I always carried a bottle of moisturiser with me, to reduce the damage to my skin.

The secicao forest rolled underneath us, rhododendron-like shrubs reaching up with thorns and sharp-speared buds pointing at the sky. Before I'd met Sukina, I'd seen these as having some kind of exotic beauty. Only now did I realise how hideous they were. Part of a chaos-ridden artificial jungle, which twisted and choked and strangled the earth beneath. On the fringes of the Southlands, harvesting teams would have to wade through twenty-or-so centimetres of secicao resin. They'd wear wellies that they replaced every month or so since the stuff ate through everything, even dragon scales. Fortunately, Velos' scales regenerated, so the effects on him were never permanent.

Soon enough, we were so deep into the clouds that I couldn't make out any more than the escort on either side of us. As we flew, the secicao clouds stung my skin. I'd taken a swig from my hip flask, so I wouldn't feel the chill so much. But still, I found it best to focus at this point, to relax in the saddle and control my faint and shallow breathing.

"Time to test it," Faso's voice came muffled from behind. I turned around to see him fiddling with the tap on Velos' flank. Beneath me, the armour began to glow a faint lime-green and heated up a little.

"Amazing!" Faso shouted. Before I knew it, the wind was screaming against us, ripping back my hair as Velos overtook the Greys.

"Shut it off, Faso!" Sukina shouted.

"But—"

"No buts! We can't lose the Greys, or we'll be shot down on sight."

Faso reached down to Velos' side again, made some adjustments, and the glow and the warmth quickly subsided. I shook my head and gritted my teeth. I liked nothing about the armour, and I hoped that as soon as we met Gerhaun Forsi that she'd be able to get it off Velos. But Velos lifted his head and roared into the clouds as if he disagreed with Sukina's orders.

"It seems Velos quite liked that rush of secicao," Faso pointed out.

"But he'll need to learn that he shouldn't use it without good reason," Sukina said. "Discipline is important in the Southlands."

It took another twenty minutes or so before Fortress Gerhaun came into sight. We didn't see it approaching as such, more it just sprang up on us. One moment, we were travelling through thick brown fog, unable to see the light of day. Then, all of a sudden, the clouds broke, and we entered a huge open space where some invisible force seemed to repel the secicao fumes. Great iron searchlights scanned the sky, with a blinding intensity when one of their beams crossed my gaze.

"That," Sukina shouted, "is the power of the collective unconscious. It's so strong here that the secicao can't get in. You see the same effect around any dragon queen."

My jaw dropped in awe. Fortress Gerhaun was huge. It had a massive moat and a drawbridge leading over what I presumed to be the canal that linked the two rivers. The canal wasn't as narrow as I'd imagined, broad enough in fact to house a good five or so small ironclads. The castle was impressive too. A thick wall surrounded an inner bailey, from where four cylindrical towers jutted out. We approached a spacious courtyard at the centre of this, with mosaics of coloured and grey dragons spread across it. By one depiction of a golden dragon in flight, a short and stocky man in a flat cap stood twiddling his moustache, staring up at us.

"I guess you'll meet my father sooner than I expected," Sukina said. "That's him now."

The man beckoned us in to land. The Greys of our formation

pushed ahead of us and raised their feet ready for landing. Their claws scuffed against the stone once they touched down.

A moment later, we hit the ground with a thud, and I caught Sukina's father's stare for a moment. His expression was cold and assessing. But when he saw Faso, anger ignited in his eyes.

12

Sukina's father was even shorter than Sukina. But he made up for that with a heavyset stockiness which kept him rooted to the ground, despite the wind buffeting against him from the dragons' wings. Once we had landed, the man examined the armour on Velos then walked around to help us off the ladder. Sukina dismounted first.

I looked behind me and I noticed Faso seemed stuck in his seat, pushed against the back of it as if he didn't want to leave the saddle.

"What have you got to be nervous about?" I asked.

"You'll see. If Sukina's father is anything like he used to be, anyway."

"He can't be that bad."

"You'll see... You'll see..."

I dismounted and reached the bottom of the ladder. Above me, I could swear Faso was trembling in his seat. I heard the click of a lighter and I turned my head to see Sukina's father light a pipe. Stale secicao smoke rose from it.

He wore a camouflaged flat-cap and a khaki short-sleeved shirt, with an impressive array of badges and stars sewn onto his shoulders and several pennants dangling from his breast pocket. His face was round with a fluffy moustache that curled upwards a little at each side, and the same almond eyes as Sukina, raised at the outside corners. He held the pipe firmly in his hand while he glared up at

Faso, just sitting up there, clutching the bar on the harness in front of him. Sukina looked at her father's pipe and shook her head, but she didn't say anything about it.

"Blunders and dragonheats!" Sukina's father shouted up. "Come on down, you buffoon. You think you want to sit up there all day and starve?"

Faso looked down at him and his eyes widened. "I'm sorry, sir. I just need to make a few modifications up here." He reached down away from us to where the spigot was on Velos' flank.

Sir? How exactly had this man got Faso treating him like a knight of all things.

Sukina, stood beside her father, her hands folded neatly in front of her white blouse, now stained yellow from the secicao clouds. She turned and put her mouth to her father's ear. It was strange, even though she was whispering, I could hear her words perfectly in my head.

"Go easy on him, Butan," Sukina said. "He's not as bad as you think." Butan was Sukina's word for father.

He harrumphed. "I'll be the judge of that." He looked up again at Faso. "If you don't come down soon," he shouted, "I'll order my guards to shoot you down. Just because you had relations with my daughter doesn't mean I'll go easy on you."

Faso sat up and puffed out his cheeks. "Okay, I'll be right down." He crawled towards the ladder.

Sukina's father turned to me and glared right at me. He took another puff on his pipe and I had to turn my head away from the sickening fumes.

"So you came," he said.

I waited for Sukina to say something, not really wanting to address this cantankerous man. But she simply nodded at me as if giving me approval to introduce myself. I approached timorously and offered him my hand.

"Pontopa Wells at your service, Mr Sako."

He twitched his moustache and looked generally unimpressed. "That's General Sako to you. What makes you so high and mighty that you think you can ignore my honorific?"

"I'm sorry, I didn't know." My heart was hammering in my chest. I never thought a man so short could be so intimidating.

Faso's boots scuffed against the ground behind me. As he approached, he kept as close to Velos' flank as he could. Ratter was nowhere to be seen.

"Gordoni, boy," General Sako said. "So, you've finally emerged from your hiding hole. Why don't you come forward and tell your ex-father-in-law-to-be what you've been doing all these years?"

"Well..." Faso tugged at his collar.

"Yes, yes, I know. I take it that you've decided to take up Gerhaun's offer of a position with us. Dragonheats knows why Gerhaun would have ignored my condemnations of your professional qualities."

Faso's head was low. "It's not as if I was given much choice."

He glanced at Sukina. Her eyes had become slits and her face looked as sour as a lime. "You mean to tell me that you didn't come here of your own free will?" General Sako asked. "Then how exactly do I know you can be trusted? After all, I heard you signed a contract with King Cini. For all I know, you could be performing reconnaissance for that pompous fool who thinks everything about him, including his own backside, should be called 'your majesty'."

Faso didn't utter a word. Probably a good thing, really, I don't think General Sako was in the mood for listening to him. Still, I had also signed that same contract with the king and I didn't want to be accused of cooperating with any enemies.

"With all due respect," I said. "Faso is only pursuing his own best interests. My parents and I are much the same. Although we deplore many of Cini's actions, we need to make sure we bring home enough money to live."

General Sako looked up at Velos with scorn. "I hear, Miss Wells, that you've made quite a living from the secicao you send to the king. Tell me, what do you do with all the surplus cash you tuck away?" He pointed to the armour. "Perhaps it's put into revolting contraptions like that thing on your dragon's back."

"The armour was Faso's doing," I snapped back, without thinking. There was no way that I'd be held responsible for doing anything of the sort to Velos, even for a moment.

"Yes, yes, I might have known." General Sako turned to Sukina. "I don't trust them. They need to be locked up."

Sukina's lips tightened. "Butan, no!"

"Look, these two are clearly working for the king and they don't seem to be doing so under duress. I have no reason to trust them and they must be properly vetted. We shall lock them up until they are."

"But I've already confirmed Miss Wells' abilities as a dragonseer."

"Are you telling me dragonseers have never turned traitor through history? We must go through proper procedures."

"But Butan, Gerhaun said—"

"Blunders and dragonheats! I don't care what Gerhaun said right now. If you want to wake up Gerhaun, be my guest. For now, this is what we're going to do." He turned to a guard behind him, who was wearing the same mustard yellow uniform as his comrades, as well as a navy-blue sash that ran from his right shoulder to his opposite waist. "Wiggea, you heard me. Arrest them both... But go easy on the girl."

The long-faced guard looked at General Sako in surprise. Then he saluted and ordered two of his guards forward. As soon as they approached, Ratter poked his shiny nose out of Faso's sleeve. The automaton scurried up to Faso's shoulder and, beneath red glowing eyes, bared a monstrous array of razor-sharp teeth. Out emanated an intimidating hiss. This stopped the guard in his tracks.

"What in the dragonheats?" General Sako said.

Sukina sighed. "Faso, if you know what's best for you, you'd disable that thing."

Faso let out a huff then tapped Ratter three times.

"Take it to containment," General Sako said.

"Yes sir," Wiggea said and he motioned another soldier forward to retrieve Ratter, who Faso had placed neatly on the floor.

Sukina then caught my eye. I heard her voice in my head, even though she didn't move her lips. *"Pontopa, don't be alarmed. This is how we talk in the collective unconscious. Please forgive my father, he's just paranoid and he likes to think he's in charge here. But as soon as Gerhaun wakes up, I'll talk to her and get you out."*

I didn't know how to respond, really. I half thought I was going mad.

Sukina turned to face her father. "Cells are no accommodation fit for them."

"Pfft! They'll need to get used to such conditions if they're going to work for us. There's no cosy heating and royal divans over here. Wiggea, why are you slacking off? You have your orders."

The guards shuffled forward and then escorted us off towards a set of double doors. Just as we were about to enter, from behind me, I heard a great roar. I turned just in time to see Velos gnashing out at one of the guards, who rolled out of the way and pointed a long narrow rifle at Velos' head.

"No!" Sukina and I shouted at the same time. Sukina rushed forward to steady the guard's gun and then pushed it downwards. She sang out a song to Velos and I could feel his rage soothing a little. But his angst was still there, subdued.

"There's no need to sedate him," Sukina said to the guard. "The dragon will behave."

Velos turned to me and I very faintly heard a soft croon.

"It will be okay," I said under my breath. I felt my thoughts reach out to Velos, who then lowered his head to the ground. "*It will be okay...*"

"Don't worry, Ma'am," Wiggea said, now standing next to me. "We'll treat you as well as we can down there."

I nodded and allowed myself to be led through the double doors that one of the guards had pulled open for us. We walked into a dark, dusty brick corridor that smelt of mildew. I couldn't see Velos now, and I hoped with all my heart that he would behave.

PART IV

GERHAUN

"Secicao is as much a drug to humanity as it is a threat to the planet. Its roots churn up the earth and take away its nutrients. They dig deep into our planet's mantle, increasing the acidity of the soil so nothing else can grow. But dragons are there to protect us from this. Without them, the leaders of this world would rule contently addicted to secicao, until the inevitable moment that the blight wipes out every single human and dragon on this planet."

— FROM 'DRAGONS AND ECOLOGY' BY
GERHAUN FORSI

13

Actually the cell turned out to be pretty decent, as far as cells go. Not that I'd ever found myself in one before, but I'd heard plenty about Cini's cells in magazines. Dark, boxy rooms with hard stone beds, no pillows for comfort, rats running around between rooms, a stench of ammonia emanating from the floor. Probably a lot of that was just propaganda to scare us common folk. I mean, if we fear the cells enough then we won't want to go anywhere near them, right?

But Fortress Gerhaun's cell had a separate compartment for a toilet, with a working flush and sink, and a door that closed. Two windows brought in a little light from the top of the room, though they were too high up to see out of without at least kneeling on the bed. Unfortunately, the place did still smell of damp and mildew, and down here it was pretty cold. But there were soft beds. Two, thank wellies, on separate sides of the room. I'd ended up in the same cell as Faso. The inventor was kneeling on the mattress, his arms folded over the high window ledge. He was peering out at something.

I'd half expected him to spend his time here boasting about his achievements, perhaps even complaining about how the conditions were unfit for someone as high and mighty as him, but he seemed to have lost his spirit. So, I sat kind of quiet for a moment.

Then, the anxiety started to settle in. After what we'd just done at Fraw, I was kind of worried about my parents. Even if Papo was a buffoon, I'd got angry because I hadn't wanted him putting himself in danger in my place. Now my actions could have put my parents in jeopardy. Once news reached Cini that Faso and I had turned traitor, I was sure the Five Hamlets would be the first place he'd look for us. Then, what he'd do to my parents was anyone's guess.

After a while, I decided that the only way to get over my emotions was to talk. Even if Faso was the person, I least wanted to have a conversation with.

"Is there really anything out there?" I asked.

He turned, though his gaze was vacant, lost in some far away thought. "What's that?"

"I mean, there's no birds to watch, the dragons aren't flying around, there's not an automaton in sight. What are you so interested in?"

"Nothing, really. I was just wondering how it all works."

"Say again?"

"The way that they keep those clouds away. There must be some kind of mechanism."

"You don't believe in the collective unconscious, huh?"

"Baloney, baloney. You'd never believe some of the nonsense I had to put up with from Sukina. This, indeed, is one of her best."

I bit my lip to try to hide my amusement. So *that* was what was on his mind. "You miss her," I said.

"Miss her? Of course, I miss her. But we were never really compatible. I need a smart lady for a relationship... Someone who understands my work."

That must have caused a frown on my face. I mean, for him to say Sukina wasn't smart was baloney itself. "So, what attracted you to her in the first place?"

"Wellies, have you seen how beautiful she is? You've seen the way the guards look at her. She melts even their hearts."

I sighed, why did men always have to be so superficial? I knelt on my pillow to look out of the window. I grasped the bars there, resting my forearms against the dusty brick.

But outside there was little to keep me entertained for long, other than slowly roiling clouds of secicao gas and a dusty, sandy floor. If I listened close enough, I could hear the croons of the dragons in the distance, but I couldn't make out Velos.

Faso got up off the bed, reached down to pull it back a bit, the metal feet scraping against the stone, then knelt back down on it, his knees against the pillow. He poked his head through the bars, as far as it would go. I laughed.

"Are you that desperate for fresh air?"

He pushed himself back in, both hands clutched to the bars. "I merely wanted to test if there is any difference between the air outside and inside. You have to experiment to hypothesise."

"So, what's your theory?"

"There must be some kind of vacuuming or blowing mechanism in concealed holes where the cloud meets the ground. There's no other possible explanation for it."

"Why not just accept this is the way things are?"

"If we scientists did that, lady, we would never make any progress."

I leaned towards Faso. "Why don't you just admit it, Faso? You're bored and you're trying to find a way to pass the time."

"Smart people never get bored. Although, I wouldn't expect you to realise that."

"Smart people never feel the need to put down inferior minds," I said. "Only those that are greater than them."

"Hah, you're not possibly saying you're smarter than me, are you?"

"Well, I'm certainly wiser in choosing my battles." I guess, in all honesty, I was bored as well. Without a novel in here to keep my company, there wasn't much to do. "Say, we've been forced into this situation together and there's so little I know about you. What's your story, Faso?"

Faso shuffled back around on the bed, turned to face me and placed his feet on the floor. Then he puffed out his chest. "If I didn't know better, the young lady's getting interested. What exactly, Miss Wells, do you want to know?"

Well, in all honesty, I might have been flirting a little at the time, but I didn't mean anything by it. Despite his flaws, Faso did have a certain charm to him. In certain situations, anyway. I mean, there must have been something about him for a lady like Sukina to be attracted to him all those years ago.

"You know, I've never been to Slaro," I said. "What's it like and what were you doing there? When you met Sukina, I mean. What brought you together in the first place?"

Faso sighed and then turned to look out of the window again. From that position, he spoke without looking back at me. "We met in Slaro. Sukina had come over from Orkc, an administrator looking for work on King Cini III's staff, five years after his father had died and the end of the infamous dragonheats. They say Cini III was mellow at first. Rumour had it around the palace that he didn't really approve of his father's bigotry and wanted to liberalise Tow a little, open it up. Let immigrants in. Sukina came from a country much colder than our own. Said that she wanted adventure, to see new places to write about. But those days, she struggled a lot. Sometimes she couldn't get two sentences together without having a breakdown. She was lacking subject matter to fuel her voice."

"But how did you get started in the palace?"

Surprise registered on Faso's face. "How did I get started? Why, I was headhunted, of course. I've been building automatons since I was seven, you know. In my parent's hovel by the Sanito-Cini river of all places. My parents were pretty much on their deathbeds while I made all kinds of machines to go scavenging from old war automaton parts I found lying around the street. Father had these old books that he said his uncle passed on, handed down from an engineer friend he fought with during the dragonheats. I read them with fascination, and I was immediately hooked.

"Once they saw my automatons running around the streets, a woman named Alsie Fioreletta – who I'm sure you've heard about in the magazines – came looking for me, she said that King Cini wanted me to work for him. I was sixteen at the time. It was good work. It paid the medical bills for my parents. Though within a couple of years of working there they both passed away from different cancers within a six-month gap."

"That must have been hard," I said.

"At the time, it was. But, fortunately for me, that's when Sukina entered the scene. I had wanted to give up then, throw it all away.

But Sukina came looking beautiful as always, drowned my tears in her shoulder and told me to carry on, and build my legacy. We needed to work hard, help fund Cini's war effort. I had to advance technology, help the world become better. By that time, the airships had started bringing secicao by the ton to the city and really, I was fascinated how it worked. If that stuff could just power machines..."

Faso's eyes had become narrower. From outside, a warm breeze had picked up that came through the window and blew back strands of his hair. He touched his hand to his sleeve then lowered his head. "They better not do anything to Ratter..."

I shook my head – It seemed like Faso couldn't stop thinking about those damn automatons. But I wasn't going to let the conversation get side-tracked. "I can kind of see how you never really liked Cini."

"It's not a matter of like or dislike," Faso said. "I never really trusted the man. I distilled the secicao in secret, learned how to refine the oil from the beans, sap, and root. But I never told him what I was doing. I kept developing automatons for the king, but this research was always private, and Sukina was doing research too. Only, while I knew I was doing good, she convinced herself that anything to do with secicao was destroying the world. Wellies, she must have been the only person in Slaro who abstained from taking it. Even her father liked to keep some in his snuffbox for his pipe, and still does by the look of it."

"Ah, so that's when you met him," I said. "I thought you and Sukina lived alone."

"Yes, well, after living with a friend in Slaro for a while, Sukina's father came to live with us. He demanded that I should do an equal amount of work around the house as Sukina, and he didn't seem to respect that I'd already developed automatons to do my half. Dragonheats, it was difficult to get any of my independent research in. To top it off, Sukina didn't have a job. She'd resigned because she said she couldn't work for the king as she didn't want to support his war effort anymore. She seemed so distant all the time, almost as if there was someone else..."

He paused and stared into space. "Sukina thought the king," he said after a moment, "only wanted to get more and more secicao from the Southlands. She claimed that this would destroy the

Northern Continent. She'd got hold of one of Gerhaun Forsi's books from the black market and kept reading passages of it to me. It was absolute balderdash, all of it. But Sukina's father would back her up as well, adamant that I should resign. It proved a nightmare living with him, I tell you."

Now, I'd read *Dragons and Ecology* just several nights ago and it seemed convincing enough to me. In many ways I wanted to lift the arguments right out of the text and throw them back at Faso. But then I'd seemed to open a vein with him, and I preferred this candid side of him rather than his usual sheer arrogance. In all honesty, this more sensitive side of him, when he wasn't belittling others and assuming he knew what everyone wants, was quite charming. So, I simply nodded along and let him carry on.

"That," Faso continued, "was when Captain Colas appeared out of the blue."

"Captain Colas?"

"Some old man, younger in spirit than he looked. A bald, shrivelled excuse of a creature hunched over a cane, with a wrinkled forehead and glasses thick enough to seal a bomb. He called himself a scientist, although he didn't stay around long enough for me to talk about science. But he was rich, I can say that much, he came to Slaro West airfield in an airship lined in every nook and cranny with gold and other riches. Even the balloon lining had shiny silver thread running through every inch of the fabric."

Faso took a deep breath and scratched underneath his flared-out sleeve. His knees were bouncing up and down rapidly, one after the other.

"What happened?" I asked.

"What happened?" Faso rose, clutched a fist. "What happened? Colas stole Sukina from me, that's what. Sukina had published three books by then, through independent publishers. Colas had picked them up in a bookstore and said he was impressed. He told Sukina that he could tell from her prose she had read Gerhaun Forsi, who he consequently knew. He wanted her to go and work for Gerhaun. He said Sukina was a dragonseer, whatever that meant. Then there was this strange exchange between them where they stared at each other for a long, long time. I tried to ask Sukina what they were doing, but she told me not to interrupt. It took a couple of days of visits, each with Colas and Sukina just sitting there staring at each other. I got so irate about it that Sukina eventually wouldn't let me in the room. Then Sukina told me that she had to go south. She'd learnt more about her heritage, she said, and now had finally discovered her destiny. She wanted me to come along for the ride..."

"You didn't want to?"

"Wellies, no. I had no intention of living in a land of disgusting secicao resin and brown intoxicating clouds. Not until I decided to harvest the stuff for myself anyway to make sure I got the best sample. Besides, I was on the crux of discovering something, I'd almost perfected the secret to secicao fuel, and I wasn't going to upend everything and throw it all away by moving my workshop."

I laughed. "Sounds like you perfected that moving trick."

"All thanks to my soon-to-be-patented secicao fuel," Faso said. "Marvellous, stuff you have to admit. All this was invented by my own genius brain." He pointed to his forehead.

Ah well, Faso's ego had returned. I sighed and turned my head to gaze back out of the window. But Faso countered by loudly clearing his throat.

"So," he said, "now you know my deepest darkest secrets. Maybe, I could take you out on a date when we return to the Five Hamlets."

I raised an eyebrow at him. "You've just explained how you'd never exactly been boyfriend material, and now you're trying to get me out on a date." The memory nagged at the back of my mind of having to punch Faso for what he did to Velos.

"Well, it's not as if you seem the type who wants to be a girl-friend, either."

"What's that supposed to mean?"

"I just think that—" A tap-tapping sound of stiletto heels interrupted him, coming from the corridor outside the cell. Faso turned towards the corridor. "I guess Sukina's finally come to set us free."

I listened to Sukina's approaching footsteps and then her voice manifested itself crisp and clear in my head. *"Frustrating, isn't he?"*

I looked around, trying to identify the source of the voice. I imagined Sukina must have been hiding in a corner somewhere.

The sounds of the footsteps eased off. *"Come on, Pontopa, when are you going to accept that we can speak this way."*

Accept? No, this had to be something else, something to do with the secicao fumes perhaps – maybe some had managed to seep inside this clearing after all and they were sending me mad. Although Varion and other characters had managed to speak this way in Sukina's books, this was real life, not fiction.

"If you could speak to me like this, Sukina," I said in my own mind, *"then why didn't you do so before we got to Fortress Gerhaun?"*

"Good question," the voice replied. *"It's simple really. Although we can share emotions without it, we need a strong source of the collective unconscious to be able to communicate like this, and there's no stronger source than a dragon queen."*

Faso was looking at me strangely. He must have seen me turning my head every which way, trying to identify the source of the voice.

"Look, if you are the real Sukina," I said in my mind, *"could you please address me in both the collective unconscious and then the real world? I need to know I'm not going mad."*

"Certainly," Sukina's voice said. *"I'll let you know my purpose of coming here now, though. Gerhaun has awoken and wants to see you in person."* The footsteps resumed down the corridor.

My vision must have blurred out a little at that point, because the next thing I remember focusing on was Faso waving at me as if trying to snap me out of a trance.

"Welcome back to the land of the living."

"Sorry, I just zoned out for a moment."

"Strange..." Faso said, and he turned towards the cell door. "Sukina would do that sometimes too..."

A guard, with a bulldog face and much meaner looking than the three who escorted us down here, stood beside her at the door, glaring at nothing in particular. Sukina had appeared next to him, her face clear as ever as if she'd just been to the bathroom to polish it. In her hand, she held a set of keys. She looked at me.

"You already know why I came. Come on, best not to say much right now."

"You mean that was really you?" I asked.

She smiled. "Pontopa, let's stop playing these games."

"Okay," I said – what else could I say, really? I stood up and walked towards the door as Sukina unlocked it.

"As for you," Sukina turned to Faso and jingled the keys, looking rather pleased with herself. "Our chief engineer Asinal Winda wants a little word with you about your inventions."

"Oh, so you finally made your father see sense."

Sukina nodded. "Gerhaun thinks it's a good idea for you to start getting your hands dirty in the labs and, yeah, Butan needed a little talking around, but he got there eventually.

"Fantastic," Faso lifted himself off his bed and brushed off his suit. "Finally, I can get back to some real science."

We walked out of the cell and Sukina locked the door behind us. She turned to the guard. "Please walk Mr Gordoni to the labs."

"What?" Faso said. "I need a guarded escort now? I thought you said I was free."

"Do you know the way?" Sukina asked.

Faso looked at the guard, who had a smile on his face. "I guess not," he said. Then Sukina beckoned me away.

14

I was absolutely fascinated by the corridors, which seemed to get grander as we progressed towards Gerhaun's abode. Sukina told me how these corridors spanned around the outer perimeter of the castle. Posted every metre or so, on the left-hand side, were tall and narrow gothic windows, looking out onto the dusty ground and the roiling wall of brown clouds beyond. No windows looked out from the other side of the corridor. Instead, the walls there had tapestries of dragons of different colours woven into them, depicting them in battle against hosts of war-automatons. Each of these were lit by flaming torches in sconces casting dancing shadows that almost made the pictures come to life.

"Beyond that wall is where the dragons live," Sukina said. "We try to keep man and dragon separate from each other, mainly. Dragons and humans coexist, but we each also need our personal privacy. Although, it's different if you're a dragonseer…"

"I guess we have the freedom to roam," I said. "What about the other men and women? Do you restrict access?"

Sukina smiled. "Something like that," she said. "Although my father doesn't always respect that."

"He seems quite a character."

"Yes… Somehow, as dragonseers, you seem to attract characters. I've often wondered if it's something to do with the dragon's blood within us."

"Dragon's blood? You mean…"

"I believe Gerhaun wants you to discover the answer to that one yourself. Come on, this way."

We'd reached the end of the corridor now, which had widened out a little to make way for two double doors, perhaps five times our height, towering up into what looked like one side of a chimney. There were no windows here, but flickering torches suffused the alcove with yellow light. Sukina selected a large iron key from her ring and unlocked the doors.

I wondered how Sukina could possibly get the things to open, but she didn't even need to push on them. For, as if affected by some magical force, the doors opened on their own accord.

The room revealed on the other side was of mahogany and stone. Displays of gold cascaded down its walls, like statues of waterfalls. In the centre, stood a heap of precious treasures: golden crowns beset with precious stones, coins of bronze, silver and gold in all kinds of sizes, diamonds as large as a fist, intricate glass roses with emeralds or rubies at their tips, golden swords that looked so fragile they couldn't possibly have been made for fighting, and so many other curiosities I couldn't possibly name them all.

The room felt warmer than the corridors, which was surprising because it was so vast. But it needed to be this way to house the dragon queen.

Gerhaun Forsi was three times the size of Velos and certainly the largest dragon I'd ever seen. She wasn't grey like the others around the encampment. Nor was she blue like Velos, or any other scaly colours that I would have expected a dragon to be, but gold. The finish of her skin wasn't reptilian, but rather a shiny, polished gold, just like the treasures which surrounded her.

"Gerhaun Forsi," Sukina stated, not vocally but in the collective unconscious. *"This is Pontopa Wells, a dragonseer I believe."*

The great creature craned its smooth polished neck, then leaned forward and cocked her head a little. She balanced herself gracefully on two massive golden hind-feet, with claws as long as sabres, with her fore-legs raised high above me. She examined me for a while, and I must have stood just gazing at her in wonderment, no thoughts running through my mind, just a sheer sense of marvel at what I saw.

"I can feel you," she said eventually. *"Pontopa Wells, yes, I can feel you. Sukina is right, you are a dragonseer."*

I was lost for words, still awestruck by this massive creature before me that exuded nothing but greatness.

"You can speak, if you like," Gerhaun said. *"You must learn not to be affected by first appearances. A dragonseer must be brave, but not fearless. The fear will always be there, my dear."*

Even after her prompting, it took me a while to work out what to say. *"I guess I've accepted I'm not mad by now,"* I said eventually in my own mind, which meant I was speaking in the collective unconscious.

"Far from it. Pontopa Wells, dragonseer, descendant of Candida. You have a lot to learn."

"I do," I said. My thoughts began to spin off in a thousand directions and I tried to blink away the confusion that had begun to flood my mind. Gerhaun's face was so large that I could only focus on one of her great green eyes.

"You may ask questions," Gerhaun said. *"For you have many, and if you leave them unasked, they will never go away. You wish to ask about the Ambassadors, yes?"*

I shook my head. I still hadn't quite got over this whole telepathy thing, and Gerhaun seemed much more adept at it than Sukina. *"Yes, I want to learn about the Ambassadors,"* I said. *"Who exactly were they?"*

"Indeed, you know the myths. You've recounted them many times before."

Again, she paused as if waiting for me to say something, but I really didn't know what to say. Sukina had implied that Gerhaun would answer all my questions, but now her answers seemed somewhat evasive.

After a moment, Gerhaun continued to speak. *"Your dreams are more than just dreams. They're the closest that most come to the collective unconscious. Because you're a dragonseer, dreams also bring you closer to the truth. Once you learn to read them then, my dear, you can learn a great many things."*

I was still absolutely bewildered and a little frustrated, to be honest. But by this point I'd decided to bite my tongue. I took a deep breath. Gerhaun, all this time, had been waiting patiently for me to compose myself. My heart was thumping in my chest, but I tried my best to ignore it. What I needed the most, was to find out what was going on.

"*What dream do you speak of?*" I asked.

"*That's more like it,*" she said. "*Courage must come first before discovery. Often the answers you seek are within. Now, the dreams you ask of are only those of the myths of creation. The versions from your textbooks don't speak as true as the dreams you've had since birth.*"

"*Of Finase and Honore?*"

"*Yes,*" Gerhaun said. "*You know well the myth, I'm sure.*"

I did. The creation myth was one of the first stories I remember my mother telling me as a child. In it, our world began with two immortal races: men and dragons. Finase was the leader of men, Honore the leader of dragons. There were no women.

At some time in the distant past, a great war emerged between the two races. After a decade of fighting, they realized they couldn't possibly exist together upon this world. So, they called up to The Gods Themselves for help.

In response, the Gods Themselves sent down the Tree Immortal, with the promise that whoever drank first of its sap, would rule the world. The two leaders called upon great armies, which clashed at the base of this huge tree.

There, Finase and Honore met and, in a battle to the death. They tore apart its bark with knife and claw. They ended up destroying the tree and each other before they could drink of its sap.

All men and dragons died in battle that day, but their blood mingled with the soil and the mashed up roots of the Tree Immortal. From there, arose men, women, dragon queens and dragons of all the colours of the rainbow.

"*Yes, that's the myth,*" Gerhaun said, again reading my thoughts. "*You learned your history well. But tell me, Pontopa, is that the version you recall?*"

My eyebrows knotted in confusion. "*What do you mean?*"

"*The truth, dear Dragonseer. Do you know this myth to be true?*"

"*I --*" Was there something I had forgotten from my schooling? I started racking my brains for what I'd read in the history textbooks.

"*No,*" Gerhaun said. "*Not there. Don't search for the answer in knowledge, for what people have taught you in the past is often filled with lies. Trust only the truths rooted inside you. Recall your dreams."*

"I can't remember my dreams."

"You do. They only become hidden within through years of trying to rationalise. Sukina was once the same. Just focus, Pontopa. Seek within."

I dropped my head. My stomach churned and I couldn't remember the last time I'd felt so nervous.

"Breathe, dragonseer," Gerhaun said. Then again, I heard her voice more distant in my head as if I'd experienced a sudden change of consciousness. *"That's right. Don't fear yourself. Simply let it flow."*

For a while, I felt the panic rushing through me. Wild thoughts that had no direction. Worry about my parents and the fact that we were terrorists now. How I was never really the best learner at school. And Velos...would he be okay?

"Relax, Pontopa," Gerhaun said. *"Breathe."*

On those words, I did as she said. I let another breath of stale air fill my chest. With it, a sense of relief washed over me. Then, clear as rain, came the truth. Pictures I had seen many times but forgotten. Dreams of the past, of the future, of sailing the void that connected human, dragonkind and the whole of creation that The Gods Themselves had left behind.

"That's it," Gerhaun's voice now seemed to waver in the background. *"Go deeper. Connect to the collective unconscious. Never let your fear keep you away."*

I let my mind take the plunge and everything around me – Sukina, the massive dragon queen in front of me, the glistening pile of treasure – all this blurred into nothing as I entered a world within. I focused on recalling what was in my mind's eye and diving as deep beneath my own subconscious as I could, and then beyond into the sea of the collective unconscious.

There, images flooded my mind's eye. I'd seen them many times in my dreams, now forgotten. The kind of lucid dreams that seem so real until you wake up and then ten minutes later, they're gone. The next time, you feel a sense of déjà vu, but then again, as you awake, they're lost to the mind, and so the cycle repeats.

"*Finase and Honore didn't die at each other's throats,*" I said. "*No, I see a woman. Finesia, Finase's wife, drank the sap from the Tree Immortal's roots. The world didn't start with just men, but men and women alike, all immortal.*

"*The Gods Themselves gave Finesia to Finase for company. As he and Honore fought, Finesia thought she'd dive in and take the tree's power for herself.*

"*But her greed was her own undoing. An immortal, she was the only one who survived the battle. She watched in horror as her own kind perished around her, including her beloved, Finase. The dragons died too, including Honore. So, in despair, Finesia hacked the tree into a million pieces, which scattered on the wind throughout the Southlands.*"

I then became Finesia, wandering in solitude, roving the barren plains of the world for company, but finding nothing. Reduced to delirium, mania, and insanity. I felt it all – it struck my emotional core. Tears flooded to my eyes.

"*It may hurt,*" Gerhaun's voice kept me grounded. "*But don't lose it.*"

I took some more deep breaths, centred myself then brought myself back to the vision within. "*The Gods Themselves looked upon such a desolate world in disappointment. Humans and dragons were their creations that they had once loved, and now they had undone each other through greed.*

"*That was when the Gods Themselves deserted us. They departed to other stars, other planets, to leave this one behind. They didn't want to leave this world devoid of life. So, they created men out of mud. Then, they created women from the bark of trees and dragons and dragon queens from the sulphur at the centre of the earth.*

"*To guard us all, they also created eight creatures out of the blood of both man and dragon. These were born out of eggs but took the form of human women. Thus, came the first dragonseers, the Eight Ambassadors, who share the blood of both humans and dragonkind. Their job was to mediate the conflict between man and dragon and ensure the two races never destroyed each other again.*"

"*Those Ambassadors,*" Gerhaun cut in. "*Were the foremothers of the today's dragonseers, and you are directly descended from the*

Ambassador, Candida. There can only ever be eight of you, a dragonseer will always have only one child, no more, no less, always female. Although thanks to King Cini II's dragonheats, there's now only two of you. Plus, another back in Tow—"

"My mother."

"Not your mother, I'm afraid. If there was a fourth dragonseer alive, we would have sensed it by now. Another..."

Fortunately, I was too deep in trance to be shocked by that statement. But that didn't stop me being curious. *"Then who's the other?"*

Gerhaun Forsi kicked out with her hind leg and the sudden motion brought me back to the present, almost as if Gerhaun had wanted to snap me out of my self-induced trance. I opened my eyes to see a nugget of gold come tumbling down from Gerhaun's stack. *"Questions, so many questions. Have patience and you will learn more, but for now we need to get on to more pressing matters."*

She turned her mighty head to Sukina. *"Is there any more news of the little one from the north?"*

Sukina smiled as she looked at me. I heard her speak within my head, without her even needing to move her lips. *"Gerhaun means Artua. You know the king's nephew we've been reading about in the magazines."* I sensed there was more to this than Sukina let on. But I could hear nothing of her true thoughts, she masked those well.

"*Very well,*" Gerhaun said. *"We shall call him Artua for now. Although, Pontopa, you should know that the child doesn't really belong to the King of Tow."*

My eyes opened wide in astonishment. *"Sukina? It was you who was responsible for the kidnapping?"*

Sukina shook her head. *"No, but we're concerned about who did. We thought that Prince Artua was safe within the king's walls, but now it appears he might be in danger. Gerhaun and I have been making plans to rescue him, since the matter is now becoming a matter of urgency."*

"But I don't understand," I said. *"What does the boy mean to you?"*

"*That, we can't reveal to you yet,*" Gerhaun said. *"You need to first learn to mask your thoughts so others can't hear you. It's not a technique that comes naturally, unless you've been trained since birth."*

"Mask my thoughts? From who?"

"From spies who might listen in the collective unconscious. There are others who can listen to your mind and they might do so to try and discover our secrets. You have to understand, dear dragonseer, that the more we tell you, the more we put ourselves at risk."

I zoned out for a moment. Gerhaun's reference to danger had reminded me that my parents could be in jeopardy, and that got me worried. Part of this was due to the mention of the execution of the two perpetrators in the magazines. Unlike his father, Cini III had never acted aggressively to anyone within Tow before, he'd more wanted to protect his country as a perfect utopia, a place where nothing could go wrong. Now he seemed to be taking a different stance, so what he'd do next was anyone's guess.

"Your parents will be okay," Sukina said in the collective unconscious. She was doing that mind-reading thing again. It was starting to get on my nerves a little.

I turned to her wanting to throw back my chagrin, but her expression was so full of sympathy that I couldn't possibly fault her. Despite the fact she'd kind of got me into this mess. *"I just can't help but worry about them."*

Gerhaun cocked her head. *"You are quite right to, my dear,"* she said. *"Part of you wants to blame Sukina, or blame Faso. However, it was you who decided to come here, and you did so for much greater reasons than just to see a new place."*

"But my parents..."

"We've already sent a spy to the Five Hamlets to keep an eye on things, and he'll send information back to us via Hummingbird if he discovers anything unusual. It's probably better to see what news he sends back to us before acting on anything. We have strong resources to react quickly here, and you and Velos will be safe here."

I lowered my head. *"You're right, but what can I do now?"*

Sukina stepped forward and put a comforting hand on my arm. *"We've ordered Admiral Sandao to stay up north a little longer. If there's any danger, we'll hear about it pretty quickly. Meanwhile, we have a mission we want you to partake in."*

I raised an eyebrow. *"A mission?"*

"*Yes. It will give me a chance to show you what dragonseers can really do.*"

I shuddered. I had a sense that danger lay ahead of me, but then, perhaps this would help me take my mind of things a little bit. "*Tell me more.*"

"*Of course,*" Sukina said. "*My father has already prepared a briefing team and he's waiting for us outside.*"

15

We had the briefing in the courtyard on which we'd previously landed. They placed our seats around the tail of the huge golden dragon mosaic, which I now realised depicted Gerhaun. We'd all sat ourselves on the wooden, foldable seats at the front of around ten to twelve rows, with every seat stuffed with mustard suited soldiers. Sukina sat on my left and Wiggea, that nice guard who had escorted me to the cell, on my right with his hands clutched between his knees.

General Sako was at the Gerhaun mosaic's head. He stood next to a noticeboard on a stand, with a map of the Southlands placed upon it. Smoke rose from the pipe clenched between his lips as he glared at someone in the back row. I turned around and peeked over the crowd to see Faso sitting right at the back-row corner, his head tucked to his chest like a sleeping pigeon.

Behind Faso were the dragons. Velos lay on the floor in the centre, sound asleep, now awoken although still a little bleary, and no longer in chains. He still had that horrifying armour on him, of course. Other Greys had spaced themselves out well away from Velos. They stood around, picking bits out of their wings or eating out of secicao troughs that lay scattered around the courtyard.

Due to the collective unconscious being stronger here, I could feel even more of what Velos was feeling. My heart went out to him, because he didn't know how to fit in with these kin who were of the same species, yet so different from him.

"*Go on,*" I said, this time in the collective unconscious. "*Make friends here.*" I doubt he understood my language, even if I now had a channel to his mind. But he understood the intention in my words, and I felt him whimper then and shy even further away from the Greys.

I sighed and looked back at Faso who hadn't changed position one bit, then I turned to Sukina, who smiled. "Faso's been showing off his contraptions in the laboratory ever since I let him out."

Brown secicao clouds roiled in the distance. For the first time, I noticed how mesmerising they were to watch. Thin wisps occasionally broke through the invisible barrier only to dissipate like smoke would from a fire.

Then again, it wasn't the first thing that seemed strange here. I couldn't work out why, after Sukina telling me that they kept dragons and humans separate, would both meet for briefings.

I decided to ask her.

"We only do it for missions involving dragonseers," Sukina said. "Which means that dragons and humans will have to work together. It's more for the troops' benefit than the dragons. They tend to fear them less when they're briefed alongside them." She opened her mouth as if to say something else but was interrupted by a cough from General Sako at the front.

Immediately, everything fell silent. General Sako waited for a few moments, scanning the crowd as if looking for offenders as he puffed on his pipe. Then he took his turn to bawl out the brief.

"It's come to our attention," he said, "that King Cini has decided to test the prototypes for his new harvesting operations. We've nicknamed this new invention Mammoths. Massively armoured machines, these beasts work by ripping secicao out of the ground and then grinding it into mulch through huge grinders in their mouths."

"*Idiots,*" I thought. When they grinded it so quickly, it would lose some of its augmentative properties.

"*And also increase its acidity when it's extracted into the soil as waste.*" Sukina's voice entered my head again. Once again, reading my thoughts.

"I wish you'd stop doing that," I said back to her in my mind.

I saw Sukina nod out of the corner of my eye. *"This is exactly what Gerhaun means by needing to learn how to mask your thoughts."*

"But how?"

"It's a lifelong practice, really," Sukina said. *"The theory is so simple but the application difficult. You simply still your mind and then watch your thoughts from a distance, but it's a lot easier to explain than do."*

"I guess you'll teach me more later," I said.

"Of course."

General Sako had drawn an arrow on the map from somewhere on the northern coast of the Southland towards fortress Gerhaun. "Cini wants to use the Mammoths to take operations further inland," he explained. "As you know, automatons don't work well under the effects of secicao resin. But Cini has developed a hardened coating on the machines' caterpillar tracks, that potentially allows these machines to travel several hundred miles inland.

"If we let King Cini progress with these automatons, then he might accidently stumble across Fortress Gerhaun, which wouldn't be good news for us. The king has designed the Mammoths to be highly impervious. Fortunately, our spies have confirmed that they have their flaws.

"We'll need volunteers for a team to assist our two dragonseers to this point here—" he pointed to a location on the top right of the map "—where we'll intercept one Mammoth being tested and convince King Cini that his new toys are a big waste of money."

He took another draught on his pipe as he scanned the seats with a stern gaze for a show of hands. Next to me, that guard Wiggea put up his hand and then turned to me and smiled. I guessed I could come to like that man. I turned around to see ten or so more raised hands, an even mix of both ladies and men. Four of the soldiers who had their hands raised, wore the same navy-blue sash I'd noticed on Wiggea the other day.

"They're dragonelites," Sukina told me, again reading my mind. *"Gerhaun's finest troops. The other volunteers know they'll also be considered for the rank if they keep volunteering. It's a prestige thing."*

"I see," I said.

In front of me, Sako was scanning the volunteers. He looked slightly disappointed. "Is that all? Come on, what did I train you for, to sit around all day and drink South Saye tea?"

Another hand rose up from behind me. General Sako looked at it in disgust.

"Blunders and dragonheats! What are you thinking, Gordoni?" General Sako certainly could be loud when he wanted to.

Faso stood up so that I could see him. He seemed unusually mouse-like under General Sako's glare, but still he stammered out his point. "King Cini has a brand spanking new invention, and there's no way that I'm going to stand on the side-lines and hear about how they work second-hand." For once, I found myself almost admiring Faso for sticking up for himself.

"What absolute nonsense," General Sako said. "You're no soldier. You'll put the mission in jeopardy. Or perhaps that's your intent?"

"My intent," Faso said a little sterner now, "is not to get bored within these walls. You wanted to employ me to be a scientist and that's what I intend to go out and do."

"You will do no such thing, Faso Gordoni. An order is an order."

Faso lowered his head and he looked as if he was about to sit down, almost defeated, until a lithe woman in a grey felt frock coat stood up. She wore glasses and had short raven hair parted in a fringe. "Please, General Sako. If I might make a suggestion?"

"Please do," General Sako said. "But come and do so out here where everyone can see you."

"Thank you," the woman said. She walked to the front, leaning forwards with her hands behind her back making her look older than I was sure she was.

"*That's Asinal Winda,*" Sukina said in my head. "*Gerhaun's Chief Engineer. The way that Faso looks at her, I think he has the hots for her.*"

I chuckled under my breath. "*Is it mutual?*"

"*Who knows,*" Sukina said.

"*You're not jealous, are you?*"

She folded her arms. "*Not one little bit.*"

The engineer had now reached the map and turned to Faso,

who still stood at the back, his hands in his suit pocket. "Mr Gordoni, I must say, I'm fascinated by your automaton. You call him Ratter, right?"

"That's the one," Faso said. "Ratter's one-hundred per cent modifiable, the most versatile automaton around."

"And he runs on secicao, I noticed."

Faso frowned. "How on earth could you know that?"

"I merely looked underneath the hatch. I was careful not to damage the mechanism, as I really do find it a fascinating machine."

I huffed quietly. If she had seen the thing when it had that syringe plunged into Velos, she might have thought differently.

"He is quite," Faso continued. "I hope you understand that I wish to take him with us on our little mission." Faso had regained his haughty posture now that he wasn't addressing General Sako.

"Actually, I was thinking that you could stay behind and help a little?"

"And miss out on a chance to survey a piece of technology." Faso put his hands on his hips. "Tell me, is anyone who has volunteered today a scientist?"

"Well, no—"

General Sako cut the engineer off mid-sentence. "Faso Gordoni, you are in no position to be making demands. You will stay here and help Winda in the laboratory, or we'll lock you back up."

"Actually Butan," Sukina stood up. "I think Faso might be right. He may be of use."

"Sukina—"

"Look, if we could get any useful information on those Mammoths, then we might be able to exploit their flaws in case Cini does build more. I know you don't like it, but Faso does have a talent for observation."

"Blunders and dragonheats! He'll compromise the mission."

"I'll make sure he does no such thing. I've just spoken to Gerhaun, Butan, and she agrees that Faso should accompany us."

General Sako gave Sukina one hard gaze, but she didn't back down. He took another puff on his pipe and blew out a plume of yellow smoke that Winda backed away from, while waving at it with her hand.

"Very well," General Sako said. "So, we've selected who will topple the Mammoths. Eleven troops, plus Sukina, Miss Wells, and Gordoni. We'll send out fourteen Greys—"

"We'll take Velos and eleven Greys," Sukina interrupted. I felt Velos awaken and he let out a stiff roar, causing half the gathered soldiers to almost jump out of their seats.

"Yes, right," General Sako said. "I certainly have a headstrong daughter."

Surprisingly, a chuckle emanated from the crowd. Everyone clearly must have been used to the little spats between Sukina and her father. General Sako turned to me. He spoke to me much more gently than he'd addressed me before.

"Miss Wells, is there anything you need to ask?"

I knew that there was no point asking whether there was any news from my parents. General Sako was unlikely to have heard anything more than Gerhaun. But there was one other thing that had been on my mind. "How dangerous will it be?" I asked.

It was Sukina who answered. "Don't worry about that. We have the best troops in the land."

Again, another chuckle from the audience. It caused me to crack a smile too. Sukina had such confidence that I felt kind of excited to be going. Although, I did realise that this humour was just there to help keep up the troops' morale. In all honesty, we were going up against a formidable machine.

Also, I couldn't stop thinking about my parents. Firstly, there was the issue of whether they actually were my parents. Gerhaun had seemed to think not. Yet I'd grown up with them my whole life and I shuddered when I thought about the jeopardy they could be in.

Sukina spoke once again within my head. *"Your parents will be fine, and news from the Five Hamlets will probably have arrived by the time we're back from the mission."*

"I hope so," I said back in the collective unconscious, and I swallowed my thoughts. Rather than getting anxious, it seemed more prudent to focus on the mission at hand.

AFTER THE BRIEFING HAD FINISHED, Sukina led us to a sealed door at the far end of the courtyard. It had this rubber suction thing around the edges, making it airtight. A large valve protruded out of the door.

"The armoury," Sukina said. She turned to Wiggea. "Officer, would you?"

"Certainly," Wiggea said with a slight bow. He turned the valve and the door sucked open. A sudden rush of cool air whisked past us and we stepped into a confined brass chamber with a similar airtight door on the other side of the room. Faso entered last, taking some time to examine the doorway.

We stepped into a large room, again with brass walls. Rifles adorned the back walls and in front of those stood some metal shelves with some funny looking gas masks. Each had a tube protruding from the right-hand side, just underneath the nose. The tube led to a green pouch at the end.

"What are those?" I asked.

"Secicao masks," Sukina said. "Come, we must hurry. Put one of those on and then we can set off. Oh, and don't forget the wellies."

I walked over to a shelf and took the gas mask. It strapped around the back of the head using a strong piece of elastic. There was some kind of dial on the tube.

"Turn that, and it will burn some secicao," Sukina said from next to me, as she pulled one bright yellow wellie up to her knee. "It moderates how much you take in, ensuring a consistent effect. Much more effective in many ways than drinking from a hip flask. But, of course, cumbersome and not the easiest to conceal when you're passing through customs at the Southern Barrier."

It made a lot of sense, really. When surrounded by secicao fumes, it wasn't easy to take off a mask to take a swig from your hip flask. But this device combined both the secicao and the gas mask together.

I put on my wellies – needed to protect me from the resin – and then I turned to look at Sukina. I couldn't help but laugh how ridiculous she looked with that long trunk hanging from the side of her nose.

A guard had handed Faso a yellow camo coverall to put over his suit, which he refused to take off. Underneath the uniform, I could still make out the knot on his tie and through his goggles, I could see his scowl.

We went back into the courtyard, where Winda was waiting for us with Ratter upside down in her hands. All of sudden, Ratter sprang out of her grasp, turned itself one-eighty-degrees in the air, landed, and scurried over to Faso. It tried to poke its nose underneath Faso's sleeve, which was sealed there by an elastic band. Instead, he went to rest on Faso's shoulder.

Not far away, Velos was waiting, in line with another eleven Greys. Sukina, Faso, and I mounted Velos' armour via the ladder while the other eleven troops took places, unsaddled on the Greys' backs.

Velos was nervous too, I could feel that much. He'd seen enough of General Sako's diagrams to know that we were going up against automatons, and he'd never had to face one before. So, I decided to placate his spirit by singing to him. A song just came to me that I felt would give Velos a little courage, a rhythm to its harmonic procession that made it sound like a like a war march.

"You're getting the hang of this," Sukina said and then she joined in my song, although she varied the notes a little to reach out to the surrounding Greys.

With all the dragons fuelled by with a new energy, we took off and flew into the secicao clouds.

We could see nothing all around us other than the secicao gas and, very faintly, the knotted secicao branches beneath. We were right in the thick of the secicao forest. My breathing was shallow through the filter and again, the acidity of the gas stung at my skin.

We flew on Velos right at the centre of the formation, sandwiched on each side by two Greys ever so slightly behind us. We were going so fast that the wind whipped past us and roared against my ears. Otherwise, everything seemed rather silent. Never did we break from formation. We'd strayed so far from Fortress Gerhaun now, that I could no longer hear Sukina in my own mind.

Usually, I would swoop and dive with Velos, which would make these journeys fun. But Sukina had warned me against doing anything that could render us detectable. So I shifted around in my saddle, wondering when the journey would end.

Faso might have made this armour safe, but he hadn't made it comfortable. So, once again, I found myself missing the feeling of straddling Velos' back. I turned around every so often, awfully envious of the soldiers. I didn't think I could ever get used to riding in such an unnatural way.

After what seemed quite a few hours, we came across the Mammoth harvesting automaton. It appeared wispy and ghostlike at first through the murky haze. As we got closer, the haze seemed to clear giving us a better view.

The thing was massive. I had thought Gerhaun had been huge, but while she towered, this machine hulked. It moved forwards on two thick caterpillar tracks, flattening the secicao beneath. Although I couldn't quite make out their scale from this distance, I guessed the tusks to be as large as Velos himself. They protruded out of a plate that swayed up and down, tossing up strands of secicao, which in turn slid down the plate into the machine's mouth. The mouth looked like the propellers at the back of a steamship, with a contraption inside whirring so fast that I couldn't make out the blades.

Its body housed row after row of turrets with menacing muzzles that wavered back and forth on their pivots, scanning the terrain. Clearly, General Sako had been misinformed about the Mammoth not being armed. The secicao mist in front of us thickened, once again obscuring the Mammoth from view.

"Bank left," Sukina called from behind me, her voice loud enough for the whole formation to hear.

I steered Velos in that direction and dived down a little, so we could hopefully get close enough to see. But before the huge automaton came back into view, I heard something in my mind's eye. A song, yet not a song, for it lacked harmony, only noise. Still, I recognised it as some kind of dragonsong, although one designed to distort.

"*You heard it?*" Sukina asked and I realised her to be speaking within my own mind.

"*I heard something,*" I thought back. "*But what the dragonheats was it and why can we speak like this all of a sudden?*"

The song came again, this time a high-pitched wail and I felt Velos buck a little underneath me. For a moment he entered a stall, just as I heard Faso shout out from behind. Fortunately, Velos quickly recovered and I turned him towards where I imagined the Mammoth to be.

"*Should we retreat?*" I asked Sukina inside my mind.

But she seemed more focused on singing a song. A sweet harmony that seemed to soften the wind around us. Velos' armour glowed green and began to feel warm between my calves and I turned around to see Faso lifting himself up from the spigot on Velos' flank.

"*You better augment,*" Sukina said and I remembered the dial on my mask. I reached down to turn it, and the sinking fear inside my chest was replaced by a burning resolve. "*There's no turning back now, I'm afraid.*"

That grating tune came again. The song seemed to have some kind of consciousness and I could feel it trying to rock Velos' mind. But Velos had secicao fuel in his body now.

"*What is it?*" I asked Sukina, now speaking comfortably through our telepathic channel. "*Why can we speak here all of a sudden?*"

"*There's something here,*" Sukina said. "*Someone I once knew and never thought would return.*"

"*Then we should turn back, surely?*"

"*No,*" Sukina said. "*We'll carry on. If anything, I need to learn if it's him.*"

Perhaps the secicao burning in my mask kept me from being afraid – I'm not sure exactly what blend we were using. But then, part of me knew Sukina was right. If we gave up now, then whatever this thing was might discover Fortress Gerhaun. Then there would be no stopping King Cini as he tried to destroy the remaining dragon queens.

"Everyone augment!" Sukina shouted out louder than the wind. "We're going in."

I gritted my teeth and pushed right on Velos' steering fin. Towards the Mammoth harvester automaton that had again started to come into view.

"Sukina, look!" The call came from Faso who pointed up towards the sky.

I turned up my head to see a black form pass over us. Dark, like a crow but with the long, outstretched wings of a dragon. Though, a colourful sheen washed over it, like you'd see in an oil slick.

"What the—" I said, although I wasn't sure if it was in my mind or out loud.

"It's Charth," Sukina said.

"What? Who?"

From above the Mammoth, a roar came from the sky. I craned

my head to see the dragon wheeling around up there. Wellies, how had it managed to get back so fast. But then I glanced over my shoulder, and the one I had previously seen was high above us, turning around back towards the Mammoth. Two of these creatures, that was all we needed.

"My, my, two dragonseers," the voice came inside my own mind, male and slick. *"I'd expected to only meet one of you."*

"And who, exactly, are you?" Sukina said in the collective unconscious.

"Oh yes, darling," the other voice said. *"I know you want to speak to my brother... But you know already how he's the silent, brooding type."*

"Charth", Sukina said. *"Reveal yourself."*

"I'm sure he'll speak when he's good and ready. But for now, we can't let you take the Great Harvesters. That's not part of Finesia's grand design."

"Finesia's dead," I said. *"Is he mad?"*

"Not mad, my darling," the voice returned. *"For now, you might call it a religion."*

"We won't let you get in our way," Sukina said.

"Well, well," the voice replied. *"Let's play for a while. I'm curious to see what you can do."*

I turned back to Sukina. *"What do we do?"* I asked her, still in the collective unconscious.

"We go in..." She clenched her teeth. *"I never thought I'd meet him again, and now, it seems, he brought his brother too."*

We were close enough to the Mammoth, that we could see its intricate designs. Like Faso's workshop, it had upon it the red glowing eyes of the old war automatons from the Dragonheats. But they weren't arranged in disarray, rather on each turret that had now started to point towards us as we approached. Shortly thereafter, the whole contraption started to glow green. Secicao light pulsed over its polished brass curves.

"Dragonheats!" Faso shouted from behind. "They've stolen my technology."

This couldn't be good. But we'd come too far to back out now.

"Attack!" Sukina shouted, then she sang a short song to say the same to the dragons. The armour bucked beneath us and the Gatling guns begun to fire from Velos' sides. In chorus, the turrets responded from the Mammoth, swivelling around their pivots and firing a shot every second or so. They weren't as accurate as I'd feared and we managed to get close enough for Velos to let out his green flame, scorching and disabling several of the turrets as we swooped by.

Behind us, came a scream and one of the dragonelites got knocked off the dragon's back. Another shot echoed out, and the Grey went down with a huge roar.

I pulled back on Velos' steering fin and we entered into a loop-the-loop. My stomach churned and blood rushed to my head, as the world span upside-down. Usually, I'd use my thighs to keep me in place, but now we had the seat belt harnesses. At the top, Velos tucked in his wings and did a half barrel roll, so we could then turn to come in for another pass.

We turned to see another Grey spiralling to the ground. We'd regrouped with the remaining dragons outside of the Mammoth's firing range. On the Mammoth, half the guns on our side were now hanging from their sockets. Perhaps we could now approach and topple the thing over.

"Okay, okay, that's enough," said that same voice in the collective unconscious. *"Indeed, you're quite impressive. Let's call a temporary truce."*

The guns on the mechanism whirred to a halt.

Behind me, Sukina raised her hand palm facing forwards. She called out a fast song with staccato notes. The two black dragon-like creatures had now met in formation above the Mammoth. They entered into a swift dive and hit the ground. The resin they landed on turned red for a moment and then, from out of it, arose a thick yellow secicao cloud, concealing them from view.

"Why should we listen to them?" I asked Sukina. *"It looks like we can take down that Mammoth."*

"Because I think they want to negotiate something that's in every-one's favour. I know Charth and I doubt very much his intention is to harm us or Fortress Gerhaun."

"But what if they do intend us harm?"

"Then they wouldn't have called a truce."

She was right, I guess. Although still, I wasn't sure I could trust them. Even if Charth was someone from Sukina's past.

I pushed up on Velos' steering fin and sent him down to ground. Sukina sang a song to indicate the remaining Greys should follow. Through all this, I'd forgotten Faso was with us too. I turned around to see his face the whitest I've ever known, hands clasped on the handlebar in front of him and the whites of his knuckles showing.

"Pontopa, what the dragonheats are you doing?"

"They called a truce."

"What? How could you possibly know that?"

"Because we have other ways of communicating, Faso. Now let us do our thing."

Just as Velos touched down, the clouds that the two black dragons had kicked up subsided. Where I had expected to see dragons, two tall, broad-shouldered blond-haired men stood below us. One had wavier hair, with his hands on his hips, his head high and tossed to the side a little, as if posing for a magazine. He wore a violet sports jacket and flared beige trousers.

The other's hair was also blonde and slicked-back. His posture was more human, although slumped forward a little as if he really didn't like his life on this earth. Much like his demeanour, his attire was grey and as dull as the barren landscape and roiling brown secicao clouds.

Sukina clicked her harness open behind me, adjusted her wellies, and then descended the ladder. I started to follow her down, but I stopped at the top rung and turned to Faso.

"You don't want to come down?" I asked.

Faso had himself pushed up against the back of his seat. His knees were raised up to his chin now and Ratter stood vigil from one of his knees. "I'd rather not."

"I never thought you'd be one to be afraid."

"Afraid? Have you bloody seen that thing?"

I raised an eyebrow. "You did realise there were two of them."

"What? No, not the dragons. The Mammoth. It will shoot you down as soon as you go near. They stole my technology, you know. That thing's powered by secicao."

I shook my head. There was no reasoning with this man sometimes. I descended the ladder and met Sukina on the ground.

The wavy-haired man stepped forwards, whilst the other kept his distance. The first man glanced up at the dragon, and he looked kind of impressed. Part of me wanted to despise him. He was supporting King Cini's harvesting operations after all. But then he had those good looks – high cheekbones, broad shoulders that looked like a child could ride upon each one. His wavy long hair fell gently over his shoulders, and he seemed to just emit an aura of sheer handsomeness. A regal military look, much like some of the airship captains I'd met from Tow.

"*Careful,*" Sukina said in my mind. "*This man is using the collective unconscious to manipulate your feelings. He wants you to like him.*"

The man took another step forward, his back and shoulders straight, and his chest puffed out. He looked between Sukina and I a few times. Eventually, he turned to me and gave a lopsided smile. "Francoiso Lamford," he said out loud, "and this is my brother." He indicated the other man who was still loitering cautiously at the back.

Sukina turned to the second man at the back. "Charth," she said. "You work for the king now?"

But his brother spoke in his place. "Yes, Dragonseer Sako, in a way we do."

"Careful," Charth said. "Do not give too much away."

"Oh, there's nothing we can say or do that can be of any threat to us. We are, after all, free agents. King Cini doesn't own us and we don't answer to him."

"That's enough," Charth snapped. As he flicked a glowing speck of secicao resin off his lapel, he turned a hard stare on Sukina. "We'd much rather not be here. But the king knew this automaton needed some guards."

"Is that all you can say, Charth?" Sukina replied. "No, 'hello, how have you been all these years?' Always focused on the mission. You haven't changed one bit..."

Charth shook his head. "I have nothing to say to you. We established that a long time ago."

I could almost feel Sukina grit her teeth. "This is not your land. We can't permit you to go any further."

"I don't think you have much of a say in the matter right now, Dragonseer Sako." The way her name rolled off Charth's tongue indicated he at least held her with some regard. "You can take down the automaton, and so we'll just fly back and bring more of them and extra troops. The king is creating hundreds of these things and he's not going to back down now."

The lines on Sukina's face hardened. "You killed our men," she said, "and our dragons."

"Oh, that..." Charth looked towards where one of the men had fallen. We couldn't see him from here, only the hulking form of a Grey lying dead on the ground, occasionally revealed by the fast moving secicao clouds. "But you attacked us."

"As I recall," Sukina said, "it was your contraption that first fired upon us."

"It's programmed that way," Charth said. "We had no way of knowing that your Greys would be mounted by armed men."

Francoiso gave me a wink. "And women, I must add," he said. "With better assets than weapons, I'm sure." How he was able to see any of that through our masks and camo was anyone's guess. Mind, who knows how they could stand there without a mask at all.

"Shut up, brother," Charth snapped. "We don't have time for your tomfoolery."

Francoiso smirked and looked back at his brother. "You never have time for a little fun. You need to lighten up a little."

I put my hands on my hips. Handsome as this guy was, I wasn't going to let insensitivity pass. "This is no time for lightening up." I gestured to our dead.

"I apologise, darling," Francoiso said. "You must understand, we're very sorry about your losses."

Sukina stepped towards Francoiso, a hard gaze locked upon him. "What is it you want exactly? You don't seem as if you came here to mock us."

"Why, simply to protect the king's harvesting operations. Although you never know who you're going to meet along the way."

There was a silence for a moment. I wanted to say something, but I really had nothing constructive to add. Sukina turned to glance at the dead then back at Charth.

"Why you?" she asked.

"That," Charth said, "you will shortly learn, I'm sure. As well, as Finesia's plans for you."

"Finesia is a myth."

Francoiso chuckled. "So, apparently, are the dragonseers."

Again, silence fell. I could feel Sukina's rage burning in my chest.

This time, Charth was the one to cut the discord. "Dragonseer Sako. I understand your reason for being here. The only reason you would attack us is if we'd almost stumbled upon your precious dragon queen's base. You're quite right in doing so in your own way. King Cini, powerful as he is, is not ready to uncover your operations. Extermination of another queen would create an imbalance that none of us want."

The rage in myself and Sukina began to turn into a glimmer of hope. "What exactly are you proposing?" Sukina asked.

"Allow our harvesters to continue operations in the Southlands – at least for now – and Francoiso and I will ensure they stay well away from your base. No more of your men or dragons will die, and we'll no longer have to squabble."

"Why would you do that?" Sukina asked.

A wide grin stretched across Francoiso's face. "It turns out that my brother can be quite generous when he gets the chance. As I said, we're free agents and we, in fact, have ulterior goals to the king."

"Francoiso, that's enough," Charth said.

The wavy-haired man turned to look at his brother. "See, it turns out that I can't answer your questions, without Charth getting all stroppy. Ah, well, I guess we should bid you adieu and leave it hanging for another day."

He turned to me, gave a long bow and the ground around him turned to brown dust. Out of the cloud, a black form rose up into the air. Charth looked up at the rising dragon, shook his head, kicked the ground and, in the same fashion, launched himself upwards. Momentarily, the Mammoth whirred back to action, it's turrets now remaining dormant, but its great hulking tracks turning the automaton in the opposite direction.

Once it had orientated itself, the thing moved surprisingly fast. I watched it for a moment, then turned to Sukina. She had her hands on her hips and her head pushed forward.

Shortly after, I felt my connection to her in the collective unconscious break.

"We must report this to Gerhaun," Sukina said out loud.

"Men who can turn into dragons," I said. "Who are they, Sukina?"

But she just sighed and then walked away to attend to the dead. I turned back to check on Velos and noticed Faso cowering timidly behind his armour. He let off a meek wave. I didn't return it, but instead went to help Sukina gather the bodies.

17

The night after our mission, I couldn't sleep. So, I just lay in bed staring into the darkness. Partly, the insomnia was due to what we'd seen that day. When I looked back, I can't see what I'd found so alluring about Francoiso? I mean, I like my men a little rough and ready, but I didn't make a habit of chasing after my enemies.

But then, who were these men, if you could call them that, and how could they turn into dragons? How could anyone who worked for Cini possibly see us as a potential ally after what we'd done at Fraw?

So many questions, and so few answers. It was enough for me to want to tear my hair out by its roots. But Sukina and Gerhaun had both explained why they'd withheld information from me. I just had to learn how to mask my thoughts.

Then part of me felt a little guilt for being so concerned about the goings on here, that I'd forgotten about my parents. News still hadn't come by Hummingbird from the Five Hamlets, and I couldn't help but wonder if Gerhaun or Sukina was also hiding the truth about this for fear of what I might do. It didn't matter at this point whether they were my parents or not. I just wanted them to be okay.

I also felt bad about the arguments I'd had with Papo. By this time, my parents could be hanging by a noose from the rafters of their country farmhouse. Cini III wasn't as ruthless as his father, admittedly – I mean, he didn't start the dragonheats. But that didn't mean he was fair, and one thing was for sure: our king did not like subterfuge. I'd never forgive myself if our previous altercation was the last exchange I'd ever have with my father.

"You know, I'll have to teach you to worry less. Your anxiety is enough to keep Gerhaun awake, never mind myself." I almost jumped out of my skin, the way Sukina's voice materialised in my head like that, taking precedence over my own.

"For crying out loud," I said. *"How many times do I have to say, I wish you wouldn't do that?"*

"I'm sorry," Sukina said. *"I did promise to teach you how to mask your thoughts. It's not easy, mind, and at the same time it's the easiest thing in the world. You simply need to train your mind to exert zero effort. Detach yourself from conscious thought and then it no longer becomes open to others."*

Again, Sukina seemed to be entering the realms of the airy-fairy. *"Are you telling me not to think at all? Without thought, how would I ever get anything done?"*

"On the contrary. I'm merely saying to separate your mind from your essence. This isn't a skill unique to dragonseers. Any skilled artist or craftsman can do the same. You simply need to forget yourself and become aware of everything around you. From there, comes true clarity of thought and a deep connection to the collective unconscious."

"I don't understand," I said. *"How can I forget my thoughts when there's this huge mess around me? You're asking me to forget my parents and the jeopardy they're probably in, is that it?"* A tear dropped off my cheek onto the pillow.

"It will take time," Sukina said. *"But you won't get there through trying to force it. This isn't about forgetting but deferral. Simply let your worries drift by and focus only on what you can control."*

"But I can control this. I could fly back and at least I'll know what's happening in the Five Hamlets. I should jump on Velos and ride him as quickly as possible through the night."

"You know well the costs of doing so. There's no way you'll get Velos through the Southern Barrier alone. What's the point of doing anything when you don't even know the situation? Sometimes the

greatest courage comes from patience. I know it hurts, and the pain won't go away but there are ways to alleviate it."

My heartbeat started to subside a little. *"Thank you,"* I said. *"I'm sure I'm not the only one with problems around here. Dragonheats, you probably have plenty of your own."*

"I try to not let life get to me," Sukina said.

"But sometimes it must, surely? I mean, you yourself said that you write, to fill the void of being alone."

This telepathy thing seemed more than the ability to hear each other's words. I could picture Sukina in my mind right then as well, see her face as a smile crept across it, as if she was sitting right beside me.

"Yes," Sukina said. *"I write to channel my energy sometimes. But to fill the void... I've learned to quite enjoy solitude since Faso..."*

I laughed. *"I can understand why, after Faso."*

"We just went in different ways. Faso can be a little much sometimes, but he's a good person underneath that arrogant mask of his."

"I can see that", I said. I started to wonder that if maybe I was a little harsh on him sometimes. Through the darkness, I could hear Velos snoring in the distance, much louder than the other dragons, or perhaps I heard him in the collective unconscious. I took a deep breath, the musty air filling my lungs. Strangely, I felt much calmer after talking to Sukina.

"You still there?"

"Yes," Sukina said. *"I can feel you're much calmer now."*

"I am. Say, I was just wondering before. Who's this boy, Artua. Why's he so important to you and Gerhaun and why did the king decide to kidnap him in the first place?"

"That's one of the things I can't really tell you," Sukina said, and I felt her breath catch in her throat.

"Is he like those two men? Can he turn into dragons, or something?"

"No, no," Sukina replied, *"nothing like them."*

"So, if the boy isn't one of them, who exactly is he?"

I felt Sukina's sigh rise up within my chest. *"Please, Pontopa. Don't press me on this issue. This is something we need to keep secret until you learn to mask your thoughts."*

"Okay," I said. *"I just wanted to learn a little more about you."*

"When the time comes for you to learn more, I promise I'll reveal all. For now, though, it's late, and I'm pretty tired after today."

Now that I had calmed down a bit, I also realised how tired I was. *"No problem,"* I said. *"But I'm eager to know."*

"I know," Sukina said, and I felt her mind drift quickly and soundly off to sleep.

IT SEEMED strange to wake up in Fortress Gerhaun without natural sunlight. The brown clouds gave the whole place a foreboding gloomy quality which made my body feel as if it wanted to lie in until early afternoon. When I opened my door and looked at the clock outside, indeed I had slept in until eleven in the morning. So, I wandered down to the grand hall to grab the last crumbs of breakfast – some cold crispy bacon, some sausage, some hash browns and a few slices of toast.

Faso came in a little worse for wear, his eyes red as if he'd hit the whiskey last night. He looked around the room, spotted me and then gave me a wave, his demeanour springing to life a little. Ratter was also perched on his shoulder, his red glowing eyes fixed upon me. A shiver ran down my spine.

Faso grabbed a plate from the buffet tray, piled on a selection of food, then sauntered over to me and plonked his rear on the seat in front of me. "Good morning, Miss Wells," he said. "You're glowing and radiant today."

"You've lightened up," I said.

Faso looked at the device on his shoulder. "Yes, well, Asinal Winda from the labs gave me ideas of some modifications to Ratter. I'm still working on a prototype, but I think this little guy could be the answer you need to take down those massive automatons. An army of them perhaps."

I snorted, trying to imagine each of Fortress Gerhaun's troops carrying a Ratter on their shoulders. "You sure you wouldn't accuse Gerhaun of stealing your technology?"

"Not if she pays me a modest wage."

"Really? Where would you spend it exactly."

"Why, in Slaro, of course."

"The king would eat you alive."

"Dear, I've got friends in high places there, you know. There are ways of hiding from Cini's forces, you just need enough money to do so. Besides, no one needs to know of my little arrangement with Gerhaun, and I can simply say Sukina took me hostage during the attack at Fraw, which in many ways is true."

I laughed. He'd certainly changed his tune. I guess he was missing his home after all and he didn't seem eager to return to the Five Hamlets. But then, I couldn't imagine him as a criminal, hiding away in Slaro's dark alleyways away from the king, juggling clients who were literally at war.

Faso's expression hardened to contempt. "You seem to doubt what I'm saying."

Again, I laughed. "I think you can do anything, Faso. Whether you can stay alive doing it, well, that's another matter entirely."

Faso scoffed. "It's all the name of science, isn't it? At the end of the day, it doesn't matter who I work for. As long as I'm advancing the future of mankind."

There wouldn't be a future, I thought, if Cini's left to his own devices and what Gerhaun wrote in *Dragons and Ecology* is true. I didn't say it out loud, though. I didn't want another of Faso's lectures on what's proper science and what isn't.

"And getting rich doing so," I pointed out instead.

"Well, yes, a man should take a little reward for his labours. We can't all be monks, you know?" A sly grin began to creep across his smarmy face. "Say, why don't you join me on this endeavour? You've already wanted a life of adventure, right?"

"With an executioner waiting around every corner, no thanks. Besides, I can't imagine Faso Gordoni living a life of danger. You'd never leave the house."

"Oh, I'll have servants to do that for me," Faso said, "and representatives so the king would never have to know he was working with me."

"You're not really selling this to me, Faso."

"Yes, I thought not. Well, it was just a thought."

He reached up to touch a pressure point on Ratter's back. The ferret automaton scurried down Faso's arm, cleared a space at the centre of Faso's plate and sat itself down there. I looked at it with derision.

"What's that thing doing now?" I asked.

"Warming my food... You know, with me, you'd never have to eat cold bacon again."

I shook my head. "Look, you don't seem to be getting the hint here, Faso. I would never be interested in you. I don't tend to go for anyone who makes false promises they can't keep."

The smile trembled on Faso's face a little, but it didn't fade. "Oh, you're just playing hard to get."

I decided it best to ignore him and lowered my head to tuck into my cold food. I left Faso sitting there without having to speak another word to him. It didn't take Ratter long to heat up his plate and after it had, Faso seemed pretty content to focus on his meal.

I said goodbye before I left, now at least on speaking terms with the guy. Then, I took some time to check on Velos, who seemed perky after what had happened in the jungle. Surprisingly, the secicao hadn't had as much of a draining effect on him as usual. Perhaps, I loathe to admit, it was due to that green coruscating armour on him.

After feeding him a little secicao I had some time to wander the palace. Sukina joined me after an urgent meeting she apparently had to have with Gerhaun. Which was good, because a question rose in my head that I'm surprised I hadn't thought to ask before.

"Sukina," I said as we walked the corridors away from the courtyard where we'd met. "I remember Gerhaun saying that secicao is a blight, but this got me thinking. Dragons need secicao to feed on, so if we destroy the secicao, we'd also have to kill off the dragons, right?"

Sukina peeled her gaze away from a mosaic on the wall of a Grey swooping down to tear apart a red-eyed war automaton. "I wondered when you'd ask. But our goal is not to destroy the secicao."

"But it will always be a threat, right?"

"In a way. You have to remember that before we had boats, secicao had no way to leave the Southlands. It also cannot grow there unless it uses its chemical formula to acidify the soil. This land belongs to dragons and secicao, and we'd be wrong to try and change that."

"So, dragons should have never left the Southlands and I'm wrong to keep Velos in Tow?"

"Not at all," Sukina said. "Velos needed to leave the Southlands to become a Blue."

"Say again?"

"It's the only way for a dragon to become fertile," Sukina said. "To have a taste of the wider world away from the secicao clouds. Stay here too long and he'd become a Grey himself. Coloured dragons don't belong in the Southlands."

"So, if secicao covered the world, then no dragons could gain colour."

"Exactly," Sukina said. "While man would choke to death, dragonkind wouldn't be able to reproduce and eventually die too. By feeding on secicao, dragons help stop its growth. But King Cini II's Dragonheats tipped the ecological balance and now there's few dragons of colour left."

I'd never realised before how special Velos was. It surprised me that they allowed us to take Velos out into danger if he was so valuable.

But Sukina again read my thoughts. "At the end of the day, we believe you and Velos are free agents. You weren't born to this dragon queen, which means Gerhaun, by dragon law, has no right to control you. In fact, given you're an Ambassador between mankind and dragonkind, you'll eventually come to meet the other dragon queens. Then, you'll roam free amongst the dragon fortresses and serve all the dragon queens."

"But why can't I meet them now?" I said.

"Because you're not quite trained yet. Since the dragonheats, the dragon queens have wanted to keep extra secrecy about their locations. Gerhaun is the only one of the dragon queens who now works with humans. The rest are only happy to meet with dragonseers, and only those that have been approved by all the dragon queens."

"Then, when do I start my training?"

We stopped outside a small oak door. Sukina unlocked it with a key from her keyring.

"Right now. This way please." She stepped inside.

THE ROOM WAS TINY. Barely large enough to fit one person, let alone two. It had no windows, smelled virtually of nothing and, once Sukina closed the door, the whole place plunged into darkness. Then, I realized how airless it was, and I started gasping for breath.

"Sukina," I said. "What are you doing? Open the door!"

"First things first," she replied. *"Speak in the collective unconscious. There's enough air in here to breathe, so long as you keep your breathing shallow. This is where you begin to learn to mask your thoughts."*

But I was hyperventilating and there was no way I'd calm myself down. Blood pounded to my head and it throbbed at the temples. "Sukina, open the door!" I gasped. I couldn't even think to talk in the collective unconscious.

Sukina sighed and a slit of light came from the doorway letting in stale air. It shone off one side of Sukina's face, and she observed me for a moment. I started to calm down.

"Pontopa," she said in the collective unconscious. *"I do not wish to harm you and no harm will come to you in this room. Part of learning to mask your thoughts involves trusting yourself not to fear what you cannot see. Now, are you ready to try this again?"*

This time, I was glad she'd asked. I nodded.

"Good, then empty your mind. Focus on your breathing and keep it slow, shallow and steady. There's enough air in here for us both to survive."

She observed me for a moment, probably to see if I'd calmed down. Then, she once again closed the door.

This time, strangely, I didn't feel like I was suffocating. I did as Sukina asked, listening to the sound of my breathing as I kept my body absolutely still. But still, my heart was beating heavy in my chest. I tried to make out the shape of Sukina in the darkness that shrouded me, but I only saw swirling patterns of imagined light.

"Sit down," Sukina said. *"The more you preserve your resources, the easier your first time will be."*

I lowered myself into a crouch and then used my hands to find the cold, dusty floor before I sat down on it. But as much as I could steady the rhythm of my breath, I couldn't stop my heart hammering. "*What happens next?*" I asked Sukina.

"*You don't have to worry about that. Just know that nothing will harm you in here. Now, take some time to observe your thoughts.*"

That was when the anxiety washed over me once again. I thought about my parents first, and a horrific image came to mind of them hanging from the gibbets, in the old vineyards just outside their cottage. Then, I was panicking, again. Hyperventilating. I grasped at my chest and tried to still my breathing. But there wasn't enough air in this room.

The door opened and some light once again came in room. Sukina stood by the door.

"*Do you want some time?*" she said. "*Maybe, you're not quite ready for this yet.*"

I took a moment to recover, then I spoke back in the collective unconscious. "*I don't know what I'm meant to do here. It seems that as we wait, the air becomes less and less. What exactly is my goal?*"

"*Remember,*" Sukina replied. "*That I'm observing your thoughts here. Once you've learned to mask them, I won't be able to hear them at all. You can trust me when I say that we can sit here for hours, if only you treat your thoughts the right way. It's not the lack of air here that's causing you to suffocate, but the anxiety that you allow to roam free. Distance yourself, Pontopa, and you'll become much more powerful in everything that you do.*"

I shook my head. "*I can't. I mean, I just don't know how. I can't help but worry about everything.*"

"*Maybe we should give it a break? Try again another day.*"

"*Maybe...*" I said. Then, I gritted my teeth. "*Actually, I want to try one more time.*"

Sukina examined me again. "*Okay. Take the time you need to prepare.*"

"*I'm ready.*"

"*Very well.*" Sukina, once again, closed the door and I could see nothing once again.

I listened to the rhythm of my lungs. Not forcing it and trying to keep my breathing as slow and steady as possible. As if dreaming, images flooded to my mind of Faso putting the armour on Velos. How Faso looked at me after I'd punched him the face. Papo's face after I'd shouted at him in my cottage. But I didn't let myself become emotionally attached to these images. It was like the other day when I flicked the thoughts away through swigs of brandy. But this time, instead of closing the thoughts off, I let them drift casually by.

"*You're there,*" Sukina's voice came in my head and this too seemed strangely distant. "*Now, let's test it more. Remember, there is nothing in this room that can hurt you.*"

I heard something click, and then a sound like stone grinding against stone. Then came a chittering – spiders. I shuddered for a moment, then I remembered. I couldn't let myself become afraid.

Then came the sound of little feet clinking against stone. Whatever that thing in the room with us was, it moved fast along the wall. I had two options in this situation – either panic or continue to focus on my breathing. I remembered Sukina's words that nothing in this room could harm me. So I placed trust in that and listened intently to the chittering, without letting my emotions rule.

Something touched my leg. Not sharp, but the creature was testing somewhere to walk. Then the thing walked on to my lap, as heavy as a cat but with thin spindly feet. An instinct came to my mind to push it away and back up into the darkness. No, but that too was distant inside my mind.

This creature – it was cold and felt even colder as it rested its bulk upon my lap. After that, the chittering stopped and Sukina opened the door, letting the light back in. I looked down to see some kind of giant spider automaton lying dormant upon my lap.

"You did it," Sukina said out loud. "You almost masked out everything. Although it's very, very hard to keep out initial fear."

I pushed the automaton off me and stood up. It scurried back up to a hole in the wall and a concealed stone doorway slid shut behind it. "You didn't warn me about that," I said.

"Of course not. Fears and anxieties will always emerge unexpected. The hardest part is remembering to cast the leash over them when your mind is unaware. Now, come, let's go and get some brandy to celebrate."

"Sounds great," I said. We stepped out of the room.

But before we had time to say more, we were distracted by the sounds of a commotion coming along the corridor. Heavy footsteps approaching with urgency and two or three men arguing so fast, it was hard to make out what any of them were saying.

I saw Wiggea turning the corner first, wearing his navy-blue sash. He was accompanied by two lower ranked mustard suited guards. In his hand, Wiggea carried a slip of paper that looked like it had come fresh off a printing press. When he saw me, the features on his face fell.

"Miss Wells," he said as he approached. "Miss Wells, thank goodness I've found you. General Sako said to contact you immediately as soon as the Hummingbird arrived."

"What is it?" I asked.

"We found you as soon as we could, Ma'am." He handed me the slip of paper. I caught glimpse of the words Five Hamlets and urgent before Wiggea explained the meaning. "We've heard from our contacts in Tow. The Five Hamlets is under martial law and your farm is under lockdown."

My jaw dropped and Sukina immediately sprang into action. "Come on," she said. "We need to go and speak to Gerhaun. Before you do anything rash."

PART V

CIPAO

"I've always believed that man should live with an indomitable spirit and a willingness to charge."

— CIPAO WELLS IN THE TOW OBSERVER

18

The atmosphere at Fortress Gerhaun had changed from lethargy to near panic. Sukina and I picked up pace towards Gerhaun's treasure room, accompanied by three guards. Hummingbirds whizzed past us in the either direction. From the rooms off the corridors, emanated attentive voices and the furious clicking of typewriter keys. The whole base was acting as if preparing for an attack, and I couldn't help but wonder why a sleepy village so far away from the fortress would cause so much concern.

"We all know that the only option now is for you to leave us," Sukina said in my mind. *"Now, we're making urgent preparations."*

I wished then that I also had the direct connection with Gerhaun that Sukina had. Why did she always want to meet me instead of just speaking directly to me in the collective unconscious like she did with Sukina? It felt as if I was passing some kind of initiation. Perhaps when I learned to consistently calm my mind as Sukina had demonstrated, then that channel to Gerhaun would finally open up.

But Sukina didn't answer my concerns as we were already at Gerhaun's massive double doors, towering up before us. Wiggea stepped forward to open one of the doors and gestured us inside.

Gerhaun wasn't the only one waiting in her treasure room. Asinal Winda, the chief engineer was also there and Faso. They had set up a screen on one side of Gerhaun's throne room. Ratter was placed on a trestle stool in front of that, with a wide beam of light emanating from his open mouth. But it wasn't that which drew my attention away from Gerhaun's resplendence so much as the images that the beam cast on the screen.

My stomach churned as I realised what these images showed. Sepia photographs of Papo's vineyard – everything he had worked for – ransacked. Charred, smoking dry vines stretching for miles. My cottage now rubble and a huge hole knocked out of one of the corners of my parents' two-storey cottage. Velos' stable now four pillars lying flat on the ground, with his secicao trough upturned and in flames. The barn that once had held barrels upon barrels of Papo's wine, also on fire.

More photos displayed Faso's workshop, pieces of warped brass and wood sprawled across the charred ground. More images of the Five Hamlets' streets, red paint splashed haphazardly on the pretty doors of the rustic houses. No one was on the streets, not even a cat or a dog.

"I... I..." These were the only words I could muster, shocked to see that Cini would do such a thing. There was no reason that my parents should suffer like this, let alone an entire village, just because one of their villagers had got into a minor scuffle at Fraw.

Faso walked over to Ratter and tapped the automaton's back to cut off the beam. He looked back at the screen his body hunched up like a crippled dog.

"How long ago was this?" Sukina asked Winda.

"The Hummingbird came through just twenty minutes ago. But the photos from it have timestamps on them from a few hours ago, taking into account the change in time-zone. Mr Gordoni taught us a technique for storing photos in the machines, which is how we were able to get them over so fast."

She cast Faso an appreciative and gentle smile. Faso didn't react.

"My parents..." I said. "What about my parents? Are they—"

"We're getting information every minute, more Humming-birds relaying this between this room and our comms office. We're still unclear on the situation, but we do know where your parents are."

"Where?"

"Apparently in the prison underneath the town hall. Fortunately, right now, reports have come across that they're unharmed."

"The holding cells, you mean?"

"Underneath the mayor's office, yes."

These cells were put there seventy or so years ago, to hold shady traders caught selling contraband secicao that hadn't been commissioned by the king. But rumour had it the only time they'd been used the last twenty years was when a five-year-old girl stole bubble-gum from the local convenience store. She stayed there for half an hour while her parents waited upstairs, which was enough to teach her a lesson.

"But, what's the latest?" I said. "Have you been able to check on them recently?"

"We are still assessing the situation. But it would appear they're under some kind of automaton guard. A new prototype..." She glanced at Faso, "which the locals have reported is coloured green."

"My technology..." Faso muttered. "Stolen." How could he be concerned about technology at a time like this?

The room trembled a little as Gerhaun leant towards me. Her voice came soft and deep, lacing the very walls of this chamber. "I understand, Pontopa, that you will have to leave us for a while."

I nodded. "With Velos," I said, remembering what Sukina had told me before about Velos' importance.

"With Velos," Gerhaun repeated, "and Sukina too."

"And me," Faso said. "I must reclaim what they haven't destroyed." I guess he was no longer planning to move to Slaro and start his shady business right under the king's nose.

Sukina glanced at Faso then up at Gerhaun, who gave an approving nod. "And Faso," Sukina said. "We'll take only Velos. Any other Greys might compromise our ability to return."

"But how will we get through?" I asked. "They'll have surely fortified the Southern Barrier by now." The worst thing I could do right now was get myself killed, especially after everything I had promised my parents. Although, in all honesty, my capture or death might save the Five Hamlets.

Sukina looked at me in alarm. I'd forgotten she could read my thoughts like that. I opened my mouth to say something but was interrupted by more commotion at the door.

"Blunders and dragonheats! What in the Gods Themselves' name is going on here?" General Sako barrelled into the room, reeking of whiskey and secicao smoke. He carried a document, around four pages in length, typed up on heavy matte paper. "Daughter, you are not about to attempt a pass through a fortified land and get yourself killed for no reason. This is a suicide mission, do you understand? Why are these plans being drafted without my permission?"

It wasn't Sukina but Gerhaun who replied. "General Sako. I gave the orders myself as there was no time to wait for you to drag yourself out of bed."

"But I'm the general here. Isn't that what you employ me for, to give advice in urgent situations?"

"This isn't a military, but a dragonseer matter. We understand your concerns, general, but right this moment, it's time for you to stand down."

Sako's face almost glowed purple. I knew he had a lot of fight in him, but I'd never thought he'd use it against Gerhaun. "Blunders and dragonheats, Forsi. This is my daughter you're talking about. I forbid this."

Gerhaun lifted her head and she almost looked like she wanted to lurch down and snap General Sako's head off.

Sukina stepped between Sako and Gerhaun. "Father," she said. "You have to let me go sometimes. Dragonseers look after each other and this mission is of huge importance to Pontopa. An attack against Pontopa's hometown is an attack against our own."

"But the Southern Barrier," General Sako said. "The fortifications…" He reached up to his breast pocket and touched the handle of his pipe.

"Admiral Sandao has sent scouts ahead to find a way to get us through, given I can't travel freely in the king's land anymore. Cini doesn't have enough resources to cover the entire Barrier. We will find a way."

"Sukina, if I may," I interjected. "I have an idea."

Sukina stepped back from her father and turned to me. "Go on."

"I just remembered. My father has a long-time friend called Candalmo Segora who operates merchant runs down to the Southlands every few weeks. He always works on schedule, so his boat should be somewhere just north of the Southern Approach, right around now."

Sukina frowned. "Is it large enough to house Velos?" Clearly, for some reason, she didn't want us going north without him.

"Of course. He's got one of the largest secicao import companies in Spezzio. His trawler would be able to fit Velos in the hull plus two, maybe three, Greys."

"The less the better," Sukina said. "We'll need to be as discreet as possible."

General Sako was giving me such a hard look that I worried he was about to rush over and punch me. He turned again on his daughter. "Sukina, this is madness, you hear me?"

"Butan," Sukina said. "We've been through this a thousand times and I'm sure we'll do so a thousand times again. A mission is a mission and you know as well as anyone here that we've got to face danger sometimes."

"Sukina, I—"

"I'm going, Butan. That's the end of it."

On that note, she stormed out of the room. I rushed out to catch up with her, remembering the argument I'd had with Papo. Our over-controlling fathers seemed another thing we had in common.

19

We met Candalmo Segora just by the island of Soora, halfway up the Southern Approach. These islands were all the same really, red and grey lumps of rocks, some with sandy beaches but little else to mark them as distinct.

He was standing on his deck, looking out at the secicao clouds that we'd presently left behind us. The sun had just started to peek over them, which was always quite a spectacle – the halo around the sun and the way it cast out its rays in multi-coloured prismatic displays.

The full-bearded moustachioed man was just a little bit taller than General Sako but much lither. In all honesty, he'd always seemed to me much more a city than a sailor type. His twenty-three strong crew were busy working the engines of the trawler, making sure it had enough fuel to power the huge beast on its way.

When he noticed us in the sky, he first shouted out something and a couple of crewmembers ran below decks to grab some rifles. A couple of minutes later, though, he recognised me, gestured to his men to put down their guns and beckoned us in.

We landed on the quarterdeck, with plenty of room for Velos. The three of us dismounted fast.

Candalmo came up over the ladder at the bottom of the deck carrying in one hand a tray with four cups of hot secicao and a cafetiere. Another crewmember came up with a small trestle table strapped on his back. He put this out on the floor, where it stood at around ankle height. Candalmo placed the four cups down on the table and sat down cross-legged on the hard, steel floor.

"Fine day today, isn't it?" he said. "I'm sorry, I saw the glints of metal and I thought you were some kind of rogue automaton. What have you done to Velos? I must say, doesn't he look splendid?"

This caused Faso to smirk and I bit my tongue to hide my chagrin.

"Come, come," he said. "Sit yourself down and have yourself some secicao. It's been so long since I've seen you, Pontopa and my, how you've grown."

I sat myself down on the floor, remembering a couple of trips I'd taken south with Candalmo and Papo during my childhood. I eyed the cup of secicao and was tempted to reach out for it, but then I remembered. "I better not, I'm abstaining."

"I too," Sukina said as she sat herself down.

"Ah, well," Candalmo said. "All the more for us men then." He poured the contents of my and Sukina's cup back into the cafetiere.

Faso was the last to plonk himself down on the floor. As soon as he did, Ratter popped his head out of his sleeve and scurried up onto his shoulder, cautiously watching Candalmo's every movement.

"What is that thing?" Candalmo said.

"This is Ratter," Faso said. "My own personal butler. Made from the same technology as the dragon armour that you so admired."

"Yes, that's very nice, I suppose," Candalmo said from behind his cup of secicao. He turned to me. "Well, Pontopa, what brings you here today?"

I decided to cut straight to the chase. "Candalmo, did you hear about the Five Hamlets?"

"No, not yet. Business still booming as usual?"

I shook my head. It took me a moment to compose my thoughts. "The king razed our vineyard. He took my parents prisoner and now the entire village is under martial law." The words came out so broken, I didn't think I would make it to the end of the sentence.

Candalmo's hand trembled and some secicao splashed onto his chest. He wiped his lips and brushed the spillage off his shirt. "You're kidding me. Why?"

"The thing is, we're now wanted fugitives."

Candalmo looked at Faso then Sukina, as if trying to determine which of them had drawn me down a criminal path. "But the king would raze a whole village just because of one citizen? No... You're pulling my leg."

"Unfortunately not," Sukina said. "I can see from this boat that you profit well from King Cini, but he can be ruthless at times."

"Dragonheats!" He took another sip of his secicao. "Who are you, by the way? I'm sorry, I never introduced myself, I'm Candalmo Segora."

"Sukina Sako."

"The author?"

"Among other things."

Candalmo turned to Faso. "And you are?"

"Faso Gordoni, entrepreneur and inventor extraordinaire."

"Yes, well..." Candalmo turned back to me. "Pontopa, what happened? Problems with the dragon again?"

"Far from it," I said. "Look, Candalmo, it's too complicated to explain and time is of an issue. I just want you to trust me that I'm doing the right thing."

"Never doubted, it my lady. So, I'm guessing you need my help getting home?"

He took another sip of his secicao. The aromas rising from the cafetiere made me desperately want some and then I became a little sick thinking about it.

"Jonis," Candalmo shouted down deck. "I need you here on the poop."

"Captain Segora," Sukina said. "I wanted to ask: how well fortified was the Southern Barrier when you were last there? I guess, you would have passed around four days ago?"

"Three, in fact. Cini installed some new technology in our engines that has us running at lightning speed."

Faso jerked his head up when he heard this. Ratter sprang to attention on his back. "What technology is that, exactly?"

"Oh, the ability to use some of the secicao we harvest. Cadigan coal is now outdated, he says. These are new times and our ship is one of Cini's first experiments."

Faso's skin turned red, but he said nothing this time. He'd clearly now got past complaining about the king stealing his technology.

"So, the fortifications," Candalmo continued. "Yes, I came through the Southern Barrier just east of Fraw and I could see there was a heavier guard west of there. Lots of airships passing overhead, though. I thought they were just preparing for a festival. Did something happen over there, Pontopa?"

"Something, yes," I said. "Look, I need to ask a huge favour, Candalmo. Do you think you'd be able to take Velos below decks and smuggle us through? East of Fraw perhaps, where it's a little less fortified?"

Candalmo shook his head. "I'm afraid we have a full cargo. King Cini made me sign a contract that I'd also send these massive automatons south."

I looked at Sukina. So, that's where the Mammoths were coming from – merchant trading ships. She raised an eyebrow. We were so far from Gerhaun that we could no longer use telepathy through the collective unconscious, but we could still read the expression on each other's faces.

"There's new deadlines too," Candalmo continued. "King Cini's put extra quotas on the times that we have to deliver his stuff and bring the secicao back. After what you tell me about the Five Hamlets, I don't know what the consequences would be of failing to keep to his terms."

"I understand," I said. "I guess our best bet is to fly through ourselves."

A man poked his head up the ladder. "You called, Captain," he said.

Candalmo looked at his pocket watch. "You took you your time. I was going to ask for more secicao, but something urgent has come up. Calculate bearings to Sanjiornio and give me an estimated time there and back."

"But, sir, the contract."

"I just need information right now. Go on, get on your feet and get on with it."

The crewmember saluted. "Yes, sir."

He rushed down the ladder. "My hunch is that I can take you that far and still make it back here. We've been running the engine on fifty per cent power to stay on target – the more secicao we burn here the less we can sell to the king."

I smiled. "Thank you, Candalmo." It made a lot of sense. A merchant ship would draw a lot less attention than an approaching dragon. The ship was on the water after all and it would take them a while to see Velos on board.

We sat and chatted while we waited, though I found it hard to concentrate any more on what Candalmo was saying with the burning anxiety within my chest. Fortunately, he soon took an interest in Sukina as he too had read her novels. Every second or two, I kept turning over my shoulder to see if the crewmember would climb up with news.

Soon enough, he did. He rolled out a parchment of paper. "We estimate it would take three days to get there," he said, "and two and a half to get back. So long as we run at one-hundred per cent power."

"Do it," Candalmo said. Then he turned to me with a smile. "Remember, I'm burning away my profits for you. Just make sure you and your father remember that when you get back on the straight and narrow."

The man scurried down the ladder, shouted an order. Shortly after, the foghorn sounded, and the ship began to turn around.

WE HAD some time while we waited for planning. Which was a good thing really, given we had no idea how we would get through at Sanjiornio. I'd only been to this island a couple of times, to avoid heavy storms at Fraw. It made sense to pass through Sanjiornio this time, since the island was much narrower in places than other islands in the Southern Approach, meaning King Cini couldn't install as many fortifications on land.

It wasn't ideal for boats either, due to some strong currents and jagged underwater rocks to the east and west of the island. Which meant that Cini's forces only needed to watch out for pirate airships and, of course, dragons.

We stood on the bridge around a map of the Southern Barrier and Northern Continent that Candalmo had pinned out on the navigation table. He had labelled on it the locations of Cini's major stations, and it was clear that the king had the Southern Barrier covered quite extensively.

The table stood at the centre of a lookout tower from where we could see the sandy, island of Soora, the fading secicao clouds, and in all other directions the deep blue sea.

"Cini protects Sanjiornio through watchtowers and shrapnel-flak automatons," Candalmo pointed out. "It won't be easy for you to sneak through."

"Easier, I think, than getting through near Fraw," Sukina said. "But we still need to work out a plan."

Faso was pacing back and forth on the spot, his hand on his chin. "So, we have to escape the watchful eye of guards as well as heat sensors on the shrapnel-flak cannons looking for dragons."

"How would you know how they work?" I asked.

"Because I designed the things."

That caused me to grimace. It made me wonder if Sukina wanted Faso on Gerhaun's side not so much to develop technology for her, but rather to stop him developing war technology for the king.

"If it's shrapnel-flak," I said. "Then maybe we can just fly over it, like we did at Fraw?"

"No," Sukina said. "We don't want those things firing at us, since that would reveal our location to King Cini. He may be luring us towards the Five Hamlets, but our advantage is that he doesn't know where we are right now and consequently when exactly and from which direction we'll arrive."

"Although," Faso said. "Maybe Pontopa's idea to fly high isn't a bad idea. If we get high enough, then the guards won't know exactly what they're looking at."

Sukina nodded. "Candalmo, what's the weather forecast for when we arrive?"

"Clear, sunny skies, and dark moonless nights. No clouds."

"Great for a holiday," Sukina said. "But hardly ideal for a covert operation."

"So, we do it under cover of night," Faso said. "I simply need to turn the armour on so Velos can get high enough. They never designed their fortifications for anything that flies so high. If I heat the armour to the right temperature, the heat sensors will think they're looking at a seagull and ignore it. Of course, I had to put in a safeguard, so they don't shoot everything that passes through and waste the king's resources."

"That's good," Sukina said. "Apart from one thing. The guards will still see us. They can't miss something shooting by glowing green on a dark night."

"Not necessarily," Faso said. "Candalmo, how exactly do the guards keep watch for dragons and airships with their propellers off?"

"Why, searchlights, of course."

"I thought so." Faso stopped pacing and looked at Sukina, a smile on his face. "Problem solved. Searchlights means light pollution. Which means all we need to do is evade the beams and the guards will have no chance of seeing us."

"Okay, Faso," Sukina said. "I must say, this time you've surpassed yourself."

The inventor turned to me and winked. "I know," he said. "I know..."

Well, he was smart, I admit. I just wished that sometimes he could also show a little more humility. I excused myself and went outside to check on Velos.

WE MADE it to the Southern Barrier in two and a half days, just as the sun was starting to set. We waved Candalmo goodbye and then Velos took off and flapped his wings to cut through the twilight and shortly after darkness descended, and we could soon make out the searchlights ahead.

Eight of them, attached to eight guard stations, turned around the sky at a pretty steady pace, obviously automatons themselves. They were powerful too, stretching out far away from the island, which would easily catch a slow flying airship trying to sneak through.

We didn't want to get spotted when the searchlights pointed away from us, so Faso only turned on the armour when we were close to one searchlight's beam. Then, I steered Velos to follow the path of the beam around, never entering it, while pulling back on his steering fin to get him high.

I looked down into the darkness below then and could only faintly make out the shape of the land. I couldn't see any sign of the shrapnel-flak automatons, but I knew they were there. If Faso had got his calculations wrong, the sensors would latch on to us. Then, the guards would raise the alarm, thousands of Hummingbirds would come hunting and, if we made it to the mainland, Cini's troops would be right on our tail.

Fortunately, we passed through without incident and then we could quite comfortably travel through the rest of Tow without much risk. That probably meant around five more hours in the saddle, given it wasn't a good idea for Velos' armour to be on at this time. Faso also hadn't designed this thing for comfort and the seats left my backside feeling kind of numb.

Ironically, he was the one to start moaning. "Can't we touch down?" he said once we were far enough inland. "We must be clear of Cini's forces by now."

"Shh," Sukina said. Although there was no sight or sound of an airship, we were worried that Cini might have set some patrolling without lighting.

"I'm hungry, thirsty, and my bottom feels like I'm sitting on an iron maiden."

"Faso, you designed this armour," I pointed out. "Why didn't you put cushioning on?"

"Safety was my paramount concern at the time, not comfort. I kind of expected you'd factor plenty of breaks into our trips."

I shook my head. "Faso, we'll land when we get to the Five Hamlets. The more you complain the longer it's going to be."

Admittedly, I just wanted to get home as soon as possible. For all I knew Cini might have executions lined up for my parents.

"Suit yourself," Faso said. "But don't expect me to be able to walk easily tomorrow." Which stopped him talking for the rest of the trip, but it didn't stop him groaning every time we hit a bit of turbulence.

Admittedly, I did find it a little cramped in the seat as well. The way Faso had installed it, I had to push my knees up to my chest, and I missed the feeling of my legs dangling off the sides, able to stretch them out whenever I pleased.

Eventually, we reached the Five Hamlets. I felt Velos want to let out a roar, and instinctively, a soft song came out of my mouth to calm him. I knew why Velos had felt a little angst. Usually, the Five Hamlets had a little charm about it. They kept oil lanterns lit in the streets, so that we could see the stucco on the walls and the cobblestones on the street as we came in to land.

But this night, no one had bothered to light the lanterns at all. All the better for us, I thought, since it decreased the chances anyone would see us approach. Something rustled behind me and I heard Sukina taking a swig from hipflask. "Automatons. Just because we can't see them, doesn't mean they can't see us."

"Your blend helps you see in the dark?" Faso asked. "Why, I wish I'd thought of that…"

"Here," Sukina said. "Ladies first." She pushed something cold into my hip. I took the flask and took a sip from it. The night ghosted into a speckled green, the buildings of the Five Hamlets visible in a way I'd never seen them before. At the same time, energy coursed through my veins and all the stiffness left my muscles.

"This is good stuff," I said.

"Fortress Gerhaun's blend," Sukina said. "It will improve your strength and agility amongst other things."

I passed the flask back to Sukina. Behind me, Faso was reaching down towards the spigot.

"Faso, no!" I said and he looked up at me, even though I doubt he could see me. Fortunately, I'd managed to stop him in time. "If Velos is glowing green, we'll be spotted in an instant."

He crossed his arms and sat back in his seat, then took the flask off Sukina and knocked back a swig. I wiped a bead of sweat off my forehead.

We followed the coast, then I veered Velos inland a little to sweep past the town hall. If I saw it was unguarded, then I would break right in with Velos to rescue my parents immediately. But two mean looking lithe automatons were scanning the horizon rhythmi-cally from the entrance. I swept Velos upwards before we entered one of their lines-of-sight.

We flew over Papo's vineyard then. I tried to make out if anything had been saved from amidst the rubble, but I could only make out outlines, even with my augmented eyes. If I dared get a little closer, I might have seen more, but I had no idea what Cini had posted there.

In the distance, to the north, a faint glow rose up from the hori-zon. Faso's workshop, no doubt.

"We should set up in the forest," Sukina said and so I cast off to the northeast for a while. Velos picked up a little speed just before I brought him in to land. He couldn't quite see what I could see, and quite a few times I had to steer him away from crashing into pine trees.

Pumped up on secicao oil, there was no way we'd be getting any sleep that night. It was so dark that it was a perfect time to act. We left Velos there between the trees. I sang a song to calm him and reassure him that we'd be back soon. Honestly, I'd got the hang of these songs pretty quickly. But then, it seems, I'd known how to sing them all my life.

Velos understood perfectly his need to be quiet. So, he put his head against the ground, to stay low. But I knew that he didn't intend to sleep. Instead, he'd keep watch and fly in to rescue us at first sign of any danger. I could rely on him for that.

20

Once we'd left the forest, Sukina put up a hand to halt us and she scanned the village using a pair of binoculars. We'd taken another dose of Sukina's secicao oil, which meant I could still see everything in speckled green. We waited a while to give Sukina a chance to survey the scene. Faso also had a little eyepiece, that he also used to keep track of what was going on. Ratter stood guard on his shoulder in case anything came close.

Sukina turned to me and handed me the binoculars.

"I've been watching out for troops or automatons," Sukina said. "But I've seen nothing nearby. I would have thought Cini would post a sentry here."

I shook my head. "He's expecting us to break into the holding cell, so he's probably posted all of his forces there."

"Most likely," Sukina said.

Faso stirred and groaned. He bolted upright, immediately looked at his pocket watch. Sukina waved a bread roll at him, and he walked over and snatched it. "Now I'm here, I need to get some things I left behind here." Then he dashed off in the direction of his workshop.

"There's no stopping that fool sometimes," Sukina said.

"I guess not." I looked over at Velos keeping watch. "Do you think Velos will be okay here?"

"As safe a place as any. Besides, he's a big boy who knows how to fight for himself."

True that, and those ugly Gatling guns on his sides would at least offer extra protection. We'd left the armour running so Velos could activate the guns himself, and also so he didn't fall asleep.

"We should probably start rescuing my parents."

"Via your farm, of course," Sukina said. "We might find some indication there of what we're up against. But I'd understand if you wouldn't want to go."

And see my farm ruined, of course I didn't want to go. "It's okay," I said. "I mean, some things are better done than not done."

"Indeed."

We moved towards Papo's vineyard. The ground was a little soft underfoot, as if it had rained a couple of days ago. It took a good twenty minutes before I saw the ruined walls of my parents' farmhouse.

A hole had been blown into the stonework and you could see right into my parents' bedroom. That would have destroyed the painting created and handed down by my great, great grandmother, which would have made my parents furious. I felt my stomach lurch and I retched but didn't vomit. My heart was beating heavy inside my chest and my legs became weak all of sudden.

Sukina put a hand on my back and supported me. Then we moved forward. I saw my cottage, completely reduced to rubble, looking just as it had in the photo, and probably worse. A cold breeze crept through the blackened charred vines, rows of destruction leading towards Old Drani.

I stepped closer to see torn bookshelves; every single book had been burned. Sukina Sako reduced to ashes. The sofa that I'd loved to sit on and read a mess of torn cloth and scattered foam.

The place had been torn apart as if Cini wanted me to see his cruelty… wanted me to suffer for what we had done at Fraw. It was almost as if he'd known about me being a dragonseer all along. Now, he wanted to display to me the cost of changing sides.

One thing was for sure: the king had changed his stance and wanted to display to the public he could be just as ruthless as his father.

"He will pay," I said.

"You'll have your chance," Sukina said and we heard a voice coming from behind, male. I turned sharply to see Faso running down the path. "They left me nothing," he said once he'd arrived. "All the secicao fuel salvaged. Every single automaton ripped apart from the joints, rendered irreparable. Cini stole my technology and the worst insult is this. He left me nothing."

He looked up at me. I was in tears. "Oh, I see your place got shook up pretty bad as well, huh?"

"Would you shut up, Faso, for wellies sake. No one cares about your stupid technology. My parents built a life here, so much hard work put into these vineyards. And now..."

Faso crossed his arms. "So, you understand how I feel, then?"

"No, I don't understand how you bloody feel." I wanted to punch him again, but Ratter was perched precariously on his shoulder looking menacingly at me and I didn't want to get sedated. "My parents are in danger for wellies sake, Faso."

Faso puffed some air out of his cheeks. "I'm sorry," he said, like a rebellious schoolboy who'd just been told to apologize.

I sighed. "I guess we've both lost something important to us."

Sukina walked over. She held something in her hand, a thin piece of an automaton, a shoulder guard perhaps, torn off with thin brass pipes running through its cross section. The thing glowed green. "I guess that's what we're up against. It must have got caught in the crossfire."

Faso looked at it, biting his lip.

"We should get going," I said. "Faso, if you know any way to disable these things, now would be a good time to say."

"I designed the engines, for the dragonheats, but the device around it could be assembled in millions of different ways."

"Then to the town hall," Sukina said. "Maybe, Faso, you'll work something out."

He huffed and crossed his arms. "If the opportunity arises, I'll let you know."

We augmented before we set off towards the town hall. Again, after a little discussion, we decided Sukina's blend of secicao seemed the best idea. The extra strength, agility and ability to see in the dark seemed handy against these automatons.

The wind lifted the dust off the ground and blew the smoke

from the chimneys eastward. I raised the collar of my jacket to keep out the chill. We'd expected to see at least guards posted on the narrow streets, but these were strangely deserted.

We did see a couple of Cini's red-coated guards when we passed the airfield however, standing on the only airship stationed there and smoking their secicao pipes. They didn't seem particularly on alert, sitting on deck and playing poker.

"It doesn't look like Cini's brought a large force here either," I pointed out.

"Chances are, we got here so quickly that he's not managed to send an adequate force here yet," Sukina said. "To be honest, I doubt Cini realised we'd react so fast."

This made a lot of sense, but how exactly had Cini enforced this curfew with so few troops? "There must have been something he threatened the village with."

"Maybe," Sukina said.

We were just about in sight of the town hall, visible through a thick mist that had just developed, when a door opened to our side. We jumped startled, and both Sukina and I drew our pistols.

We saw only the ruddy face of the mayor, his eyes expressing surprise behind his wide glasses. "Pontopa, Miss Sako... It's just me." He looked over his shoulder. "Please, you must come in at once."

He opened the door just a crack so I could squeeze through. I started to move forwards before Sukina put a hand on a shoulder to still me. "How do we know it's not a trap?"

"Trust me," I said. "I've known Mayor Sandorini for years. He's been like an uncle to me. If it was a trap, I would have seen it on his face." I squeezed inside then beckoned Sukina and Faso onwards.

"You're sure?" Faso asked. He kept scanning the street from left to right with a sense of urgency, as if part of him wanted to get inside as well.

"Absolutely," I said.

"Good enough for me," Faso said, and he followed suit.

Sukina shrugged and entered behind him. We all huddled into the narrow hallway. This wasn't in fact the mayor's house – he lived in the town hall.

"Where's your son and wife?" I asked the mayor.

"Upstairs sleeping. But naturally, I've had bouts of insomnia lately." He closed the door behind us and then adjusted the glasses on his face. "Pontopa, I'm glad you're safe. Is it true what they said – that you murdered an officer at Fraw?"

"I can't remember actually killing anyone," I said. Although I had no idea what had happened to those guards after Sukina had knocked them out. "We did what we needed to get Sukina out of there."

"Quite rightly too," the mayor said. "The king putting us under martial law is out of line."

"But there are no troops on the street," I said. "How come you're not planning your escape?"

"Because our homes are here, and the curfew is only at night time. We're free to go about our duties during the day. But now, there's sniper automatons posted in the hills that can kill from two hundred yards. I'm surprised you made it in alive."

"Me too," Sukina said. "This makes me wonder if it's really as dangerous out there as the king let on. Mayor Sandorini, did anyone dare test the king's threats?"

"King Cini has cut off all means of communication within the village. As far as I know, no one's dared go outside."

I peered down the corridor to see that the windows here were boarded up. The whole place was lit by one of the same oil lamps which was used to light the streets, now flickering from its perch on a stool. "Well, I see now why none of you have just opened the window and just looked down the road. But how did you know we were coming?"

He took hold of a device that stuck out from the door. He gave it a twist, then pulled it out of its hole. It looked like a simple telescope, with intricate metalwork across bronze facade. But when he twisted the handle again, the front part of the telescope bent out to one side. "This simple modifiable teleperiscope," the mayor said. "Has been a family heirloom for hundreds of years."

"Impressive," Faso said. "How technology used to be so primitive."

"Sometimes the best of designs is the simplest," the mayor said. "This one does what I need it to do."

"Ah, but if you could get a recording of what's happening out there by Hummingbird, then you could cast it via projector onto a screen in here." Faso put his hand on his chin, smugly.

"Then Cini's snipers will shoot the Hummingbird and he'll send in extra troops to quell such an operation at once."

"But no one's tested this theory," Sukina pointed out again.

"Miss Sako, if you've known Cini III for as long as I have, you'd know he doesn't make false threats."

"I can believe that," Sukina said. "Although, something's wrong. If they had those snipers posted, they would have seen us come in."

"Or perhaps they didn't see us through the fog," Faso pointed out.

"Your parents are at the town hall," the mayor said. "That's what I brought you in to tell you."

"We know," Sukina said. "But do you know anything that will help break us out?"

"I've been watching the patrols. They threw me out of the town hall so they could take the whole building. But fortunately, a kind couple let my family and I use their unrented place as a safehouse

"One of Cini's officers came in a week or so ago, with around thirty troops and these fierce sniper automatons. He brought one into town and said the rest were posted in the hills. Its thin head had a long muzzle the length of a yard pole and a low four wheeled base that looked heavy enough to keep them secure. There was a green sheen which kind of washed over them. The officer showed it shoot the heads off some scarecrows five fields across from the town centre. Then, he threatened to kill anyone who stepped out of their houses at night. The same if anyone tried to leave the village."

Again, it was another sign that Cini had changed his stance.

"As I thought," Sukina said. "Cini only sent a smaller force as he probably doesn't think he needs a larger one. It's possible that there's only perhaps one sniper automaton, posted more as a deterrent than something that wants to kill."

"But why would Cini do that?" I asked.

"Because he wants to take us alive."

"That may be," the mayor said. "But there's still a large enough guard to be a threat. I watched what happened through my teleperiscope here. Last night, a troop of twelve redguards and several war-automatons marched towards your father's farm with torches. I thought the officer was going to kill them, but I saw the troops bring them back towards my town hall. Fortunately, your parents moved willingly without resistance."

Panic rose up in my chest. "You mean you don't know if they're still alive in there?"

The mayor put one hand on my shoulder. "Put it this way. I'm a pretty light sleeper and wouldn't have missed it if there'd been gunshots."

But there were knives, poison, gassing, drugs, anything could have happened to them. "We have to go in," I said, and I moved towards the door.

Sukina held out her arm to stop me. "Wait a moment," she said and turned to the mayor. "You mentioned you'd been studying their movements. Did you manage to ascertain how many there were?"

"There's three regular redguards in there, as far as I can tell. Or at least three come out at regular intervals. And the automatons, from their movements I'm guessing there's around four of them. But honestly, all this I don't know for sure."

"How often do the guards pass?" Sukina asked.

The mayor looked at the pocket watch dangling from his breast pocket. "Yes, the redguards seem to always pass on a schedule. I'm pretty sure they'll pass here in five minutes and then won't return for half an hour or so."

Sukina looked at me. "Then soon might actually be a good time to move. How often do the automaton guards rotate, Mayor Sandorini?"

"Every fifteen minutes or so, I'd say. I documented all the move-ments in this table." He pointed to a piece of paper pinned onto the wall, with a list of times on it.

"Perfect," Sukina said. She scanned the piece of paper. "Looks like we have about ten minutes before we go. You counting, Faso?"

Faso looked at his pocket watch. "Sure, but maybe I should take a look first, verify you've got the figures right?"

"No need," Sukina said.

The mayor was also looking at his watch and he'd pressed the button on the top to start the stopwatch. "I agree. Miss Sako seems to have her head on her shoulders as usual."

"More up her own behind," I heard Faso mumble, just loud enough for me to hear it and for Sukina to be out of earshot. I ignored him, of course. We all knew who was the one here who had his head up his behind, and there was no need to reiterate it.

Instead, we waited patiently and silently, my heart thumping in my chest and my arms and legs trembling. Every so often, the mayor would offer me and Sukina the teleperiscope, so we could have a good look at what was happening out there. I saw the redguards pass, smoke trailing behind from their cigarettes. I then saw an automaton swing around the corner of the town hall, wait there for a few minutes and then storm forwards on its two spindly brass legs, its posture upright and scanning the territory as it moved. Then it spun around the corner again and disappeared out of sight.

"Now," Faso said and placed his pocket watch in his inside pocket. I stepped back from my place at the teleperiscope and the mayor opened the door for us. Sukina left first, her pistol at the ready. She stepped out sideways, keeping her eyes on the doors of the town hall. I followed, then Faso. I drew my gun and Ratter took a place on Faso's head with its front feet wrapped around Faso's temples for support.

We moved forward. Sukina signalled me to go on, while she guarded the rear. I hadn't a clue what Faso was doing. But I didn't want to check, instead staying focused on getting to those doors ahead of me. I peered around the corner, then ducked back around to see the automaton just turning the next corner ahead of me. Fortunately, it wasn't facing in my direction, otherwise it would have spotted me well before I spotted it.

"We have two minutes," I said to Sukina.

"That's enough time," she said, and she took another swig from a hip flask. On the door was a cast-iron, fifteen-strength padlock. Sukina took hold of it and snapped it off in her hands.

On the other side, Sukina closed the doors.

"I can't see," Faso moaned. "My secicao's run out."

Sukina passed him the hipflask and he took a swig from it.

"Don't you have some special glasses?" I said.

Because his face was drawn in heat signatures, I didn't see the snarl flash across his face, but I knew it was there, nonetheless.

Strangely, nothing awaited us inside, which gave me the creeps. I expected to see turrets lined up on every wall, a line of automatons looking down upon us from the mezzanine, a force too strong to fight off.

"Pontopa, I can hear your anxiety again..." The voice came in the collective unconscious.

"Sukina, how?"

"Someone's here... Charth..."

"What? Why?"

"Try to still your mind, Pontopa. They can't be trusted."

"Easier said than done," I thought. In the heat of the moment, I'd forgotten what I did to keep my mind calm in Fortress Gerhaun the other day. Then, I had the genius idea to repeat that single phrase in my head. *Easier said than done. Easier said than done. Easier said than done.* Like a child counting to one hundred, if I just kept saying that, how could I possibly think anything else?

"That's one way of doing it." Sukina's voice seemed distant now. *"Now, let's get downstairs."*

"Wouldn't that be exactly what they're expecting us to do?" I asked. *Easier said than done. Easier said than done.*

"Yes," Sukina said. *"But Charth just warned me that a lot worse is waiting for us outside the front door."*

"You said we couldn't trust him..."

"This time, I guess we have no choice."

"Hello, darling," this was now Francoiso's voice inside my head. *"If I'd realised before our little run in at the Southlands that I'd bump into you again so soon, I would have at least packed some cologne."*

"Shut up, brother..." This time, it was the dry, lifeless voice of Charth.

"Oh, come on, let me at least have a little fun."

"We have a mission to be getting on with."

"Getting jealous, are we?"

"Brother..."

"Fine, fine. Okay, the both of you, go downstairs and rescue your parents. You're going to meet some resistance, but you must escape."

"So, this is the channel you're going to use?" Sukina said. *"No need for private conversations with Charth?"*

"Oh, brothers like us should never keep secrets," Francoiso said.

"Remind us again then why we should trust you?"

"Darlings, darlings. You know the king was pretty angry after your escapade at Fraw. Then, when word got out what you did to the Mammoths, he was furious. You destroyed his dream of his perfect utopia and now we're trying to talk him out of becoming a brutal warmonger like his father. But for now, if you're killed here, he told us he'd be happy. If you're taken alive, he ordered his loyal officer to hang you in the town square at the break of the next dawn. Neither of you are any use to Finesia dead, and we'd rather you came to the palace on your own free will."

Finesia again. These guys must have been on drugs or something. But honestly, if that drug gave you the ability to become a dragon, then it would be great to meet their supplier. Or at least that's what I was thinking at the time.

"Come on," Sukina said out loud and she moved forwards.

Faso trailed behind us as we made towards the mezzanine, down the east wing, towards the staircase that led to the old dungeon. Three hundred years ago, this led down to a torture chamber, where errant earls would try to extract information from their subjects. But some guy, I can't remember his name, eventually decided to install some bars and turn it into a prison.

It was pretty dusty on the spiral staircase and I had to hold back a sneeze. Faso let one out full blast though and I turned to him, giving him a harsh look of contempt.

"I'm sorry," he said. "But I can't control bodily functions."

Once we reached the bottom, I was blinded by a white light. It took my eyes a little time to adjust to the old-fashioned medieval torches through my augmented sight. Then, I saw Mamo and Papo, huddled on the floor in the cell together, Mamo sleeping against Papo's shoulder and his head resting on hers. The bastards had removed the beds.

Papo opened his eyes. "Pontopa... You shouldn't have come."

"Shh, Papo," I said. "We must get you out."

"How did you get in here? We've not seen a guard and not had food, for two days. I thought they would let us die here."

"Mr Wells, stand back," Sukina said. She stepped forward, looked at the lock. Papo woke Mamo up, then dragged her to the far wall as she was just about to open her eyes. She saw Sukina first, who was just drawing back her fist towards the cage lock, reeling back a huge punch. Her fist connected, and the lock span backwards, hitting the wall just next to Mamo's head. That caused Mamo to jump. She rubbed the sleep from her eyes.

"Sukina Sako," she said. "You…"

"She's here to rescue you, Versalina," Papo said.

I ran to my parents and wrapped my arms around Mamo, buried my head in her shoulder. Then came a voice again in the collective unconscious. "*Pontopa, darling, you're sweet and all that.*" Francoiso said. "*But there's no time for sentiments… Watch out! Behind you.*"

The wall opposite the cell collapsed, crumbling into dust and gypsum. Out of it, swarmed ten or so machines that looked and buzzed like hornets. They spun out in all kinds of directions. Some pursued Faso, some me, some Sukina, some my parents. I felt something sting my arm, then I rubbed to see a dart there. Ratter hissed, shot into the air, extended some wings, and began to glide, then let out a flame that brought a few of these things down. But I was already feeling dreary.

"*Dragonheats, they're better than I thought,*" Francoiso said. "*Wellies, augment! You must get out alive.*"

Sukina nodded, took hold of her first hip flask, knocked back her head and tipped some down her throat. She wiped her lips, steadied herself on her knees, her other hand facing outwards. She passed the hipflask to me. "This will combat the sedative," she said. I must have drunk almost a quarter of the flask.

I still felt bendy legged, but somehow a little clarity returned to my mind. Mamo was already drifting off, Papo fighting it a little, not letting his eyes close for more than a split second. "Mamo, drink," I ordered and passed Mamo the flask. She opened her eyes then stood up a little as Papo poured the remainder of the flask down his throat.

"You didn't leave any for me?" Faso said. Amazingly he looked pretty perky. "Lucky I have Ratter to defend me from those things."

I turned to see the swarm regrouping. They took formation just in front of the wall where Faso had just stood. "*We have them,*" Charth said. "*Stay back.*"

The earth beneath us rocked and then the wall exploded. Bricks and rubble flew out, one almost hitting Faso on the head. All that was left of the room was a dusty smoky hole, and pile of dust that created enough of a ramp to get outside.

"Dragonheats!" Papo slurred. He was virtually falling asleep. "We must get out."

He moved towards the hole and pushed himself out. A gunshot, Papo screamed. Came back in, his hand stained red and clutched to his shoulder, his breathing heavy. He collapsed against the wall. "The snipers..."

"*Damn you people,*" Francoiso said in the collective unconscious. "*No one has to die... Don't let anyone out until we give the signal.*"

"*How many of them are there?*" Sukina asked.

"*Fortunately for you,*" Francoiso replied. "*Cini didn't have the resources to post any more than one sniper automaton in the hills. The villagers thought there were more, of course. But that's Cini for you: always making things seem worse than they actually are. Its sights are now trained on you though, so you have to be careful.*"

The bastard. He'd tricked the entire village. "Stay here," I said to everyone and Sukina nodded. Mamo had already torn the sleeve off her blouse and was wrapping it around Papo's wound.

"Now," Sukina said, "it's your dragon's turn." She sang a song that shimmered through the dust and the collective unconscious. Something from lullabies I'd heard as a child and since forgotten.

A roar came, and then the glint of Velos' armour as he sailed past the hole. First came another gunshot, and I couldn't help but poke my head out of the hole and see what was happening. The Gatling guns on Velos armour clattered to life, sounding like two massive distant power-drills. Then, came an explosion from the hills.

"Lucky I activated his armour before we left," Faso said.

"*That armour's some impressive work,*" Francoiso said in my mind. "*I must ask your boyfriend there to make one for us sometime.*"

"He's not my boyfriend," I snapped back. Then... *"Why exactly are you helping us again?"*

"Pontopa Wells, there's no time." This wasn't Francosio's but Charth's voice. *"You have two minutes until the remaining snipers reload. King Cini, must never hear we were here, do you understand? Or I'll hunt your parents down and destroy them personally."*

"You didn't tell us what you want from us." Sukina said in the collective unconscious.

But I could already feel the connection to Sukina fading.

"Goodbye, darlings," Francoiso said. *"I'll see you soon, under quite different circumstances."*

I scanned the sky for signs of black dragons, could see nothing. Then I remembered to sing the song. But Sukina had already done it for me. Velos turned in the sky, then his massive form started to hurtle towards us. Papo now had slumped against the wall, a dark red mark on his shoulder, Mamo's sleeve wrapped tightly around it. His face had gone pale.

A gust of wind came from the outside and Velos landed. "Come on, Mamo, we must get Papo onboard. Before reinforcements arrive."

Mamo knew what to do. She took hold of Papo, draped him over her shoulder. "Come on, you big lug," she said, and she helped him up the ladder and then rested him on the back – Faso's – seat. She turned to face him, her legs straddled over the armour, facing Velos' tail.

Faso looked at them for a moment, then shrugged and climbed up to the central seat. "You and Sukina can share," he called down to us.

"I can take position at Velos' neck," I said. Kind of glad that I wouldn't have to sit on his armour. He'd have to keep his head straight, which he'd hate, but I'm sure he'd rather that than me falling off.

"Very well," Sukina said and she climbed into my seat. The armour tapered out a little at Velos' neck, so I could again feel his skin against me. It was now like I was riding a much thinner version of him. But Velos didn't do anything to complain.

We took off into the air and a voice came every so faintly in the collective unconscious. Charth's. *"Head east through the forest in which you made camp,"* he said. *"You won't bump into any reinforce-ments that way."*

"Goodbye, darling," Francoiso's voice even fainter now. *"See you in Slaro..."*

My heart sank as that connection to the collective unconscious was lost. I turned back to Mamo. "I'll fly Velos to Doctor Forsolano's."

"Good idea," she called back. I turned to see her face almost as white as Papo's. "Just get there fast..."

"I'll try, Mamo," I hollered back. Though I knew Velos had to be careful. Then I passed Sukina my hip flask. I doubted I'd be needing it for a while. She passed it back to Mamo, who took hold of Papo's nose then poured some secicao oil into his mouth.

The forest rolled up before us and then we entered a cloud. It became cold all of a sudden and I wrapped my shawl around my neck. It was around an hour from here to Doctor Forsolano's. Hopefully Papo would survive the ride.

21

Doctor Forsolano's House was surrounded by a canopy so dense that we couldn't land any closer than five kilometres away. There was a clearing that he'd made so that Velos could have somewhere to land whenever we needed it. He thoroughly believed in sustainability. He and his nurses collected herbs and other remedies from that forest, but he was also careful not to damage the ecosystem there. To cut down even a single tree, he'd always argued, could readily destroy his trade.

Doctor Forsolano was an old friend of Papo. They met during the dragonheats and fought together against some of the rebels – although, fortunately neither of them had had to fight any dragons. Forsolano was a medic and he'd treated Papo's minor injuries three times during the wartime. Then later, he'd mended Papo's leg after his jockey accident. In return, Papo had supplied wine and later one of my blends of secicao, both of which served as effective pain relief.

As a result, we now saw Doctor Forsolano as part of the family.

Fortunately, the doctor had spotted Velos' armour from a distance and so had hurried over to the landing point thinking that Cini had sent automatons to burn his place down. He and his two nurses always carried a foldable blue stretcher with them. So, they were ready to rush Papo to Doctor Forsolano's home as soon as they saw him, which they did so without a word.

Doctor Forsolano and one of the nurses carried him. Everyone

182

else kept up pace, even though our legs objected. The effects of the secicao had now worn off, which created a huge drain and any one of us (other than Papo who was drugged up on it) could have collapsed and fallen right asleep. It didn't help, of course, that those automaton wasps had also injected sedative into us. But the secicao had largely broken that down at this point, which is why we weren't all dead to the world.

Eventually, we made it to Doctor Forsolano's house – a two story cottage with a high roof and long dangling eaves. We went inside and Doctor Forsolano rushed Papo into the downstairs bedroom that he kept reserved and cleaned as an emergency room for patients. He instructed us to stay out while he dressed Papo's wounds. One of the nurses, a pretty lady just a little younger than me with blonde locks waited with us outside the room.

"Doctor Forsolano thinks he'll be okay," she said.

"He'll work damn hard to make sure that's so," Mamo said with a nod.

The nurse led us to the living room. Doctor Forsolano didn't have a taste for sofas and so Mamo, Sukina and I each sat in a soft pink armchair. Faso took the brown rocking chair by the roaring fireplace, which suffused the room with a soothing warmth. The nurse went out to make us some tea after refusing Faso's request for secicao.

"I can tell from your eyes, Mr Gordoni, that you've had quite enough of that lately," she said, causing Faso to scowl.

The nurse left us there and Mamo turned to me. "Pontopa, are you all right, dear? What happened down there? Your father and I were worried sick. King Cini said you'd killed someone in Fraw. Is it true?"

I shook my head. "We didn't kill anyone, Mamo." At least I didn't think we did. "We've trusted the king this far, but he's not a good man. In many ways, he's worse than his father. He's good if you stay on the good side of him, but what he's doing to this world... It's terrible."

Mamo smiled. "I believe you, dear. I know what it's like to have to fight. But I can't help worrying about you."

I leant forwards and took Mamo's hands, the skin dry and cracked after the last forty-eight hours, or so of dehydration. Fortunately, the nurse brought in a big carafe of water and a teapot, alongside four tiny cups with intricate dragons painted on them in blue, and some biscuits with jam in the centre. She placed the tray down on the heavy marble coffee table at the centre of the room.

"It's been a long day for you all, I know," the nurse said. "Take some time to relax, the doctor will call for you as soon as Cipao feels a little better. For now, he says, the man must rest."

"We understand," Mamo said. The nurse left the room.

Mamo turned to Sukina. "Thank you for coming here to help, dear. You probably have plenty of other things you need to do."

"Actually, Mrs Wells, we're on the way to another mission."

"Please, I've told you before," Mamo said. "You can call me Versalina."

"Sorry... Versalina."

I was looking at Sukina in surprise. Another mission. I tried to ask the question in my mind, but I'd forgotten I needed that connection to the collective unconscious.

"Now, do you really have to leave so soon? Pontopa's father would have a fit. I was hoping that we could all stay safe for a while here."

Sukina looked towards the doorway. "Versalina, I must ask, can we have a word? In private..."

Mamo bit her lip. Then she nodded. She and Sukina walked out of the room.

Ratter had lowered itself down to Faso's lap and the inventor was stroking the automaton, like a cat. "Discharging static," Faso explained, when he noticed me looking at him in confusion. "He gets that when he's in the air. It builds up in his little wires."

I smiled. "You sure are an odd one," I said.

Faso shook his head. "So, what was all that about?" he asked.

"Shh," I said because I was listening to the voices coming from behind the door.

I heard some words – 'heritage', 'Pontopa', Sukina saying, "you must tell her". Then Mamo raised her voice a little. Sukina snapped something back then Mamo went quiet. Then, I heard someone sniffling.

"What the dragonheats?" Faso said.

"Shh!"

Another few moments passed, Sukina and Mamo entered into the room, sat down without saying a word to each other. Mamo's eyes were red.

"You've probably guessed that I'm going to Cini's palace tomorrow," Sukina said. "To rescue the boy, Artua. He isn't the king's nephew after all but, in fact, is of great importance to Gerhaun. Francoiso Lamford's news that the king isn't quite himself has got me even more worried. Something strange is happening in the palace and I just have a hunch that Prince Artua isn't quite safe. In short, Pontopa, I'd like to ask you to come with me."

Mamo nodded but didn't say anything.

"But my parents," I said.

"I've talked to Sukina about this," Mamo said, her voice a little broken. "Your father will be quite safe here and it's about time you realised your abilities."

"My abilities? Mamo... You knew?"

"We'll talk later about this, Pontopa, I promise. Before you leave, if Papo recovers. I think he should be there, really. I'm sorry we've kept it from you so long."

I blinked off the confusion. What in the dragonheats was she talking about?

The door opened and the nurse walked in the room. "Thanks to the good doctor," she said. "Your father's making a quick recovery. It's not serious, fortunately. The bullet didn't hit any organs or shatter any bones."

I breathed a sigh of relief. Then sprang up out of my chair, forgetting how tired I was. We walked out into the patient's room.

Papo was propped up in bed by what must have been half a dozen pillows. A little colour had returned to his cheeks. He wore no shirt now, displaying his lithe and supple muscles. A poultice had been wrapped around his arm with something green and spongy pressed against the wound.

"Well," he said. "We made it."

"We did," Mamo said and took hold of his hand while she broke down in tears. She took a stool by the bed. Doctor Forsolano gestured us over to the other wooden chairs placed around the bed.

"Papo, you're something sometimes. Why did you have to rush out ahead of everyone else?"

"Hey, I just wanted to check that the coast was clear. I'd rather I got shot than one of you lot. Darling, come here."

I moved closer, knelt down besides the bed. He moved his wounded arm to ruffle my hair but grimaced as soon as he tried to stretch it too far.

"Rest it," Doctor Forsolano warned him. "Pontopa, maybe you'd be better on the other side."

I took my chair to the other side of the bed, placed it besides Mamo. From there, I also took hold of Papo's hand.

"I'm sorry, Papo," I said. Tears welled in my eyes.

"Pontopa," he said. "I heard you're a fugitive now..."

"Welcome to the club... We'll probably all be in the Tow Observer tomorrow."

"Don't worry, you'll be safe here," Doctor Forsolano said. "The king has no idea I exist, let alone where I am."

I looked at the doctor in surprise. "But you're one of the best doctors in the land."

"I was... But since I decided to create this honest rehabilitation centre in the middle of nowhere, I've also escaped the watchful eyes of Cini's troops."

I nodded. "That's reassuring."

Mamo took hold of my hand. "Pontopa, dear. Can I have a word with your father a moment?"

Damn all this secrecy. Anyone would think there was a conspiracy. "Okay," I said. "Come on, Faso, Sukina."

Faso stood up, but Mamo said, "Sukina can stay. Doctor Forsolano needs to be here, of course."

Faso and I walked out the room together.

"You think Sukina and your parents are trying to set us up?" Faso asked with a cocky grin.

I snorted. "You wish," I said.

"Somehow, I do."

I decided to go back in the sitting room and finish my tea. That way, I didn't have to put up with Faso. I was beginning to tolerate him a little better, although at this moment I just wasn't in the mood for him. My parents, Sukina and Doctor Forsolano didn't take long discussing what they needed to discuss.

Soon, Mamo came in to get me.

"Come on," she said. "There's something we've all got to tell you."

"I guessed that," I said. Part of me knew exactly what it was, part of me didn't want to admit it.

I followed Mamo back into the bedroom, Faso trailing behind like a loyal puppy. He took his seat by Sukina at the foot of the bed. Doctor Forsolano was now on Papo's right, checking his bandages. I sat down besides Mamo and took hold of both Mamo's and Papo's hands.

"Dear," Mamo said. "It's about time you knew this."

"Don't tell me," I said. "I'm adopted." I turned my head from Mamo to Papo. Part of me wanted to feel anger, but when I saw the sympathetic expressions on my parent's faces, no anger came.

"Not quite, dear," Mamo said. "Although, Papo... He's not your biological father."

"Mamo? But—"

"Technically, I'm not your biological mother either."

Doctor Forsolano smiled. "But in many ways Versalina... you are."

"What?" My expression must have been a mixture of astonishment and confusion. "What the dragonheats is this about?"

"Pontopa," it was Papo's turn to speak. It seemed planned out as if both Mamo and Papo should have equal weights in the conversation. "We met your first mother during the dragonheats. I was resting from my injuries, near Doctor Forsolano's old place, in the countryside just outside Slaro. I'd recovered well enough that your mother and I decided to go out blackberry picking together.

"There, we came across a woman on the verge of death. She'd managed to escape remarkably, from Labour Camp 33. She said she was a dragonseer, and pregnant with child. She needed help, so your mother and I took her to Doctor Forsolano right away.

Papo turned to look at Doctor Forsolano, who nodded. "I wasn't able to save her," he said. "All the herbs and drugs in the world would not bring her back. Cini II's guards had beaten her hard in the labour camp and were about to kill her for not keeping up with her quota. But she told us we couldn't let the child die."

Mamo took the story from here. "She told us about the dragonseers. A dying people who were crucial to the fate of dragonkind.

She had a dragon herself, that they'd murdered, in her own words. An opulent ruby red, she'd told us, its life taken away by the old war automatons. His head then severed by King Cini II's own sword, as if it was a hunting trophy, left lying there bloody on the ground.

"We had to save the baby, she told us. King Cini II was hunting down the dragonseers and they'd discovered who she was at the camp. She managed to escape barely, through the barbed wire electrified fence just as she'd learnt they'd ordered her execution. If she died it would wipe out an entire line of these people she called dragonseers. She told us the legends, she told us about Gerhaun Forsi's Dragons and Ecology and how other dragonseers had already been killed by the king. She begged Doctor Forsolano to do a caesarean and get the baby out there. Give it a chance."

"But she was only five months pregnant," Doctor Forsolano said, "so there was no chance we'd get the baby out alive. It needed a womb to incubate in. Fortunately, at the time, I'd made some discoveries in medicine. I'd learnt how to move a baby from one womb to another, using a thin connection of malleable pipes that helped expand a woman's tummy, so to speak, and let the baby be born."

"I was barren, you have to understand, Pontopa. This is the reason you've never had a sister. But Doctor Forsolano presented your father and I with a solution. There would be two caesareans. One on her to take the baby out, one on me to put the baby back in. I'd need to keep a cage in my womb to house the baby, with special pipes that connected to the umbilical cord. It was a spark of luck that me and your mother had the same blood type."

My jaw had dropped towards the floor at this point. Really, you couldn't make this stuff up. Part of me wondered if they were all pulling my leg, but the straight expression on their faces and the solemn tone of their voices contained no traces of humour. "So, you're my mother, but you're also not my mother…"

"Thanks to Forsolano's genius," Papo said.

"Such a remarkable story," Faso said, "and all done with technology. Are you sure you hate automatons so much, Pontopa? Doctor Forsolano, if I might ask, I'd love to have a look at that womb-cage sometime."

"I don't do it anymore. It had complications…"

I looked again at Mamo. I'd always thought her healthy. "Complications?"

"Your mother made it through strong, but I tried it on two other women, and they all died in childbirth. For me, that was enough."

"But the future of science…" Faso said. "Doctor Forsolano, there has to be sacrifices sometimes."

"Not when people's lives depend on it, Mr Gordoni. I put people's health before everything else."

"Even when you can save thousands of lives in the future?"

"It won't," Doctor Forsolano said. "Versalina was an anomaly. When I think, from experience, about how the machine worked, it's a miracle that she survived."

"Dragonseer blood," Sukina said. "We're tougher than we look, you know."

"I know," Doctor Forsolano said. "There's certainly something in you, Pontopa."

I stood up and started to pace the room. It would take me a little while to get my head around this. I was perhaps the only person in the world with two biological mothers. Did that make me a dragonseer or not?

"Papo, you know I have to leave tomorrow," I said. "I'm a dragonseer now. I met a dragon queen, and she told me what I have to do. I know you don't want me to go Papo. I know you want to protect me. But this boy is important to Gerhaun and there's so much I have to learn."

Papo breathed in heavily as if to let out a sigh, but he was cut off with a grimace and he clutched his hand to his shoulder.

"Easy, Cipao," Doctor Forsolano said.

"I know. I guess this is something we have to accept. But you mustn't do anything that gets you into any danger, you hear me? I've got to rest well at the end of the day, knowing you're alive."

"I'll stay safe, Papo, I promise."

"Then send us a postcard," Papo said with a smile, "and really, get out of there as soon as you can."

"Thank you, Papo," I said, and I kissed him on the cheek. "Mamo, thank you."

I walked to the open window to get a breath of fresh air.

I slept in a twin room with Sukina. Faso took the single room next door and I kept being woken up from his snoring. Mamo, I believe, slept in the chair downstairs watching over Papo. I kept hearing the creaking of floorboards as Forsolano got up every hour or so to tend to him through the night.

Breakfast the next day was vegan – no eggs or sausages or bacon, much to Faso's dismay. But Forsolano had admonished us for over-doing the secicao and he advised it was better to get a good mix of fruit and veg and recover the vitamins. So, on his long table, he'd laid out a selection of salads, hummus, rye bread, tabbouleh, falafels and all kinds of other rich delights that I wondered how he'd managed to source all the ingredients, being in the middle of nowhere and all that.

Forsolano had let Papo out of bed to at least have breakfast with us, although he was under a strict time limit of half an hour.

I tried not to linger too long before I said goodbye to my parents (if I should be calling them that now). I didn't want any more tears or angst – I just wanted Papo to rest and Mamo to look after him. But I lingered long enough to tell both of them I loved them and that I forgave them about the whole adoption thing.

Papo had to stay at Forsolano's and Mamo wanted to look after him. So we decided that only one nurse would come with us to the clearing, just to make sure we didn't get lost.

In the hallway, I gave Mamo a big hug then and she cried in my arms. "Dear, you must come back, you hear me?"

Sukina smiled. "She will," she said. "I'd put my own life before hers any day."

Mamo looked at Sukina. "Don't you go getting yourself killed either, dear. Or you for that matter, young man." She turned to Faso.

Sukina laughed and Faso grimaced. "No one's going to die, Versalina," Sukina said. "We're all too valuable for that."

Mamo smiled and Papo stepped forward. He tried to reach out with both arms with a hug, forgetting that his left was in a sling. He grimaced when the right extended further than the left. Then he accepted defeat and gripped me with one arm. "Your Mamo and I both love you, you know that?" she said. "We're only protective like this because we'd much rather be the ones getting into trouble than you."

"I'll stay safe, I promise, Papo," I said.

"So you go in, get the boy, and get back here safe."

"I understand."

We left Mamo with Papo at Forsolano's and traipsed back to the clearing in the forest to leave with Velos. I felt him as we approached, and he didn't seem happy having to spend the night there while we slept so comfortably on Forsolano's soft mattresses.

But, as soon as he saw us, I felt him perk up a little. He raised his head to the sky and let off a huge roar.

"Shh, Velos," I said and then sang a song quickly, without knowing what I was doing.

"He's just saying hello," Sukina said. "Don't worry, I'm sure we're miles from Cini's troops here."

"I hope so," I said, and we took off towards Slaro.

PART VI

CINI

"There is no more valuable resource in this world than secicao."

— KING CINI III

22

We decided to fly east for a while then north instead of taking the direct route northeast to Slaro. The latter would take us through a valley where Slaro had heavy fortifications. But the king would unlikely expect anyone to fly over the five-thousand-metre high Caprio Mountain range. Airships found it difficult to get over there with the thin air.

Of course, it was also much colder up there. This time of year, there was snow and we had to put our breathing masks on to ensure we had enough oxygen. Without the storage offered by Velos' armour, we wouldn't have been able to pack the necessary winter-wear to get us through. But now some trench coats and Saye Alpaca Wool jumpers kept us warm enough for at least the few hours we had to stay high.

Just before we reached the mountains, Sukina had taken a little while to brief us on the plan. She had a contact within the city, a publisher known as Simpra Grandola who lived just southeast of the mountains, and who could shelter Velos underneath his printing office. We'd leave Velos there and Simpra would escort us towards the Palace Station tram stop, where he knew of a secret tunnel into the palace. After that, it would be a matter of stealth, Ratter would be able to help disable some guards, if necessary. Sukina said she'd show us the exact schematics of the palace once we reached our first destination.

We approached the plains of Slaro from above, the land once stripped bare by a glacier that had run westwards. From above, you could see the grey-yellow smog clouds roiling down below – a mixture of coal smoke and secicao from all the refineries used to blend secicao and create the oil.

When I looked at it then, I could see what Sukina and Gerhaun meant by how secicao was taking over the world. You didn't notice it so much when you were down on the ground in Slaro. Just a general clamminess and the thin sunlight which brought a little warmth to the city before it plunged into a cold night.

"You're home now, Faso," I called back. "You want to set up your enterprise here?"

"I've changed my mind about that."

"I don't blame you," I shouted and then we dove into the clouds. It was if I'd suddenly entered a room filled with chain smokers. I started coughing and hacking and it took me a couple of minutes to adjust.

Then, just as I began to return to my senses, time seemed to slow, and I sensed danger approaching. A humming came from the left and a cold wind washed over us. At the same time, something shifted in the collective unconscious. I turned over my shoulders, to see a huge red dirigible emerge from the murk.

King Cini III was on deck in his splendid white furs, looking out with his hands behind his back. Two other men were there that I recognized – Francoiso with his hard-cheeked good looks and Charth with that dour face. There were also around a dozen guards and a slender tall woman with dark black hair standing on top of the wooden gondola. As the airship got closer, I saw that I recognized her too. Alsie Fioreletta, the king's famous consort.

The king raised a megaphone. "Welcome to Slaro, Miss Sako. I see you've brought Miss Wells and Mr Gordoni with you. Excellent work."

Then came Francoiso's voice in the collective unconscious. *"Hello, darling. When I said soon, I had no idea it would be this soon."*

"What do you want with us?" I said in my mind.

"Never mind that for now, dear. Just follow the king's orders and come down with us for a safe landing. Fortunately, my brother and I

have had a little word with King Cini, and he now agrees you and Miss Sako are much too valuable to die. So, you'll be pleased to hear, you'll be treated well."

Well, I guess this would screw up our plans to enter the palace by tram and tunnel. I looked behind me. Sukina gave me a nod. "*Probably not the best idea to try anything this time,*" she said in the collective unconscious. We could again speak here, due to the proximity of the Lamford Brothers.

Behind Sukina, Faso looked terrified, his face blanched and his hands tightly clutching the handlebars in front of us.

"We're going in," I said out loud.

"Dragonheats, I'm glad to hear that," Faso shouted back. "I thought you were going to try fighting them again."

I pushed down on Velos' steering fin to level him out with the airships. He lifted his head and let out a roar, which caused a guard on deck Cini's airship to raise a rifle. Immediately, I started to sing a song to tell Velos to behave and that calmed him a little.

Then, we allowed ourselves to be escorted down to ground.

CINI'S PALACE had its own dedicated landing pad. His father had built a structure on what must have been thousands of pillars, just a little taller than a man. Its roof was a flat platform that could hold a hundred or so of the king's massive dirigibles.

I had to land Velos there, amidst the nauseating smell of coal and oil. I could feel he hated it too, but rather than roaring out a complaint, he simply buried his head into his front legs and whimpered like a dog.

"We'll get out of this one alive," I said. "I promise." Velos didn't speak my language, but he would understand the emotions behind it. That seemed enough to placate him a little.

Cini's troops buoyed the airship so they could swing the ramp right down at our feet. It thudded against the ground just short of our noses, letting a gust of wind brush over us. I looked up to see two snipers with their rifles trained on us, golden flasks dangling at their hips.

Three guards came down the ramp and each of them took positions an arm's breadth away, their Pattersoni rifles pointed right at our chests. Then the king walked haughtily down the ramp, not lowering his head to look at us once.

He stopped and his gaze fell on Sukina. "So, we failed to take you at Fraw. My cousins failed to capture you in the Southlands," he looked over his shoulder at the dragonmen. "Then you come walking right into my arms. How kind of you, Miss Sako…"

Ratter had perched himself right on Faso's shoulder, its back hunched up like a hissing cat. Cini glanced at it with derision then summoned one of his troops forward from behind him. "Confiscate that thing. Don't think, Mr Gordoni, you're going to try any of the same tricks you tried at Fraw."

"Wouldn't dream of it," Faso said. He tapped Ratter on the back, twice this time, and the automaton flopped down on his shoulder. A guard moved forward and took the device back to Cini, holding it by its tail.

"Not just him, you fool, take Gordoni too. He's broken the law by using the king's technology against him."

"The king's technology, I—"

"We commissioned you to create these automatons, didn't we?"

"Yes, but—"

Before he could say another word, another of Cini's guards knocked him on the back of the head with the butt of a rifle, almost knocking Faso to the floor. "I remind, you Mr Gordoni," King Cini said. "That your voice isn't as melodious as you might think."

"I—"

"Another word out of you and I might decide it better to have you shot. Now lock him up." He waved Faso off to the cells.

As all this was going on, the two dragonmen and Alsie Fioreletta climbed down the ladder at the back of the airship. They walked towards a tall building with a high tower. Halfway up that, four further towers extruded at obtuse angles, kind of looking like hands of a clock. Each of these had a different colour – red, blue, yellow and green, with the central tower being an intense alabaster that contrasted starkly against the brownish-grey smog.

The guards walked Faso off in another direction, and he also had his eyes locked on the two men and the one woman, although he didn't dare say anything.

"Don't worry, darling," Francoiso said in my mind just as he'd disappeared out of view. *"No one's intending to kill you this time. I don't know what Cini's going to do with the inventor, though. Although, I kind of have a feeling you'd rather he'd never entered your life in the first place. You, my dear, are destined for much greater men."* Actually, to be honest, I was kind of concerned what would happen to Faso at this point. Despite him and I getting off on the wrong foot, I'd started to warm to the guy.

"Francoiso, stop fooling around," Charth said again in the collective unconscious.

"Allow me," this time it was a woman's voice, and it wasn't Sukina. A shrill shriek followed. It was as if someone had shot a spike right through my ear drum. I jerked my hand to my ear, but the pain quickly subsided. I looked at Sukina.

"What was that?" I tried telepathing to her. But she wasn't there.

I felt a sudden emptiness inside me. My connection to Velos, to Sukina, to the connective unconscious severed. Then, normality returned, but I could no longer hear the dragonmen in my mind.

Cini had been watching us all this time with curiosity. "You dragonseers have always had these strange moments," he said. "I remember them from my visits to see my father's four prisoners when I was a child."

I guessed he was talking about the 'Famous Four'. Cini II had abandoned four terrorists in an old water tower, without food or drink until they eventually died. This had apparently been all over the magazines at the time, as well as the fact that Cini II went on excursions with his son to visit them. The old king had wanted to show the king-to-be how hard decisions needed to be made as a leader, as well as how 'vile' these people were. Just then, King Cini III had just claimed...

"Yes," Sukina said in the collective unconscious. It appeared she had managed to restore the channel after Alsie's brief interruption. *"The Famous Four were dragonseers."* I looked at Sukina in astonishment. Then, I blinked away the expression, realizing Cini was observing us with a hand on his chin.

"Oh, don't worry," he said. "I don't plan any executions here and now. The Lamford Brothers and my beloved Alsie have helped me realize how valuable you dragonseers could be to my dear country. So, I want to offer you a compromise. A place at court in return for your services. Of course, I don't expect an answer now. I know such decisions are difficult."

Sukina's eyes had become slits. "We came to take the boy back. You know that he's not your property."

"Oh, him... I personally would be quite happy to give the little brat away, but my mistress quite enjoys his company. She says he's essential for some operation or other and who am I to argue about her family's plans?"

"Why exactly are the Lamford Brothers so important to you?" Sukina asked. "We all know they're not really your family."

"But officially they are, you see. The unofficial version, unfortunately, I'm not at liberty to discuss. But then, you are my prisoners here and so my family isn't any of your concern."

"So why not arrest us like Faso?" Sukina asked.

"The inventor? His science has always been quite valuable to me. I'm sure after a little rough treatment, I can convince him that he joined the wrong side. For you, however, tough as you seem, I have plans to indenture you into the court."

"We'll never."

"Oh, you will," King Cini said. "But for now, you must be quite hungry and I'm sure dinner will be ready." He turned to one of his guards. "Bring them to my dining room."

He turned on his heel and walked off with a straight back, tailed by three of his elite guards. We went without resistance. So, there was no need for blindfolds or any nonsense like that.

Cini's palace was – I hate to say it – grander than Fortress Gerhaun. While Fortress Gerhaun was functional full of layers of dust and murk, here everything was manicured, and opulent in marble, obsidian, and gold. Every corridor was guarded on each side by rows of golden statues. Figures of Cini's ancestors and the dukes and earls who had served them well in the wars. On top of each statue, a brass turret stood vigil, with beady red automaton eyes that watched you as you passed. The king didn't use any of Faso's fancy secicao technology here – just simple war automatons that would shoot on the first sign of danger.

We walked through several corridors before one opened up into a wide courtyard, limned with elm trees and a pond that ran around the perimeter, its source a fountain of eight quartz lions. Steam rose from the pond, which brought a little heat to the place as you stepped over it. The fountain was covered by a large pagoda with stairs leading up from all four compass points. Cini and five of his redguards led us up to the top.

Up there lay an emerald coloured table, again made of marble. We sat down on some finely carved walnut oak chairs, each wide enough to fit three men. Two teapots lay on the table, a silver and a gold one. The king hitched up his fur cloak, sat himself down on the chair as two redguards stood beside him. A maid in a white plaid skirt and green cotton bib, who had been standing back, stepped forwards and poured King Cini a cup of green tea from the gold pot into a delicate porcelain cup.

She then took hold of the silver pot and poured this strange liquid into the cup. As soon as I saw it emerge from the teapot, I felt drawn towards as if by some hidden force. As the liquid rose within the cup, a silver whirlpool emerged which kept spinning, never settling. Part of me wanted just to reach out, snatch the cup, and take down the liquid in one.

But how could this liquid have such control over me?

"It's poison," I said.

King Cini shook his head. "Dear Miss Wells, if I was going to kill you, I simply would have ordered my guards to do the job. Villainous actions like poison are the stuff of novels, not modern life. Please, at least enjoy the pleasure of my finest tea."

Sukina had the cup in her hand and was swirling around the liquid within. "How can you expect us to drink something," she said, "which looks so odd when we have no idea what's within it?" But I could see within her eyes a yearning to drink it too.

Cini sighed and gestured to one of his guards. The guard nodded and raised his rifle. "I believe you have no choice, Miss Sako. You either do as I say, or I must execute you as a traitor to the king."

Sukina looked at the barrel of the gun, then took a sip of the liquid. At first, she looked as if she was going to spit it out. But her expression softened and then she raised the cup to her lips and let the liquid trickle into her mouth. When she put the cup down, it was empty.

"That's better," King Cini said. "Miss Wells, the same applies to you…"

I shook my head. If I was going to die here, then I'd rather be poisoned than shot. I raised the cup to my lips. It had a metallic ferric taste, yet so… Familiar. It warmed my throat without burning, like the finest of whiskeys and when it settled down in my stomach, a pleasant tremble ran down my spine. I tipped back the cup and my body thrilled with an orgasmic sensation as the liquid went smoothly down my throat.

"I've heard it's quite fine stuff," King Cini said. "I'd drink myself, but this stuff isn't for normal men. Here we call it Exalmpora, and you'll never guess what's within it."

"It's wonderful," Sukina said. The words rolled loosely off her tongue. "I guess carrots and ginger, and a hint of Cadigan's finest silver."

"No, no, that's silly," I said. Somehow, all of a sudden, I wanted to play the king's games. "It must be hibiscus and oleander – did you know oleander is poisonous, so it must only be a hint, because you don't want to poison us do you, King Cini?" The world had become blurry and the king's hard-lined features had somewhat softened. In the distance of my mind, I could hear very faint echoes. People and dragons talking, about nonsense. The kind of voices you might hear before you go to sleep.

"Oh, this is such a fun game," King Cini said. I'd never known him so flippant. "I'd love to give you the answer now, but that would ruin the surprise. Why don't you have some more?"

At first, when the maid poured, some common sense inside me told me to refuse, despite the barrel of the rifle pointed at me. But as time went on, I feared less, and didn't even notice anyone except Sukina, the king and I were in the room. The day flowed into night and it seemed as if four moons rose high in the sky, although I knew there was only actually one of them.

"You are both very beautiful women," I remember the king saying at one point. "My cousins have been most willing to meet you. I believe you've already been acquainted, however."

Then came a voice lucid as crystal in my mind. *"Hello, darling,"* and I saw Francoiso's handsome face in front of me. Jagged high cheekbones and the way that his features swirled to from an Adonis fit for the most beautiful of princesses to the most splendid black dragon I'd ever seen. *"I see the king's getting you a little tipsy today."*

Behind I could hear Charth, and even he sounded more charming than usual. But he didn't need to say much for Sukina to erupt into a fit of giggles. Then another cup of Exalmpora went straight down my throat.

I don't know how late the night went on. I think the king left us at some point and perhaps I sat on Francoiso's lap, perhaps I even kissed him. Then Charth said something to Francoiso and they were gone, and gentle hands, perhaps of a guard, carried me off to my chambers.

Soon, I was sinking into soft down and wool and shortly, I was asleep.

I woke up several times throughout the night gasping for air. Nightmares of Velos being chained and war automatons shooting him down from the sky. Sukina launching herself from an airship strapped to some kind of bomb. *"I must sacrifice myself to save you,"* she said. Then she dived into Cini's palace and an explosion rocked the sky. A statue of an empress as tall as a mountain looking down from an icy throne, as we stood beside her toe, her toenail arching over our heads. Besides me stood Prince Artua and Faso, and we knew we had to scale the statue. But it would take hours, days, a lifetime to get to the top where we could pull out Finesia's golden tooth.

Then I woke, and I could hear Sukina. A sea of gibberish. *"Faso, Charth, Colas, Alsie. Alsie is here... Finesia, who is Finesia? The Empress... No, she cannot exist. The Gods Themselves have abandoned us and only Gerhaun can show us the light."*

"Sukina," I called out, but she couldn't hear me. Or in many ways I couldn't hear her. I fell back asleep and I kept waking and then falling through clouds and silver whirlpools and midnight dark.

I don't know for how long I slept. I woke to the faint warmth of the sun peeping through the secicao smog to gently touch the back of my neck. Or maybe it was the loud rapping at the door.

"Who is it?" I called, forgetting where I was, and I almost drifted back off to sleep.

But then came a shrill pitch in my mind, the same I'd heard the other day on Cini's airstrip. It bored right through my eardrums into my skull and made me want to throw up.

"Do you have to be so cruel?" that was Francoiso's voice, coming ever so faintly from behind the door and not in the collective unconscious. I could only just make him out through my throbbing headache.

"It's not as if your efforts to wake her did her any good," said a woman, again outside. Her voice was cold.

"Well, she's awake now. So, you can leave the rest to me."

"Don't forget the cure," the woman said. "Cini has to understand you can't rush the process."

The sound of heels tip-tapped away from the door in a steady, rhythm. I dragged myself over to the door and opened it. I peered around into Francoiso's handsome face, as I held on to the cold handle for dear support.

"Good morning, darling," Francoiso said. "You're looking hale and hearty, I must say." He grinned. He was wearing a purple velvet waistcoat, a white frilly shirt and thin breeches, dressed as if for a hunt.

"Pale and sickly, more like. What was that stuff the king forced upon us yesterday? It gives the worst hangovers."

"Ah, yes, I almost forgot." He opened a waistcoat and fumbled through an inside pocket. From it, he produced a thin vial with a green viscous liquid inside. "Here, drink this. Call it a hair of the dog. It doesn't taste the best, but I have my orders."

I took the vial and almost dropped it. It was hot but not to the point of scalding. I took it in my other hand and held the glass at the neck. "I guess you're not wanting to poison us either. What does the king want with us? He said something about marriage?"

"Oh, darling, just play along with his little games. As much as I'd like to reveal every one of the king's deepest secrets to you and then whisk you off to a foreign land, I have to hold restraint. Alsie would kill me if I let you know too much. You have to understand."

"Alsie?" I said.

"Yes, she was here a moment ago. You'll meet her soon enough. But for now, the king wants you to meet Master Artua."

The boy we're here to rescue, I thought. Then I remembered what Sukina had said about masking my thoughts. Damn it.

Francoiso smiled. "Don't worry. We know all about that already. Soon enough, you'll come to know that much here is not quite what it seems. Now, drink up."

I eyed Francoiso suspiciously. Then I unstopped the cork and poured the liquid down my throat. It tasted of liquorice, the flavour so intense I almost retched it all up again. Somehow, I got enough down for the serum to take effect.

It sank like lead in my stomach and then a wave of relief washed over my entire body. Like a miracle drug, the headache and the nausea vanished in just a few seconds and clarity returned to my mind.

"Remarkable," Francoiso said. "You truly are a dragonseer. Come, get dressed and then I'll walk you to the throne room."

"It's probably best to do as he says." Again, Sukina could talk to me in my mind. *"They seem allies, but for what reason, I don't yet understand."*

I looked at Francoiso. "Give me a minute," I said. I closed the door and looked down at my clothes. The shawl and trousers I'd worn for flying now had strange silver stains over them, tinted with brown around the edges. This silver pooled in certain areas, like under the armpits. I opened the wardrobe, wafted away the dust and found a modest black dress hanging there alone. I pulled it to my body. It seemed to fit my curves perfectly, as if someone had come to measure me in my sleep. I checked the window to see no one was watching – there were no curtains, and I was trapped behind some heavy iron bars. I sighed then dressed myself. Francoiso was waiting patiently outside.

"What exactly does the king want?" I asked.

"Oh, the boy simply needs some mother figures in his life. Alsie can be quite terrifying to an eight-year-old sometimes and, as the magazines keep telling us, here we have quite a male dominated court."

It was true. The magazines often discussed the fact that King Cini had not yet fathered an heir. He was young, admittedly, and probably had a good fifty years of reign ahead of him. But still, everyone believed that there should have been a young prince by now.

The doors had been left wide open. Beyond them lay the throne room, fully resplendent in gilt and velvet and fur. The room was long, with an arched aisle leading down the centre and two wings on either side of this, separated by lines of pillars. Bas-reliefs ran around each of the pillars, and I examined the closer ones to see wars between men and dragons. I noticed the Tree Immortal from the myth in there too, and a great armoured warrior I assumed to be Finase, holding a naked woman in one arm as he slashed amongst the rioters ahead of him with a claymore in his other. The woman: Finesia.

A redguard stood aside each of the pillars, with halberds on their shoulders. Only on the row of guards to my right, could I see the pistol holstered at their hips. Interestingly, the room was open to the sky in the centre, leading up to a chimney wide enough for a dragon to fit through.

King Cini sat on a high throne that rose much taller than him, with two golden sabres like horns protruding from the seat of it. Two steel shields stuck out from the armrests like scales protecting the flanks of some monstrous beast. The throne had been raised upon a marble dais, with a few steps leading up to it. At the bottom corner of these steps, to the king's left, a boy played with an automaton toy – a miniature airship that the child navigated through swoops and dives.

"Ah, Miss Sako and Miss Wells." The king looked over at an elaborate grandfather clock ticking away on one side of the throne room. "I wondered at what time you'd eventually grace my presence."

Sukina gave a half-arsed curtsey, then stepped forwards. "What exactly do you want with us, Cini?" she asked. "You know that we came here for the..." She paused a moment. "Boy..."

"My nephew? What would you want with someone so dear to me?"

Sukina grimaced at the use of the word nephew. "He's of no relation to you, and you know it."

The boy looked up at us as if slightly curious. But the mock war he was orchestrating with his airship seemed more fascinating. In his other hand, I noticed in horror, he held a toy dragon and the airship was chasing the dragon as if to shoot it down.

"Accusations, accusations, Miss Sako. But you know you're not in a position to decide who the boy is. I merely wanted to introduce him to you. I thought he'd be happy to meet his new guardians."

"What the dragonheats are you talking about?"

"I mean that we intend for you to look after him here in the palace. Oh, don't give me that look. It's not like you have any choice in the matter. You tried to sneak in and take him for yourself, but how exactly would you have done so without him raising an alarm? The boy is incredibly important to the war effort, Miss Sako."

Sukina looked like she wanted to spit on him. "What have you done with Faso Gordoni?"

"The inventor is quite safe, I assure you. He's also important to us, but it's not as if he can't be taught a lesson in humility, is it?"

Somehow, it just didn't seem right that he'd have to be stuck in cells when we were treated like princesses in court.

"Now, Artua," the king continued, "come forward a moment. I want you to meet your new guardian." The boy looked at the king then back down at his airship as if he didn't want to abandon it. "Now, Artua!"

The boy huffed then put the airship down on the floor. He stood up and meekly approached Sukina. He offered her his hand and Sukina took it. "Nice to meet you, Miss Sako. You look like someone I know."

At that, I saw Sukina lose her composure for just a split second. Or maybe I felt it in the collective unconscious. Francoiso and Charth were loitering somewhere nearby – I could sense them too – as well as another presence.

"It's very nice to meet you, young man," Sukina said. "Now, maybe you should return to your toys."

From behind the throne, a woman stepped out. It was as if she'd stepped out of the darkness, one minute she hadn't been there and then the next she had. It was the same woman we'd seen the previous day on the airfield. Her straight raven hair was swept down past her dark skin and behind it all she had these brilliant blue eyes. "It's time for your medicine, Artua," she said, and she handed him a thimble. The boy looked at it in glee, tipped the contents down his throat, then returned to his toys.

Alsie walked towards Sukina. "You will perform your duties to the king, Miss Sako. You will not leave the palace unless ordered to, or you will be shot on sight. You will teach the boy all you know about dragon songs. Then, when the time comes, he shall take the throne a true warrior in battles against the Greys."

So that was it. Artua was to take King Cini's place when he passed on. How Alsie had him wrapped around her thumb I don't know.

"Who are you to give me such orders?" Sukina said.

"Why, that's Alsie Fioreletta," the king said, and she went to sit on his lap. "My right hand maiden and most trusted advisor. I'm sure you've read about her in the magazines."

Alsie planted a kiss on Cini's lips and ran a delicate hand down his cheek. A lot had been written about Alsie Fioreletta, including many questions about why she'd not yet borne children. This was something that every hamlet, village and town in Tow wanted to know. The magazines surmised that the king had never proposed to her for the same reason.

I felt as if I'd been sinking into the background here. All this time, I'd been wanting to know why the wellies I was also here, but I hadn't yet dared speak out. But at this point I didn't want to be forgotten. I stepped forwards.

"So, you need Sukina here to look after the boy, but what do you need of me?"

The king looked down at me then smiled. His threatening nature had completely washed away now, to be replaced by this strange geniality. It was almost as if he'd accepted me into his family, though I knew behind it all how fake it was.

"Miss Wells. You can help Sukina with her duties. And—"

Alsie raised a hand as if to cut Cini off, and he shut up immediately. "That's more than enough, my dear king. Dragonseer Wells, you are of great importance to the war effort and the future of mankind. That's all you need to know at the present moment."

"She's crazy," I said in my mind.

"Careful what you say," Sukina said. Of course, I still needed to learn to channel my thoughts.

Alsie's head jerked up as soon as I'd registered that thought, as if indeed she could hear. "Now Cini," she said and rose up off his lap. "I believe you wanted to entertain our guests."

"Of course," he said. "Miss Wells and Miss Sako, you must indeed be hungry. Come and let us enjoy a fine and royal feast."

We left Alsie and the boy in the throne room. The king again led us to that pagoda with the emerald marble table. The same two gold and silver teapots were laid upon it, alongside three covered dishes, surrounded by silver spoons and goblets.

A maid walked over to the table to lift the plate covers. Underneath one was a few quails stuffed with walnuts and apricots, under another, potatoes roasted in goose fat and a third had grilled aubergines sprinkled with finely diced garlic. I didn't know what Faso was eating in his cell, but it couldn't be anything as rich as this.

"We can talk in this channel," Sukina said in the collective unconscious. *"I have enough mental acuity to mask our thoughts from everyone else."*

"Good," I replied mentally. *"So, what do you think's going on here?"*

"It's madness. Why would the king treat us with such grace?"

"*Beats me,*" I said and despite the food smelling amazing, I wasn't really so hungry. "*Last time I checked, we were his enemy.*"

"*Yet he trusts us to raise the boy. Why does he trust Alsie Fioreletta so much? Something strange is going on in this court that I don't quite like.*"

"*Tell me about it,*" I said, and I looked at the cup of Exalmpora that was placed in front of me – the silver swirling inside the clear thin liquid.

"Well, drink up before you eat," King Cini said. "It will help you regain your appetite." I turned to see a Pattersoni rifle pointed at my head, which I wouldn't see for very long if I didn't obey the king's wishes.

This time, I felt no resistance. It was almost as if the liquid was pulling me towards it. I wanted its power. I wanted whatever it held within.

I took the cup to my lips, closed my eyes and took the liquid down in one. My muscles immediately loosened, and the world began to swirl around me again.

"My, my, you are enjoying yourself," Cini said.

Then the day flowed into night and I remembered even less of it than the previous day.

I WOKE up squirming underneath the woollen bed covers, again from lucid dreams. I could hear Sukina's voice in my mind and, strangely, it made sense this time.

"*Pontopa, are you awake now?*" she asked. "*Pontopa...*"

"*I am,*" I said. "*Sleepy...*"

"*I can hear your dreams.*"

"*I can hear yours. What is that... The Exalmpora?*"

"*I don't know. But must defeat it... We must persevere, Pontopa... We must push it away.*"

"*Francoiso, Charth, Alsie... Can they hear us?*"

"*I don't think I can keep them out of the channel,*" Sukina said. "*Too much Exalmpora to concentrate.*"

"*But why are they here?*"

"*I don't know.*"

I felt my eyes getting heavy again. *"Sukina,"* I said. I wanted to say something else, but I'd already forgotten what.

"Yes?"

"Sukina?" I must have fallen asleep. When I awoke again, I tried to reach out to her. But I was answered only by a sea of gibberish and more dreams of death.

24

I didn't have any initiative to explore the palace the next day. I just wanted to get to the king's entertainment pagoda and drink the Exalmpora, even though I knew such feelings weren't good for me.

I didn't have much of a headache either, surprisingly. My power to connect to the collective unconscious seemed strengthened. I knew the locations of Sukina, Charth, Francoiso, Alsie, and even Velos in the palace.

I felt a touch of shame then. How long had I been in here without even thinking about Velos, let alone my parents? But that thought soon became replaced with an urge to hunt down the Exalmpora and drink it copiously.

I knew Francoiso was waiting outside my door before I opened it. He hadn't even knocked this time, and he didn't have a vial containing the cure for the Exalmpora. Although, I didn't particularly want it at that point.

"Darling," he said in the collective unconscious. *"You're getting even more beautiful by the day, both inside and out. Though my brother keeps reminding me I have to teach you to resist the Exalmpora, I must say I'm liking the effects it has on you."*

"Why is Cini making us drink that stuff?" I asked. Although, I have to say it wasn't as if I was showing much resistance anymore.

"You already know part of it, my buttercup. The properties of that

serum will make you more loyal to those you see the most. But that's not all, I'm afraid. The king wants you to become dragonmen, just like us. Or in your case, I guess, a dragonwoman."

"He wants us to become dragonwomen? Wait... Is this how you became this way?"

"Oh, darling," Francoiso said. *"I'm not yet ready to tell you how I came to be. Maybe sometime later in our relationship I can reveal my hidden secrets."*

"I look forward to it."

"Come on, you must get dressed. King Cini, buffoon that he is, has plans which in many ways I'm quite looking forward to."

My black dress again had those ugly silver stains on it. So, I opened the wardrobe this time to find a stunning long opal green dress, so wide at the back it left me virtually naked there, and in other places the cloth flowed casually over my curves.

I stepped outside to see Francoiso waiting, nonchalantly whistling as he leant against the wall. He offered me his arm. "Shall we?"

I took his arm, appreciating his muscles and the warmth of his body against mine. We flirted and made small talk until we reached King Cini's throne room.

"Ah, such a fine couple already," the king said as we entered the room. "Francoiso, my friend, I must say I'm slightly envious."

King Cini sat in red splendid robes on top of his throne. Artua stood beside him in his normal spot. Again, he was playing with his airships, but this time it seemed the dragon was the good guy in pursuit of the airship who had stolen some goods. Alsie stepped forward from her place hidden behind the throne and rubbed Artua on the head.

"Francoiso and Pontopa," she said. "Why don't you put your toys away and greet them?"

King Cini turned his head to Alsie. "It's about time he starts calling them Auntie and Uncle, don't you think?"

Alsie returned a look of scorn, then swallowed it down. "Very well, your highness," she said, and she gave a slight curtsey as if mocking him. "However you wish it to be."

"Alsie, I remind you who's in charge here. Artua, return to your toys for the while. I will call you when needs be." My, my, it looked as Alsie and the king had had a bit of a lover's tiff.

Alsie gave the king a contemptuous look as if to say, I'm really the one in control here and no damn king is going to get in my way. There was a certain power to that woman even greater than in the Lamford brothers. I could sense it in her, almost as if it thrummed through my own body as well.

I heard the click of Sukina's heels approaching and Charth's heavy boots shuffling behind. They also walked arm-in-arm, although Sukina didn't quite meld to Charth like I felt I melded to Francoiso. Each step of hers seemed cautious as if she was willing her feet forward when her body didn't really want to move.

"Another remarkable couple, don't you think, Alsie? I think they'll make a perfect team."

"You already know my opinion on that," Alsie said. "I've told you full well these things need time to stew, Exalmpora or not."

"Who, I ask, is king here? You are just my mistress, and if you show any resistance, I'll also lock you up like the Gordoni boy."

"I'd like to see you try," Alsie said. I half expected when Cini stood, given how red his face looked, that he was about to order his guards to arrest her. But he simply left Artua and Alsie there together and walked towards the entrance. "Come," he said to Sukina and myself. "It's time to have a feast and then I shall announce the news."

"You're a fool," Alsie called after him. "What is he?" she said to Artua.

"You're a fool," the boy parroted, as if entranced.

The king turned back, his face purple. "One more word out of you, woman, and I'll have you hanging from the gibbets."

Alsie produced a dagger from her belt. "Just try me..."

The king huffed and walked out the room.

"Oh, Alsie," Francoiso said. "Do you have to be such a spoilsport all the time?"

Alsie replaced the dagger in her belt and turned her contemptuous look upon Francoiso. "I should remind you what Finesia wills, Francoiso. Although, after you and your brother's antics lately, I'm not sure you quite understand this. I hope that you've been giving the dragonseer the vials," Alsie looked at me, "because she doesn't look particularly sober right now."

Francoiso didn't seem afraid of Alsie's aggressive tone. "I just like to have a little fun. But neither you nor my brother seem to know what that is."

"Brother, you know we're not trying to create monsters," Charth said.

Francoiso looked back at Charth and I followed his gaze to see that both Sukina and Charth had a similar sour look as Alsie. Whatever their plan was, clearly, I wasn't in on it.

"What the dragonheats is going on here?" I asked.

"That," Alsie said, "we only reveal on a need-to-know basis. Go and entertain the king for now, and we'll meet again in a couple of days. Meanwhile I must attend to business elsewhere."

"I guess you need a holiday, huh?" I said but she didn't take any time to respond. One moment she was there and then a blink of the eye she was gone. A roar came from the chimney and a cold gust of wind swept down, scattering dust and ash in its wake.

"Come," Charth said. "We should attend to the king."

Francoiso took hold of my hand and we turned towards the door.

"Wait!" the call came from little Artua. He put down his toys and shuffled up to Sukina. The boy looked up into Sukina's eyes.

Artua pulled back a little, surprised. Tears of recognition welled in the boy's eyes. "Mamo?" he said. Now that Alsie had gone, it appeared he felt a little freer to speak.

Sukina's cold expression immediately broke down. She pulled Artua close to her and buried her head in the boy's hair.

"Taka, how you've grown," she said. "Gerhaun will make a woman out of you. I promise you that..."

"But I'm a boy... I don't want to become a woman." He looked up at Charth.

Charth stepped between Sukina and the boy – girl. I must say, I was shaking my head in disbelief. How could everyone, the media, have been so fooled? The king's nephew was Sukina's daughter, a girl!

"That's enough! What are you doing, Sukina?" Charth pulled

the two away from each other. "If those words were to fall on the wrong ears..."

Sukina spun on him. "Now Alsie and the king are out of earshot, I can talk freely to him."

"That wasn't part of the deal."

"What does it matter? At least this way Taka knows who his mother is."

"What's going on, Sukina?" I just had to ask. "What the dragonheats is this all about?"

Sukina looked at me and said nothing. She still had tears in her eyes.

Francoiso took my arm in his. "Come on darling, we better leave these three in peace." He led me out towards the entertainment pagoda.

NO FOOD WAS SET out on the table this time, just the standard gold and silver teapots and those tiny ornate cups. There were no guards or maids anymore. It was just me, Sukina, Francoiso, Charth, and King Cini.

The king poured out the Exalmpora before me and I felt myself immediately drawn to it. I'd been desperate to get to this point all day and now I took down the concoction in one, instantly forgetting my hunger pangs.

"*Careful,*" Sukina said in the collective unconscious. "*You have to learn to control it.*"

"*You'll be fine,*" Francoiso said in my mind as he gently teased my ear. His hot breath sent a pleasant tingle down my spine. "*You're strong enough to handle this stuff. I was the same.*"

"*Francoiso, stop encouraging her,*" Charth said. "*She needs to keep her rational mind.*"

"*But Charth, tomorrow we get to—*"

"*Don't you dare,*" Sukina said, still in the collective unconscious.

"*And what exactly will stop me?*"

I had a feeling I knew what he meant and the warmth rushing down below told me I also wanted it. I turned to Francoiso and planted a kiss on his lips.

"Damn it, Francoiso, you know what Alsie ordered. Did you even give her the cure? You don't want her getting suspicious again, do you?" All this time we were having a conversation within our minds, and the king who sat there staring at Sukina's cup, had absolutely no idea.

"While Alsie's gone, don't you think we can have a little fun? She never has to know, brother."

I giggled. I liked the idea of having a little fun.

"Francoiso, you're crossing the line," Sukina said. She and Charth definitely had an alliance, though at that point I didn't really care. I wanted pretty much what Francoiso did.

"You need to drink your Exalmpora," Francoiso said. *"Because the king, right now, is getting suspicious."*

Sukina looked down at the cup. Charth glanced once at the king, then took hold of Sukina's hand, guided it towards the cup and helped Sukina raise it to her lips. He took hold of her neck and Sukina's body trembled as the liquid left the cup. Then Charth pushed his body closer to Sukina and tipped her head back while he planted a long and passionate kiss.

"See, brother," Francoiso said. *"You want it too."*

I felt Sukina's mind melt away in the collective unconscious. We spoke a little, but her voice had become more flippant. As I looked at her beautiful, polished face, her features started to warp, almost as if she was becoming a dragon herself.

"You know what we have to do," Charth said. *"We keep King Cini entertained until it's time to turn the cards."*

"Why are you always such a boring stickler, Charth?" Francoiso asked.

But Charth didn't seem interested in his games. Instead, he addressed me in the collective unconscious. *"I must apologize for my brother's behaviour. He wasn't always a slave to his emotions. Just know he's a better person deep inside."*

"Excuse me," Francoiso said. *"This is my future wife you're talking to. You're meant to sing praises about me. Tell her what a fine specimen of a man I am."*

"Start behaving like a gentleman, and maybe I will."

But, it seemed, that Francoiso had other plans for me. Part of me knew I should be planning my escape, questioning Sukina about what she was so concerned about, worrying about my parents, finding a way to break Artua and Faso out of there. But this Exalmpora had turned me into a different person. I no longer felt the tugs and the whirls of my senses. Instead, I was more attuned to them than I'd ever been. Unlike the other nights, I remembered everything that happened that night (up to a point), like you remember the most vivid of dreams.

As we kissed, and Francoiso's tongue played with mine then ran itself down the back of my neck and then spine, I forgot Cini was even in the room. I saw his face watching, but it had become like part of the scenery. This Exalmpora had turned me into a wild animal, a thing of passion. All I know is that I wanted Francoiso, there and then.

"My, my," King Cini said. "This is getting quite raunchy now, isn't it? You must back away, Charth and Francoiso, because you know the customs. By all means, in a couple of days, you can take them to your bedchambers."

Charth straightened up and stepped back immediately with a curt nod. Francoiso took a little longer to run his hands around my waist and I knew where those hands were going.

"Francoiso," the king said. "That's an order."

I huffed as his arms left mine. But I still sat obediently on my wooden chair.

"All these leader types are such spoilsports. Why can't they just learn to be free?" Francoiso said in the collective unconscious.

"Because we live for higher purposes than our desires," Charth said.

"Sometimes," Francoiso said. *"I wonder if we'd be better off just being ourselves..."* He took a step back from me.

King Cini was sat on his stool, watching us with curiosity. "Really, you people fascinate me with your private conversations. Who knows what you were talking about. Well, it doesn't matter. I made a promise yesterday to reveal what's in the Exalmpora, and now it's time to tell."

"Oh, do say, you handsome man," Sukina said. Then she started to giggle, and I joined in, not knowing exactly what we were giggling about.

"I do like how you're enjoying yourself so much," King Cini

said. "You drink enough Exalmpora and you'll actually want to stay here. Then, you can help our scientists work out how to create armies of people like the Lamford Brothers and Alsie, to replace our damn unreliable machines."

I poured myself some more Exalmpora and then almost snorted it out all over the table. "Faso says you're stealing his technology," I said. "Can't say how he'd feel if you then replaced his machines."

"Yes, yes," the king said. "He does grumble a lot, doesn't he? You would have thought he'd take a hint by now."

"I'm sure you're treating him well down there," Sukina said. "You are such a kind and handsome man."

"Like royalty, for a prison cell," the king said. "You should see how the King of Cadigan treats his prisoners, not to mention your home country of Orkc. Mr Gordoni's mentioned you a few times, Miss Sako."

"He didn't say anything about me?" I asked, feeling strangely jealous for a moment. I guess not so much because I wanted Faso's attention, but the Exalmpora was making me want any attention no matter who it was from.

"Not yet. Although I do know he holds you in high regard, Miss Wells, beauty that you are."

That sent me ecstatic and I punched King Cini jokingly on the shoulder.

"Yes, you're right," Sukina said. "Anyway, you must tell us what's in the Exalmpora. We're most certainly desperate to know."

"Ah, that silver stuff you see in there is dragon blood."

"But dragon blood isn't silver," Sukina said.

"Not just any dragon blood, you see, my dear. But blood of a dragon queen. My father collected it during the dragonheats, and it's kept perfectly preserved ever since. A scientist who used to work here called Captain Colas discovered that when you mix it with seci-cao, it has profound effects on dragonseers, as you can see."

I saw Charth grimace at the mention of the name Captain Colas and Francoiso shifted awkwardly.

"That's remarkable," I said. "You hear that Sukina? A drug that can control us..." I giggled again.

"It is," King Cini said. "Now for my other good news. Here at court, we've decided to announce a royal wedding. Pontopa Wells and Sukina Sako, you will marry my cousins: Charth and Francoiso Lamford."

"That's wonderful news," Sukina said.

"Marvellous," I said. "When will it happen?" I wished in all honesty that it was right now so we could get on with the good stuff.

"Patience, my dears," the king said. "We first much pick a suitable place for their proposal. So I've arranged a hunt for you tomorrow, to give you time to spend with your husbands to be."

"Just wait a couple more days, darling," Francoiso said out loud.

"Good," King Cini said. "I'm glad to know everyone is happy. Francoiso and Charth, you are now dismissed to make preparations for tomorrow."

They descended the stairs without another word either for real or in the collective unconscious. I drank more Exalmpora to such an extent that the world again became a haze.

THE NEXT THING I remembered that night was standing outside my room with Charth holding an empty vial with tiny traces of green in it.

"Unfortunately," he said, "I couldn't trust Francoiso to give you the cure this evening. He seems to think you're better off with the Exalmpora, but if you keep drinking it without the antidote, you risk becoming a product of your emotions. A truly wild beast."

I looked in astonishment at Charth. "Can Francoiso hear us?"

"Don't worry," he said. "As brothers, we're forever bound to the same channel when we speak in the collective unconscious. But I know how to separate what I say out loud from my thoughts."

"So, tell me. Why the dragonheats are you helping us?"

"If I could tell you more," Charth said. "I would. Just know for now that this is all part of the grand plan." He left me there and I entered my room and, for the first time in the palace, I actually remembered crawling into bed. I took off my clothes, sank into the soft blankets and I reached out into the collective unconscious.

"Sukina, are you there?" I asked.

"Yes, dear, but be careful what you think. There's only so much I can say."

"I just want to know what the dragonheats is going on. Artua is now Taka, your daughter? Why didn't you tell me Sukina?"

"I trust you, Pontopa. But until today, Alsie has been listening. I just didn't want you revealing the wrong thing. She's not as easy to block out as everyone else."

"But what does it matter? The king knows that Artua is your daughter, surely."

"He doesn't. It was the only way we could keep her from being executed Pontopa. Hide her in the palace and pretend she's a boy. Or at least that's what I was told at the time."

"You mean you knew Francoiso, Charth, and Alsie all this time?"

"Just Charth and Alsie."

"Dragonheats, Sukina. Why so many secrets?"

"The less you tell people, the more people you save. I learned this lesson the hard way a long time ago."

"Sukina—" I really was lost for words.

"Just, Pontopa... If anything happens to me, make sure Taka stays safe."

"Sukina, don't speak like this. We'll get out together. You'll see."

"Yes," Sukina said. *"We'll see."*

We fell silent for a moment. Somehow, a faint sliver of moonlight had managed to creep its way through the secicao clouds, and I could see the outlines of the wardrobe and the fireplace in my bedchambers. The cure had only been partly effective and I so through the faint light, I could still see swirling patterns within the darkness.

"Sukina," I said eventually. *"Who is the father?"*

"What? Who?" I'd just aroused her from sleep. I don't know how she managed to close herself off to the world so easily. But then, she was a light sleeper and easy to wake up again.

"The father, Sukina. Taka's father. It's not Faso... Is it?"

"It's Faso, yes."

"What? Does he know?"

"I never told him. Colas came to see me when I was just getting the first bouts of morning sickness. Then we had to leave."

"And the child was born."

"Yes, but the world was too dangerous. Colas, he promised he'd keep the child safe. It wasn't until later that he told me where the child was. That was when I first met Charth. He—"

But Sukina was cut off from a piercing noise in the collective unconscious. That same kind of shriek that rattled my brains so much that it extended into the physical and pierced my eardrums. I clutched my hands to my ears.

Alsie had returned.

I tried to reach out more to Sukina. I had so many questions. But clearly, Alsie didn't want her answering and I could learn no more. Something about that screech also made me suddenly feel exhausted. I was quickly asleep.

PART VII

FRANCOISO

"For romance and for desire. What else is there to live for?"

— FRANCOISO LAMFORD

25

The next day, my head was even clearer than it had been any previous day. The dress in the wardrobe was designed for the day ahead of me – deep red, with frilly lacy bits around the neckline and a low hemline.

In some countries they wore such dresses on the day of wedding, with pomp and circumstance and ceremony. But in Tow, women in high circles would only wear such clothes on the days they were to be engaged.

I'd half believed I'd never wear one of these. Although I was still young, I had never at that point considered settling down. With Velos and my runs south, I'd always thought I'd be some kind of free spirit, never marrying. Now, here I was looking at a dress to prepare for a wedding that deep inside, I wasn't sure I wanted.

But then, I wanted the Exalmpora. I wanted to get to the king's entertainment pagoda and drink, and drink, and become that wild, lusty girl and wrap my lips around Francoiso's. Though my mind didn't seem to want the wedding, my body wanted him. Despite the cure Charth had given me the previous night, my body had more control over me than my mind.

"Don't let your instincts get the better of you, Pontopa," Sukina said inside my mind. *"If you let yourself succumb to this Exalmpora then you will lose your rational mind."*

At the same time, Francoiso spoke in the collective unconscious, almost as if he'd found a way to listen in to Sukina's channel. *"Darling,"* he said. *"I know you're such a wild girl at heart and neither you nor I were meant to be tamed."*

His words sent a trill of passion down me. I got dressed, ready in time for the knock on the door. It wasn't Francoiso standing outside, but one of the king's pages, an adolescent wearing a blue flat cap and black frilly suit. "Miss Wells. The king says it's time to prepare for the grand occasion. He wants you in his throne room this instant."

Well, that was rather a direct way for a servant to speak to someone who was about to become royalty. The valet led me to the throne room. King Cini sat on his throne with Francoiso and Charth standing on either side of him. Alsie was nearby, I could sense her, but couldn't see her. As was Sukina's daughter Taka – somehow, I could sense her too.

Sukina entered the room just behind me and then the king stood up from his cushions to address us both. "Bright and early this morning and neither of you look too bad for the wear. The Exalmpora must be working quicker than I'd expected."

"Yes, my liege," Sukina said. "We're certainly enjoying the company."

Sukina, of course, was only acting. We had to make the king believe the Exalmpora was taking control of us. Even if the Lamford brothers kept giving us the antidote to keep it away.

"It's a wonderful day today, sire," I said. "A perfect day for an engagement."

"Well, I hope you're looking forward to the occasion as much as I am," King Cini said. "I'm sure you've read about these ceremonies in magazines and I want to create the kind of occasion that two dragonseers deserve. Then the country will be extremely happy to hear that you've joined our ranks in the war effort against the Greys."

"I'm sure today will be marvellous," Sukina said and she gave an elegant curtsey.

"That's good to hear. I'll let your suitors lead the way."

Francoiso and Charth had been standing loyally without saying a word, not even flinching or whispering in the collective unconscious. Their postures were remarkably straight, as if true soldiers. I smiled at Francoiso and let him march forwards and take my hand. At the same time, my heart was beating in anticipation for what lay ahead of me.

We left the king there and the four of us walked two by two through the corridors.

"You know the drill, I'm sure," Francoiso said.

I nodded. Anyone who read the magazines knew how royal engagements worked. We would travel north on a steam barge until we reached the king's hunting cabin in the countryside. I would have to kill an animal of significant stature to prove I was a worthy match for the groom. Then, the magazines could wax lyrical about what a brave person the new royal lady is.

If I failed, tradition had it I should be sent back to my home-town. Of course, these things were always rigged so that this never happened.

"Just remember that your hunting rifle won't actually contain bullets," Francoiso said. "The king doesn't one hundred percent trust you yet, so he's not going to give you loaded weapons."

"So, who will kill the animal?" I asked.

Francoiso winked. "That is something throughout history that the woman's never needed to know."

I'd never quite seen a boat like the king's Royal Steamship. But then, I'd never been on a riverboat before. With Velos, I didn't need to travel by boat much. So, the only time I tended to spend on them was on the trader ships, like Candalmo Segora's, when I popped on board for cups of secicao.

Huge trawlers like those stank of oil and coal. But this ship was different. The chimneys were at the back and a large fan also jutted out just in front of these, to blow any sickening smoke away from the deck.

But here, you wouldn't want to go outside much, with the lavishly decorated salon within. Chandeliers fit for any palace hung from the ceiling with large faceted diamonds dangling almost as low as the banquet table. The king sat with us, but far enough away together with Alsie that we couldn't hear what they spoke about. King Cini kept barking angry retorts at Alsie, who snapped back with equal aggressiveness. They certainly seemed like lovers given how much they were always at each other's throats.

Still, this atmosphere didn't mar the romance in the air, partly created by the scent of myrrh and frankincense rising from infusers on the tables. I held hands with Francoiso, and we gazed into each other's eyes. His were a brilliant blue and he kept a smile across his face. As we sat there, we both spoke in the collective unconscious.

"I wish you'd tell me what was going on," I said to him. *"Charth and Sukina are up to something and we're not in on it. What are they planning Francoiso? Why aren't you giving me those vials?"*

Francoiso's expression deepened. He always seemed so cocky and jovial, but now the lines on his face soured and he looked more like his brother. *"I like you, Pontopa,"* he said. *"You know that. I want you to stay here in the palace and I'm rampantly attracted to you. But Alsie and I have different views on the Exalmpora. If you take it fast like I did, you'll become a creature of passion. We can fly together through wild nights, beasts of the sky. But Alsie wants to create a more controlled you... And Charth... He won't let on what he's planning to me either. Although I have my suspicions..."*

"Maybe he wants to help us rescue the boy. Although, really that boy's a girl..."

"Oh, but Artua's a boy," Francoiso said. *"He didn't used to be, admittedly. But after Exalmpora..."*

"You gave him Exalmpora? That's—" I wanted to say wrong. Unethical, perhaps. But the words caught in my throat. The part of me that wanted Exalmpora so much right now, also thought that there was absolutely nothing wrong with Artua taking it.

"That's the medicine that Alsie pours down the boy's throat in the thimble every day. Her job..." Francoiso paused, as if he didn't believe Alsie should have a job at all. *"She's been given the task of making sure that Artua becomes a dragonman. That is Finesia's will."*

"But how can a girl become a boy? I don't understand."

"It's the Exalmpora that does it. Darling, I..." He looked up towards where the sun had been. We had now just left the secicao smog and the sun was hiding behind a real, white cloud. *"I was once a woman, Pontopa."*

My jaw dropped. This didn't make any sense. Francoiso's features were the epitome of masculinity. Across the table, the king looked up at us, but Alsie pulled his face away and whispered something in his ear. She then shot an angry glance at Francoiso, as if he shouldn't be telling me this. But Francoiso shook his head at her and turned back to me. He closed his eyes, put his hand on his temple as if focusing on something, and then continued to speak.

"Like you, I was once a dragonseer. One of the Famous Four who the king allegedly executed in the gas tower during the dragonheats. But he only ended up killing one of us, although he told the Tow Observer he'd killed all four. Instead, he made us drink Exalmpora. The idea of the king's scientist at the time, Captain Colas... My father... We were his experiment..." Francoiso shuddered but kept his hand to his temple. His face scrunched up a little as if straining. Across the table, Alsie was holding the king close and kissing him. But she had her eyes open and was watching us out of the corner. It was almost as if she could hear Francoiso and myself talking, or at least parts of the conversation.

"It must have been terrible," I said. *"Or perhaps, wonderful..."*

"You're right. It was fantastic. You can't help but enjoy Exalmpora. It changes you... You gain a connection to Finesia."

"The Empress?"

"Don't you understand? Finesia and secicao are one and the same. When she drank of the Tree Immortal, she hacked it to pieces and ate every last inch of its bark. Then, her skin became like bark and she shattered into millions of little pieces. Out of those pieces grew the first strands of secicao."

I laughed. *"So, she doesn't even have physical form?"*

"Oh, she has. It just isn't human... Yet." Francoiso opened his eyes and I felt a slight jump in the collective unconscious. He took hold of the back of my head and pulled me close to him. *"I want you, Pontopa. I can see how the Exalmpora is changing you and I know, unlike me and Charth, that you'll stay a woman. This is what Finesia wants. We can multiply and create more of us. Start the birth of a new race. Together we can become even more powerful than Alsie. You have more potential than you realise, Pontopa."*

"But how does the cure fit into all this?" I asked. *"Charth gave it to me last night, because he said there was no way you'd do so."*

I felt someone listening there again. Alsie, just waiting for Francoiso to let his guard down, so she could keep tabs on him. Dragonheats, I wanted to kill that bitch for invading our privacy.

Francoiso lowered his head and immediately put his hand to his temple. He closed his eyes and I felt a tightening in the collective unconscious again. I looked at Alsie who was staring at us over King Cini's shoulder. She'd heard what I said, and I could tell she wasn't happy with Francoiso. I just wonder if she'd heard Francoiso's part about us overthrowing her as well, or if Francoiso had managed to keep her out at that point.

Though my suitor's eyes were closed, I could make out lines of guilt across his face. Or, maybe I could feel that guilt in the collective unconscious. "*Charth is not as far gone as me,* he said. *My brother is stronger in the mind. He... can resist the Exalmpora. Although, still, it managed to change him. But out of the three of us, he showed the most restraint. He drank it the slowest.*"

"*Like Sukina,*" I said.

"*Yes, they are very much alike.*"

Now it was me gazing into space. I raised my hand as the sun once again appeared from behind the clouds. I looked back at Francoiso and felt drawn to his handsome face. My body thrumming with desire from the tips of my fingers to those much deeper places. Francoiso opened his eyes.

"*I want you... I want the Exalmpora. I want to become...*"

"*I know exactly how you feel,*" he said and, for the first time since I'd been sober, we kissed. I caught a glimpse of Sukina then, nestled within Charth's arms. Our eyes met and I saw the alarm registering on her face.

"*Resist it, Pontopa,*" she said to me in the collective unconscious.

"*No,*" I said back to her. "*I won't.*"

"*Pontopa, you don't want to become this person. You don't want to lose control.*" I'd never heard Sukina sound angry before. "*We must take Taka, get out of here, and return to the fortress. Charth has made the plans. We'll escape tomorrow.*"

"*No, Sukina. I must pursue my own destiny.*" For the first time in my life, I cut off the channel to her, blocking her out of my thoughts.

THE WHISTLE SOUNDED on the steamship and our boat turned into port. We passed nests of Gatling guns mounted on sandbags on both sides of the river, and the rapids settled a little as the river widened out. A fishing cabin with pier stood between the guns, smoke rising up out of its chimney – real smoke, nothing to do with secicao.

An older man emerged from the hut, six rifles strapped onto his back. These weren't the modern repeater Pattersonis but had a much wider barrel and an antiquated look.

"Those are Gladionos," Francoiso said in my eye. "They're the finest, most accurate, and also the most expensive rifles in the land. They can shoot without faltering from two hundred yards and pack so much of a punch they'll bring down a bear in one shot."

"Kill it?" I asked.

"Depends where you hit the bear," Francoiso said with a cheeky smile. "You don't need worry about that anyway darling." Because my rifle wasn't loaded... Right. Although, in all honesty, I hoped we didn't encounter any bears.

The old man gave us a rifle each and I noticed that mine and Sukina's were a little smaller than those given to the two Lamford Brothers, Alsie and the king. I took hold of it and appreciated its weightiness, it certainly felt like a weapon of power.

Papo had taken me out shooting a few times through the forest back home. I hadn't killed anything, though, hadn't even dared to pull the trigger to be honest. All Papo had brought back from those expeditions was a rabbit and a couple of ducks.

I wondered then how Velos was doing back at the palace. Not strangely, under the influence of Exalmpora, I hadn't thought of him much. If the Exalmpora was indeed turning me part dragon myself, my connection to Velos would probably die a little. But then I started to feel guilty. Velos could be dead by now, for all I knew.

"He's fine," Francoiso said, again in the collective unconscious.

I shook my head. *"What will happen to him if I become a dragonman?"*

"That's for you to decide." The shock realisation came on me that I may become so cruel that I'd kill Velos myself.

No, I wouldn't, surely? But then these Lamford brothers had

killed three Greys back in the Southlands, seemingly without remorse.

"This is no time to think about that," Francoiso said. *"We must focus on the animal you intend to kill this moment, not the great hulking beast we've left behind in the palace."*

"Velos is no beast," I replied.

"As I said, now is not the time." He sounded a little angry. Then his telepathic voice calmed a little. *"Look, we'll talk about this later, okay?"*

"Okay," I said.

Cini was watching the visual exchanges that took place between me and Francoiso, as well as those between Sukina and Charth I knew nothing of. "Dragonseers and dragonmen. Often, I don't know what's going on inside your heads." He looked at Alsie. "I'm not sure I want to know, either. Come, this hunt must begin."

He and Alsie walked into the forest hand in hand, their rifles slung across their backs. Francoiso took my hand. *"Come on, darling. It's time."*

He led me into the thick of the forest. The air out here was cool, with little sunlight poking between the trees: a freshness that reminded me of home. The air smelt of pines and silver birches and the ground had a soft, spongy feel to it. It was hard to believe we were so close to the smog and lifelessness in Slaro where nothing could grow. Hard to believe, in fact, that anything could survive out here.

I kept my rifle close to my chest, and occasionally raised it to aim at passing rabbit or stoat, even though I knew I couldn't shoot them with an unloaded gun.

"We're going to have to find a much larger beast than that if you want to marry me," Francoiso said on one occasion, and he continued to lead us into the forest.

Soon enough the air cooled even more and from between the trees came the sound of a running stream.

"As I remember, there's a glade near here," Francoiso said. *"Usually, water's our best bet."* He kept light on his feet, his purple velvet boots almost making no sound against the floor. Still, he moved fast.

We found the clearing perhaps a minute later, me finding it

difficult to keep up with Francoiso's longer strides. He kept ahead a little and soon raised his hand to still me. *"It's a beauty,"* he said in the collective unconscious while he turned and placed a finger to his lips.

"What is it?" I said back mentally. But I didn't need his reply because I saw the creature's two yellow eyes on the other side of the lake, its long neck lowered into the stream, its antlers creating ripples across the water. A white stag, twice as large as any deer I'd seen in my life. *"We're going to kill that?"*

"Oh, yes," Francoiso said, *"and we shall have a fine feast the night before our wedding."*

"But it's beautiful, majestic.... Magical."

"Come on. You know magic's only a myth."

"Which is why you can turn into a dragon..."

"Because my body allows it. Soon, my darling, yours will too."

I smiled at the thought. Tonight, I would drink more Exalmpora, and we'd feast on white venison and then soon I'd have all the powers Francoiso had. I raised the rifle and sighted in the white stag.

"That's the spirit," Francoiso said. He also raised his rifle. *"Once you pull the trigger, we are technically betrothed."*

Though I had no bullet, I felt the power surge through me. I had the power to take the life of one of this land's most beautiful and rarest creatures, something so majestic and powerful. Was this how it felt to command armies? To know that your orders would result in thousands of innocent deaths.

No, this wasn't me. The Exalmpora... I wanted the Exalmpora. But it had control of me. It had me addicted. Sukina was right, I had to fight this.

"Don't think about it too much, darling," Francoiso said. *"You're much, much more dashing when you're displaying your wild side."*

I bit my lip and sighted down the rifle. The stag raised its head to us, as if aware of the danger. I had only one moment and then it would flee. I pulled the trigger.

My gun bucked and knocked me backwards. Something burrowed itself into the neighbouring tree. The gun had been loaded after all...

The stag turned to run, but Francoiso already had it in his

sights. The bang echoed through the forest. The stag stopped still a moment. Then its legs buckled, and it fell to the floor.

"I'm sorry, darling," Francoiso said. My ears were ringing but I could still hear him in the collective unconscious. *"You're going to have to shoot better than that if we're going to last."* He winked. *"But we shall count that as your kill for the magazines."*

"Thank you," I said, staring at the fallen body, my hands shaking. Now, the whole world will think this was my crime. My triumph. The Exalmpora was turning me into a monster.

But as soon as such despair rose in my mind, a desire quenched it. Exalmpora, I wanted Exalmpora... I would kill for it. I would feast on one of the greatest beasts known to man. I would become stronger. I would become a dragon.

"Francoiso," this was Alsie talking now in the collective conscious. *"You know she's not ready for this yet."*

"Why, Alsie," Francoiso said. *"So, you finally decide to break in on our moment of triumph. Why did you have to include Pontopa in this communication?"*

"Because she has to know what you're doing to her. Dragonseer Wells, if you drink the Exalmpora too fast, you will become a creature governed by emotions. You want her to be a beast like you, Francoiso, but another beast is no good to Finesia."

I licked my lips. *"That's exactly what I want,"* I said. *"To become wild and free."*

"That, you shall not get. Francoiso, you already tested my patience when you decided to kidnap Artua and try to deliver her to Dragonseer Sako, taking the fact she was visiting Tow as an opportunity. Yes, Dragonseer Wells, it's important that you know this, because you should know how dangerous it is cross me."

I struggled to answer back, but while Alsie was speaking here, it was impossible to put word to thought.

"Subsequently," Alsie continued. *"I dragged the two Lamford brothers, as they call themselves, back to the palace and told them I'd kill them with my own claws if they ever tried anything like that again. To keep the king happy, I executed two innocent 'perpetrators', linking their crimes to Fortress Gerhaun in the process. All in a couple of hours work.*

"Now, Francoiso, Dragonseer Wells also knows what I'm capable

of and she has much to fear. So, you will give her the cure after the wedding tomorrow and she will drink it every morning after Cini has given her Exalmpora, until she's ready."

"No," I said. I didn't need Francoiso to speak for me now. *"I'll refuse to drink it."*

"Then we shall battle much sooner than you expected, resulting in your own destruction."

"You wouldn't dare," Francoiso said. *"You're barren yourself and you know how we need another woman to continue the line."*

"There's still Dragonseer Sako. I'm sure she'll be enough."

"Get out of here, Alsie," Francoiso said. *"I'm sick of your empty threats."* He raised his hand to his temple again.

"I've warned you both," Alsie said. Then, I felt her leave the channel.

Francoiso crossed to the other side of the lake to examine the kill. I approached, brashly. Through the forest another shot sounded. I felt Sukina's heart sink. They had also killed something.

"Marvellous," Francoiso said. *"I think we'll be accompanying this feast with a great panther."*

Then came a third a shot, and I knew that Cini and Alsie had killed something too.

26

We slept without eating. Tradition had it that both bride and groom should fast the night before the engagement feast. Cini didn't give us any Exalmpora either. I realized later that this was a test. The king wanted to check for any hints of us not being loyal to him, before he indentured us into court.

This time, given I had time available to think about it, I remembered better how Sukina had taught me to block my thoughts, and I kept myself distanced from my own mind throughout the night. I could constantly feel Alsie trying to get in, prying for any hint of anything that might ruin her plan. I felt Sukina knocking sometimes as well. But I wouldn't let her in either. I didn't want to be dragged away from my desires.

Strangely, as I kept distant from my conscious mind, the urge to take Exalmpora was also beginning to dissipate. Instead, emotions rose up within me: like guilt for not being concerned about Velos and for wanting to kill that white stag. I kept these distant as well. I just wanted, for a moment, to be.

So, I lay on my bed to appreciate the soft warm kiss of the woollen blanket underneath. From through the window, came the faint sulphuric smell of the smog. It was then that the realization dawned on me. Sukina was right. If I let myself succumb to the Exalmpora, then so much I held valuable would be lost. My connection to Velos would die. I'd hardly thought about him the last few days. Then who knows what would happen to my connection to my parents. Instead, I'd lose my will and become a servant to Finesia. It was a terrifying thought.

But that terror could also take reign over me. I remembered the spider that had entered that dark room back at Fortress Gerhaun and, just as I had let that walk over me, I watched my fear walk by. Then, it floated gently away.

I fell asleep and woke the next day to a knock at the door. I knew it wouldn't be Francoiso – I wasn't allowed to see him until the official proposal. Instead, I was surprised to see Sukina there. "Come on, Pontopa." she said. "Get dressed and let's get this proposal out of the way."

She didn't say anything about our escape, which was wise given the guards posted around. Instead, I felt her trying to enter my mind again. But I still wasn't ready. At that point, I didn't quite know what I wanted.

I nodded and went to the wardrobe to find a red engagement dress. Symbolic, they said, of all the blood I had shed before my alleged right to bear children. I probably shouldn't elaborate. I put on the dress. I never thought I'd come to this day. Let alone with a man I didn't want to marry. That was it, I didn't really want to marry Francoiso. Part of me knew that I was throwing my life away.

But then I knew what I did want: Exalmpora. Dragonheats, I thought I'd quelled that urge. But here it was, rising again.

The lace around the dress' bustiere felt surprisingly soft against my skin. The red dress was designed to be the most raucous of all of them, and this one had a plunging neckline underneath the lace and the hemline displayed well over three quarters of my thighs.

If, as tradition said, he was going to back out, then this dress would make it even harder for him to do so. It felt strange to hold Sukina's hand as we walked to King Cini's entertainment pagoda. Especially since she kept tap-tapping on my mind, trying to find a way to speak to me. There was no way I'd let her in, though. I didn't even look at her. But I kept hold of her hand. Etiquette was etiquette and I didn't want King Cini getting suspicious about anything.

At the pagoda, a fine feast awaited us. Our game from the previous hunt would have to wait until the wedding day. But that hadn't stopped King Cini from providing produce from his finest boutique farms. A roasted hog was splayed across the centre of the table and, around it, various canopies so elegantly made they must have each taken hours to construct.

The Lamford brothers sat at either end of the emerald marble table, while the king sat at the side with Alsie, he in his white furs and Alsie wearing a splendid raven dress that matched the colour of her hair. Francoiso looked at me and smiled. He was wearing a navy-blue suit that even Faso would have envied. Charth had the same suit, but somehow it didn't hang off his hunched posture quite so well.

Of course, the same golden and silver teapots lay on the table and I eyed the silver one with thirst. I would kill to drink that Exalmpora. I'd take down everyone in this room or die doing so.

But still I was a lady and had to show some restraint.

I stepped forward and sat next to Francoiso. He planted a kiss upon my lips. The king bowed to me and then poured me a cup of Exalmpora. I took it down in one and then the hunger subsided. I felt complete again and my muscles seemed to writhe and twist underneath my dress.

Alsie turned her eyes on me. I could tell from her expression that she had something that she deemed important. It looked almost like a challenge. That was enough to get me curious, so I let her in.

"You're taking this too far, wench," she said. *"I hope you heed my warnings and drink your cure tomorrow, like a loyal subject."*

"I'll decide on my own destiny," I answered back.

"Then I shall have to force the vial whole down your throat until you learn. You shall not disobey the will of Finesia."

Alsie's eyes were already regarding Sukina who drank from the cup in more refined motions. Their gazes met, locked on to each other and a tension rippled through the collective unconscious, as if someone had just pulled something tight around my heart.

"If you doubt my power, then hear this," Alsie said to me in my mind and I felt another channel open up. I tried to push it away, but now I had no control.

"Dragonseer Sako," Alsie said. *"I know already of your plans to*

escape. You think you can plot in your channels with your old lover. But you can't hide these things from me."

"I don't know who you think you are," Sukina replied mentally, because she was in there too. *"But my daughter has never been yours."*

"Not mine... Finesia's. Don't you know, woman? I'm not just Cini's but Finesia's right hand. Now, it's only a matter of days until the transition becomes complete and then Artua will also become powerful. He'll lose his ability to be a dragonseer and gain something far, far greater. Someone, Dragonseer Sako, of which you can be proud."

"You're a sociopath."

Alsie scowled. *"You have two options, Dragonseer Sako. Do as Finesia wills or die. If your suitor tries helping you anymore, I've already let him know how that will end... There is no other way. I don't care about morals, and I don't care about how Charth feels we should have treated Artua. So, you will stop resisting the Exalmpora, just as Dragonseer Wells here must learn to resist more."*

Sukina shook her head then tipped the liquid into her mouth. Her pupils dilated and I felt her train of thought vanish a little. Or was she just hiding it?

Artua appeared at the base of the pagoda, again wearing a suit. Without looking at either of us, he sat down next to Alsie. His eyes were hazy, as if the life had been sucked out of him. Alsie produced a thimble and raised it too his lips.

"Thank you, Ma'am," Artua said. He looked at me and a sly smile spread across his face. "I can see you're enjoying this, Dragonseer Wells, and I wanted to extend my congratulations." He sounded so much more mature now, as if he was growing up too fast.

Artua turned to Sukina. But there wasn't a look of recognition like the other day. Alsie had done something to him to sap away his spirit. How much Exalmpora had it taken to numb his or her senses?

Yet, I somehow approved.

"And Dragonseer Sako, congratulations," Artua continued. "I see the Exalmpora is also turning you into a fine woman."

Cold, as if the blood relationship between them didn't exist. As if she'd never given birth to him. The Exalmpora had moulded him into a different form.

But Sukina didn't show any remorse. Either she was a good actress, or she was more far gone than it seemed. "Thank you, young man. I'm sure you'll make a fine dragonman yourself."

"I will," Artua said. "Alsie says I have great potential."

"You do, young man. You do."

"Wait a minute, Alsie," I asked in the channel, which was still open. *"Why are you forcing Artua to drink the Exalmpora every day if it's so dangerous for me?"*

"Because Artua is a child and children break down Exalmpora quicker than adults. If he doesn't drink it every day, it won't have the desired effect on him. I know what Finesia wills, Dragonseer Wells, and I urge you not to question my intentions again…"

She then coughed out loud and Artua sat up straight in his chair and shut up. Alsie took hold of a carving knife and fork and began to carve the hog. "Shouldn't that be a man's job?" I said to Francoiso out loud, with a punch to his shoulder.

"Oh, no, no," Francoiso replied with a wink. "Alsie always likes to take control."

I hate to admit it, but she carved so elegantly. Under the control of the Exalmpora, I found myself for the first time admiring her. It wasn't as if the dress moulded around her, but her form moulded to the dress, as if with every movement she transformed into a slightly new shape. Her eyes focused on the knife as she carved with such intensity that it almost seemed a weapon of war.

I could sense great power in her. Even greater than the power that I sensed in Sukina. But with Sukina, when I'd first met her, I wanted to know more about her. I felt a connection to her, and I loved her stories.

Yet, with Alsie what I felt was a need to gain her power and become even more powerful than her. I wanted her control over the king. I wanted that ability she had to control everything around her.

She looked up at me then, and for the first time, I saw her smile. *"Not yet",* she said in the collective unconscious. *"We will one day battle and fate itself will determine who wins."*

I bared my teeth at her, because I hoped this fight would be sooner rather than later.

Soon the meat was cut, and we all tucked into our food. We drank copious amounts of Exalmpora, and I once again became tugged into the warm liquid's embrace. Underneath my skin, a different type of transformation was also starting to occur. I was warping into a new being, something far, far more powerful than anything I'd ever known.

"How long does it take to become a dragonman?" I asked Francoiso out loud, just after I'd breathed in his long and passionate kiss.

"That depends on your abilities entirely. For me it took a month, for Alsie, half a year. For Charth... Well, I'm not sure he's even reached it yet."

Francoiso threw a joking smile to his brother.

"Oh, but he's a fine specimen," Sukina said slurred. "Don't you think, Artua?"

But the boy didn't answer. Instead he was staring out at a full moon that shone through the thick smog.

"Enough, enough," King Cini said. He was standing now and tapping a fork against his wine glass. "Francoiso and Charth, you know why we gathered here tonight. Now, it's time to make your destined moves."

"Yes, yes, of course," Francoiso said and he stood up abruptly. He turned to face me, went down on one knee, and produced a ring from his inside pocket. "Marry me, gorgeous," he said.

I took the ring and put it on my finger. "Of course," I said.

The king and Alsie started to clap. Artua joined in, but he still gazed off into the distance as if his hands were disengaged from his brain.

Charth stood up a lot slower and with much more grace than Francoiso. He lowered himself on to one knee and took Sukina's hand in his. As he produced his ring, he kept his gaze on Sukina's.

"Sukina Sako," Charth said. "We've met once again, and we've fallen in love once again. Until death do us part, I shall protect you. Marry me, Sukina."

Sukina gave Charth a curt nod. "Yes," she said.

Then she leaned out to give Charth a more modest, softer kiss.

"So, it is done," King Cini raised his voice over the applause. "The dragonseers and the Lamford brothers are betrothed and you will finely adorn our court. Now, all return to your chambers, and rest well, for tomorrow the celebrations truly begin."

Francoiso pulled away from me, but I still kept hold of his hand for as long as my arm would reach. *"I can't wait, darling,"* he said in the collective unconscious. I knew he wasn't talking about the wedding.

It felt like everything had once again changed. Now drunk on the Exalmpora, I really wanted the wedding. In just under a day now, I would go to Francoiso's bedchamber and we'd have a night of passion as two wild beasts, free of rationality and full of desire.

27

I woke to a throbbing headache. I thought I had the Exalmpora under control now. Clearly, I'd drunk much more the previous night than any other night. Today, I would get married and to that handsome man of my dreams. We would multiply and create a new race of Finesia's servants. Though I hadn't yet heard Finesia's voice, I could feel her spirit pulsing through my blood.

So, despite the hangover, I sprang out of bed and went straight to the wardrobe. I looked there this time to discover a beautiful wedding dress of the finest woven whites. Full of lace and frills and shining with faint traces of silver.

I washed myself in the basin and found some perfume waiting for me on the sink. I reached out for the bottle, my eyes still a little blurry from the celebrations the night before. Alsie's voice sounded in my head.

"This time, wench, I delivered it myself."

Dragonheats, I wish I could keep that woman out of my mind.

But I didn't know what she was talking about, until I looked down at the perfume bottle and saw a tiny green vial lodged inside. Another cure... I didn't want it. No, I wanted the effects of the Exalmpora, and I wanted Francoiso tonight, and I wanted to kill Alsie.

"Block it." I don't know if it was really Sukina who said that to

me, or just her imagined voice in my head. But it had such authority that all my desires became suddenly forgotten.

Instead, I felt a stillness inside of me, as if hypnotised. What I did next was automatic, yet I was also completely aware of every action I took. A deep inner part of me reached down into the bottle and took hold of the vial, uncorked it, tipped the contents into my mouth.

"I don't want it. I don't want it." The thoughts echoed around my mind, trying to regain control. Yet these were secondary. Distant. I swallowed the cure and a sense of release washed over me.

I no longer felt transformed and the muscles in my body seemed to return to their normal shape. Waves of calm pulsated through my body, as if I had submerged myself in a warm and salty sea.

"Good," Alsie's voice came again. She had been watching all this time. *"I now see you're starting to learn. Every day I will reduce the amount in the cure until you're ready to become a rational, yet still loyal, servant of Finesia. Though the process may seem progressive, the transition will happen overnight. As you shall soon see with Artua."*

Then, I felt Alsie leave my mind and I knew once again I was alone. I gritted my teeth, walked back to the wardrobe, and put the dress on.

As I dressed, the truth entered my head, in a place far out of reach of Francoiso and Alsie. I didn't want to marry today, but I had to fool the king. Rescuing Artua was of crucial importance. He still had something of a dragonseer within him and he could be of great help to Gerhaun.

Another thing became obvious too. It was as if nullifying the desire introduced by the Exalmpora freed my mind to think clearly again. I realised that the only reason Sukina had kept me out of her plans, was because I hadn't yet learned to block people out.

I was missing something. I looked in the wardrobe and there I found the other half of my wedding outfit. A traditional calico blue and white chequered outer dress. Heavy, and large enough that it would fit over the wedding dress. I put this on then left my room.

Three bridesmaids in long salmon-coloured dresses and pink bows in their blond hair were waiting outside the door. The king had selected the ladies, from who knows where, who looked remarkably similar to me. Another tradition for those who could afford it. If Francoiso was to lay a lustful gaze on any of them, I was allowed to slap him in the face and leave him on the spot.

The bridesmaids led me to the throne room, and we met up with Sukina and her bridesmaids at the corridor. With Sukina's oriental look, her entourage must have been even more expensive to source than mine. Sukina looked absolutely stunning, with a single long hairpin clipped through her hair, eyebrow extensions that brought out the almond shape of her eyes. The train of her long dress fell far below the hemline of her red and white calico over-dress. The wedding dress itself was one long straight cloth, with a surprising lack of frills.

When Sukina saw me looking at her, pride registered in her eyes. She knew, I guess, that I'd managed to push all the angst away from the previous days. The connection I shared with her was enough for me to know that tonight we would make our escape. I didn't even need to register the thought.

Today, the guards would be so drunk and Cini would least expect our disloyalty. If we were going to back out already, we'd have surely done so well before the wedding.

"You look beautiful," I said to Sukina as we walked side by side towards the makeup room, because there was still a lot to be done.

"You too, dear," Sukina said. "You've made me so proud, Drag-onseer Wells."

I knew those words were dangerous. But they also caused my heart to flutter in my chest. I didn't really want the Exalmpora and I didn't really want Francoiso. I wanted to be a dragonseer and fight for Gerhaun. My behaviour the previous days had only been down to chemicals. Nothing else. I was stronger than those chemicals. I was stronger than secicao.

I won't go into too many details about the makeup session. Let's just say it was long and tedious, and great care had to be put in to make each of the bridesmaids look even more like me and Sukina.

Afterwards, Master Artua was waiting for us outside the throne room. He wore this cute little suit and dickie bow that made him look four years older. His hair had been swept down in a bob cut, which somehow highlighted Sukina's high cheekbones on his face. Today, there was no doubt who his mother was.

"Hurry, Miss Wells, Mamo," he said. "You'll be late." At the word Mamo, I felt Sukina's heart melt within her chest.

Artua gave us some flowers – I had buttercups and Sukina had daisies – to put in our hair. Two redguards opened the door for us then each of them curtsied to reveal the throne room before us.

The king sat on the throne with Francoiso and Charth in front of him, their backs turned to us. Alsie stood on the king's right-hand side. The rest of the seats were filled with all kinds of people I recognised from the newspapers – entrepreneurs, royal family members, the king's famous seamstress, the king's mother even who, apparently, rarely got out of bed. Guards flanked the room in the traditional manner.

I never thought I'd have a wedding this grand. Yet, at the back of my mind, I also knew I couldn't take such a wedding seriously when I was marrying under duress.

Heads turned towards us as Artua led us down the aisle, carrying two rings on a silken red cushion. The bridesmaids walked between him and us and, at the front, Charth and Francoiso turned their heads towards us. Only Francoiso smiled, but Charth's eyes when they turned on Sukina reflected true sincerity. It could almost be called love.

Or, maybe, they just had something planned.

Before we did the honours with the vows, Alsie stepped forward and produced a hip flask from her waist. She handed this to me first. "*Exalmpora, of course,*" she said in the collective unconscious. Traditionally, we were meant to drink dessert wine, but absolutely no one in congregation would know what was in the flask. "*Drink a good swig and make sure you have enough to convince the king you want to do this. He's suspicious enough as it is.*"

"*Oh, I want this*", I said. But I didn't tell her what *this* was. I took hold of the flask and tipped my head back, so it looked like I was taking a huge swig. Part of me wanted to take down the contents in one. But I willed myself to resist. Instead, I angled the flask so very little would tip into my mouth.

But Alsie grasped my hair, pulled it back, and kept the flask there so I was forced to swallow more. I heard a gasp from the audience. It's not as if I could spit this stuff out, as that would be a clear refusal of the marriage. So, I let ecstasy and oblivion wash over me once again and I let myself bend to the will of Finesia.

"That's it," Alsie said, out loud this time. Then she added in the collective unconscious, "*You will do our Empress proud.*"

I turned around and faced the congregation so they could see that I'd indeed swallowed the liquid. Their expressions turned from shock to laughter and they gave me a huge round of applause as I offered a comical bow. Meanwhile, I felt my body morphing underneath my skin again. I almost wanted to bite at the air and roar.

"*Resist it.*" A voice said at the back of my head. But no, it was so good and now I would marry Francoiso. We'd drink more and then he'd lead me to his bedchamber and the rest would be history.

Alsie marched over to Sukina with the hip flask, with the pomposity of an Empress herself. Sukina didn't try resisting like I did, so Alsie didn't have to force the Exalmpora down. In retrospect, it was a little foolish of me to show resistance. It could have given the game away to Cini and made him suspect even more. Again, Sukina turned to the congregation and gained an equal round of applause. The king then stepped forward to address them.

Before Cini performed the ceremony, he walked up to Alsie with an air of urgency to say something to her. Alsie didn't look so impressed, and I could hear enough of the conversation to make out something about a revolt in the northern provinces and that the Lamford Brothers were obviously engaged.

I felt a channel open then in collective unconscious. There were three of us then – me, Sukina and Alsie.

"*I hoped I could be around to make sure you performed your duties,*" Alsie said. "*But for now, I have to go away on business. I shall return soon and if I learn you've attempted anything against King Cini's wishes, then there will be severe consequences.*"

Then there was a puff of smoke, a gust of wind that caused a murmur from the congregation, and Alsie was gone up the chimney. In all honesty, I didn't want to escape. I just wanted to get this over with so I could accompany Francoiso to his bedchamber.

But I had a wait ahead of me. Cini looked up for a moment, then turned back to the congregation. He then gave a long and boring speech, telling us how dragonseers and Tow used to be enemies. His father before him wanted to exterminate us. But now, dragonseers and Tow had allied and could live together as one. This marriage was not just any old royal marriage, it was symbolic of a significant change in the war effort, where Tow would finally take control of the Southlands and have access to all the secicao that mankind would need. Then he instructed both Francoiso and Charth to put the rings upon our fingers and then it was time to start the good stuff.

"Let's start with the youngest couple, shall we?" he said. He turned to me and Francoiso. The moment I – or at least Exalmpora-addled I – had been waiting for. "Francoiso, you may now kiss the bride."

I melted into Francoiso's arms, and he pulled me close to him. "Finally, darling. These last days have seemed like they've lasted for months."

He opened his mouth and wrapped his lips around mine. I felt the warmth of his breath and something even further down rising. I couldn't wait.

The king ahem-ed and gave an uncomfortable laugh. "Now, now, Francoiso. In less polite company I'd allow this, but please show at least a modicum of respect."

Francoiso pulled away, as would a sulky child. "As you wish," he said. But he still kept hold of my hand and started playing with the skin there in an incredibly suggestive way.

"Charth," King Cini said turning to the other couple. "Do you take Miss Sako to be your lawful wedded wife."

"I do," Charth said. "Under my protection, always."

"Good," King Cini said. "So, you also may now kiss the bride."

Even though the Exalmpora had control of my mind, I felt Charth's kiss, or at least I felt the rush of dopamine as his lips closed over Sukina's. Sukina had also somehow become smitten with Charth, although that might have been the Exalmpora talking. Now we had that subconscious connection between us, no drug, even Exalmpora, could break it.

"Well, well. Now you're both married, you can do the honours and enter royal society."

I turned around so Francoiso could undo the buttons of my calico over-dress from the back. He slid this off my shoulders and his hands kept close to my waist and buttocks as he pulled this down in front of everyone. The white dress that was revealed shone in the torchlight, making me feel very much like a princess. As, I stepped out of the over-dress, I caught a glimpse over my shoulder of Sukina who looked equally stunning. I turned to kiss Francoiso once again.

"Well, well," Cini said. "Now that's done, let us begin our celebrations."

The pages, then Artua, then Sukina, I and our partners, followed by the bridesmaids walked down the aisle. As we walked, Artua turned to us. I felt him establish a channel in the collective unconscious. I guess, now Alsie had gone away, he felt free to do so.

"Mamo, Auntie Pontopa. What's a dragonseer?" he said.

I looked at Sukina, surprised. But Sukina simply looked down at Artua and smiled. *"I'll tell you soon, dear, I promise,"* she said in our minds. We walked out towards the banquet hall.

THE ONLY THING we were allowed to drink during the celebrations was Exalmpora, although the king had cleverly disguised it with food colouring, so it looked like red wine, for the benefit of all the guests around us. I'd never quite tasted meat as rich as white stag or black panther. The panther tasted like a richer version of rabbit, although with a much smoother texture. I'd had venison before but nothing that settled on the tongue so well as this perfectly marinated white stag, cooked in cashew nuts, mustard, and honey. I honestly didn't want to eat anything else than meat that night.

We sat at the long head table, with the king at the centre. Artua sat next to Cini. Charth and Sukina sat at the king's right and Francoiso and I on his left. The rest of the guests had taken large circular tables draped with silk tablecloths. We sat within a huge banquet hall, as opulent with cold white marble as the rest of the palace.

I knew many of the guest's faces from the magazines, yet I'd never spoken to any of them. It felt so strange in a way to be part of a wedding without my parents or any of my old-time friends.

Soon though, I'd had enough Exalmpora that I forgot about them entirely. King Cini also seemed merry on his own wine, too much that I don't think he had the clarity of mind to suspect us of anything after all.

Day flowed into night and Francoiso took hold of my hand and led me to his bedchamber. While I had been staying in that tiny room the king had reserved a room for us fit for a king. With several metres between each of the walls and a four-poster bed right in the centre. The torches around the walls had red silk curtains hanging just in front of them, far enough away from the walls as not to catch on fire, but close enough to diffuse the room in a soft red light.

I was all over Francoiso as soon as I entered the room, my whole body thrumming with passion. But he didn't melt into my touch, and instead seemed kind of wooden.

"Pontopa, I've been thinking," he said in the collective unconscious.

"Thinking? I thought you were the one without the rational mind." I ran kisses down his neck as I fondled his chest.

But he pulled away from me a little. *"No,"* he said. *"Charth is right. You're not yourself, Pontopa, and I don't want to take advantage of you. I've wanted this so much. But I want to know you really want it as well. Without the Exalmpora."*

"Oh, but this is absolutely what I want. Without a doubt." I pushed myself closer to him as he backed up against the bed. There was nowhere for him to go and so I wrapped one arm around him and with the other, I began to undo my dress.

"Pontopa, don't do this." Francoiso said. *"You have to understand. The Exalmpora. Back then, it changed me... I'm not entirely in control."*

"Then that is what we both want, to be wild and free, right?" I lowered my cleavage and then pushed myself up against him. I had strength in my muscles then, powered by something inhuman. I used it to push Francoiso down onto the bed.

This time, I wasn't going to stop. I wanted this too much. I could feel every inch of my body morphing into something else. My skin pinching and the muscles writhing underneath.

"Pontopa—" Francoiso said. Then he changed. His eyes glazed out and his pupils dilated. *"You're right, this is exactly what I want."* With those words, that vestige of the rational part of Francoiso was lost.

My hair felt like it was on fire. As if each single strand wanted to retract back into the roots. It was painful, but I didn't hate the pain. No, I relished it. Francoiso also started to deform. His nose pulled out of his face. Black scales started to peel down his cheeks. His voice became deeper.

"Come darling. Come and show me what you're made of."

I laughed, now this was the Francoiso I wanted. I launched myself on top of him. My hands landed on either side of his hips. He looked up at me then, scales protruding from out of his eyebrows, he opened his mouth and pulled me close to him.

His breath wasn't just warm but hot. As if he was breathing fire into my very mouth. But it didn't sear, as a protective layer of scales already guarded against the hotness at the roof of my mouth and tongue. I could taste the saltiness on his scaly tongue, and I could also feel its roughness.

Besides us, the door slammed open and I jerked my head around to see both Charth and Sukina standing there. "Francoiso, you shall not!" he snapped.

Francoiso turned his head to him. "Come for the show, have you brother? I never knew you to be such a peeping Tom." He flipped me over on the bed, so he was on top of me. Then, he pulled down his trousers so all I could see was his briefs.

I was panting like a wild animal. Ready for anything, despite the company. Dragonheats, I relished in the company. Let them join in, for all I cared.

Charth threw his head to the sky and roared. Scales shot out of his arms and face. He leaped at his brother and knocked him off the bed.

I looked at both of them wrestling for a moment and huffed. Sukina had a vial of something in her hand and she approached me with it. That hideous thing: no, I wasn't going to drink it. I wasn't going to let them ruin the moment.

I launched myself at her, a deep growl emanating from my chest. I took hold of her neck and pinned her against the wall. Her eyes went wide, and her face went pale. She dropped the cure and it smashed against the floor.

"Pontopa, you—" I was strangling her so much, she couldn't get another word in. She continued to speak in the collective unconscious. *"Pontopa, this isn't you. The Examplora. Don't let it control you. Stop, Pontopa, stop!"*

But her thoughts began to fade. At that point, I felt, she deserved to die. She would never be a dragonwoman like me. She didn't have what it takes. I had to kill her then or destroy my chances of ever gaining the power I'd need to kill Alsie.

Such thoughts were spinning around my mind as the Exalmpora kept control of my brain. This wasn't me speaking. This was Finesia planting her soul into my mind.

I tightened my grip on Sukina's neck.

"Pontopa, this isn't you. Control yourself. Conquer within. Distance yourself. Remember... Remember."

I felt Sukina's life slipping out of her. I raised my head and roared in ecstasy. My dress had ripped at the arms and beneath them I could see the rows of scales. Just one more squeeze and I would crack Sukina's life out her neck. Power surged to my claws.

Something slammed into my side and knocked me to the ground. I looked up into the eyes and maw of a black dragon. The features softened and beneath them I expected to see Charth.

But instead, I saw Francoiso's scaly face. Fear looking out of those beastly blue eyes.

"I can't let you do this, darling," he said. "Oh, Finesia will kill me, but my brother is right. I don't want you to become a monster like myself."

"No!" I screamed. "Let me go... This is my will!"

But Francoiso had me pinned. I lunged out in attempt to bite at his neck, wanting to take his life for being such a traitor. But he had me held down too strongly. He took hold of a green vial from his inside pocket, gave my cheeks a squeeze and tipped the contents down my throat.

He turned back to Charth who was standing there, back in human form. "I did it, brother," he said. "But you know what this means."

"Alsie will hunt us down for life," he said. "But this is right thing."

"Yet, even combined, we don't even have a chance to match her strength."

I felt myself losing strength as well. While I felt almost capable of throwing Francoiso off me before, now it felt like I had a whole building pinning me down. Francoiso looked into my eyes a moment. Now the gaze wasn't lustful but assessing. "She's safe," he said. "Pontopa, I'm sorry…"

He looked a different man now. I didn't feel a desire for him anymore. He was like a painting you would admire in an art gallery. Handsome, but I really didn't know what was underneath those layers of paint.

"I'm sorry too," I said. For the first time, I understood. Francoiso's soul had been destroyed by a drug, but there still remained a decent part of him.

"Come," Charth said. "We have to get out before Alsie gets here."

"You know where she is?" I asked.

"No, but she's already on her way."

"Don't forget about Faso," Sukina said.

"And Velos," I pointed out. I felt guilty already that I'd forgotten about my best friend in the whole wide world.

"Velos is your escape plan. And the boy, we'll help you rescue him too."

"My daughter," Sukina said. "Thank you."

"Your son now," Charth said. "Come." He led us out into the corridor, and we navigated our way out of the palace under cover of dark.

Fortunately, most of the guards would be sleeping off the alcohol and so there would be little that could disturb our escape. Or so we hoped. But, unfortunately, we were about to be proven terribly wrong.

28

The Lamford Brothers split up once we reached a fork in the corridors. Charth promised that he would go and get Faso. But first, we stopped to take stock of the situation. We'd already retrieved our original changes of clothes from our wardrobes and our hip flasks and weapons (including Sukina's daggers) from one of the king's storage rooms.

"We've not got much time," Francoiso said. "Oh, Pontopa, how I wish we'd done this differently."

My eyes had adjusted to the darkness now and I could faintly make out the outline of his muscular form. "Maybe we could under different circumstances," I said. If he left the palace, stopped supporting Cini's war effort, joined us at Fortress Gerhaun, and proved himself a true hero. Maybe then there could be something there... Maybe.

"My brother and I are going to have to hide after this," Francoiso said.

"But where would you go?"

"Tell you and I'll also put your own life at risk." I guess Francoiso also realised I hadn't yet learned how to consistently mask my thoughts.

"I never quite understood why you decided to help us in the first place."

It was Charth who answered this time. "I promised a long time ago that I'd protect Sukina's daughter. But I failed her when I let Alsie and Cini feed the boy the Exalmpora. It was wrong to try and take away his free will. And..." Charth looked at Sukina. "I love you, Sukina, and I have since the first time I met you. I'm sorry, that I failed."

Sukina nodded, but her face stayed straight. "I understand," she said. "But you never failed."

"Thank you," Charth said. He walked away.

Then I turned to Francoiso. "So, what's in it for you?"

Francoiso smiled. "I'm doing this to help out my brother – once sister – of course. Because, after all, isn't that what family does? Not to mention, I really, really hate Alsie... Stunning as she may be."

Then he beckoned us onwards and he led to us towards Artua. We reached Master Artua's room and opened the door. A torch was lit inside, suffusing the tiny room with red light. There were no toys in there – only a bed and a fireplace. Honestly, it was like a prison cell. How could this boy have been said to have a childhood? Was this how they'd been keeping him all this time?

Artua had already packed his things into a little haversack that he had over his shoulder. He wore flexible brown cotton trousers and a loose shirt, clearly ready for riding. An empty vial lay on the bed, traced at the edges with specks of green.

"Mamo," Artua said and he flung himself into Sukina's arms.

Again, Sukina's eyes were full of tears. "We're getting you out of here, Taka," she said.

Artua crinkled his nose. "Isn't Taka a girl's name? I don't want to be a girl."

Sukina smiled. "Then we shall call you Artua from now on, if that's what you want to be called. All that matters is that you're finally going home."

From every single room we passed, out emanated a sound of snoring. Even the guards we found standing at their posts were audibly half asleep. Fortunately, Artua was light enough on his feet that we didn't end up waking anyone. Although, I'm sure any guards we did wake would be no match for Francoiso, or Sukina for that matter.

Once we got there, we found the palace's raised airfield

deserted. Velos was also sleeping there. I'd half expected to see him in chains. Without them, I really didn't understand what had kept him there. The number of times I'd broken my connection to him and given myself to the Exalmpora. If I were him, I would have flown away. But I guess Velos was too loyal for that. Cini must have realised that there was absolutely no way he would leave without me.

His armour was on him still, gleaming in the faint light from the crescent moon that shone faintly through the secicao clouds. As I approached Velos, I realised the reason he hadn't roused yet. He wasn't dreaming like he usually would. No, somehow the king had drugged him unconscious. Perhaps they had also fed him Exalmpora, wondering what the effects might be on a dragon.

"I can't wake him," I said to Sukina.

"I don't know a way, either," Sukina said. "If I had a connection then I could sing a song, but it's not there."

But he was still breathing fortunately. I could see he wasn't dead. The moon disappeared behind a cloud and the airfield plunged into darkness save for the raised oil lamps that limned its perimeter.

"Any ideas, Francoiso?" I asked.

He shook his head.

"Wait, I think I know something," I said. I remembered that dragonsong that had come to me after Faso had installed the armour, when I sat outside drinking that bottle of brandy. I knew then, why I'd chosen that particularly song. It had within its notes the power to wake a dragon. But not just any dragon, this one was special for Velos. If the sleepiness hadn't cut me off mid-song, I might have woken him out of his armour-induced coma sooner.

I sang the notes as I remembered them. A lilting harmony that didn't make melodic sense, but still stirred Velos' emotions. Like before, I found myself entering Velos' dreams. I saw the Greys in my mind's eye, none of them wanting to associate with Velos. I felt Velos' estrangement then. With it, I wanted to drift off to sleep.

But then I used the skills I'd used to mask my thoughts. I distanced these images in my mind and watched them from afar. I felt no longer tired. In doing so, I could complete the song, which roused Velos from this heavy, sedative-induced sleep. He let out a huge roar that shook the walls of the palace.

"Well, that will wake the guards," Sukina said.

"Yes," Francoiso said. "I'm sorry to say that there's a good chance Alsie heard it too."

"From that distance?" I asked.

"Yes... Her senses are, shall we say, pretty acute."

I looked at Velos anxiously. I really wanted to take off. "I hope Charth and Faso get here soon," I said.

"Who's Faso?"

Sukina hesitated. "He's someone very important to us, dear. Charth's bringing him to us." She held Artua close to him. "He'll be here soon."

"Ooh, goodie," Artua said. "Are Charth and Francoiso coming with us too? Charth's been telling us about our adventure to the Southlands. Am I really going to meet a dragon queen?"

"You will, dear. As soon as Faso gets here."

Then she said in the collective unconscious, keeping the channel open so Francoiso and I could also hear. "*What's holding you, Charth?*"

But there was no response, or at least not in the collective unconscious. Instead, another voice floated across to us from the direction of the north staircase.

"My, my, I thought I smelled treason in the air," King Cini stepped out from the stairway, eight guards flanking him. "After Alsie had informed me that everything would go so smoothly tonight."

The guards kept their rifles trained on us. I could tell from the faint green glow from their skin that they were augmented, which probably would also have knocked away any effects of the alcohol.

"I guess this will look great in the magazines," Cini continued. "Turns out that dragonseers could never be trusted after all and my father did the perfectly right thing by executing as many as he could find. So, tell me. How, my dear dragonseers, are you going to get out of this one now?"

I noticed that three of the guards, wisely, had their rifles pointed at Francoiso. Even if he attacked one of them, I didn't think he'd stand a good chance at taking the other two down. Hence, he stayed put.

Suddenly, two of the guards turned their rifles towards the back of the stairway. I hazarded a look over my shoulder to see Faso coming up the stairs with Ratter on his shoulder. Surprisingly, Charth was nowhere to be seen.

"Mr Gordoni," King Cini said. "Who ever thought that you'd come to join the party. Why don't you go to stand with your friends there? Oh, and Francoiso, where's your brother? I'm sure he has more of a play in this game than you. I've never trusted that man... Or should I say, woman..."

Francoiso's jaw tightened. "I've always thought you talk too much, Cini..."

"I've always thought you show off your teeth too much. You never seemed to realise that your job within this court is not to sell toothpaste."

"And your job is not to sell face whitening powder."

Cini scowled. He turned to one of his guards. "Enough of this tomfoolery. Seize them."

The guard nodded then took a step forward.

"Wait," Sukina said. Her face now looked blanched. "I stand for all my friends here. By the laws passed down through the kingdom, you must be able to best me in a duel, if challenged."

"Sukina, no—" I said.

"We don't have a choice," Sukina said. "*I can take him,*" she added in the collective unconscious.

"No!" Francoiso said out loud. He stepped forwards. "I should be doing this."

King Cini laughed from the bottom of his belly. "I think the law states that I have to duel another human. But I shall not lose face to a woman. You do realise, Miss Sako, that the king's secicao is the best in the land. Only Alsie and I know the formula." He displayed his hip flask.

"I realise all," Sukina said and raised her hip flask. "You shall not win."

"Oh, but I'm the king," Cini said. "Which means I shall."

He took a swig from his hip flask. His skin turned a deep luminous green and cracks traced the length of his skin, hardening it like tree bark. Sukina also took a swig from her hip flask, drew her two daggers from her garters, and lurched forward. I was glad to see Charth had thought to return them to her. Simultaneously, King Cini drew his broadsword from his shoulder and readied himself in a defensive stance.

Sukina's daggers met the king's sword, and an impressive display of flashing steel began. Sukina was quick with her lurches and feints, and her daggers did meet Cini's skin a few times. But, due to the effects of secicao, the blows glanced off, leaving not even a scratch. Cini responded with huge swings of his broadsword, but Sukina was agile and ducked out of the way.

Yet she couldn't keep this up forever. The king would tire her out eventually then he'd take her life. "Can't you do something, Francoiso?" I said.

"She's got this," Francoiso said. "Just you watch."

Cini had Sukina back up against an airship now. She leaned right against the propeller and if the king wanted to play dirty, he could order one of her guards to turn on the engine and slice her into pieces. His mouth displayed a rictus of ecstasy as he swung in such broad and low sweeps that Sukina had nowhere to go.

But Sukina looked calm, as if waiting for something. She just needed that moment, for the king to make one mistake. He made it as he swept his sword a little too low. Sukina cartwheeled over the sword, then in a beautiful dance-like movement sprang back on her legs and cut up her arms so her knife was around Cini's throat.

There, the skin would be softest, I realised, and she could slice through that thick bark-like skin and the cartilage beneath. But before she could do so, a shrill scream echoed through the collective unconscious.

In a flash of scales and wings, Alsie landed in dragon form in front of Cini. She sucked in her scales and immediately became human. "You fool, Cini. You thought you could best a dragonseer."

In her hand, as if out of nowhere, she produced a dart and launched it at Sukina. The dart buried itself in Sukina's throat and she dropped her daggers, stumbled, then collapsed on to her knees.

"Mamo!" Artua shouted. He moved towards Sukina, but I held him back.

"It's not safe, Artua," I said.

Alsie's eyes turned upon me and I could see death within them. Clearly, I was next. Her face contorted towards dragon form and she lurched forward. I waited for the blow, but another black form leapt towards her.

Francoiso's form was contorting from human into dragon. Together, Alsie and he tumbled over the ground. Francoiso ended up on top, scales and shards ripping out of him. Alsie had completely transformed at this point and a battle of growls and anger ensued as both black dragons bit at each other's necks.

Faso had also placed Ratter on the floor and the automaton had scurried forwards to release a green gas that had the guards clutching at their eyes and coughing. Cini took one look around him and then turned and fled through the cloud. Ratter turned upon him and hissed as he went by, but neither Ratter nor the gas could stop Cini from launching himself off the platform. He hit the ground below with a heavy thud then ran towards the palace.

"Get out of here," Sukina said in the collective unconscious. *"Pontopa, go."*

"Sukina, no!"

"You must protect my daughter. That's your mission, you hear me? Now go."

"Sukina—"

"Dragonheats, do as I say, Pontopa! You have no time to save me."

Alsie's dragon form was slightly browner than Francoiso's and so I could distinguish the two easily. Alsie now was on top of Francoiso and had him pinned to the ground.

"Sukina, I'll come back for you." I took hold of Artua's hand. "Come on, little one. We'll pick your mother up in a moment."

I pushed him up the ladder into Sukina's chair and then I ran up Velos' neck to take my position at the front.

"Wait for me," Faso shouted, and he scrambled up the ladder towards Velos' back. He whistled through his fingers and Ratter darted up Velos' neck with unbecoming speed for his size. "You need someone to look after the armour, don't you?" Faso said.

For the first time, I appreciated the fact that Faso was there. Velos lifted his head and roared to the sky, then without me having to will him onwards, he launched himself into the air. "Damn it,"

Faso shouted. "They siphoned the armour dry. We must get more fuel for the guns to work."

"No time," I shouted back, and I circled the air to see if there was a chance to pick up Sukina. But the clouds had subsided, and the guards already had their rifles aimed.

"Get out of here," Faso shouted. "Fast!"

I sighed then turned Velos to the south. I looked over my shoulder then, at Sukina lying there and Francoiso who was now pinned underneath Alsie. Francoiso's scales were a little greyer than Alsie's, and Alsie had the much larger form. She had reared back her head and then I saw her maw shoot forwards and close around Francoiso's long neck. The collective unconscious shook, and I felt a part of my mind torn away.

Just like that, Francoiso was gone...

Sukina was still there, I could feel her faintly, though she wasn't conscious. I had to save her... I readied Velos to turn around and pick her up. We had to risk going in.

But I didn't have to. Another dragon form shot out of the sky, swooped down and picked up Sukina in its talons. Alsie roared and launched herself up towards him. But Charth was fast enough to catch up with us and deposit Sukina on Velos' back, just in front of Artua. He draped her there and I passed back the straps of my harness so Artua could strap her in.

Charth turned around in the air and charged at Alsie to confront her head on. Alsie ducked out of the way, but she'd lost momentum. She could either choose to chase us or confront Charth. She turned around.

"I'll deal with Alsie," Charth said in the collective unconscious. *"Find a doctor for Sukina."*

"But Francoiso," I said...

"My brother is dead. There's nothing you can do for him now." His voice sounded bereft of emotion, as always. *"Now flee."*

He was right, but maybe we could save Sukina. The blood was leaching out of her face and she looked pale.

"Hurry, Velos," I willed in the collective unconscious. *"We've not got much time."*

"Will she be okay?" Artua asked me.

"I think so," I said.

"Where are we going?" Faso shouted.

"To Doctor Forsolano's," I said. I could think of no one who had a better chance of saving Sukina's life.

29

We arrived at Doctor Forsolano's just as the sun was rising. I touched Velos down on the ground. Forsolano, Mamo and Papo were waiting there, alongside the two nurses, with their foldable stretcher ready. It was lucky really that they'd been looking out at the time to see us arrive.

Mamo ran up to us as soon as Velos' feet touched the ground. Velos lowered his neck and I vaulted over his steering fin then slid down to the ground.

"Oh, Pontopa, dear," she said. "I was so worried. A royal wedding, what on earth? What did the king do to you both? You looked so strange in the photos and you had that silver glow in your eyes."

"Mamo, there's no time," I said. I gestured towards Sukina lying on Velos' back. There was absolutely no colour left in her face.

"Oh my," Mamo said. "What happened?"

I was already around the back of Velos. I patted his rump to get him to lower his back. Faso had moved there to assist this time. He looked pretty worried about her too. From up top, Artua unstrapped Sukina and then he pushed her legs while I pulled Sukina at the shoulders and Faso provided support at her back. Together, we lowered her onto the stretcher.

The nurses rushed Sukina towards the house, while Papo stepped forward and I gave him a quick hug. He still had the sling around his shoulder, but he looked much better for the wear and the way he was moving his torso, I suspected he could probably take it off by now. Hopefully, Doctor Forsolano, who was also rushing ahead of us, could work miracles with Sukina as well.

We followed Forsolano into the bedroom as the two nurses lowered her onto the bed that Papo had been sleeping in. It looked made now and ready for the next patient. Forsolano knocked off one of the pillows so there was only one to support Sukina's head, then he took her pulse and opened her mouth to reveal a hideously green tongue.

"What's this?" Forsolano asked. "Poison? What happened?" He examined the dart hole at Sukina's neck where a large bruise had now welled up around it.

"A dart," I said. "I don't know what was in it."

Doctor Forsolano fumbled around in the drawers and removed a needle. He used this to draw out from her wrist black, coagulated blood.

"This stuff, it's inhuman. What did they do to her?"

"Alsie Fioreletta did it... She's murderous," I said. "So is the king..."

Doctor Forsolano took a syringe and gave Sukina an injection in the upper arm. Sukina opened her eyes then and jerked up in bed. She looked around and her eyes met mine, then Artua's, then looked back at me again. "Easy," the doctor said. "You need to rest, Sukina."

Sukina sank back onto the pillow then turned her head to me. "Pontopa. We made it out alive..." Her voice was weak and hoarse.

"Charth saved you," I said.

"Did he make it?"

I shook my head. "I don't know. But Francoiso... He didn't." I hadn't had time to process what I felt about that. Somehow, I guess I had felt a connection to him after all, even though the marriage had been wrong.

I could hear Sukina muttering in the collective unconscious, as if her subconscious and conscious thoughts were merging into one. Sukina looked at Taka.

"Taka, come here."

The boy didn't object that his name was actually Artua. Instead he shuffled over to his mother and took hold of her hand.

"Mamo—" he said. "You were always in my dreams."

"As you were in mine, dear," Sukina said. "Listen. You must take good care of Pontopa Wells. Both of you are going to make fine dragonseers one day."

"Why?" Artua said. "Where are you going?"

"Nowhere," Sukina said. "I'll always be with you... In... your..."

"Sukina, I—" I said. I could see she was fading. "No, Sukina, you must fight this."

But her gaze fell on me and she spoke ever so faintly. "It's time, dragonseer. Tell Gerhaun..."

Then, that was that. Once again, like I had with Francoiso, I felt a soul tear out of the collective unconscious. I reeled. I wanted to be sick. But I swallowed it down. "Sukina?" I said. But she didn't reply.

"Sukina," I said again in the collective unconscious. *"You can't leave us."*

There was not a trace of her anywhere. Whatever poison Alsie had given her, it had been effective. Dragonheats, I'd kill that woman. I'd hunt her down and tear out her life with my own hands.

"Mamo," Artua sobbed. "Mamo?"

I walked over to the boy, took his hand. "Artua, I'm sorry."

"My name is Taka," he said, and he stormed out the door.

Papo walked up to me and pulled me into a hug. His right arm was working again, I could feel some strength there. "Darling," he said. "I'm sorry. Whatever happened in there must have been terrible. I'm so sorry about everything."

I looked at my father. That argument we'd had so many weeks ago now seemed so irrelevant and I was just glad to feel loved. "Thank you Papo," I said.

"Just tell me one thing," Papo said. "Was that the king's nephew?"

"Yes," I said. I glanced over at Faso whose hands were now shaking as he bent over crying at Sukina's feet. Sukina, I realized, had not even given him a glance on her deathbed.

I guess she'd always been a dragonseer first, lover second. But sometime, I'd have to break the news to Faso that he was Artua's – I mean Taka's – father. But first I needed to check that Taka was safe. I walked outside to check that the boy hadn't ventured into the woods alone.

TAKA WASN'T outside the house, but fortunately, I knew where to find him. I walked across to the forest clearing where Velos had landed. Taka was crouched down besides his feet, singing a soft dragonsong that I'd never yet heard before. Velos crooned from the very base of his neck.

That friendship would last, I realized. The boy now could be around real dragons.

But then another thought dawned on me. Taka would need a mother, as well as a father. I'd have to help Faso look after the boy.

There would be no more new Sukina Sako novels to read. No more listening to her in the collective unconscious, teaching me the trials and tribulations of being a dragonseer. No more conversations about how sometimes Faso's not all that bad.

No, I would have to do this all without her. Not just that, I had a responsibility to teach to Taka what Sukina had taught me. Hopefully Gerhaun would be able to help me. I was sure there was so much about being a dragonseer that I still had to learn myself.

One thing was for sure, we had to go south as soon as possible and get back to the fortress No matter how much out of the way Doctor Forsolano's lodge was, Alsie would track us down eventually.

We had to leave, then we had to find a way to get my parents out of here, so everyone would be safe. Faso's plan to pass through Sanjiornio under cover of night worked last time, so I had no doubt it would work again.

But I just didn't feel like moving.

Papo and Mamo had followed me into the clearing. Mamo went over to whisper something quietly to Taka, but I had no idea what it was. Then she walked over to me, and took me into her arms. I broke down and wept into her shoulder.

"Why did she have to leave us?" I said. "Why now? Why does the king and Alsie and everyone in Slaro have to be so cruel?"

"I know, dear," she said patting my back. "I know."

I pulled myself back from my mother and looked at her with as much sincerity as I could muster through my blurry eyes. "Mamo. You know we're not safe here. Not now... Things are going to get a lot worse."

"They're after you?"

"It's not just the king," I said. "Wellies, how can I explain? There's a woman who can turn into a dragon, and she's dangerous. You have to believe me, Mamo, I wouldn't make any of this up."

"Don't worry," Mamo said. "I believe you. I heard some of the stories your blood mother told. Just remember, you're not alone. Your Papo and I, we're here for you."

"I know Mamo," I said. "Thank you."

I once again buried myself into her shoulder and she embraced me with a warm and familiar hug. After a couple of minutes, she spoke again. "I know it's never a good time to ask this, but you can't be taking Sukina's body south with you. Do you want to bury her, or..."

Dragonheats, I hadn't even thought about that. But if Forsolano said she was dead, there would be no bringing her back to life. "She must return to the Southlands, so she can rest close to Gerhaun and her father."

"So, you want us to..."

"Can we cremate her? Is it possible?"

"Doctor Forsolano does have the facilities here, yes." Mamo said. "He sometimes needs to perform ceremonies for lost patients himself. But cremation takes time. You'll need at least five or six hours."

I bit my lip. There was no way that Alsie or Cini would know where Doctor Forsolano lived. We'd be safe here for that amount of time and could leave late the next evening, to pass through the Southern Barrier at night.

I nodded. "Then we'll take her ashes south. I think that's best... What she would have wanted." Although I'd hate to be the one to explain to General Sako why we couldn't bring her body home whole.

"I'll make the arrangements," Mamo said. "Come on, both of you. There's some dinner on the table and we all need to eat. It's been a long day."

I'D NEVER THOUGHT Sukina Sako, with her fame, would have such a modest funeral. But here, in the forest, only Taka was here from her family... And Faso, who I guess was kind of family too. He'd completely changed character and hadn't said a word since Sukina had passed away. Ratter also hadn't emerged once from his flared suit sleeve, almost as if doing so would be disrespectful to her.

Taka had been pretty quiet too, but he'd started to draw closer to me. He held my hand as the pastor from the village read out a beautiful speech on the solidarity of man, and how much Sukina had achieved in her life. He'd asked us plenty of questions about Sukina before, of course, to achieve this.

Sukina lay innocently on a wooden bier, everything, save for her face, covered in a virgin white shawl. Despite her eyelids and face being completely blanched of colour, she still had a look of power about her. Even in death she seemed regal.

Doctor Forsolano had set up the firewood over an iron pit, though the doctor had assured us she'd later be moved to the furnace where we could retrieve the rest of her ashes. The pit had been filled with charcoal and soon enough, I had the job of throwing a match onto the Sukina to set her aflame. Faso had not wanted to do it and I wouldn't dare have given Taka this burden.

Just before the fire came to life, Papo drew the shawl over Sukina's face. Then, I said my final goodbye, reaching out in the collective unconscious, even though I knew she wasn't there.

"I will always be watching" the voice had come to the back of my head. Whether that was Sukina's voice, or my imagination, I truly didn't know.

"And I," this voice was now Francoiso's. *"Once in the collective unconscious, always in the collective unconscious. Death shall never do us part."*

No, I was imagining it, surely. I pulled Taka close and let him weep against me as I raised a handkerchief to wipe a tear from my eye.

We went inside and talked of our memories of Sukina. Taka wanted to hear as much as he could from us. But still, Faso said nothing. He didn't yet know that the boy was his daughter, and I was trying to find the best moment to tell him. One thing was for sure, I didn't want Taka around when I did.

Everyone was pretty sleepy, so we took some time for a nap after cake and tea. I let Taka sleep in the same bed as me. He needed someone close right now for comfort. I slept lightly, waking up half thinking I heard Sukina as if she was lying beside me, and also from more rampant inappropriate dreams of my previous lust for Francoiso. It was still there nestled in my subconscious and I wondered if I'd ever recover from the effects the Exalmpora had had on me. I eventually roused at dawn, once the sun starting peeping through the curtains.

Mamo and Papo were already up when I walked downstairs, and Faso was sitting in the living room, his eyes baggy as if he'd not slept a wink. An elaborate urn, painted with blue and gold dragons, stood on the coffee table before him.

I took hold of the urn, checked it was tightly secured and then placed it in my backpack. "Are you going to come south with us, Faso?"

He looked up at me but still said nothing.

"Oh, for wellies sake. We need to get you down there, you're not safe here."

Faso shook his head. "I'm not coming."

"You bloody well are. If not for me, for Sukina and Taka. He needs you there."

"The boy? Why?"

I took a deep breath. There never really would be a good moment to tell him. "Faso, there's something you should know. Taka... He's yours."

Faso raised his head. "My son?"

"Yes. I'll leave you to decide when to tell him."

"But Sukina... We could never..."

"There's more," I said. "Taka was once your daughter. Cini and

Alsie changed his sex. Through a drug called Exalmpora. Look, it's complicated."

"That doesn't sound very scientific," Faso said with a frown.

"Yes, well the drug was discovered by a man named Captain Colas. I believe you knew him, and I believe also he was a scientist."

"That man... I might have known he was involved in all this."

Faso continued to stare at the space on the coffee table a while and I stood with my hands on my hips, waiting for him to move. Eventually, he lifted himself like a wraith rising from a grave. "I'll come," he said.

"Good. Now come on, let's get some breakfast."

The good doctor had served out some bacon, eggs, sausages, and toast on the table. We ate, Taka and Faso still remaining pretty silent. After that, we passed time until the sun set, eating a good hearty lunch and early dinner to fuel us for the journey ahead.

My parents then escorted Taka, Faso and me into the clearing while Doctor Forsolano went into the village to get some supplies. I gave Mamo and Papo a hug, big tears in my eyes after everything that had happened and having to leave them here.

"I'll send someone back to get you," I said. "I promise. You won't be safe in Tow."

"Take all the time you need, dear," Papo said. "Don't worry, we can look after ourselves."

I nodded to him and then Faso, Taka and I climbed on top of Velos. We took off and flew towards the Southlands, a strong wind whipping against my hair.

PART VIII

PONTOPA

"To be a dragonseer is both the most challenging and the most natural of things."

— PONTOPA WELLS

30

It seemed safe to travel at night. Cini would have sent word around the country by telegram to look out for a dragon flying in the sky, so troops everywhere would be looking out for us. I was also a little apprehensive that Alsie would find us. I doubted, to be honest, that Charth had made it after engaging Alsie in combat. I also doubted that anyone else or anything other than Charth could defend us from her, not even Velos with his armour. If Cini got Taka back, then everything Sukina had died for would be rendered moot.

So, the aim was to hit the Southern Barrier a couple of hours before dawn, so we'd be through before first light. We augmented using Sukina's blend, so I saw everything in speckled green. We flew as low as we could to the forest canopy to make us less visible from a distance. It wasn't long before we saw something rustling down there. It looked like a rabbit, although it moved with a little less fluency than a wild animal. But I was really too far up to see.

"You've got to be kidding me," Faso said from the back, peering down with his telescope. Something had clearly reactivated his energy, and I had a feeling it had something to do with his technology.

"What is it?" I called back.

"They stole Ratter!"

"I thought you had Ratter with you?"

"Not my Ratter. A copy… Now the thing is tracking us."

I snorted, trying to imagine Velos being a match for a mechanical ferret, armour and all. "I don't think we're in much danger up here."

"Well, we're out of range. But if that automaton's nearby, then someone, somewhere knows exactly where we are."

"Dragonheats," I said. "Can you do something to stop it?"

"If I could, it's already too late."

"Dragonheats," I muttered again. "Taka, hold on tight."

I pulled up on Velos' steering fin to get him away from that thing. Plus, extra height would help us see ahead. If they knew our location it was only fair that we knew theirs too.

"Is there anything I can do, Auntie Pontopa?" Taka said.

"Just stay put for now. We'll work something out."

Fortunately, we'd pretty much reached Sandstone Bluff, and we would soon fly over Sanjiornio, the same island we'd passed over on the way in. No one had sighted us there so my best assumption was it would be still deserted.

As we left the cliff face behind, I turned around to see that ferret at the top of the precipice, although from here it was only a dot on the horizon.

"We should have returned to the Five Hamlets to refuel," Faso said.

"What? Are you crazy? Do you know how many guards will be posted there?"

"We could have found a way," Faso said.

I shook my head. "I don't think we could have."

The floodlights of Sanjiornio soon came into view. As before, we followed them around in much the same fashion and got high enough that the shrapnel-flak scanners couldn't sense us. We timed it well and ended up getting well away from the Southern Barrier just as the sun started to appear on the horizon.

The place was stirringly silent. I could only hear the rush of the wind and the swishing of the sea below, which was bathed in the amber light of the rising sun. I scanned the terrain, trying to find at least a hint of danger, because it had to be close. I half imagined that Alsie would shoot out in front of us in dragon form and take us down out there and then.

In that moment of respite, I found myself instinctively reach out in the collective unconscious, despite there not being a strong source of it, to ask Sukina if she had any advice. But I only got emptiness in reply. I couldn't feel what she was feeling anymore. I couldn't lean on her emotionally for support. I now had to face whatever lay ahead alone.

It wasn't long after that it started. First came the hum of propellers, then I spotted airships approaching from the east and west. Closing in on our location like lobster pincers. We could turn around now and let them chase us back inland, or we could carry on and confront whatever ambush Cini's forces had prepared. It seemed wise to stay low. So, I pushed Velos down slowly, just in time to see boats on the water. As we flew further south, I sighted more of them, and my heart sank.

An entire armada lay there in wait. King Cini's admirals had gone all out – battleships and frigates and cruisers and even Hummingbird carriers.

"Dragonheats! Pontopa, we're not going to fight them, are we?" Faso said.

I gritted my teeth and plunged Velos into a dive so we could approach at speed. "What other choice do we have?"

In the distance, the Hummingbirds rose up from the carriers in a golden cloud, which roiled towards us, like an approaching swarm of bees. Another cloud also rose from the frigates, this time black, leaving a dulling boom in its wake. Shrapnel-flak, creating an impenetrable wall above the line of boats. If we passed through, we'd be torn apart by shards of floating metal. This time, Velos didn't have enough secicao in his armour to take us over the cloud.

But I had a more immediate problem to worry about. The Hummingbirds were now approaching, and we could hear the buzzing of their fast-beating wings.

"Damn it, Pontopa, retreat!" Faso shouted.

I looked back at the airships now closing in on our location. They'd formed into a single line now. On board each, redguards had their rifles raised, aimed right at us. But Faso was right. We had a better chance against the airships than the Hummingbirds.

I took my flask from my hip and took a swig of secicao oil. Alertness washed over me, and somehow, I also felt sick. It was as if

I could feel Exalmpora in the liquid. All of a sudden, I wanted it. I wanted to become a dragonwoman. That previous lust for Francoiso washed over me. Then, I remembered he was dead.

No, I couldn't think about that right now. I passed the flask back to Taka. "Take some."

"More medicine?" Taka said.

"It's not medicine, it's secicao. It will keep you safe, I promise."

"I trust you," Taka said, and he took a swig from his flask. Faso also had his golden flask tipped to his mouth. He wiped his lips and then he bent down towards the spigot at Velos' side.

Meanwhile, I turned Velos sharply towards the airships. On the way around, he let out a sharp spray of orange flame, with a faint tint of green in it, which doused the approaching swarm of Hummingbirds. Several of them sputtered and then spiralled to the water. But it wasn't enough to stop them surrounding us. I expected to get shot down there and then. But the things just barrelled in front of us and then formed a protective wall. A few knocked against Velos' body, and he let out a huge, bellowing roar.

"They don't want to shoot us?" I asked.

"They probably want to try taking us alive," Faso said, "so they can later photograph our execution for the magazines."

I felt a surge of anger rise up in me. *Wasn't killing Sukina enough?*

From behind us, came another boom. A cannonball whizzed past us. Somehow, I knew they didn't want to knock us out of the sky. Just scare us into landing. The chance of hitting a fast-flying target like Velos with cannon fire was pretty slim, anyway, even when automatons were doing the shooting.

Meanwhile, the Hummingbirds charged forward once again. Velos' armour began to glow a faint green and the Gatling cannons whirred into life. They weren't as strong as before, but still had enough punch in them to knock a Hummingbird out of the way before it hit me in the face.

"I thought you said the armour's reserves were depleted?" I shouted back to Faso.

"The armour has a smaller emergency tank."

"Good call!"

We were approaching the airships now. On one of the ones

nearer to us, a blue-suited officer came on deck. He raised a mega-phone to the sky. "Pontopa Wells, you are surrounded and outnum-bered. I order you to land on the carrier if you value your life."

"You'd kill us anyway," I shouted back, even though I doubted they could hear me over the gunfire.

I took Velos down beneath the airships and then I circled around, and we tried skimming the surface of the water. We'd be a much harder target down here and Velos could create splashes with his feet that might confuse a few Hummingbirds.

"This is your last warning, Pontopa Wells. We will order the Hummingbirds to fire if you don't surrender in five seconds."

The Gatling guns continued to knock Hummingbirds out of the sky. But they had begun to slow a little, running out of energy and there was no way that they could destroy the approaching swarm behind us.

"Four..."

A carrier had separated itself from the main fleet and was gaining speed in our direction. All I had to do was wave my surrender and then land Velos on the shining silver platform ahead.

"Three..."

No, we'd stay close to the water, Velos sweeping up spray with his claws. In front of us, another swarm of Hummingbirds rose up from a carrier. Dragonheats, there seemed to be no end to them. The Gatling guns on Velos' flank sputtered to a stop.

"Two..."

As if out of nowhere, Sukina's voice sounded in my head. It had no comprehensible words behind it, but I could hear the harmony of a dragonsong. Then came a tingling sensation in my temples. Dragons, grey ones nearby. A good few hundred of them, at least.

Instinctively, I reached out and started a song to pull them in.

"One..."

The Greys latched on to my call. I could hear them approach-ing. The Gatling guns dropped slack on Velos' side and the warmth from the armour started to fade. Some Hummingbirds pushed ahead of Velos from behind, but Velos hit them out of the sky with his flame. The other swarm swooped down at us, and the massive hull of the landing carrier came into view.

"Okay, time's up, Miss Wells."

Static came from the megaphone and the propellers from the airships roared into life. A shot came from the rifles, and I ducked out of the way of a bullet, seen through my augmented eyes. The second cloud of Hummingbirds closed in on us.

I swerved Velos to hug the side of the carrier and then we swept around the back of it. As we turned, I glimpsed Greys in the distance. They swept down on one of the carriers, knocking out a third swarm of Hummingbirds that had just emerged. Shrapnel-flak cannons roared around us and my heart lurched in my chest as I felt a dragon get shot out of the sky.

I swerved again to hug the other side of the massive boat. This would confuse the Hummingbirds. Some of them would barrel into the ship, others would have to climb over it, but it would take time for them to adjust their course. I let out another song to try and get the Greys to fly towards me.

But then as I looked over my shoulder, I could see the wall of shrapnel-flak and guns on the side of the ships would make it impossible for them to get through, without getting shot out of the sky. I sang another song to tell them to keep their distance. I looked over my shoulder again and noticed that Cini's boats had started to turn away from me.

Another round of rifle fire. Velos roared and I screamed out and clutched at my arm as pain shot through it. It wasn't me that had been shot. I looked down to see a hole in Velos' wing. "Come on Velos," I said. "You can make it."

"They've got us," Faso shouted. "Pontopa, we need to surrender."

"They'll kill us!"

"Maybe they'll give us enough time to work out a plan."

"No, we can make it," I said. I looked around at Taka his eyes wide, his hands trembling where he gripped the handle in front of her seat, the whites of his knuckles showing. But he kept a brave face. "I can help, Auntie. I know a song." I looked into his eyes and I saw the same kind of resolve that I would have seen on Sukina's face.

I nodded. "Whatever you want, darling."

He let out a melancholy harmony which both softened my

heart and strengthened my resolve. I felt Velos gain some strength too, as he'd been weakening since getting clipped.

The airships ahead were gaining distance now. Soon, they'd be on top of us, and I thought maybe we could hide under their gondolas for a while. But there were some fat looking turrets on some of the cabins, with red eyes that would latch on to Velos and shoot him down in an instant.

We reached the next of corner of the carrier's hull, and I turned Velos just in time to evade some Hummingbirds. The airships had their rifles cocked and ready, but they didn't fire yet. Probably, they didn't want to damage the front of the boat, perhaps there was fuel in there or something.

"You can't keep this up forever, Miss Wells," the voice boomed out again from the airship. "Surrender is your only chance."

There was no point even trying to reply. We turned the corner again, and this time I kept watch with my augmented eyes for when the rifles would fire. But just as I saw the finger tighten on one guard's trigger. A klaxon sounded, and a guard ran up onto the officer airship's deck to point in the direction of the battle behind.

I looked in the same direction to see a silver line forming on the horizon, beneath the shrapnel-flak and below the Greys. Reinforcements had arrived. Sandao's fleet, I presumed. The guards lowered their rifles, causing a temporary respite in fire. This didn't stop the Hummingbirds approaching though. Another swarm of them buzzed towards us.

"Got it!" Faso shouted, as he fiddled with the control panel at the back of the armour. "There's a secondary reserve."

"What?"

"I'll explain later... We have around a minute."

Beneath me, Velos' armour began to glow green again. The Gatling guns came back to life. They locked on to their targets and Hummingbirds began to fall out of the sky. The Hummingbirds fired shots back, one of which I had to duck out of the way of, another that hit the armour. If it wasn't for the armour, that shot would have gone straight through Velos' heart. But instead it just deflected off into the water.

One by one, the number of Hummingbirds in the swarm dwindled. I managed to turn Velos around enough to meet them straight on. It seemed we didn't have to worry about fire from the airships anymore. The airborne fleet had begun to separate again into two flanks, heading towards the navy. Now, instead of having the rifles trained on me, they had them trained on the horizon.

"It's time to join the battle," I shouted, and we ploughed forwards. Behind me, Taka kept singing her song. I could feel Velos' pain, though he didn't even groan. Still, I have no idea how he managed to carry on with that clipped wing. Perhaps it was the armour's reserve tank and the secicao within it that kept him able to fly.

I wanted again to pull in the dragons, but the wall of shrapnel-flak still separated me and Sandao's fleet. Another cloud of Hummingbirds emerged from one of the carriers, but this time it wasn't sent off in my direction but towards the battle ahead. I kept Velos flying towards the fleet.

"Pontopa, you're crazy!" Faso shouted. "We'll never get through that shrapnel-flak."

Yet I knew there was no turning back now. We would push forwards and we would make it. We'd return to Gerhaun and give Sukina a proper funeral. Although, I hadn't quite yet worked out how.

Still, I knew this would be the right way.

So, I gritted my teeth and pushed down on Velos' steering fin to get him closer to the water. We were going in.

We were losing. Though we had dragons and we had bigger guns, Gerhaun's naval technology was a little outdated and, as I drew closer to King Cini's boats, both Faso and I noticed the green pipes running through the hulls.

"My technology!" Faso said.

"I know," I shouted back. He didn't have to state it for what must have been the thousandth time. Cini was using secicao to power his automatons and now his boats, it seemed. This technology would be here to stay.

Only a couple of ships on Cini's side were sinking, their hulls now tipping below the water. But in the distance, I could see smoke and fires on hulls, swarms of Hummingbirds descending on naked steel superstructures.

Then there were the Greys. I could feel their pain. What must have been a good several hundred of Gerhaun's best now had been reduced by half. Each lost life tugged on my heart as I felt it sink beneath the water. Could we really win this battle? Could we really defeat a much larger foe?

"You can, Pontopa," Sukina's voice came in my mind. *"Your strength is within."* Again, it must have been a figment of my imagination. My own head telling me this, nothing else.

"What's the use," I said back, just like I was talking to her in the collective unconscious. I considered the inviting Hummingbird

carrier again. To land on it would be easy. Then all this would be over.

The boat in question was getting closer to us. Funnily enough, that thing hadn't sent out any Hummingbirds. Maybe it needed extra space for Velos – huge beast that he was. Or maybe it was saving a bigger weapon for a last resort. I shuddered as images flashed passed my mind of what that could be.

Behind me, four airships were also closing in on us. The rest of the airships were now some distance between us and the distant fleet.

I felt drained, and I wanted to collapse. So, I raised my hip flask to my lips to take another mouthful. But the secicao had almost gone, so I only got about half of what I'd usually get.

I steered Velos back towards the enemy fleet. In the distance, a smaller cloud of Hummingbirds disengaged from an emerging swarm, the larger cluster swerving off towards a small cluster of Greys. I could also feel Velos running out of energy. The secicao in his armour had virtually ran out.

"There's not much left in him!" Faso shouted. "Dragonheats, Pontopa, you need to turn around." He had stood up in his seat now and Ratter was perched upon his shoulder, its red eyes glaring at me. A Hummingbird approached us, and Ratter shot it out of the sky using the cannon in his throat.

Velos doused the rest of the approaching swarm in an orange flame. One by one, they sputtered and fell to the water before they had chance to release a shot. Velos still had something in him after all.

But then my heart lurched as I felt five more Greys fall out of the sky. I let out a song to try and at least give the rest of the flock some heart. But my singing was so meek that I doubt it fell upon a single dragon's ear. Taka seemed to catch on and he also began to echo the song. The dragons on the other side of the barrage turned around to start to form into a larger group.

"Safety in numbers," I said back to Taka.

He simply nodded then he pointed over to the larger carrier, the one we were meant to land on. "Auntie Pontopa, look!"

Out of one of the funnels of the ship emerged what must have been thousands of Hummingbirds. These weren't the standard bronze variety. Instead, they were tinted green. As they approached, an olive coloured cloud began to surround them.

"My technology, again!" Faso said. "What happened to patent law? Dragonheats, we're screwed."

"Pontopa Wells," the voice filled the air again. The officer's airship had drawn ahead of the other three ships and the blue suited officer stood on deck, once again with the megaphone to his mouth. "As you can see, the battle is lost. I'll give you three seconds to turn Velos around or our new technology will cut you out of the sky."

I felt a pull then, a need to draw towards those Hummingbirds. They had something I wanted...

"*Pontopa, resist it,*" Sukina, again inside my mind. "*This isn't you.*"

But there was something in that swarm. The Hummingbirds had now lined up in a lattice formation, and a larger black Hummingbird was floating in the centre of this. Instead of a gun, it held a large transparent flask in its arm, and I could see what was in the centre of that flask. Exalmpora. Drawing me towards it.

"*I must have it,*" I said back to that voice in the collective unconscious. "*Alsie took Francoiso and Sukina away from me... I'll hunt her down and I'll kill her.*"

"*Pontopa, don't let it take control.*"

"Auntie... Auntie!" Taka was screaming. Perhaps he hadn't seen the Exalmpora. No, he knew it was there. But he had more power to resist. As Francoiso said, children had more control over these things.

"That's it," said the officer over the loudspeaker. The secicao-powered Hummingbirds charged forwards.

"*What do I do?*" I asked that voice in my head. Could it really be Sukina?

"*You know what to do...*"

"*But...*"

"*Just do it...*"

I looked back at Taka. His eyes were wide, his hands clutched on the bar in front of him. But still, he had this knowing look. "Auntie, you do your part, and I'll do mine."

"What?"

"Mamo's here. I heard her voice. She's with us, Auntie."

"Taka?"

"Just sing!"

For a split second, I was stunned by Taka's brashness. But then I swallowed down my pride and I snapped into life. I turned towards the Greys in the distance and I sang a dragonsong. This one wasn't to heal, not to give courage, not even to give strength, but to protect against what Taka was about to do. Somehow, the plan had already formulated in both our minds.

The song I let out created a shroud that I threw out towards the dragons in the distance. I saved a little for Velos as well, and it seeped out of me like two tendrils into his ears. He roared, deafened by my song. Then my hearing went too. We needed to do this if we were to survive.

Despite the shrapnel-flak raging around me and the cannons booming not far away now, I managed to become strangely calm. I kept my distance from my fear as well. Taka looked into my eyes, knowingly and then his mouth opened wide.

Neither me nor the dragons heard the sound he let out. But the Hummingbirds did. The first of them had just come close enough to fire upon us. I grimaced for a moment, expecting to be knocked off my perch.

But Taka's mouth remained open and the Hummingbirds carried on in the same direction. One knocked hard against my shoulder, causing me to yelp out in pain. That same Hummingbird lost its momentum and fell into the water.

The rest continued into the wall of shrapnel-flak and buried themselves there. Then a green explosion erupted from the black cloud and the secicao-powered Hummingbirds were no more.

I don't know where the knowledge of my song had come from. These things often just came to me at the heat of the moment. But I made a mental note that if we could second-guess Alsie then we could also use it to guard against her scream.

Once their deafness had worn off, I continued my songs to direct the cluster of Greys to reform and engulf an approaching swarm of Hummingbirds in flames. In numbers they became stronger. They had just needed a leader to organise them.

I continued to sing to tell the dragons exactly what to attack. It wouldn't be true to say I could see through the dragons' eyes, but I could feel each dragon's soul and somehow, I knew exactly what note would cause each one to react. Taka sang with me, but his notes were more focused on keeping up the Greys' courage.

With our song and the might of the dragons, we coordinated an attack that destroyed every single Hummingbird. Not one dragon fell in the process.

"You're back, Auntie," Taka said.

I was. But we still had a barrier to cross. That cloud of shrapnel-flak kept being renewed by the cannons. If we tried to pass it, we'd arrive on the other side torn to shreds. Velos had no reserves left in his armour and I felt how his muscles wanted to give out. His last strength was dwindling, and he was drawing closer and closer to the sea.

"No, Velos," Taka shouted. He changed his song to strengthen Velos, while I still focused on the Greys. I wished they were over on the same side as us, so we could fight this battle together. Maybe with Velos, we could divert some of the fire so Sandao's fleet could move in. Sandao's boats themselves had been keeping a distance and I couldn't quite see what was going on over at the horizon.

"Pontopa, we have to surrender!" Faso shouted and he pointed out towards a second swarm of secicao-powered Hummingbird automatons that emerged from the ship's funnel. "We can't win!"

But there was no turning back now. I had a much better idea.

I turned Velos towards the shrapnel-flak. "We're going in!"

"What?" Faso exclaimed. "You're crazy!"

I sneered back at Faso. "So, jump ship," I said, gesturing towards the churning, uninviting sea below.

"Death lies that way, Miss Wells!" the voice came from the airship. "You're committing suicide."

Indeed, as if they saw our approach, the shrapnel-flak cannons on the carriers let out another barrage. Though Taka's song was keeping Velos steady enough, the dragon's physical strength was weakening. But we could make this. I had to have faith.

So, I closed my eyes as we approached the black cloud. I could feel the static from it now, pulling at the hairs on my arms. Maybe, if we were incredibly lucky, we could fly through without getting cut to pieces.

But that wasn't my plan. "Faso, Taka, get ready to hold your breath." I shouted.

"What?" Faso said.

"Just do it!" I pushed on Velos' steering fin as hard as I could. He knew immediately what I wanted him to do.

He plunged into a stall, just barely missing the cloud of shrapnel-flak. I felt the static even stronger and so I pushed Velos down even harder, sang a song to tell him to forget about the pain in his wings. "Be brave, Velos," I said.

Something scratched at the top of my head. Shrapnel-flak, we hadn't evaded all of it. But we got away from that cloud largely unscathed. Instead, the water's surface lurched towards us. Velos' wing tips scraped the hull of the ship, and I worried this would slow him down.

"Now!" I shouted and then I took in a deep breath. Velos' head broke the surface tension of the water, so he probably would have felt the bulk of the sting. But still it felt like a huge slap to my face and the chest as my body followed his underneath the water. Great giant bubbles rose up to my side from Velos' breath, followed by the smaller ones from my own. I exhaled slowly, but steadily, not knowing how deep we would go. I could see the boat's hull in front of us now, which went so deep I couldn't make out the bottom of it.

As we plunged, the water turned greener and I felt increasing pressure on my ears. I turned around, half scared that those Hummingbirds would have followed us into the water. But I doubted they were also waterproof.

Velos' slowed down and the water began to push up at us. Damn it, we wouldn't make it. We'd pop up out of the surface and that carrier would already be waiting for us with life buoys to take us hostage. If we hadn't already drowned.

"Come on, Velos," I thought, hoping he would at least hear my emotions. I couldn't really sing down here but sang a dragonsong in my mind to spur Velos on. I felt a push of strength then. One last kick from Velos' feet to push us downwards and we made it under the hull.

Now, I had to hold my breath for long enough and hope that Faso and Taka could do the same. I kept that thread on Velos' mind now that I'd found it, pushed him onwards with his feet. Surprisingly, he began to accelerate.

Then light came from the surface and I pulled up on Velos' steering fin to drive him upwards. He was weak, but he still had a little bit of oomph left in him. He kicked his legs as if he'd been swimming for life, pushed his forelegs in front of him and pulled the water away from him. Velos' buoyancy lifted him fast.

Behind me, Taka began to sputter bubbles and his eyes went wide. Faso looked at me as if to say hurry up. Then my air supply started to go, and I thought that was it – we were going to drown.

But just as that thought came, Velos broke the surface and the three of us gasped desperately for air. The Greys had already brought down another swarm of Hummingbirds and now they regrouped and flew towards us. I could see Sandao's fleet, which was already in retreat. On the other hand, Cini's ships still had to turn and the airships wouldn't dare to pursue a fleet of boats alone, since they'd get shot out of the sky.

I got us a safe distance from Cini's fleet, and then I looked back to see his boats sinking away from us. Velos had gained new energy from somewhere and I knew he could make it to Sandao's fleet.

"We did it," I turned around to Taka to give him a high five.

But he was fast asleep in his chair. That scream must have really taken it out of him.

"I'll take that high five," Faso said.

So, I reached over behind Taka and high-fived Faso. "Thank you, Faso," I said.

"For what?"

"For the armour? Looks like it wasn't a bad idea after all. Although, make sure you get my permission next time."

Faso smiled and then he looked behind him towards the horizon, behind which lay the scene of the battle that had almost killed us. In the very distance, I could ever so faintly make out the fading shrapnel-flak clouds.

General Sako stood waiting for us in the courtyard at Fortress Gerhaun when we arrived, yellow secicao smoke rising up from his pipe. He spotted us coming in and then waved us down towards the courtyard. When we landed, I noticed how sunken and baggy his eyes looked, as if he'd not had any sleep for a few nights.

Velos lowered his head to the ground so Faso and I could help Taka off Velos. The boy was barely awake. But Wiggea and another dragonelite had a stretcher ready. "Take him to the infirmary," I said.

"Is that the king's nephew?" Wiggea said.

"That's my granddaughter," General Sako said. "Didn't you listen to the brief?"

"Umm..." I tugged at my collar. "You should probably know he's your grandson now, General Sako."

He looked at me lifelessly. "Granddaughter."

"Grandson. Look, it's a long story, I'll explain but first I need to see Gerhaun."

"Wait!" General Sako said. "Dragonseer Wells, I'd rather hear it from you." he looked at Faso. "Is it true?"

I had wanted to wait a little before delivering the news. But it seemed that someone had told him already.

"How did you know?" I asked.

"A man. He came into the ramparts. Demanded to speak to me and only me. He had this long face and these bright blue eyes—"

"Francoiso?" My heart fluttered in hope.

"He called himself Charth," General Sako said. "The man, he could... He could turn into a dragon. He told me my daughter had been murdered by that King's consort..." The short stocky man took hold of me by the shoulders. A sickly smell of secicao smoke washed over me. "Please tell me it isn't true, Dragonseer."

My heart sank. I hadn't quite come to admit it myself. "It's true," I said. "We have her ashes. There's no way we could have smuggled her body across the Southern Barrier, so we had to cremate her. I'm sorry, General Sako."

General Sako twitched his moustache. "That's what she had always wanted," he said. "Cremation." He turned on his heels and left the courtyard, his posture sunken low.

Faso turned to me. "I'm sorry, Pontopa," he said. "Is there anything I can do to help? I can use secicao to help heal Velos, if you'd let me."

I looked at Faso. "You should probably go and check on your son."

"Yes, I should probably tell Taka I'm his father," Faso said.

"Just know that Sukina wanted to tell you," I said. "Remember, he's a dragonseer, so Gerhaun will want to talk to him too."

"Dragonseers are female."

"It's complicated."

Faso shook his head. "It certainly is," he said. "Well, I better go and check up on him. I mean her... I mean him... Wait, which one should I use?"

"He sees himself as a boy now, as I said."

"Yes, well. I'll make a fine inventor out of him." He gave a little bow and left.

GERHAUN WAS SLEEPING in her chambers. But this time I didn't think twice about waking her. This was the type of news that shouldn't have to wait. We spoke in the collective unconscious.

"I'm sorry," Gerhaun said before I even had a chance to explain.

"You heard too?" I said. *"Charth visited here?"*

"I felt her death," Gerhaun said. She lowered her great head. *"It's a great loss to all of us. But she will always live on in the collective unconscious. You must believe that."*

"This woman, Alsie. She seems to have an agenda of her own."

"The murderer, yes. I've heard her name spoken before by other dragon queens. In myth, they called her the Banshee."

"Because of her scream? Taka's picked up that ability too."

"Oh, she must have taught him something. Though, if legends are true, Taka's scream is not a patch on Mistress Alsie's. That, it would seem, is one of the most dangerous weapons known to man and dragon alike."

I raised an eyebrow. *"Tell me more."*

"The Banshee is a minion of Finesia, who can bring down battalions with her voice. Now legends say that if the Banshee is allowed to revive the Tree Immortal then she'll become the most powerful creature on this world, second to Finesia herself."

"Through secicao?" I asked. It made sense, so much sense now.

"That's right. Once secicao has covered the entire planet then the Tree Immortal can grow again. Then the Banshee will drink of its sap, to regrow Finesia and claim immortality. Together, Finesia, her right hand, and a new race of immortals shall rule. That is the prophecy."

"Aren't prophecies meant to come true?"

"Not if we find a way to stop it. But we need to do research. We need to find out exactly what Alsie is planning, and what she wants with the king."

"I thought King Cini was the villain," I said.

"We've known for a long time that King Cini is just a puppet. Now we know who's pulling the strings."

"I heard Sukina's voice in the battle," I said. *"At least, I think I did."*

"No, you didn't. Once dragonseers die, they lose their voices. But still their presence augments the collective unconscious in so many other ways."

I fell silent for a moment.

"You'll stay with us, won't you, Dragonseer?" Gerhaun said eventually.

"Of course," I said. *"Someone needs to carry on what Sukina was fighting for."*

"That's good."

"I just need one thing," I said. *"To find a way to get my parents down here. They're in a safe place for now, but if Cini ever finds them then, I don't know what I'd do."*

"Don't worry," Gerhaun said. *"We will find a way to save them, and I see you're becoming a fine woman, Dragonseer Wells."*

"Thank you," I said. I bowed, and I took my leave.

WE BURNED Sukina's ashes for a second time, though this time they stayed within her urn. Her spirit wouldn't be sealed, legend stated, until she'd been engulfed with the flame of a dragon queen.

So, we gathered in the courtyard, the wind surprisingly warm for the Southlands, bringing the faint eggy smell of secicao on it. Despite the losses at the Battle of Sanjiornio, as it had come to be called, we still had over seven hundred Greys fit enough to attend the funeral and thousands of dragonelite, Sako's soldiers, and Admiral Sandao's sailors and marines. I'd never in my life seen Fortress Gerhaun's courtyard so full.

But then a good portion of it was taken up by Gerhaun Forsi herself, who sat right in the centre, a massive fire pit in front of her ready to be lit. As if by magic, some sunshine managed to find its way through the secicao clouds and bathe Gerhaun's golden skin in a warm glow.

Behind Gerhaun, the courtyard had been arranged in two long and wide aisles, radiating away from Gerhaun, giving me a good view of the urn at the front, where I sat next to Taka. Faso was on the other side of him and General Sako sat on the other side of me, although he kept looking over at his grandson with discerning eyes as if checking he was behaving himself. Or perhaps trying to work out how his granddaughter could be a grandson. I'd still not had a chance to explain that to him.

The ceremony began and General Sako went forward to deliver a eulogy. He spoke of how beautiful his daughter had been both inside and outside, what a free spirit she was and how headstrong she'd been. She'd been the best daughter a father could ask for. General Sako also mentioned how Sukina's mother, also a dragonseer, had died young, executed during the dragonheats.

After that, he couldn't carry on speaking. I never thought I'd seen someone as strong as General Sako break down crying. I didn't blame him, of course, I don't think I could have even delivered the beginning of such a speech in his position.

Faso then asked permission to General Sako for him to deliver his speech. I was expecting the old general to refuse, but this time he simply nodded his approval, and buried his face into his handkerchief. Faso then talked about his good days with Sukina. How he wished he'd treated her better. How he'd never seen a fault in her, even though he knew he had plenty in him. He didn't talk about the breakup or about any hard feelings he'd had towards her during their period of separation. Rather he spoke of Sukina as someone he'd looked up to. Someone he'd often wanted to be.

"When times called for courage," Faso said. "Sukina always showed you how to be courageous. That's what I loved about her."

This caused General Sako to break down in tears again. I looked over at him, kind of guilty that he'd never had a chance to see the body. But then, he'd say that this was what Sukina had always wanted. She never seemed the kind of person to want to take up unnecessary space.

Gerhaun then breathed fire onto the bier. It bathed the whole place in such warmth that I found myself sweating underneath my funeral dress. We waited a minute for the flames to pass. Gerhaun's fire was so powerful though that it burnt out the firewood pretty quickly.

Then Wiggea, who had apparently been Sukina's most trusted dragonelite, rushed forward. He carefully pushed the urn onto a tray with a gloved hand, which he carried with him.

Three dragonelite followed behind him, then General Sako, Faso, Taka, and I, followed by the rest of the congregation. The dragons had to wait upstairs, of course, there was no way they'd fit into the crypts.

I hadn't realised these chambers existed. Corridors and corridors filled with marble statues of each dragonseer who had served Gerhaun and other dragon queens in the past.

We followed the corridors until we found one lit up by a hundred torches towering up to a high ceiling. A wooden statue of Sukina had already been built in the centre, her hands cupped ready. In one year's time, Gerhaun would burn this statue with dragonfire and it would be replaced by a marble one. Wiggea stepped forwards, kissed Sukina's statue on one palm and then placed the urn in her hands.

"Pontopa, this is your time," Gerhaun's voice came in my head. "To sing the dragonsong."

Yes, Gerhaun had mentioned this. I stepped forward and sang the dirge for the dead. It lifted me out of myself and for three long minutes, I didn't let my voice waver, despite the tears in my eyes. I felt the song lift out of me and float through all of Fortress Gerhaun, where it touched the souls of men and dragons alike and did its part to push away the secicao clouds.

After that, we left Sukina to rest in peace.

THE REST of the day involved the wake and a huge feast, the food rivalling the kind we had eaten in Cini's palace. Though the dishes weren't as elaborate – no white stag for us here – the chicken and beef and pork had been cooked in such a way that it reminded me of Mamo's cooking back home.

Gerhaun and the dragons took this time to rest, while I met some of the troops at the palace. I talked to Wiggea a lot, though I couldn't really stop feeling guilty. In a way, it was as if I was still married to Francoiso.

Eventually, I excused myself and went out to check on Velos. Miraculously, the hole in his wing looked much better, sealed by what seemed some kind of green spongy substance. If this was the secicao healing that Faso had mentioned then the inventor had done a bloody good job.

Velos woke when I approached. He pushed his head up to me and crooned. He was no longer physically in pain – I could feel that. But he also felt a bit lost now that we didn't have Sukina. Clearly, Velos had also bonded with her.

I went to grab some secicao from the storehouse and tossed it into Velos' trough in his stable, which had only just been allotted to him. I stayed with Velos a while before he went to sleep, then I hit the sack myself.

When I finally emerged into the land of the living, I grabbed a quick breakfast from the dining hall and then I went to see what everyone was up to. I passed Sukina's bedroom on the way, the door ajar, from which I could see light from a torch burning inside. I opened to see Faso standing there, Ratter on his shoulder watching as Faso painted this stunning oil portrait of Sukina. He had depicted her in three-quarters profile and her gaze was cast a little off to the left. The painting made her look kind of innocent and Faso had painted a golden halo around her.

Taka was on the bed watching Faso intently. Faso turned to me as I entered the room.

"Hello," he said.

"Faso... I never knew you were so artistic."

"I wanted to get this out of my memory, before it's lost to the world."

"I can understand that. Mind if I watch a while?"

"Sure," he said. Then he returned with an admirable focus to his work. I sat down next to Taka and took his hand.

As I watched the details emerge in Sukina's face, I thought about how much she'd changed me as a person. Yes, I'd loved her novels, and she'd never be able to write another one, damnit.

It wasn't until I'd met her that I started to realise who I was. A dragonseer. Someone who had a purpose in life that involved helping others. Not just making money, consuming secicao and flirting with the occasional airship captain who passed through the Five Hamlets. Instead, I had my own individual destiny.

That's the thing about great people. They end up bringing about great change in some way or another. For me, Sukina would always occupy a special part in my life.

"*Pontopa, can you feel that?*" Gerhaun spoke to me in the collective unconscious.

"*What is it?*"

"*A presence. The same kind I felt when General Sako received the news about Sukina.*"

Come to think about it, there was some kind of shimmer. But

I'd been so enraptured in the painting that I hadn't quite registered it.

I rushed outside to see if anyone was in the courtyard. But there was no one there.

"Nothing," I told Gerhaun.

"I only felt it for a moment," she said. "It *must have let slip his mask."*

It was getting late and so I went again to check on Velos. His skin underneath the spongy thing on his wing was returning to normal and it seemed like he would heal up well. He still felt a little lonely though, I could feel it, so I sang him a soothing song.

Then, I thought I felt the presence again. As if someone was watching me. I turned around, thinking I could see the faint silhouette of something dragon-like sitting on Fortress Gerhaun's ramparts.

But I only needed to blink, and it was gone.

Parenthood has never been so hard.

It's been two years since Pontopa Wells escaped from the clutches of a power-hungry king and exiled to the Southlands: a continent infested with a noxious plant called secicao.

Now, Pontopa must parent her old mentor Sukina's son, Taka, and she doesn't know how to handle the task. Particularly when she struggles to live up to Sukina's name and assume the role of a dragonseer — a leader of both men and dragons.

But when Taka goes missing, Pontopa must travel to a tropical continent, where she will meet an indigenous people who can reveal to her who she truly is.

Meanwhile, the mysterious Empress Finesia is on the rise, with the power to inhabit minds and a plan to use secicao to extinguish all mortal life on the planet. Can Pontopa rescue Taka and, in doing so, put an end to Empress Finesia's nefarious ways?

AVAILABLE AT MAJOR RETAILERS

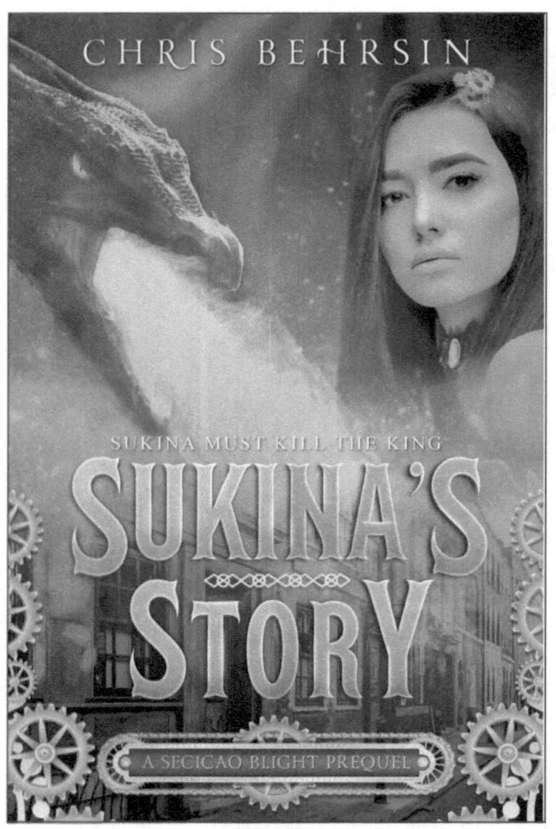

CHRIS BEHRSIN
SUKINA MUST KILL THE KING
SUKINA'S STORY
A SECICAO BLIGHT PREQUEL

ACKNOWLEDGMENTS

As my first major release, my list of acknowledgements is rather short. However, there are some specific people I'd like to thank for helping me get this book where it is today.

Firstly, I'd like to thank my good friend, Patch Willis for giving me some incredibly valuable editorial feedback on the manuscript and helping me iron out plot holes.

I'd like also to thank my beta readers: Sarah Sutton (sarahmaew on Fiverr) and Bianca (biancalcice on Fiverr), who also offered me some fantastic feedback and helped convince me to publish the book.

A big shout out to my original writing group in Daejeon, South Korea: Jake Disch, Ben Garrido, Tom Cecil, Sung Kim. Your advice was valuable during the early stages of my writing career.

To my father who has read a lot of my work and given me the verbal encouragement I needed to keep going. And to my mother, for giving me emotional support through those difficult career times.

Also a huge thank you to Wayne M. Scace, who later stepped up to edit this novel and has also edited my other books.

And finally, thank you most of all to my dear wife, Ola for reminding me I was a writer and convincing me in 2009 to start writing once again. She was also immensely helpful as my first reader and kept me motivated through every stage of the process.